DEON MEYER

COBRA

Translated from Afrikaans
by K. L. Seegers

RANDOM HOUSE CANADA

PUBLISHED BY RANDOM HOUSE CANADA

Copyright © 2014 Deon Meyer
English translation copyright © 2014 K. L. Seegers

www.penguinrandomhouse.ca

Library and Archives Canada Cataloguing in Publication

Meyer, Deon
[Kobra. English]
Cobra / Deon Meyer ; translated from Afrikaans by K.L. Seegers.

Translation of: Kobra
Issued in print and electronic formats.

ISBN 978-0-345-81491-3
eBook ISBN 978-0-345-81493-7

I. Seegers, K. L., translator II. Title. III. Title: Kobra. English.

PT6592.23.E94K6313 2015   839.3'636   C2014-905927-2

Typeset in Plantin Light by Hewer Text UK Ltd, Edinburgh
Cover design by Marc Cohen/MJC Design
Cover images: (cobra) © Vmaster, (bullet) © Al Mueller, both Shutterstock.com

Printed and bound in the United States of America

2 4 6 8 9 7 5 3 1

Penguin
Random House
RANDOM HOUSE CANADA

Advance Praise for **COBRA**

"The plot clicks along like a machine. . . . The set pieces, such as a complex train-hopping action sequence, are slickly executed. This is an author in full charge of his technique, but he burnishes the mechanics of the story with delicious Kaapse characters and richly idiomatic dialogue. The feral pickpocket Tyrone Kleinbooi is one of Meyer's best characters ever, sly and quick with a strong sense of thieves' honour."
The Sunday Times

Praise for Deon Meyer

"A defining novelist of modern South Africa."
Independent

"Deon Meyer's gritty crime novels are part police procedural, part political thriller, and have, in Benny Griessel, one of the most appealing and humane of detectives. . . . What makes Meyer such a national treasure—and as good as anyone in the world—is that even if you have no knowledge or interest in South Africa's history or present, his books are compelling page-turners."
Times Live (South Africa)

"Deon Meyer is one of the best crime writers on the planet."
Mail on Sunday

"Meyer is a gorgeous stylist, whose lush prose takes readers right into a spectacular setting at odds with the evil men bring to it."
The Globe and Mail

"Classy, edgy writing, subtly plotted and beautifully balanced between fast-paced action, pungent social comment, and the process of investigation."
Weekend Australian

"Meyer is brilliant at suspense, a skill that is coupled with beguilingly unabashed social commentary."
The Times (South Africa)

"Meyer bravely speaks about things which South African mass media doesn't like to discuss. . . . Nevertheless the author's titles remain beautifully written crime stories first of all."
Prochtenie (Russia)

"A John le Carré with a sense of humor."
Weekendavisen (Denmark)

Also by Deon Meyer

Dead Before Dying
Dead at Daybreak
Heart of the Hunter
Devil's Peak
Blood Safari
Thirteen Hours
Trackers
7 Days

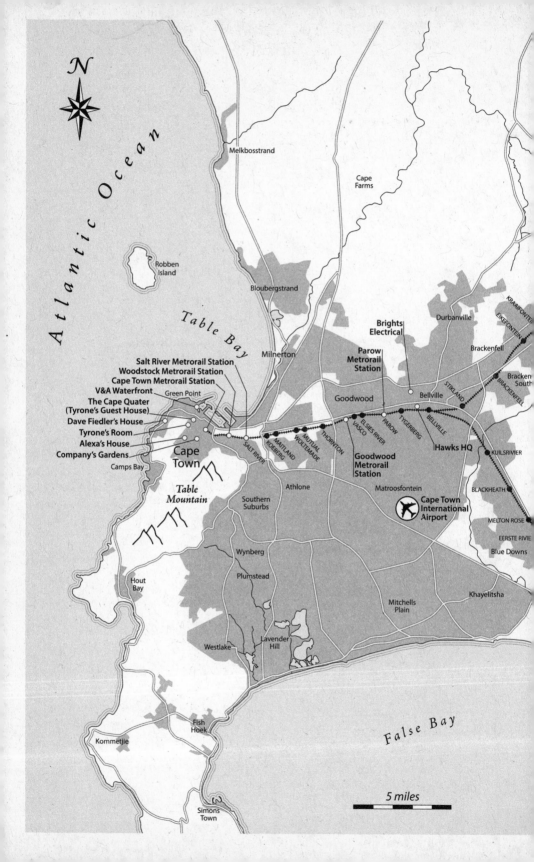

I

The rain drummed down on the corrugated iron roof. Ten past eight in the morning. Captain Benny Griessel clicked open his homicide briefcase on the wall of the wide, high veranda, removed the shoe protectors first, then the thin, transparent latex gloves. He pulled them on, vaguely aware of respectful eyes on him, the uniforms and two station detectives who sheltered in the open garage beyond the curtain of rain. His anxiety and fatigue faded, his focus was on what awaited him here in this big old house.

The heavy front door stood open. He approached the threshold. The grey morning cast the entry hall into deep dusk, the second victim appeared as a dark, shapeless mass. He stood still for a moment, holding his breath. Considering the advice of Doc Barkhuizen: *Don't internalise. Distance yourself.*

What did that mean, now?

He looked for a light switch, found it inside, just beside the door jamb. He clicked it on. High up against the baroque ceiling a chandelier shone white and bright. It did nothing to dispel the chill. The man lay outstretched on the gleaming oak floor, four metres from the door. Black shoes, black trousers, white shirt, light grey tie, top button undone. Arms outstretched, a pistol gripped in the right hand. Mid-thirties. Lean.

Griessel warily stepped closer. He saw the bullet wound in the forehead, diagonally above the left eye. A thin streak of blood, now almost black, ran down to the right. Under the head, which was turned to the left, a puddle, thicker, saucer-sized. Exit wound.

He felt relief at the simplicity of this death, the swiftness of it.

He sighed, long and slow, trying to rid his body of this tension.

It didn't work.

He surveyed the hallway. On an antique table to the right was a light blue vase filled with a green and white mass of fresh arum lilies. On the opposite side, against the left-hand wall, was a hat stand beside an umbrella rack. Six old-fashioned portraits hung on the wall in heavy oval frames. Dignified men and women stared out of each one.

And at the back, deeper in, a sitting room opened out between the two pillars.

He made his calculations from the position of the body, the probable trajectory of the shot, so he could walk where it would least disturb the invisible blood spray and spatter. He stepped around and crouched down beside the pistol, saw the Glock emblem on the barrel, and after it *17 Gen Austria 9x19*.

Griessel sniffed the barrel. It hadn't been fired. He stood up.

Most likely the shooter had stood in the doorway, the victim more or less in the centre of the hallway. If the murder weapon was a pistol, the casing would have been ejected to the right. He searched for it, didn't find it. Perhaps he had used a revolver. Perhaps it had bounced off the wall, lay under the victim. Perhaps the shooter had picked it up.

The exit wound meant the bullet would have hit the wall somewhere. He drew an imaginary line that led him to the sitting room.

He trod carefully, making a wide detour around the corpse, past the pillars, where he picked up the faint scent of burnt wood. The hall chandelier illuminated only a small track in the spacious room and it cast a long Griessel shadow, sending him in search of another light switch. He found three in a row, just behind the pillar, pressed them one by one, and turned around. Soft lighting. Thick wooden beams in the ceiling. Shelves against the walls, filled with leather-bound books. A huge Persian carpet, silver and blue, giant sofas and easy chairs arranged in two separate seating areas. Coffee tables, gleaming, golden wood. Too many lamps and vases, combined with the fussy wallpaper, all intended to create an impression of old-world elegance. In the centre, stately and impressive, was the great hearth, the embers cold. And to the right, just visible behind a dark blue chair – the shoes and trouser legs of the third victim. In the background, on the stark white passage wall, he saw a bright fan of blood spray, like a cheerful, surreal artwork.

Griessel noted the similarities, and unease settled on his heart.

The body in the passage had the same military haircut, the same build – broad-shouldered, with a lean fitness – as the one in the hallway. Also the same black shoes, black trousers, and white shirt. Another bloodied Glock beside a ruined hand. Only the tie was missing this time.

Another head wound, between the temple and the right eye. But the first bullet must have hit the hand – two joints of the finger lay rolled against the white-painted skirting board.

And then he spotted the two shells shining dully on the edge of the carpet in the sitting room. The shooter's, had to be, lying there within ten centimetres of each other. His mind started to play its old tricks; he heard and smelled exactly how it had all happened. The murderer was a shadow slipping through this space, pistol stretched in front of him, he saw the man in the passage, two shots, the hand was a small scarlet explosion. The intense agony, short-lived, before death, no time for fear, just the short silent scream into eternity.

Griessel let out an exclamation, deliberate and loud over the drumming rain, to suppress it all. He hadn't had enough sleep. The fucking stress of the past weeks. He must pull himself together now.

He walked carefully around the body, crouched down beside the pistol. Exactly the same as the other one. *Glock 17 Gen 4*. He sniffed. No smell of cordite.

He stood up, eyes scanning around him, and further down the passage he found the two holes in the right-hand wall.

He had to tread carefully, because the body, the finger, the pistol, and the blood covered the full width of the passage. He hopped from one foot to the other until he was over it. Bent down at the holes. Both bullets were there, buried deep in the plaster. That would help.

Then he went in search of the fourth victim.

The first room, up the passage to the left, had the door open, curtains drawn. He switched on the light. There was a suitcase on the double bed, open. A blue-grey tie, and an empty black shoulder holster lay on the dressing table. In the en-suite bathroom, shaving material and a toothbrush were neatly arranged. Apart from that, nothing.

He walked to the second bedroom. Tidy. Two single beds. A small travelling case at the foot of one. A jacket on a hanger, hooked into the handle of the dark brown wardrobe. A toilet bag hung from a rail in the adjoining bathroom.

He walked out into the passage again, opened a door to the right. It was a big bathroom, gleaming white, with a bath on ball-and-claw feet, a washbasin on a marble slab, bidet, and a toilet.

The next two bedrooms were empty, with no sign of occupation. The last one was right at the end, on the left. The door was open, the room inside almost in darkness. He switched on the light.

Outside the rain stopped abruptly, leaving an eerie silence.

It was a large room. In chaos. The loose carpet lay rucked up. The double bed was askew, the mattress and bedding thrown off. The chair in front of a beautiful antique desk lay on its back, the standard lamp on the desktop was overturned, all the drawers were pulled open. And the doors of the massive wardrobe stood wide too, a pile of clothes on the ground. A large suitcase in the corner, upside down.

'Benna!' A sharp interruption to the softly dripping silence, from the front door, startling him.

Captain Vaughn Cupido had arrived.

'I'm coming,' he shouted back. His voice echoed hoarsely through the huge empty house.

Cupido stood on the threshold in his long black coat, a new piece he confessed he had picked up 'at a factory shop in Salt River, for a song, pappie; classic detective style, the Hawk in Winter, I'm telling you'.

And as Griessel carefully negotiated the hall, he was suddenly conscious of his own crumpled trousers. The thick blue jersey and jacket hid his shirt at least. Yesterday's clothes. And Cupido wouldn't miss that.

'Howzit, Benna. How many are there?'

Griessel walked out onto the veranda, began taking off the gloves. The dark mass of clouds was gone; the sun was trying to break through, making him blink. The view was suddenly breathtaking, the Franschhoek valley unveiled in front of him.

'One of the farm workers is lying in the vineyard. There's been too much rain; I haven't been able to get there. And there are two inside.'

'*Jissis* . . .' Then Cupido looked sharply at him. 'You OK, Benna?'

He knew his eyes were bloodshot, and he hadn't shaved. He nodded. 'Just slept badly,' Benny Griessel lied. 'Let's go and look at the one out there.'

★ ★ ★

The first victim lay on his back, between two rows of vines – a coloured man, dressed in what looked like a dark red uniform with a silver trim. Cupido and Griessel stood on the edge of the lawn, just four metres from the body. They could see the large exit wound between the eyes.

'He was shot from behind. And dragged over there.' Griessel pointed at the two faint, washed-out furrows that ended at the man's heels. 'And these are the footprints of the labourer who found him lying here this morning.'

'It's a brother,' said Cupido, and then, accusingly, 'In a slave outfit.'

'He works at the guesthouse. According to the—'

'This is a guesthouse? I thought it was a wine farm.'

'It's a wine farm with a guesthouse—'

'As if they don't make enough money. You're sure you're all right?'

'I'm fine, Vaughn.'

'Did you go home last night?'

'No. According to the—'

'Was there a case I don't know about?'

'Vaughn, I worked late. You know how the admin piles up. And then I fell asleep.' He hoped Cupido would just let it go.

'In your office?' Sceptical.

'Yes. The station—'

'So that's how you got the call so early?'

'That's right. According to the station detectives, around about nine last night this worker was supposed to come to top up the firewood and check that all the guests were happy. When he didn't come home, his wife thought he must have gone out on the town . . . Then the morning shift found him here. Then they saw the other one in the hallway. The trouble is, they say there were three.'

'Now you're losing me, man. I thought there were three?'

'There were three guests. Inside.'

'So there shoulda been four victims?'

'Yes . . .'

'So where's number four?'

'That's the big question. The thing is . . . We have three head shots, Vaughn. The other one in there was shot through his pistol hand *and* in the head, the two shells are lying this close together . . .'

It took a second for Cupido to grasp. '*Jissis*, Benna. Double tap.'

'On a moving target . . .'

Cupido merely shook his head in awe. 'That's sharp shooting, pappie . . .'

'What bothers me most: the last bedroom shows signs of a fight. Now why would a man who can shoot like that wrestle with a person?'

Cupido looked at Griessel anxiously. 'You thinking what I'm thinking?'

Benny didn't want to say it, the implications were serious. He merely nodded.

'There's a newspaper photographer at the gate, Benna.'

'Fuck,' said Griessel.

'Kidnapping. When last did we see *that*?'

'There's more trouble. Both the men inside look like . . . If I think of their build, hair, the clothes, both carrying Glock Seventeens. I think they are law enforcement. Or military, or Spooks . . .'

'You're kidding me.'

'And a man who shoots like that, faultless . . . He's had training. Task force, Special Forces, Intelligence . . . Something like that. A pro.'

Cupido turned around and stared at the house. 'Shit. Trouble, Benna. Big trouble.'

Griessel sighed. 'That's right.'

'We'll have to get moving, pappie.'

'I'll have to call the Giraffe. They'll have to manage the press.'

They didn't move. They stood side by side, heads bowed – Cupido a head taller than the stocky Griessel – mulling over all the implications, hesitating before the chaos that they knew would ensue.

Until Cupido, with the tails of his Hawk in Winter coat flapping in the icy wind, put his hand protectively on Benny's shoulder.

'Benna, at least there's one silver lining.'

'What do you mean?'

'The way you look this morning, I thought you must've gone on a bender again. But a *dronkgat* couldn't do it; you couldn't have figured all that out if you'd been pissed . . .'

He turned and began to walk towards the guesthouse.

2

Tyrone Kleinbooi saw the aunty climb up into the third-class carriage, here where the Metrorail train 3411 stood at Platform 4 of Bellville Station, just before 8.50 on the Monday morning. She was clearly in her best outfit, wearing a sober headscarf, clutching her large handbag with both hands. He shifted up a little to make the empty seat beside him seem more alluring.

She looked at the seat, and at him, and then she headed towards him, as he knew she would. Because he looked respectable. *Even features*, as Uncle Solly used to say. *You've got even features, Ty. It's a boon in this industry.*

Industry. As if they worked for a company.

She sat down with a sigh, balancing the handbag on her lap.

'Morning, aunty,' he said.

'Morning.' She looked him up and down, taking in his tall, skinny frame, and asked: 'Now where do you come from?'

'From the city, aunty,' he said.

'And where are you going to?'

'Stellenbosch, aunty.'

'You swotting there?'

'No, aunty.'

'Then what you doing there?'

'Going to see my sister, aunty.'

'So what's she doing there?'

'She's swotting, aunty. B.Sc. Human Life. First year.'

'That's a grand course, *nè*? What do you *do* with that?'

The train lurched, and pulled out of the station.

'There's lots you can do, but she wants to become a doctor. She didn't make the selection last year, now she's trying to get in like this.'

'A medical doctor?'

'*Ja*, aunty. She's a *slim kind*, very clever.'

'I would say so. Medical doctor *nogal*. And you? What do you do?'

'I'm a pickpocket, aunty.'

She gripped her handbag more tightly for a moment, but then she laughed. '*Ag*, you,' she said, and bumped her elbow in his ribs. 'What do you do, really?'

'I'm a painter. But not pictures. Houses.'

'I didn't take you for a manual labourer, but that's good honest work,' she said, 'for a young *lat* like you.'

'So where is aunty going to?'

'Also to Stellenbosch. Also to my sister. She struggles with gout. It's so bad she has to go and lie down . . .' And Tyrone Kleinbooi, dark as full-roast coffee beans, and even-featured, nodded politely and listened attentively, because he really did enjoy it. He was only vaguely aware that the rain had stopped. And that was good. Rain was bad for his industry. Pickings had been slim this month.

The modern farmyard of La Petite Margaux was higher up the mountain, minimalist, stacked glass squares held in almost invisible frames of concrete and steel.

The German owner met Griessel and Cupido at the front door, clearly disturbed. A large, bald man with the neck and shoulders of a weightlifter, he introduced himself as Marcus Frank. 'It is a great tragedy,' he said, with just a hint of a Teutonic accent, as he led them to the sitting room. The ceiling was two storeys high. On both sides was a wide, impressive view over mountain and valley.

Two women stood up when they came in: one, young and attractive, the other, older – with an unusual, eccentric air about her.

'Captain Cupido, Captain Griessel, this is Christel de Haan, our hospitality manager,' said Frank, and touched the younger woman's arm sympathetically. Her eyes were red-rimmed behind the trendy dark-framed glasses. She gripped a tissue in her left hand and just nodded, as if she couldn't trust her voice.

'And this is Ms Jeanette Louw,' he said with an inflection that was just a tad too neutral, making Griessel focus more sharply, noticing the body language. There was something in the atmosphere here that didn't quite fit.

Louw stepped forward and put out her hand. She was possibly

around fifty, with big bottle-blonde hair, a chunky frame and a strong jaw. No make-up, and she wore a man's black designer suit, with a white shirt and red-and-white striped tie. 'Hello,' she said sombrely in a deep smoker's voice, her handshake firm as she greeted the detectives.

'Christel and I will leave you now, at Ms Louw's request,' said Frank. 'We will be in my office, when you need us.'

'No,' said Cupido, 'we need to talk to you now.'

'I want to talk with you alone first,' said the blonde woman with an air of authority.

'Please. My office is just here.' Frank pointed down the passage.

'No. We don't have time for this,' said Cupido.

'Those were my people in the guesthouse,' said Louw.

'What do you mean "your people"?'

'Vaughn, let's hear what she has to say.' Griessel didn't have the energy for a confrontation as well. And he had picked up the atmosphere between these people. Along with the loss, there was friction, a certain tension. De Haan began to cry.

Cupido nodded reluctantly. With murmured words of consolation, Marcus Frank sent his hospitality manager down the passage.

'Sit down, please,' said Jeanette Louw, and took a seat herself on one of the angular couches.

Griessel sat down, but Cupido remained standing with his arms folded over his chest. 'What's going on here?' he asked, clearly not happy with the state of affairs.

'I am the managing director of Body Armour, a private security company in the Cape. We rented the guesthouse, and our contract with La Petite Margaux includes an NDA. They have no—'

'A what?' asked Cupido.

'A non-disclosure agreement,' she said as though maintaining her reasonable tone with some difficulty.

'What for?' asked Cupido.

'If you give me a chance, I will explain—'

'We are working against the clock, ma'am.'

'I realise that but—'

'We are the Hawks. We don't have time for small talk and monkey business.'

'Small talk?' Griessel could see her control beginning to dissolve, and her expression altered to a mixture of anger and grief. She leaned forwards, thrust an accusing finger at Cupido. 'You think I want to make small talk while some of my men are lying dead in that guest-house? Drop your act, and sit down, so I can give you the information that you need. Or I will walk out of here, and you can come and find me if you like.'

'I don't take orders from a—'

'Please,' said Griessel curtly.

Louw sank back slowly into the couch. It took a while before Cupido reluctantly said, 'OK,' but he remained on his feet with his arms crossed.

It took Louw a minute to control her emotions, then she addressed herself to Griessel. 'First of all, may I ask: how many bodies are there in the house?'

'Two,' said Griessel.

'Only two?'

'Yes.'

She nodded as though that's what she had expected. 'Can you describe them please?'

'Mid-to late-thirties, short hair, lean, clean shaven, both were apparently carrying Glocks . . .'

Louw held up her hand, she had heard enough. Her eyes closed, then opened again. 'They are both my men. B. J. Fikter and Barry Minnaar.'

'I'm sorry,' said Griessel. And then: 'You mean they worked for you?'

'Yes.'

'What sort of work, exactly?' asked Cupido.

'They were bodyguards.'

'Who was the third person in the house?' asked Griessel.

'My client. Paul Anthony Morris.'

'Who's he, that he needs bodyguards?' asked Cupido.

'I . . . he's a British citizen. That's all . . .'

'Shit,' said Cupido, because he could see the complications already.

Louw misread his reaction. 'Captain, that is all the information that he was willing to provide.'

'Ma'am,' said Griessel, 'at this stage we suspect that he . . . is missing. And he is a foreigner. That means . . .' he searched for the right word.

'Big trouble,' said Cupido.

'That's right,' said Griessel. 'We need all the information we can get, as soon as possible.'

'That's why I am here,' said Louw. 'I will give you everything I have.'

'But not in front of the farm people. Why?' asked Cupido.

'Because of the confidentiality clause, La Petite Margaux had no knowledge of who was in the guesthouse. And I have a discretionary duty towards my client. That is why I must talk to you alone.'

Cupido shrugged.

'Tell us what you know,' said Griessel.

She nodded, and took a deep breath, as if to gather her strength.

3

'Last Wednesday, just before sixteen hundred hours, Morris contacted me by phone, and enquired about the nature of our services and the background of our personnel. With a . . . I suppose what they call an Oxford accent. I referred him to our website, but he said he had already studied it, and wanted to make sure it was not merely marketing. I assured him that everything was factually correct. He had a few questions about the training background of our personnel, which I answered—'

'How are they trained?' asked Cupido.

'Most of my people are former SAPS bodyguards, Captain.'

'OK. Proceed.'

'Morris then said that he had, and I quote as well as I can recall, "a need to get out of circulation for a while, and enjoy the benefit of very vigilant, discreet and professional bodyguard services". And he needed this from last Friday. I said yes, we can accommodate him, and asked whether I could work through the standard procedure to determine our service according to his needs. He wanted to know what that procedure entailed. I said it was a series of questions about his occupation, circumstances, next of kin who could be contacted in case of emergency, possible threats, time period, and budget limitations. His reaction was that there were no budget limits, and that he wished to use the services for a couple of weeks, but he would prefer not to supply any further information. I said I would prepare a plan and quote, and email it to him. He preferred to phone back, which he did an hour later.'

Griessel listened to the official tone, the precise word choice. As if she sought refuge in the familiar territory of the official statement. There was a military air about her. He wondered if she had also been in the Service.

'My recommendation was this guesthouse, and a team of—'

'Why this one?' Cupido asked.

'We use it on a regular basis. It complies with our requirements. It is less than an hour from the airport, but outside the city. It is remote, with good access control, an open, manageable perimeter, and staff that understand our needs and requirements.'

'OK. Proceed.'

'My recommendation to Morris included a team of two armed bodyguards per day and night shift. He accepted immediately, and asked what the next step would be to close the deal. I asked him to deposit one week's daily tariffs. He—'

'How much?' Cupido asked, uncrossed his arms and sat down in a chair beside Griessel's. 'How much was the deposit?'

'Just over five thousand two hundred pounds. About seventy thousand rand.'

'For a week?' In disbelief.

'That's right.'

'And he paid it?'

'Within half an hour. And the next day, the Thursday, he sent a scan of the photo page of his passport via email, which I had requested for identification and registration purposes. It showed that he was a fifty-six-year-old British citizen. He also called that Thursday with details of his arrival. During that call I notified him of procedures at the airport, and gave him a description of my people who would meet him. That was the sum total of my communication with him. Fikter and Minnaar went to meet him at the airport on Friday afternoon – he was on flight SA337 from Johannesburg which landed at fifteen ten. They—'

'Johannesburg?' asked Cupido. 'So he didn't fly out of England?'

'It's possible that he flew from the UK to Johannesburg, and caught a connection to Cape Town. I can't confirm that.'

'OK. Proceed.'

'Fikter sent me a SMS on Friday afternoon at fifteen hundred seventeen to confirm that Morris had arrived safely, and another at sixteen hundred and fifty-two that they were at La Petite Margaux guesthouse and that everything was in order. They took the night shift that Friday night, and Stiaan Conradie and Allistair Barnes the day shift. Every team reported via SMS at the beginning and end of each shift. There were no problems. On Sunday morning, at the end of the night shift, I had a telephone conversation with Fikter to check on how things were going. He said Morris was a very courteous and refined man, and that he appeared relaxed and jovial. Conradie and Barnes are here at the moment, down at the gate. They are ready to talk to you as soon as the SAPS allow them entry to the farm.'

'So let me get this straight,' said Cupido. 'All that you know, is that this *ou* is a Brit with a fancy accent and seventy thousand to burn. No address, no job description, *nada*. For all we know he could be a serial killer.'

'That's correct.'

'But you are happy to sell bodyguard services to such a person?'

'Captain, if you have cash and you want to buy a new car, the dealer doesn't ask you if you have a criminal record.'

'A cop with cash for a car? Fat chance. And it's not the same.'

'Oh?'

'Bodyguard services are sort of personal, don't you think?'

Louw began to lean forward again, and Griessel asked: 'When you spoke to him on the telephone – did he sound scared? Anxious?'

She shook her head. 'No. During the conversation I drew only two conclusions. The first was that he had not used this sort of service before, and the second was that he wanted to reveal as little about himself as possible.' She looked at Cupido. 'And that's not unusual. Personal security services are by their very nature discreet. The majority of our clients are businessmen who don't want it trumpeted about—'

'Why not?'

'A need to maintain a low profile. And I think that's also because they don't want to offend their hosts. They come to do business with local companies, and the very public display of security gives the impression that they believe South Africa is a dangerous place.'

'Then why do they use the service? There's just about no crime against tourists.'

'It's a general misconception among foreigners—'

'Which you are happy to indulge. Could you see from the email address where he works? What was the domain name?'

'It was a Gmail address. And the name was Paul underscore Morris fifteen or something.'

'And the payment of the deposit? EFT?'

'Yes. From a Swiss bank, Adler, if I remember correctly. I will confirm that.'

'Ma'am . . .' began Griessel.

'Please. I am not a ma'am. Call me Jeanette.'

'The two bodyguards in there . . .'

'B. J. Fikter and Barry Minnaar.'

'Yes. How long ago did they leave the SAPS?'

'About seven, eight years . . .'

'How long have they worked for you?'

'For the same time period. I can assure you the attack had nothing to do with—'

'No, that is not what I'm getting at. How . . . good were they?'

She grasped his meaning. 'I only appoint the best. And for the sort of work they do, there is annual refresher training and testing, and the standards of fitness, weapon handling, and self-defence is high. We even do six-monthly drug tests. I can assure you Fikter and Minnaar were outstanding operators.'

'And yet . . .' said Cupido sceptically.

Jeanette finally lost her control. She planted her feet apart, leaned forward, put her elbows on her knees. 'Let me tell you, if you weren't a policeman, I would *bliksem* you right now.'

The young woman, not much older than Tyrone Kleinbooi, looked at the pile of notes, and then at the computer screen. 'You still owe seven thousand rand,' she said, each English syllable precise.

'Why do you *gooi* English at me – I thought this was supposed to be an Afrikaans university here,' said Tyrone. 'This is all I can pay now. One thousand two hundred and fifty.'

She bristled a little. 'It doesn't matter what language a person says it in, mister, *die rekening is agterstallig.* You are in arrears. Results are only released when it is paid in full.'

It was frustration that made him tease her. 'You can *gooi* in as many fancy white Afrikaans words as you like, but I can tell you're actually a Cape Flats girl.'

'*Ek kom van die Pniel af*, I'm not from the Flats. And I can see you have more money in your wallet. Does your pa know what you're up to?'

'*Jirre*,' said Tyrone Kleinbooi. 'What name is there on your computer, dollie?'

'"Nadia Kleinbooi". And I'm not your "dollie".'

'Do I look like a Nadia?'

'How should I know? There are some funny names on this computer.'

'Nadia is my sister, dolly. We don't have a ma, and we don't have a pa. This is money that I earned with my own two hands, *versta' jy*? And what is left in my wallet, I have to go and give to her to pay her rent on her flat. So don't you sit there and judge me. Have a heart, we pay as we can, she worked flippen hard, those results belong to her, not you lot – so why can't she see them?'

'I don't make the rules.'

'But you can bend them, *net 'n bietjie*. For a brother.'

'And lose my job? Not today.'

He sighed, and pointed at the screen in front of her. 'Can you see them there?'

'The results?'

'*Ja.*'

'I can.'

'Did she pass?'

Her face revealed nothing.

'*Ag*, please, sister,' he said.

She glanced around first. Then said softly and quickly: 'She passed well.' She took the money and began counting.

'*Dankie*, sister,' he said, and turned to go.

'*Jy kannie net loep nie*, you must wait for your receipt.'

'*Sien jy*, I knew you could *gooi* Flats.'

4

They felt the pressure, the urgency of time slipping away.

'Cyril was a friend to me,' said Marcus Frank, the German owner. 'A valued employee.'

Benny Griessel knew there was a risk that Cupido would say something like, 'So why did you make him wear a slave uniform?' and so he interjected quickly: 'You have our condolences, Mr Frank. Now, one of the—'

'Our reputation is in tatters,' said Frank. 'The media is waiting at the gate.'

'I understand. But one of the guests is missing, and we have to move as fast as possible. Can you tell us what Mr January was doing at the guesthouse last night?'

Frank made a helpless gesture in the direction of the still weepy Christel de Haan.

The woman put on her glasses and said: 'He cleared the dinner table, and lit the fire.'

'What time?' asked Cupido.

'At exactly nine o'clock.'

'How do you know that?'

'That was our agreement with them.'

'The bodyguards?'

'Yes. Breakfast at exactly eight o'clock, house cleaning at nine, lunch at one, dinner at eight p.m. Final clearing, and hospitality at nine. They are very strict, they have a lot of rules.'

'Like what?'

'They screened all our people. Only six were cleared to work when they rented the guesthouse, two for breakfast, two for house cleaning in the morning, and two for dinner and evening hospitality. It made things very difficult . . .'

'Why?'

'Because sometimes members of our staff are ill, or they want to take a vacation . . .'

'So why did you rent the house to these people?'

'They pay almost double the going rate.'

Cupido shook his head again in amazement. 'OK. So Cyril January was one of the cleared people?'

'Yes.'

'How did it work? Did he have keys?'

'No, no, if they wanted to enter, they had to call one of the guards when they were at the door.'

'How?'

'With a cellphone. They had to say a code word. They had to say "breakfast in the green room" if it was safe, or "breakfast in the red room" if they thought there was danger.'

'*Jissis*. And then the guard unlocked the door?'

'Yes.'

'But you said there were two people serving dinner?'

'Yes. Cyril's daughter . . .' De Haan's eyes filled, and her voice became hoarse. 'I'm sorry. His daughter, she's only eighteen . . . She served dinner with him, and they cleared the table, and then she left with the trolley. Cyril was doing hospitality . . .'

'What does that mean?'

'Chocolates on the pillows, check the bathroom supplies, like soap and shampoo and shower gel and hand cream, and light the fire . . .'

'Do you know what time he usually finished?'

'Between nine and half past.'

'And his wife thought he went to town last night?'

'He did do that sometimes.'

'Where would he go?'

'To friends.'

'And he would stay out all night?'

'Sometimes.'

'What was the procedure when he left the house?' asked Griessel.

'He just left, and they locked the door behind them.'

'And this morning?'

'One of our agricultural workers saw Cyril's body. At about

six-thirty, on his way to report for work. And then he saw the front
door of the guesthouse was open . . .'

'OK,' said Cupido, 'we'll have to speak to the daughter . . . We have
to speak to all the staff, in about . . .' he looked at his watch, 'in about
an hour's time. Can you assemble them for us?'

Cupido began to rant as they walked towards the car, just as Griessel
knew he would.

'"They pay almost double the going rate." That's the trouble with
this country, Benna. It's just naked greed, no fucking ethics.
Everybody just wants to score, it's just *skep, pappie, skep,* before
doomsday comes. Seventy thousand bucks for a week's personal
security? We're in the wrong business, I'm telling you. And that
lesbetarian wants to *bliksem* me? What for? Because I tell it like it is?
She can't do that, I mean, what do you say? There's just no appropri-
ate response to a lezzy, you're *gefok* if you say come try me, you're
gefok if you zip your lip. There should be a law against that sort of
thing. Wants to *bliksem* me? With seventy thousand in her back pocket
and her Calvin Klein suit and that hair . . . And what is this here?
German owner of a Boer farm with a French name where a Brit is
kidnapped. Fucking United Nations of Crime, that's where we're
heading. And why? 'Cause they bring their troubles here. Like those
French at Sutherland, and the Dewani thing, and who gets the rap?
South-*fokken*-Africa.'

They got into the car.

'I'm telling you now, the perpetrator will be a foreign citizen, but
d'you think the TV will mention it? Not on your life, it'll be like "crime-
ridden society" all over again, all that *kak*. It's not right, Benna. Wants
to *bliksem* me. But they screen the little *volkies* in slave uniforms and
let them clean up after their whitey backsides until ten o'clock at night.
Chocolates on the pillows . . .'

'Forensics are here,' said Griessel when he spotted the white minibus
parked at the guesthouse, beside the SAPS photographer's Corolla,
and the two ambulances.

'They'll have to get a move on – we have to search the Brit's room.'

'And the Giraffe.' Beside the big Ford Territory of the Directorate
of Priority Crime Investigations – DPCI, or the Hawks – stood tall,

thin Colonel Zola Nyathi, commanding officer of the Violent
Crimes Group.

As the first Hawk on the scene, Griessel reported as succinctly as he
could. He was aware of the colonel's sharp eyes on him, with that
unreadable, unchanging poker face of his.

When he had finished, the Giraffe said: 'I see,' and stood with his
head bowed, deep in thought.

Eventually: 'You're JOC on this one, Benny.'

'Yes, sir.' His heart sank, because the last thing he needed in his
current situation, was the responsibility of the so-called Joint
Operations Command.

'You already have Vaughn. How many more people do you need?'

He knew the Hawks liked big teams who could hit hard and fast,
but he was still sceptical about this approach. Too many people falling
over each other, especially on an investigational level. And he knew
command didn't always mean control over the direction of the investigation. 'Four detectives, sir.'

'You sure?'

'Yes, sir.'

'I'll get Cloete out. And start oiling the consulatory wheels.'

Captain John Cloete was the Hawks' media liaison officer. And
Griessel knew they were going to need all the help they could get with
the British Consulate. For though the Brits weren't as bad as the
Canadians, and the Canadians were not as difficult as the Chinese –
embassies were not keen to share their citizens' information, especially
when there was crime involved. And in any case, they were bureau-
cratic dead-ends. So all he said was: 'Thank you, sir.'

He noticed Nyathi's gaze dwell on him a moment before the colonel
nodded, turned, and walked back to his vehicle. He knew it was
because he looked so terrible. He cursed himself again. Last night he
should have . . .

'Come, Benna,' said Cupido, 'let's check how far Forensics are.'

In Dorp Street in Stellenbosch, a tour bus was parked in front of Oom
Samie se Winkel, the now-legendary old-time store and tourist magnet.

Tyrone Kleinbooi eyed up the tourists on the pavement. Europeans, he recognised them by their pale legs, their get-up. He had given up wondering why European and American visitors were the only people in Africa who bought and wore safari outfits – the hunting jackets (with pockets for ammunition), the Livingstone helmets or wide-brimmed hats, the boots.

His senses sharpened. He focused on the group lining up at the door to get on the bus. At the back stood a middle-aged woman with a big raffia shoulder bag. Easy target. She would be expecting contact with other tour members. Her purse would be in the bag, right at the bottom, in the centre, big and fat, loaded with rands and euros and credit and cash cards, ripe for the picking. All he had to do was to take the hair clip with the little yellow sunflower that he had in his pocket, hide it in his hand, bend down in front of her, and pretend to pick it up.

Uncle Solly: *I had an appie who tried that trick with money, a ten-rand note. He flashed it at the mark, and the mark's attention went immediately to his wallet. Now that's just stupid. You use something that is colourful and pretty. But not money.*

'I think you dropped this, ma'am,' he would say quietly, intimately, confidentially, with his big innocent look-how-honest-our-locals-are smile. And his even features. With his right shoulder nearly touching her.

With her eyes and all her attention focused in surprise on the hair clip, he would slide his right hand into the bag, get a sure grip on the purse.

She would beam with grateful goodwill, because these white people from the north are black people pleasers, probably feeling guilty about their own colonial escapades. She would reach out her hand to the clip, and then shake her head. 'Oh, thank you, but it's not mine.' He would bump her lightly with his right shoulder as he withdrew his hand from the bag, and put the purse in his pocket.

The withdrawal is the key. Smooth and fast. Keep the wallet upright, don't let it hook on anything – the last thing you want at that crucial moment is a snag. And remember, there are other people who might be watching, so you want everyone's attention on the dropped object, you hold it high and handsome. And then you get the wallet out of sight, and your hand out of your pocket. Show it to the people, here is my innocent hand.

'My apology, ma'am,' he would say.

She would reply in a Dutch or German accent: 'No, please, don't apologise.' Except the Austrian woman, two years ago, who said 'thank you' and took the clip out of his hand. He had the last laugh though. The profit from her purse was nearly two thousand rand.

He would smile, turn, and walk away, look back and wave at her. *Don't rush it. Saunter, Ty. But be aware,* want jy wiet nooit . . . *You never know,* the words echoed in his head.

He was in between the tourists, next to the woman, ready, every nerve ending tingling, the adrenaline flowing, just enough.

And then his brain said, Don't.

If it feels wrong, walk away.

He saw the pair of security guards just beyond the shop, their eyes on him.

He walked past, to Market Street, and his sister's flat.

5

From the front door, Griessel and Cupido could see the two men from Forensics at work under the bright spotlights in the sitting room. And hear their heated rugby conversation .

'I'm telling you, Bismarck is not a man, he's a machine,' said Arnold, the short fat one, vehemently.

'You shoot your own argument in the foot,' said Jimmy, the tall thin one. They knelt side by side, in the spacious lounge.

'What makes you say that?'

As a team they were known as Thick and Thin, a relic of the tired old quip from the days when they first began to work together: 'Forensics will stand by you through thick and thin', which in turn had been inspired by fat Arnold's previous Forensics partner, a freckled, cheeky and pretty redhead woman, who had self-deprecatingly referred to their partnership as 'Speckled & Egg'. There was a fair bit of murmuring when she left in search of greener pastures, and Jimmy – male, and far less attractive – was appointed.

'Bismarck is a machine? How does a machine get injured? Anyway, this year we will win the Cup, because your Sharks machine is going to seize up when the chips are down. Just like last year . . .'

'May we come in?' Griessel called.

'Thank the Lord, the Hawks are here,' said Arnold.

'I feel so safe now,' said Jimmy.

'Are you wearing shoe covers?' Arnold asked.

'Haven't you finished up front here yet?' Cupido retorted. 'Maybe you should stop talking rugby *kak* and get your arses into second gear.'

'Rugby *kak*? What sort of Cape coloured are you?'

'The sort who will kick your whitey arses if you don't pull finger.'

'If you're a kicker, the Stormers need you,' said Arnold. 'All fifteen fly-halves are injured again.'

'*Fokkof,*' said Jimmy. 'Come in if you have shoe covers on. There's something very weird here you should see.'

The 'something very weird' was a cartridge case.

'It's a Cor-Bon .45 ACP +P,' said thin Jimmy as he held it up for display with a pair of silver pliers.

'Not all forty-fives can shoot the Plus P,' said Arnold.

'Only the more recent models.'

'Your Plus P has a higher maximum internal pressure.'

'And higher velocity.'

'We can explain that in layman's terms if you don't understand.'

'We know easy words too.'

'So now you are ballistics *and* language experts?' asked Cupido.

'Your modern Forensic's scientific knowledge is vast,' said Jimmy. 'Bordering on genius . . .'

'In contrast with your average Hawk,' said Arnold.

'AKA the bird brains,' said Jimmy.

'*Fokkof,*' said Griessel. He knew it wouldn't help to try to be witty, because they always had the last word.

'Benny, you look particularly appealing this morning.'

'Or is that "appalling"?' The Forensics duo grinned at each other.

'Not so very bright-eyed and bushy-tailed, eh? And not too sharp-eyed for a Hawk either,' said Arnold.

'Don't you see it?' asked Jimmy.

'See what?' asked Cupido.

'The engraving.' He held the cartridge closer and rotated it.

'What is it?' asked Griessel.

'Take this,' said Arnold, and he held out a magnifying glass. Griessel took it, and studied the copper tube.

'It looks like a snake. Ready to strike.'

'Amazing,' said Jimmy. 'That he can see anything at all through those bloodshot eyes.'

'And what's under the rearing snake?' Arnold asked.

'Are those letters?' The engraving was tiny.

'Praise the Lord. The Hawks can read.'

'We can *bliksem* you too,' said Cupido. 'What do the letters say?'

'"N", dot, "m", dot,' said Arnold.

'So what does that mean? "Never mind"?'

'Where do you dig that up?'

'NM. Never mind. Don't you understand texting language? I thought you were so clever?'

'Sophisticated people don't use texting abbreviations. Capital N, small letter m stands for "newton-metre". If both were small letter it would stand for "nanometre". But in both cases without the dot,' said Arnold.

'So what do the two capital letters with two dots stand for?'

'I thought *you* were the detectives.'

'Because you rocket scientists don't know?' said Cupido in triumph.

'We can't do *all* your work for you.'

'Or, at least we can't do all your work for you *all* the time.'

'*Fokkof*,' said Griessel. 'We have to search the last room. Are you finished there?'

'Haven't even started.'

'*Jissis*,' said Cupido.

They went to interview Scarlett January, daughter of the murdered worker, Cyril.

Cupido sat beside her on the comfortable couch in the sitting room. He held her hand, his voice gentle and sympathetic. Griessel and Christel de Haan each sat in a chair.

'I'm so sorry for your loss, little sister.'

The pretty, petite girl nodded through her tears.

'If I could, I would not have bothered you. But we want to catch these evil people. They must pay for what they have done to your daddy.'

Another nod.

'Are you OK to answer a few little questions?'

She sniffed, blew her nose, and said: 'Yes, uncle.'

'You are very brave, *sistertjie*, your daddy would be very proud of you. Did you work with him every day in the guesthouse?'

'Yes.'

'The night shift, *nè*?'

Nod.

'Did you see the Englishman?'

'*Ja*.'

'What can you tell us about him?'

'He was very friendly.'

'Did he talk to you?'

'*Ja.*'

'What did he say?'

'My table looked nice. And the food was good.'

'Is that all?'

'And it's so lovely here. On the farm. If he looks out the window. That's all.'

'OK, *sistertjie*, that's very good. Now the bodyguards. Did you talk to them too?'

'Not really.'

'Were they nice to you?'

'*Ja*, uncle. But they didn't talk much.'

'Now, last night, what time did you leave there?'

The memory of the previous evening caused Scarlett's shoulders to shake. It took her a time to say: 'I don't know.'

'It's OK, *sistertjie*. So more or less nine o'clock?'

Nod.

'And everything was OK. There in the guesthouse?'

Nod.

'The same as the other nights?'

'*Ja.*'

'The bodyguards weren't different?'

'No, uncle.'

'Can you tell us how you left? Did one of them walk with you?'

'*Ja.* The one they call B. J.'

'OK, tell me nicely.'

'I told B. J. I was finished. He went and unlocked the front door. He went out first and looked, and then he came back in and said everything is fine. Then I called Daddy, because he had to help me with the trolley down the steps. Then—'

'What trolley?'

'The trolley with the leftovers and the dishes.'

'OK, and then?'

'Then we went out, Daddy helped me down the steps, and I pushed it back to the restaurant.'

'And then they locked up again?'

'I don't know.'

'That's OK. And you didn't see anything, while you were pushing it back to the restaurant?'

'I just . . .' And Scarlett January began to weep again. Christel de Haan stood up, gave her a couple of tissues and sat down again.

When she had regained some control, she said: 'Uncle, I . . . I'm a bit shy, uncle . . .'

Cupido leaned closer and whispered in her ear. 'So just tell me, I won't tell a soul.'

She nodded, blew her nose, and turned her mouth to his ear. 'Daddy says I was born with the *helm* . . .'

'OK.'

'Because I get these *gevoelentes*; premonitions.'

'I understand.'

'When I was walking there, I got this feeling, uncle.'

'What sort of feeling, *sistertjie*?' he whispered, barely audible.

'Evil, uncle. A terrible evil. Over there by the bougainvillea.'

6

Tyrone told his sister about her results. He sat on the only easy chair in Nadia's one-bedroom flat – the one with the broken leg that he had found thrown out in front of a house in the Bo-Kaap. He had mended it. Not good workmanship, because he didn't know much about wood-work. But it was sturdy, and it was comfortable.

'So, I'm very proud of you,' he said.

She sat at the big work table with her long black hair, and delicate, almost fragile beauty. He had swapped it for a stolen iPhone at the second-hand shop in Woodstock's Albert Street.

'Thanks, *boetie*.'

'Don't worry, I'll have the money by the end of the month,' he said. He took out his wallet. 'Here's the rent for the flat.'

'No, I only need a thousand, I got *lekker* big tips.'

'That's what I want to talk about. Tips or not, you're here to study.'

'But I like the work, *boetie*.'

'I understand, but *nou's dit* crunch time.'

'I can't just sit and swot all day.'

'So go for a walk. Or socialise a bit.'

'No. We eat for free, at the end of the shift, it saves me good money. And where will you get more than five thousand rand by the end of the month?'

'Big paint job in Rose Street, a whole block of flats. I'm one of the subcontractors for Donnie Fish. And it's interiors too, so it can *ma'* rain. And in any case, the Cape economy is booming again, tourism is up seventeen per cent. *Ek sê jou*, by December there will be enough for half of next year's class fees as well. You just swot, so that you make the selection. I don't want you wasting your time with waitressing.'

'It's not wasting time.' She had that stubborn look around her mouth that he had known since they were little. 'And I *will* make the selection.'

He knew he wasn't going to convince her. 'That's what I want to hear.'

The four extra Hawks detectives arrived – Lieutenant Vusumuzi Ndabeni, small of stature, with a manicured goatee and wide-awake eyes; Lieutenant Cedric 'Ulinda' Radebe, the ex-boxer, whose nickname in Zulu meant 'honey badger'; Captain Mooiwillem Liebenberg, the DPCI's best-looking detective and most respected skirt-chaser; and Captain Frankie Fillander, the veteran with a long scar from his ear to his crown from a knife wound.

Standing on the lawn of the guesthouse, Griessel brought them up to date with the details. He had to concentrate, because the weariness was a burden growing steadily heavier. And he was increasingly self-conscious about his appearance, and the looks that he was getting from his colleagues. He asked Ndabeni and Fillander, the gentlest of the officers, to question the farm workers, and told Radebe and Liebenberg to talk to the bodyguards.

Then he and Cupido walked to the veranda to hear whether Forensics were finished yet. The wind blew suddenly chill again.

'Global warming?' said Cupido as he looked up at the dark clouds once more looming in the east. 'Seems to me every winter is colder and wetter.'

Griessel's cellphone made a cheerful sound in his trouser pocket. He knew who and what it was.

His colleague looked keenly at him. 'But that's an iPhone you got there.'

'Yes,' said Griessel.

'Since when?'

'Friday.'

Cupido's eyebrows remained raised.

'Alexa gave it to me,' said Griessel.

Alexa Barnard. The new love in his life, the once famous singer, now a rehabilitated alcoholic, one hundred and fifty days sober now, and slowly rebuilding her career.

'The iPhone 5?'

'I don't know.'

'*Jy wietie?*' Cupido chortled at his ignorance.

Griessel took the phone out of his pocket and showed it to him.

'Yip, iPhone 5C. It's not an Android, but Benny, *broe', dai's kwaai*. Welcome to the twenty-first century. You have graduated from appie to pro.'

Over the last few months Cupido had been one of Griessel's technology mentors. He had been nagging Benny for a long time to get an Android smartphone. 'An HTC, Benna. Just don't go and get a Samsung. Those guys are the new Illuminati, taking over the world, gimmick by gimmick. Never trust a phone company that makes fridges, pappie.'

At the front door of the guesthouse Cupido called inside: 'Jimmy, are you done?'

Griessel quickly read the SMS on his screen. *Missed you. Good luck. Can't wait for tonight. Have a surprise for you. Xxx*

From inside the house came the reply: 'Close enough. Just put shoe covers and gloves on again.'

They obeyed in silence, and picked their way through the hall, sitting room, and down the passage. They found Thick and Thin in the last bedroom, busy packing away fingerprint paraphernalia.

'Found a couple of weird things,' said Arnold.

'So did we,' said Cupido. '*You* two.'

'Sticks and stones,' said Jimmy.

'Water off a duck's back,' said Arnold. 'Firstly, there is blood spray on the front door, which doesn't make sense with the way the bodies are lying.'

'Inside or outside?' asked Griessel.

'On the outside of the door.'

'The door was open when I got here. The blood could have come from inside.'

'We considered that,' said Jimmy, 'but it still doesn't make sense.'

'Secondly,' said Arnold, 'we found another cartridge in the hallway. In amongst the arum lilies. The same calibre, the same cobra engraving.'

'One shooter for both victims,' said Jimmy.

'Thirdly, all the man's clothes are new,' said Arnold. 'As in brand new. And I mean everything. Even the underpants.'

'The suitcase too,' said Jimmy. 'Practically out of the box.'

'*And* his passport.'

'Where's the passport?' asked Griessel.

'Top drawer, on the right, in a little leather cover, new, fancy,' said Arnold.

Griessel stepped carefully over the rucked-up carpet and the bed linen on the floor, and pulled open the drawer of the bedside table. Inside was a shiny leather pouch. He picked it up, unzipped it. There were boarding pass stubs for Air France and SAA inside. They showed that Paul Anthony Morris had taken Flight AF0990 from Charles de Gaulle airport in Paris to Johannesburg on Thursday at 23.20, and on Friday, Flight SA337 from Johannesburg to Cape Town. Business class, both times.

The passport was tucked into a compartment of the pouch. Griessel pulled it out. It seemed very new still, the red cover with its gold lettering and national coat of arms was smooth and without creases or marks.

He opened it, paged to the photo ID. It showed a man in his fifties with a long, symmetrical face, no hint of a smile. His hair covered his ears, but neatly trimmed, dark, with grey wings at the temples. He looked slightly downwards at the camera, which made Griessel wonder whether he was tall.

To the right of the photo was his date of birth – 11 September 1956 – and the date the passport was issued. Barely a week ago.

Cupido came and stood beside Griessel as he paged over to the immigration stamps. There were only two: France, last Thursday, and South Africa, Friday.

'Brand new,' said Cupido.

'That's what we were trying to explain to you,' said Jimmy with an exaggerated long-suffering sigh.

'Did you see a wallet anywhere?' Griessel asked.

'No,' Arnold said. 'If he has one, it went along. Or it's somewhere else in the house.'

'Anything else?'

Jimmy put his hand in his briefcase and took out a transparent evidence bag. 'A cable tie,' he said, and held the bag up. 'It was here, half under the bed.'

Griessel took the bag and inspected it closely. The cable had been tied, and then cut.

'Just the one?'

'That's right.'

Griessel let the police photographer take pictures of the passport first – the outside page, stamp page, and information pages. He asked Cupido to travel with the photographer, wait for prints, and take them to the British Consulate. 'Be diplomatic, Vaughn, please ...'

'Aren't I always?'

'And phone the Giraffe first, find out if he's greased the wheels yet.'

'Sure, Benna.'

He would rather have gone himself, so he could think. About the case. About his sins. And also because Cupido was the least diplomatic of all the Hawks. But he was JOC leader. For now he would have to stay here.

He jogged through the drizzle to the garage where Radebe and Liebenberg were questioning the two Body Armour employees.

The four men stood in a tight circle, which they opened up to include Griessel. Liebenberg introduced him to the two bodyguards, Stiaan Conradie and Allistair Barnes. The same short haircut, broad shoulders, black suits, and white shirts as the victims. Their faces were grim.

'I'm sorry about your colleagues,' said Griessel.

They nodded.

There was an uncomfortable silence, eventually broken by Captain Willem Liebenberg who spoke while referring to his notebook: 'They relieved the night shift every morning at seven-thirty, and worked twelve hours, till nineteen-thirty. The procedure for handing over was a cellphone call from outside, with "green" and "red" as code words for safe or unsafe. Then the front door would be unlocked from inside, and locked again. They said the British guy ... Morris, was friendly, but not very talkative—'

'You do understand, we don't encourage conversation,' said Barnes.

'It distracts us from our work,' said Conradie.

'So they actually know very little about the man,' said Liebenberg. 'He's about one point eight metres tall, more or less ninety kilograms, black hair, brown eyes. He speaks with a distinct British accent. Every morning after breakfast, and every afternoon after four, he went for an escorted walk of about forty minutes here on the farm, and every—'

'Did he request that? The walk?' asked Griessel.

Conradie replied: 'We give the clients a portfolio of choices. That was one that he chose.'

A portfolio of choices. If Cupido had been here, he would be going on about that: *An ex-policeman talking fancy.*

'And that's safe?'

'Safety is relative,' said Barnes. 'Unless the client divulges the nature of the threat. Which Mr Morris did not do.'

Radebe shook his head. 'Did you ask him?'

'Miss Louw does that. The background research. She said the client chose not to divulge. Our responsibility is to convey the portfolio of choices to the client, and to accommodate them. If he believes the threat is of such a nature that it's safe to go for a walk, we must accept that,' said Conradie.

'He asked us if we were sure no one had followed them from the airport,' said Barnes.

'Were you?'

'If there were any signs, Fikter and Minnaar would have reported it.'

'OK,' said Griessel.

7

The bodyguards said Morris sat in the dining room during the day with his computer and iPad, and in the evening, by the fire with a book that he had found on the sitting-room bookshelves. Sometimes he just stood at the window in the dining room, looking out over the Franschhoek Valley. 'I never knew this country was so beautiful,' he had apparently once said.

Griessel asked them where he kept the computer and iPad.

'He didn't. Every time that we left, they were still on the dining-room table,' said Conradie.

'And at mealtimes?'

'Morris ate in the dining room; we ate in the kitchen.'

Conradie saw Griessel frown. 'It's protocol,' he said.

'Did he have a cellphone?'

'He must have. We never saw him with it,' said Conradie.

'But he could have used it in his room at night when you weren't with him.'

'It's possible.'

'He never asked you to phone anyone?'

'No.'

'Is there Wi-Fi in the guesthouse?' asked Radebe.

'Yes.'

Radebe made a note.

'This place . . .' Griessel indicated the wine farm. 'I still don't understand why you brought him here. It's not hard to get in, if you really want to.'

Barnes frowned, sighed softly, and said: 'Personal security is as good as the client's briefing. We have safe houses and safe apartments that a full SWAT team would not get into, if there were enough PSOs that knew what they—'

'PSOs?'

'Personal Security Operatives.'

'OK.'

'But this guy said nothing about the nature of the threat. We can't force him. The protocol is, if they don't tell us anything specific, the boss describes all the options, and then he has to decide for himself.'

'This place is fine if no one knows you're here,' said Conradie.

'But someone *did* know he was here,' said Griessel.

The bodyguards nodded, uneasily.

'How? What are the possibilities?'

'He might have told someone,' said Barnes.

'Before he came,' said Conradie. 'Or while he was here. He could have sent someone an email . . .'

'What else? The men who abducted him are professionals.'

The silence stretched out longer, before Conradie said: 'If the pros follow you . . . It's not always possible to spot. If they're very good. If they use two or three cars. If they attach a GPS tracker to your car.'

'That's it,' said Barnes. 'The only possibilities.'

Griessel nodded. 'And he never seemed afraid or concerned?'

'No. He was relaxed. And a nice guy. One of the easier clients we've had in the past few years.'

'Anything else?' asked Radebe. 'Anything that he wanted?'

'Yesterday Morris asked for South African financial magazines and newspapers. I bought them yesterday evening at the CNA at the Waterfront, and brought them along this morning.'

They took down both bodyguards' details, and let them leave.

'I will follow up the Wi-Fi, Benny,' said Radebe. 'Find out who the service provider is for this place. Philip and his guys can get the logs.'

Over the past months Griessel had worked hard at his limited technological knowledge. Cupido and Captain Philip van Wyk of IMC, the Hawks' information management centre, were good, enthusiastic teachers. He didn't know very much yet, but he did know it was possible to track someone's Internet footprints in that way.

'Thanks, Ulinda. IMC will have to look at cellphone calls as well. Morris must have had one. Any foreign numbers . . . and if we can identify his phone . . .'

'. . . we can trace him. These bodyguards would have phoned to be let in the door; if we can get the phone numbers of the two victims, it will make it easier to track Morris. Same cellphone tower, if you get my drift.'

Griessel nodded. He should have thought of that. 'Vaughn is in the city – I will ask him to get that from Body Armour. Thanks, Ulinda.'

'No problem.'

The rain whispered softly on the roof.

Griessel and Liebenberg searched the big guesthouse from top to bottom. Griessel was in Morris's bedroom carefully going through everything again when Fillander and Ndabeni returned from questioning the farm workers. They came and stood in the doorway, their heads and shoulders shiny and wet with rain.

'Nothing,' said Fillander. 'The ones who were here didn't hear or see anything unusual. There are four labourers who left on Saturday for Robertson for the weekend. Family funeral apparently, they will only be returning today. Maybe too much of a coincidence, Benny. I asked that they phone us when the people are back.'

'Thanks,' said Griessel.

'What's next, Benny?' Ndabeni asked.

'I need you to walk the farm perimeter,' he said. 'The perpetrators did not enter at the main gate, so there might be signs somewhere . . .'

'OK, Benny.'

'I'm really sorry, but I don't trust the station uniforms to do a thorough job in this weather. And if we wait until the rain stops, there might be nothing left. Ask Christel de Haan, the hospitality manager if you can borrow umbrellas.'

'OK, Benny, no problem.'

And then he was alone again, and he picked up the overturned desk chair and sat down so that he could think and get the weight off his feet.

Jissis, he was getting old. Two, three years ago he wouldn't have been so *poegaai* after an exhausting night of . . .

Better stick to the matter at hand.

He tried to visualise it, the entire event: Last night. Just after nine. The suspects hiding here somewhere, watching Scarlett January and her father, Cyril, carry the trolley down the steps, Scarlett wheeling it away.

One gunman for both victims, Thick and Thin had said. But to abduct a man would be hard for just one person.

One gunman, with helpers?

They hide until the bodyguards open the door, survey the area, and let Cyril out.

They wait until the door is closed again. They close in on Cyril. Pistol to the head. They take him back to the front veranda. *Phone them inside. Tell them you forgot something.*

Cyril calls.

They shoot him from behind. Blood spray on the outside of the front door. With a silencer? Probably, as no one on the farm heard anything, and the sound of a shot would have alerted the bodyguards inside.

Why hadn't Cyril used the alarm code over the phone?

If they don't open, if anything goes wrong, you're dead.

Shoot Cyril before the door opens. Ram the door so the bodyguard staggers backwards. Shoot the bodyguard. He falls back, in the hallway.

The second bodyguard is in his room, deep inside the house. He hears something, grabs his pistol, comes running down the passage. The suspects are already in the sitting room. The executioner shoots the second bodyguard, first through the hand, then in the head.

The executioner gets Morris. Pistol to the head, but it doesn't help, he puts up a fight. Wrestles him to the ground. Makes him lie down. Handcuffs his wrists with cable ties.

Why snip off one cable tie? Was it too tight?

Morris's wallet is missing. Morris's computer and iPad are missing. Probably a cellphone too, though the bodyguards have never seen it. The clothes were strewn about, the cupboard moved.

At first they tie Morris to the bed with a spare cable tie – or something else – while they search for something? And cut it loose when they take him away from the house?

Why take the wallet, computer and iPad?

What else is missing?

What were they looking for?

Why not shoot Morris too, why kidnap him?

There was only one person who could answer those questions: Paul Anthony Morris. And they didn't have the faintest idea who he was.

Suddenly Griessel's cellphone rang in his pocket, the old-fashioned ringtone that Alexa had chosen. He took it out.

'Vaughn?'

'Benna, the photos of the passport are now in the hands of the Deputy Consul General of the British Empire, Madam Carlisle. She says it will take a day or two.'

'I'll phone the Giraffe, Vaughn. Maybe he can do something.'

'Where do you want me?'

He hesitated before asking: 'Can you go see Louw again?'

'Of course. I'm not scared of a bit of lesbetarian,' he said with glee.

Griessel wondered if it wasn't a big mistake. 'Vaughn, we must work nicely with her. She's lost some of her men.'

'Sure, Benna, I'm cool.'

'Get Morris's email address and all the documents that he filled in. And we want his cellphone number, Vaughn. Ask whether she kept records of all the calls last week. And the cellphone numbers of the two deceased as well.'

'I'm all over it. Like a rash.'

8

On the train back to Cape Town, Tyrone Kleinbooi switched off, leaned back, swaying with the motion of the carriage. He liked riding the train. It was an escape from his industry, here in third class. Everyone poor, but there was a hint of hope, as though you were on your way to something better. When he was down, if he had had a hard day at the office, he would often take the train and go somewhere. Lentegeur, Bellville, Simon's Town, he had twice gone all the way to Worcester by Metrorail, and then he dreamed of Europe by rail, one day. To Barcelona, *the Holy Grail of pickpocketing,* Uncle Solly always called it.

He knew why his thoughts kept turning to Uncle Solly today. It was the pressure. He had lied to his sister – OK, he had been lying about his job for years now, but he had added an extra untruth today, *by December there will be enough for half of next year's fees as well,* which naturally was a blatant lie. That tourism was up seventeen per cent, that the economy of Cape Town was booming, was all true. But it was *fokkol* help to a pickpocket.

Why? The cameras, that's why.

When Uncle Solly began coaching him nine years ago, everything was different. Here and there there was a CCTV camera in a shop, but he was not a shoplifter, *shoplifting is for amateurs and teenagers, Ty, too easy to get caught, da's just one exit, and you always want more than one, always.* Never mind that nine years ago, he, Tyrone, was only twelve years old, not yet a teenager, but that's Uncle Solly for you.

Take the postcard trick – those days you could still do it. Saunter in between the outside tables of Café Mozart, there in the Church Street Mall, go up to the tourist with your twelve-year-old even features and your charming smile, and the postcards, all hand-picked by Uncle Solly, pretty ones, Table Mountain, Table Bay, cute Boulders Beach penguins, and a couple with Madiba on. New and shiny.

'Madam, have you sent your loved ones a Cape Town postcard yet?' you ask in your sweetest little kid voice.

'Oh, aren't you just the cutest. That's a great idea. George, we should send Shirley a postcard . . . Oh, aren't the penguins adorable . . .'

And he would put the postcards down on top of the wallet or the cellphone or the passports that lay there on the table, his fingers fanning them out, swift and trained like a card sharp, while he took the wallet and gripped it under the postcards. And the husband asks: 'How much?' and he would say: 'Just five rand, it's for my school fees,' and the aunty would say: 'We'll take two,' and she would reach out with her fat, beringed fingers for the postcards, and the husband would begin looking for his wallet. 'I'm sure I had it . . .'

You hadn't been able to try that trick for a long time, there were too many cameras around every corner of the city, and somewhere a *blou-baadjie* officer sitting watching the screens and telling the Metro cops over the radio that you were stealing the tourists blind. Now you had to go back to your little room in the Bo-Kaap about four times a day to change into a different colour shirt and put on another cap or beanie or hat, so that the cop in front of the screens wouldn't start noticing you.

So what's a guy to do?

In *this* industry you went where the marks were, the marks with money. And that meant foreign tourists, because your locals didn't carry cash – except for the Gautengers and the Free Staters over December, easy pickings if you get them away from a camera, Clifton beach and Camps Bay. And the Biscuit Mill on a Saturday morning, now *there's* a paradise, all those milling people, but you could only get two or three wallets before word went around.

Foreign tourists hang out at the Waterfront and in the city and that's CCTV country, so you have to steal sharp, always in the crowd, you have to move on foot between the V&A and Long Street, between the Castle and the cable car, because the weird routes of the minibus taxis take too long, and the common taxis rip you off . . .

Before November he had to get twelve thousand rand, for this year's university fees. Before the end of January, another nine thousand for next year's first payment.

Twenty-one K. How do you do that, Uncle Solly? In this grim winter, with this rain that will keep on till September? With the fences who squeezed you with 'recession' and 'tough times'?

How do you do that and stay out of jail?

Benny Griessel and Mooiwillem Liebenberg found nothing.

They searched the big old house carefully and thoroughly. Morris's computer, iPad and possible cellphone were not there.

Captain John Cloete, media man for the Hawks, arrived. They went and sat at the dining-room table in the guesthouse to confer.

'The Giraffe says it's your call, Benny.' Cloete had nicotine stains on his fingers, and permanent shadows under his eyes. Griessel suspected that that was the price that the liaison officer paid for his apparent unshakeable calm and patience, despite the inhuman pressure that his job brought with it.

'It's a foreigner, John.'

'So I hear.'

'We will have to contact next of kin first. That could take a while.'

'Shall I say "presumably a British citizen"?'

That was not what Griessel wanted. Kidnapping was a delicate, complicated, dangerous mess. If a demand for ransom were received, today or tomorrow, with instructions for no media, the cat would already be out of the bag. And there was no way to put it back in. On top of that, it would be like blood in the water for the media sharks. The fact that it was a foreigner would make them crazy. And they would ruin everything.

'We don't know enough yet. I don't want to say anything about the Brit.'

'An unknown third party?'

'No. Absolutely nothing about a third party.'

'You know it'll come out, Benny.'

He nodded. There were too many people on the farm who already knew. Colonel Nyathi would have the final approval of the press release anyway, but for now Griessel must try to do what he believed was best for the investigation.

'I'll ask the owner to talk to his people, but I think we should just say that one farm worker and two guests were shot. Nothing more.'

'The moment we identify the two bodyguards, the media will want to know who they were guarding.'

'Then we must withhold their identities.'

'Hell, Benny . . .'

'I know, John, but if the Brit is still alive, we must do the right thing. Imagine if we fuck this one up, what the UK newspapers will write about us.'

'You'll have to talk to the bodyguard people. They will have to cooperate.'

'I agree.'

Cloete sighed. 'I will say the investigation is in a sensitive stage, we will release more information when we're sure it will not hinder the process. That should cover us, but they'll know we're hiding something.'

'Thank you, John.'

'Wait until the Giraffe approves it.'

Just after one, Christel de Haan and two restaurant workers brought them food – steaming plates of *waterblommetjie* stew. Griessel thanked her, and phoned Vusi Ndabeni and Frankie Fillander to tell them to come and eat.

Then he explained the dilemma over the kidnapping and the media to de Haan.

'Can you request that no one talks to the press?'

'We would have asked them anyway. Marcus is very concerned about our brand and reputation. All our wine goes to Europe.'

He thanked her, and called Cupido.

'I have the Gmail address, Benna. Paul underscore Morris, one five. Helps us *fokkol*. And there's nothing in the contract that says who Morris is, no next of kin. I don't understand how these people do business. And you should see that Body Armour office. Grand, pappie, big bucks.'

'Where are you now?'

'N1, at Century City, I'm on my way to you. Found anything?'

'Nothing. We're nearly done, Vaughn, you can go straight to the office. Give IMC the cellphone numbers of the two bodyguards, so they can identify the cell tower and begin checking all the calls from Friday.'

'That's smart, Benna . . .'

'It was Ulinda's idea.'

'That darkie, hey. Nobody's fool, despite the battering.' Radebe was a light heavyweight who had lost all four of his professional fights on points before he left the sport. It was his capacity to absorb blows that earned him his nickname of '*Ulinda*', the hardy honey badger.

'See you at the office,' said Griessel, and rang off.

Just after dinner, he, Liebenberg, Ndabeni, Radebe, and Fillander went walking along the remainder of the farm boundary, but they found nothing. If there were tracks, the rain had washed them all away in the interim.

Just after three, when the state pathologist had come and gone, and the last ambulance had driven away, they sealed the crime scene. His colleagues went back to the office, and Griessel drove into the city to go and negotiate with Jeanette Louw of Body Armour.

He turned on the heater in the car to banish the cold and damp. The pressure of being JOC leader made him uncomfortable, so that he thought through it all, slowly and with extreme concentration. Because his head was not clear. He didn't want to make a fool of himself. Not after all the odd looks his appearance had drawn.

He swore out loud over the stupidity of last night. Because JOC leader was an opportunity to be relevant again. He had worked so hard over the last six months to catch up, to fit in with the Hawks, to accept the whole team thing and become an efficient cog in the Hawks' wheel. Despite the fact that he was the oldest detective in the Violent Crimes group, steeped in the traditional way of doing things.

And now he looked like *this*.

He would have to keep his head.

He focused on the case, ran through everything that he had seen and heard that morning. He came to the same conclusion: first they must know who Morris was.

Fuck knew, tonight he would *have* to get some sleep, he couldn't look and feel like this tomorrow as well.

What worried him most, was that he had begun lying again. This time to Alexa, to Nyathi, to his colleagues. And the déjà vu that brought back all the old, bad memories of ten, eleven years ago. Anna, at that time still his wife: 'Where have you been, Benny?'

'At work.' Breath reeking of alcohol, drunken eyes, swaying on his feet.

'You're lying, Benny,' she would say, with fear in her voice. That is what he remembered – the fear. What was going to happen to her husband, what was going to happen to her and the children?

It had been so easy to lie to Alexa this weekend, and to Cupido this morning. The old, slippery habit was like a comfortable garment, you just slipped back into it.

In those days he could justify it. Rationalise. The stress, the trauma of inhuman violence and what that did to his head, the impossible hours, the sleeplessness, dreams, and his own phobias, that something like that could happen to his loved ones.

But no more.

He didn't want to lie any more.

9

When he emerged from the lift on the sixteenth floor of the office building in Riebeeck Street, he saw what Vaughn meant by 'grand, pappie, big bucks'. Bold masculine letters on the double glass doors announced *BODY ARMOUR*. Below that, in slim sans serif: *Personal Executive Security.*

He pushed open the door. The walls and luxury carpets were grey, the minimalist furniture was of blackwood, only here and there a splash of verdant green and chrome. Behind a black desk, with only a silver Apple laptop computer, a slim green telephone, and a small aluminium name-plate that said *Jolene Freylinck*, sat a beautiful woman – long dark hair, deep red lipstick, black blouse and skirt, elegant legs ending in black high heels.

'You must be one of the detectives,' she said, her voice serious, muted.

He was all too aware of how she might know this.

He nodded. 'Benny Griessel.'

She reached out a manicured hand for the telephone, pressed a button, waited a second. 'Detective Benny Griessel is here.'

She listened, glancing at him with a slight frown. 'You may go in,' she said and pointed at the black doors with the chrome handles.

He could see how upset she was. 'Thank you.'

Jeanette Louw sat behind her blackwood desk. The jacket hung from a stand in the corner, her striped tie was loosened. She seemed older and more weary than this morning.

'Captain,' she greeted him. 'Come inside. Please take a seat.'

He could hear the suppressed antagonism. He sat down in a black leather chair.

'I understand from your colleague that you still have no leads.'

'That's correct.'

'You know he's an arsehole. And that has nothing to do with race.'

Griessel sighed. 'He's a very good detective.'

Louw just stared at him. He was unsure how to address her. 'Were you in the Service?' he asked.

'The police?'

'Yes.'

'No.' With distaste.

He was too tired to react.

'I was the Regimental Sergeant Major of the Women's Army College in George,' said Louw.

He merely nodded. It would have been easier if she were a former officer. 'It seems as though Morris has been kidnapped,' he said.

'So I understand.'

'It makes things awkward with the media.'

'Oh?'

'The trouble is . . . We assume he's a rich man . . .'

She grasped the point instantly. 'Because he can afford my services.'

'That's right. It may be that they want ransom . . . And we don't know whether his next of kin have been contacted by the kidnappers yet. Usually they demand that nothing appears in the press, and the police may not be contacted, or they will kill their victim.'

'I understand.'

'If we tell the media that there were two bodyguards, they'll want to know who was being guarded.'

'And who they were working for?'

'Yes.'

'You don't want to reveal anything for now.'

She was smart. 'Is it possible to . . . Would the families of your men understand? If we keep the names out of the media? For now?'

Louw leaned back in her chair. She rubbed a hand over her strong jaw, then said: 'As much as it will be best for the reputation of my company not to have publicity, I would have to leave that up to the families. I owe them that at least.'

'Of course.'

'B. J. Fikter has a wife and child . . .'

Griessel said nothing.

'I'll try,' she said.

At the Hawks' offices on the corner of Landrost and Market Street in Bellville, he knocked on the frame of Zola Nyathi's open office door.

The colonel waved him in, motioned him to sit.

With Nyathi's eyes glued on him, he reported back precisely and fully.

'Thank you Benny. Good work. But we have a media problem.'

'Yes, sir.'

'I've approved your strategy, but Cloete says they're going nuts. The radio stations are already throwing around words like "massacre" and "bloodbath", and are speculating about drugs and gang violence. I don't know how long we can keep this under wraps.'

'I'll move as fast as I can, sir. The Consulate . . . If we can get hold of Morris's family . . .'

'The brigadier has spoken to our Deputy National Commissioner, who has asked Foreign Affairs to get involved. So we should soon see results.'

'Thank you, sir.'

Griessel stood up.

'Benny, just a moment,' said Nyathi, very seriously.

He sat down again. He knew what was coming.

'Benny, I don't want to pry. But you understand that your personal well-being is very important to me.'

'Yes, sir.'

'Can I ask you a favour?'

'Yes, sir.'

'You have a mentor, at the AA—'

'A sponsor, sir. But I can assure you—'

He stopped talking when Nyathi lifted his hand. 'You don't have to assure me of anything, Benny. We have a few hours before the cellular data and consular information comes in. I want to ask you to go home, take a shower, and speak to your sponsor. Would you do that for me, Benny?'

'Yes, sir. But I want to—'

'Please, Benny, just do that for me.'

He didn't want to go home. As he drove, he phoned Alexa.

'You must be totally exhausted,' she answered with a voice full of sympathy.

'I'm just coming for a quick shower and change,' he said.

'Ay, Benny, I understand. Is it the Franschhoek murders?'

'It is.'

'I heard about it over the radio. Do you want something quick to eat?'

'Thanks, Alexa, but there won't be time. See you in half an hour . . .'

And then he phoned Doc Barkhuizen, his sponsor at Alcoholics Anonymous.

'Doc, I want to come and talk to you.'

'Now?'

'Around six o'clock, Doc.'

'Come to my consulting rooms. I'll wait for you.'

Doc, who never reproached him. Was just always available.

But he would have to lie to him too.

The garden gate of Alexa's large Victorian house in Brownlow Street, Tamboerskloof, didn't squeak any more. Nearly seven months' worth of restoration work completed, and the garden had been redone. Now it looked like the home of a veteran pop star.

She must have been waiting at the window, because she opened the door for him and hugged him.

'I don't smell good,' he said.

'I don't care.' She squeezed him tightly. 'I'm just so glad you're safe.'

'Alexa . . .'

'I know, I know . . .' she let go of him, pulled him by the hand. 'But that's the way it is if you love a master detective. I made a sandwich, come and eat quickly.'

He didn't like being called a 'master detective'. He had at least persuaded her to stop introducing him that way to her friends.

'Thank you very much,' he said.

'Pleasure. I will keep the surprise for later, after you've showered.'

The pickpocketing week has a very specific pattern. Fridays and Saturdays are prime time, people take to the streets, their thoughts are *los* and casual, Uncle Solly used to say, *and they are flush, cash in pocket.*

Tuesday, Wednesday, and Thursdays are OK, no great shakes, but you can work. Especially now that the clubs are pumping way into the night, lots of young people with lots of money, and you might argue you are helping, taking the money that would have been spent on cocaine.

The seventh day is for rest, Tyrone, because Lord knows da' ga' niks aan nie, *nothing at all, not even in the malls, except before Christmas, that was another story.*

And Mondays were also basically *kak*, thank you.

So he made a loop through Greenmarket Square, just to check whether there might be a lost tour bus full of Europeans ooh-ing and aah-ing over the cheap merchandise with 'African flavours' that actually came all the way from China.

There wasn't.

He bought a meat pie on the corner of Long and Wale. Walked up Longmarket, past the home-made Frederick Street sign, probably not smart and grand enough a neighbourhood for the DA government to hang an official street sign. As bad as the ANC, they were *ammal* useless. The northwester was blowing *kwaai*, it was a long steep hike to his little outside room, in Ella Street, up in Schotsche Kloof, which he rented in the back yard of the rich Muslims' grand house for four-fifty a month. One wall was kitchen counter and sink. One wall was built-in cupboards. He had a single bed and a bedside table. Tiny bathroom. At the outer door hung the intercom, a reminder that this was once the servants' quarters. And now and then the eldest twenty-something daughter of the rich Muslims would buzz him. Nag him about the garbage, or because he hadn't closed the front security gate properly. She hung around the house all day. She was a little fat, and lonely.

Shame.

He would listen to his 32GB iPod touch, the one he had stolen from a German backpacker in December, half the music was death metal, but the rest was OK.

Time to ponder.

10

Doc Barkhuizen was seventy-one years old. He had thick glasses, wild eyebrows, and long grey hair that he tied back in a cheeky ponytail, usually with a light blue ribbon. He had a mischievous face that reminded Benny of one of the seven dwarves in *Snow White*, and a surgery in Boston where he – after a short-lived retirement to Witsand at the age of sixty-five – still saw patients every weekday as a general practitioner.

And he was an alcoholic.

'I am four hundred and twenty-two days sober, Doc,' said Griessel promptly.

'Do you want to drink?'

'Yes, Doc. But not more than usual.'

'So why are you keeping me away from *Hot in Cleveland*?'

'*Hot in Cleveland*?'

'It's a sitcom, Benny. It's the sort of thing that normal, elderly, rehabilitating men watch in the evening with their wives, to keep them from boredom and the lure of the bottle.'

'Sorry, Doc,' he said, though he knew Barkhuizen was only teasing him.

'How are the children?'

He would have to get through this first, it didn't help to try to hurry Doc. His sponsor searched far and wide for danger signs, and he always wanted all the details. 'Well, in general. Fritz has now decided that he wants to go to film school next year. Just because he has shot a few music videos with Jack Parow. Now he wants to "make movies" with a passion. And the AFDA tuition fees, Doc . . . I'll have to take a bond on a house that I don't have. But it's probably better than no education. Or joining the police.'

'And Carla? Is she still going out with that rugby player?'

'Yes, Doc, I'm afraid so.'

'I can hear you still don't like the boy.'

It was the boyfriend Etzebeth's tattoos that bothered Griessel most – that stuff was for prison gangs – but he knew Doc would say he was prejudiced. 'He was kicked off the team for fighting, Doc.'

'I saw that in the newspapers. But you must admit, it's not bad to be already playing for the Vodacom team at the age of twenty.'

'He's aggressive, Doc.'

'With Carla?'

'I'll lock the fucker up if he ever tries *that*.'

'You mean on the field?'

'Yes.'

'It's his job, Benny.'

Griessel just shook his head.

'Why are you here?' asked Doc.

'Because my colleagues think I'm drinking again.'

'What gives them that idea?'

'Last night I slept in my office. Not for very long either. So I looked really bad today.'

'That's all?'

'Last week there were two nights I slept in the office.'

'From pressure of work?'

'No, Doc.'

'Are you going to tell me what's wrong, or must I drag it out of you?'

Griessel sighed.

'It's Alexa,' said Doc Barkhuizen with certainty. He had advised strongly against Griessel's relationship with her – he said two dodgy alcoholics together spelled trouble, 'and if one is an artiste as well, then you have the recipe for a big mess'.

'Alexa is one hundred and fifty days sober, Doc.'

'But?'

'I've moved in.'

'With her?'

'Yes, Doc.'

'Christ, Benny. When?'

'Three weeks ago.'

'And?'

'And it's difficult, Doc. Not to do with drink, I swear. We . . . it's easier, she understands the craving, Doc, we help each other.'

'You know I think that's a crock of shit. But go on.'

All the way here he had considered *how* he would lie; at the beginning of his rehabilitation Barkhuizen had caught him out every time – he knew all the sly evasions of an alcoholic so well. Griessel decided on half-truths, that was the safest. And now he couldn't find the right words. '*Jissis*, Doc . . .'

'Do you have trouble with commitment, Benny? Or are you still missing Anna?'

'No, Doc. It's just . . . I suppose it's the commitment, sort of . . .'

'Sort of?'

'Doc, I got used to being on my own. For two years. Coming and going as I chose. If I wanted to drink orange juice out of the bottle in the morning, if I wanted to play bass guitar in the evening, if I just wanted to do *fokkol* . . .'

'So what possessed you to go and move in with her? Wait, don't tell me. It was *her* idea.'

'Yes, Doc.'

'And you felt too bad to say no.'

'No, Doc, I wanted to.'

'And now you're sleeping at the office so you can be alone for a while?'

'That's more or less . . .'

'*Jissis*, Griessel, you're a moron.'

'Yes, Doc.'

'Did you give up your flat?'

'Yes, Doc.'

'A moronic ape.'

'Yes, Doc.'

'You know what the right thing to do is.'

'No, Doc.'

'You know, but you don't *want* to know. You have to sit down and talk to her. Tell her you need your space. And then she's going to feel threatened and insecure, because she is an artiste. And she will wonder whether you really love her. And she is going to cry, and resort to drink, and you will feel responsible. That's the problem. You don't want to face up to all those things. You've never been very good with conflict.'

'*Fok*, Doc.'

'So tell me, how long did you think you could continue sleeping at the office before it caused complications?'

Griessel stared at the floor.

'You didn't think, did you?'

'No, Doc.'

'Why are you here, Benny? You knew exactly what I would say.'

'My CO told me to come.'

'Did you tell him you haven't been drinking?'

'I tried, but . . .'

'What are you going to do?'

'I don't know, Doc.'

'You will have to do *something*.'

'Alexa is going to Johannesburg tomorrow, until Thursday. I'll think about it, Doc. When she comes back . . .'

Doc Barkhuizen looked at Benny from under his bushy eyebrows. Then he said: 'You know that we are personally responsible for ninety-five per cent of the trouble in our lives.'

'Yes, Doc.'

'Do you want me to phone your CO?'

'Please, Doc.'

'OK. And don't worry, I'll be discreet.'

His cellphone rang as he walked outside with Barkhuizen. An unknown number. He answered while Doc locked up the surgery. The wind was icy.

'Captain, it's Jeanette Louw.'

'Hello,' said Griessel, still unsure of how to address her.

'I have spoken to the next of kin about your request. It's going to be difficult. They have already notified family members, and some of them are already on their way to the Cape to support them, and for the funerals.'

'I understand completely,' he said.

'They say they'll try, but they can't guarantee it won't reach the media.'

'It'll give us a bit of time,' he said. 'Thank you very much.'

'Captain, they are doing it because they want to help catch the murderers.'

He didn't react.

'You are going to catch them, Captain?'

'I will do my absolute best.'

She remained silent for a long time, before she said: 'If there is anything that I can do. Anything . . .'

11

Griessel drove away, looking back in the rear-view mirror at the skinny, slightly bowed shape of Doc Barkhuizen standing under the street light. He felt a huge compassion for the man, for the generous heart hidden behind the strict, inflexible facade.

His sins weighed heavily on him.

Doc was the one person he did not want to lie to. It was a sacred relationship, the one with your AA sponsor, if you truly wanted to quit drinking. It was the cornerstone of rehabilitation, in the end, it was your only lifebuoy in the stormy sea of alcoholic thirst. If you couldn't trust one another, you were basically fucked. For the past few years, Doc had been the one constant in his life, the one he shared everything with.

Until today.

That's why unease stirred down in his gut: once you began telling half-truths and concealing the Big Problem, you quickly slid down the slippery slope of relapse. He knew. He had *been* there.

If he couldn't speak about the actual problem, why wasn't he at least honest about the other things that haunted him?

Because Doc would say: 'You know what to do.'

And Doc would be right.

He would say to Doc: 'I'm afraid Alexa will catch me out, I'm afraid that she will see through me some time or other. And then she will drop me. And though I'm looking for some room, I don't want *that*. Because I love her, she's actually all that I have. So, it worries me a lot, Doc.'

He would at least be able to explain where the problem began, where the origin was. It was back when he met Alexa. He had been involved in the investigation into the murder of her husband. He was the one who recognised her as the former singing sensation, it filled him with nostalgia and admiration and a bittersweet longing. And

then he was sympathetic about her drinking and he told her he was
also an alcoholic. He was the one who believed from the beginning
that she was innocent, he was the one who unravelled the whole mess,
and the one who took her flowers afterwards in hospital and talked
with her about music.

And then she thought he was brilliant.

He tried to tell her, several times, in different ways, that she was
wrong. But he hadn't made a very good job of it, half blinded as he
was by who she was, her musical talent and her Story, and her determination to get back on her feet again. And her sensuality – *fok weet*,
despite the damage, despite the years, she was a sexy, beautiful woman.
And then he went and fell in love with her. And when you are in love,
you put your best foot forward, you hide who you really are. And she
only heard what she wanted to hear.

And then, in the months since, something had developed: 'a
dynamic' Doc Barkhuizen would call it. Alexa treated him as though
he was a good, solid man. A hero. Confidant, advisor. Introduced
him as her 'master detective', and to his dismay even once or twice
as her 'rock'.

He, Benny Griessel, someone's rock? Solid? A hero?

He was an idiot and an ape, because despite his discomfort, despite
his awareness of fraud, he loved it. That Xandra, the former star who
could still bring people to a standstill in the street, thought he was OK.
It was the first time in more than ten years that anyone except his
daughter Carla thought and said he was OK, in any way. And he was
weak, he didn't want it to end.

And now?

Now he had been drawn in, and his sins had caught up with him.

It wasn't that he could no longer play the bass guitar in the evenings.
It was that he was ashamed of what he *wanted* to play when he *was*
practising.

Last week, on the way home, he heard Neil Diamond's 'Song Sung
Blue' over the radio – the *Hot August Night* recording that began with
just acoustic guitar, and where the bass guitar only kicked in halfway
through the first verse, suddenly giving the song rhythm and depth
and familiarity – and he thought he would like to play it as soon as he
was home. Only to remember he lived with Alexa now, maybe she

would think Neil Diamond wasn't sophisticated enough, that he should rather practise something else, that he had an image to maintain . . .

He had to be what he was not.

And that was just the beginning, the tip of the iceberg.

There was the money thing as well. Alexa had inherited well from her late husband – including his record company Afrisound, which brought in a constant stream of royalties. The firm was not in good shape, but she was rebuilding it with a natural, instinctive business acumen. Alexa's own comeback album, *Bittersoet*, was doing better than expected, her concerts were fully booked again.

She was a rich woman. And he was a policeman.

She had bought him the iPhone. And a new amplifier for his bass guitar. And clothes – a jacket, and expensive shirts that he didn't want to wear to work, because he knew that colleagues like Vaughn Cupido would tease him mercilessly. Not to mention the new winter pyjamas. They were an embarrassment to him – he felt like a baboon in fancy dress. What was wrong with an old pair of tracksuit pants and a T-shirt? But when he put on the new pyjamas and stood there in front of Alexa like a moron, she said, with a big, appreciative smile, 'Come here, Benny,' and she held him tightly and kissed him until his knees buckled . . .

What would it help to share it all with Doc?

That's why he avoided all mention of the Big Problem. He could never tell Barkhuizen about that. Or anyone else, that was the big fuck-up. He would have to sort it out himself, but he couldn't, not at all – he didn't even know where to begin.

And as if that wasn't enough to complicate his life, Alexa added another dilemma this afternoon.

When he had showered and was putting on fresh clothes in their bedroom, Alexa had come to sit on the bed, excited, as though she couldn't keep the 'surprise' to herself any more. She said bass guitar player Schalk Joubert was going to perform with Lize Beekman at *Die Boer* in Durbanville next Friday night. 'But Schalk has to rush to New York for a gig, and I said to Lize, what about Benny? He knows all your music off by heart and he's not only a master detective, he's grown amazingly as a musician. And then she said that's a brilliant idea. Benny, you're going to play with Lize Beekman – I'm so proud of you . . .'

At first he felt relief that it was not the surprise he had suspected.

And then the knowledge dawned on him: he was not in that league, no matter how hard he practised with Rust, his foursome of amateur-veterans. They did covers of time-worn hits, played every now and then at golden and silver wedding anniversaries in front of middle-aged audiences. But this was Lize Beekman, the singer who, the one or two times he'd been in her presence, had left him tongue-tied and dumbstruck by her immense talent and her quiet beauty and her aura.

What was he to do? Alexa sat there in joy and expectation, waiting for his response to the great gift. He had forced a smile and said '*Sjoe*,' an innocuous exclamation that he *fokken* never used. He said: 'Thank you, Alexa, but I don't know if I'm good enough,' and knew exactly what her reaction would be.

'Of course you are good enough. I didn't start singing in bands yesterday, Benny. You've grown so much in your music the past year.' One of her typical artistic expressions that he struggled to handle. 'Lize is emailing me the repertoire, and you have to go and rehearse a few times, but that's only next week, you'll be able to arrange that with work . . . Put on your new blue shirt, you look so good in it.'

So he put the blue shirt on.

He was fucked. In at least two ways.

He found his team members at IMC, the Hawks' Information Management Centre.

'You look a bit better, Benna,' said Cupido when he looked up from the computer screen he was staring at, along with the other Violent Crimes detectives. 'Nice shirt, partner . . .'

The whole room gawped at him.

'We got the two-oh-five subpoena quickly,' said Captain Philip van Wyk, IMC commanding officer, referring to the Hawks' responsibilities according to article 205 of the Criminal Procedure Act when obtaining cellphone records. 'Seems like this has really caught the attention higher up . . .'

''Cause why, it's a foreigner,' said Cupido reproachfully.

'. . . But it's the data from three cellphone towers that's relevant,' said van Wyk. 'And weekends are prime time in Franschhoek. It'll take time to analyse everything.'

'And I can tell you now, there are going to be lots of international calls,' said Cupido. 'Half of those wine farms are in the hands of foreigners.'

'The logs of the Internet service provider to La Petite Margaux show there were seven computers and three iPads on that IP address since Friday. We'll have to identify and isolate the computers and traffic belonging to the farm personnel before we know what Morris's activities were.'

Griessel tried to remember what van Wyk had taught him. 'That means we'll have to go and collect their computers.'

'Please.'

'They're not going to like that.'

'I can send Lithpel to them. It may be less disruptive, and it shouldn't take too long.'

'Maybe Ulinda as well; those foreigners won't understand a word Lithpel says,' said Cupido.

'I'm right here,' said Reginald 'Lithpel' Davids, the lisping computer whizz van Wyk had recently poached from Forensics. Davids was small and frail, with the face of a schoolboy. He shook his big Afro hairstyle indignantly. 'It'th sometimeth like I don't exthitht to you.'

'I rest my case,' said Cupido.

'I'll phone Franschhoek so long,' said Radebe and reached for a phone. 'This is new, it's the first time I've been an English interpreter for a coloured *outjie*.'

'*Jithith*,' Lithpel said, but he grabbed his worn old rucksack of computer equipment and stood up.

'Anything on Paul Anthony Morris?' Griessel asked.

One of van Wyk's researchers said: 'We started with Google, Captain. It's a relatively common combination of names, and there are quite a lot of references that don't have photos with them. But we're working on it.'

'And the snake on the cartridges?'

'That's a difficult one to isolate in the database records,' said van Wyk. 'The query is still running, we might have to refine it. But nothing so far.'

Nyathi walked in and the room fell silent. 'Benny, the British Consul General's office just called. She has news about the passport, we can go and see her now.'

Eyebrows were raised. Cupido looked at his watch. 'Twenty past seven at night? Maybe this Morris is royalty or something.'

In the car Nyathi said, 'I spoke to your sponsor. Thanks, Benny. I hope you understand.'

'Of course, sir,' he said, because he did understand. The Hawks were a team environment. The weakest link determined their success. And at the moment that was what he was. The weakest link.

'Everything else OK? Your health? The family?'

'Yes, thank you, sir.'

The Colonel nodded his bald head slowly and thoughtfully, like a man who has come one step closer to insight and truth.

They drove in silence until they reached the N1. 'Cloete has his hands full with the media,' said Nyathi. 'We need a break. Quickly.' And then, 'Do you think it's about ransom, Benny?'

'Yes, sir.'

'Have you investigated a kidnapping involving a ransom before?'

'Three or four times, sir. But not where there's a foreigner involved.'

'I've never had one,' said Nyathi.

'They're all bad news, sir.'

They parked in Riebeeck Street and first had to search for the entrance to Norton Rose House, a tower block that was deserted at this time of the night.

The British Consulate, with bullet-proof glass doors and a comprehensive security system, was on the fifteenth floor – Griessel and Nyathi had to identify themselves before a woman came to fetch them and escort them to the Consul General's office.

The dignified middle-aged woman introduced herself as Doreen Brennan. She was not alone. With her was a younger woman with dark hair cut short, black-rimmed glasses, and a pretty mouth. 'This is one of our vice consuls, Emma Graber. Please, gentlemen, sit down.'

When the courtesies were dispensed with, Brennan pushed the police photographer's photo of the passport across the desk. 'I'm afraid this is a forgery,' she said apologetically.

Griessel's heart sank into his shoes. That meant they still did not know who Morris or his next of kin were.

'Are you sure?' asked Nyathi.

'Yes. The passport number belongs to a seventy-six-year-old woman from Bexhill-on-Sea who passed away thirteen days ago. It might be her passport that was modified, but we'll need to analyse the original to be sure.'

'No, the passport is very new,' said Griessel as he wrestled with disappointment.

'Would it be possible for us to take a look at the document itself?' asked Graber. 'We have a comprehensive database of forgeries, which might help us trace its origin.'

'Of course,' said Nyathi. 'I'm sure that can be arranged eventually . . .'

'I see,' said Graber thoughtfully. Then, 'Of course, we only want to aid your investigation. As I understand it, the first seventy-two hours are usually crucial.'

'Indeed. And your offer is much appreciated,' said Nyathi.

'We actually know very little about the crime that this person was involved in,' said Graber. 'Unfortunately, the detective who brought the photographs spoke to one of the clerks. Could you tell us more?'

Nyathi hesitated, then smiled politely. 'I'm really sorry, but the investigation is at a very sensitive stage. And now it seems as if Morris may not be a British citizen . . . I do hope you understand. . . .'

'Of course,' said Graber, and she smiled sympathetically. 'We're just trying to help. And I'm curious. Was it a robbery or something?'

'I'm not at liberty to say.'

Griessel wasn't concentrating, and only became aware of the uncomfortable silence when Nyathi gave him a swift but meaningful glance. He finally grasped that there was something on the go here, a verbal chess game – Graber wanted very much to get her hands on the passport and to know more about the crime. Nyathi was most unwilling to share it with her. And he remembered Cupido's reaction: *Twenty past seven at night? Maybe this Morris is royalty or something.*

All at once he was alert, as if the fatigue had just rolled off him.

There was a snake in the grass here. And the Colonel wanted him to help catch it.

12

He knew he must now ask his questions right. 'Do you monitor missing persons?'

He noticed that the Consul General waited for Graber to answer.

'Well, only if they're reported missing, and are presumed to be travelling, of course. There is a process . . .'

'Was a Paul Anthony Morris reported missing?'

'Not that we know of,' said Graber.

'Someone of his age and description?'

'It's hard to say. The info you have provided is rather sketchy. If we could analyse the original document?'

'Do you have any idea who this Paul Anthony Morris might be?'

'Well, it's quite a common name. As you can imagine, it is going to take some time to scour the Home Office database, which might turn up nothing.'

It was almost as though she was encouraging him to ask the right question, but he didn't know what that was. 'But do you . . . have you got any idea?'

'What we *do* know, is that no person by that name has been reported missing in the United Kingdom in the past fortnight.'

Griessel tried to understand the game. She wasn't giving him a direct 'no'. Why not?

'Are there any other persons who were reported missing that you think he might be?' Not entirely correctly phrased, she was clever, he would have to think carefully.

Without hesitation Graber said, 'The Metropolitan Police in the UK run a database called Merlin, which, in addition to other information, also logs missing persons reports. We have to assume that the age indicated on the passport is more or less correct, because it has to correspond to the photograph. And of course the photograph must bear a close enough resemblance to the man who entered this country last week in order to fool customs. Now, I can tell you that Merlin provided absolutely no data on persons generally resembling this photograph, and in this broad age bracket, that have been reported to UK authorities over the past fortnight as missing.'

Why was she going on about 'fortnight'?

'And in the past six to twelve months?'

'In the previous fiscal year, Merlin logged more than forty thousand records of missing persons. That type of enquiry might take several days before I could answer with confidence.'

'Ladies, with all due respect,' said the ever-dignified Zola Nyathi quietly and courteously, 'there is a man's life at stake here.'

'I can assure you, Colonel, we're doing everything in our power to help,' said the Consul General.

'Is Morris's life at stake?' asked Graber. 'Or is he a suspect in a criminal case?'

'You know who he is,' said Griessel, because now he was sure.

They looked him in the eye, calm and direct.

'Captain,' said Doreen Brennan, measured and diplomatic, 'I receive Foreign Office bulletins about persons of interest on an almost daily basis. To be absolutely honest, this Paul Anthony Morris could be one of at least twenty British subjects of concern to our government. But at this stage – with no certainty as to his real identity, and with you not being very forthcoming about the details of the criminal incident – speculation will do more harm than good.'

From a thousand interrogations of suspects Griessel knew that when people began to use phrases such as 'to be absolutely honest', they were lying through their teeth. He suspected the two Brits had conferred at length before he and Nyathi arrived, and they knew exactly what they would say.

But before he could respond, Nyathi said, 'I'm reading between the lines that you are willing to trade information, should we be willing to divulge details about the case.'

The Consul General got up from her chair. 'If you'll excuse me, I need to call my family to tell them I'll be home soon . . . No, please sit down, gentlemen . . .' She walked slowly to the door, and closed it behind her.

Maybe he should hold his tongue and let Nyathi talk, since he had missed the subtle message entirely.

'I have to tell you that the Consulate cannot officially comment on an identity based on a fake passport, unless we've had time to thoroughly examine the document in question,' said Graber.

'And unofficially?' asked Nyathi.

'I've been known to speculate, should a conversation catch my interest . . .'

'And how do we obtain your interest?'

'That would depend.'

'We'd consider lending you the passport, in a day or two . . .' said Nyathi.

'I'd surely appreciate that, but . . .'

'You want it sooner?'

'That isn't my strongest need.'

'You want details of the case?'

'Now *that* would be immensely helpful.'

'We could provide them, if we were properly motivated,' said Nyathi with a faint smile, and Griessel realised the colonel was good at this sort of thing. The rumour was that he had been in the intelligence wing of Umkhonto we Sizwe, in the old days. Perhaps it was true.

'I'm a firm believer in motivation,' said Graber, 'but as you know, speculation is not fact. And the idea of speculative information reaching our friends in the media is too ghastly to contemplate.'

'I absolutely share that fear,' said Nyathi. 'That is why, despite tremendous pressure, the media is still very much in the dark about the details of this case.'

'How do we ensure that it stays that way?'

'By giving you our word that Captain Griessel and I will not divulge any speculative information, unless third parties are mutually agreed upon.'

'Does that include your colleagues at the Directorate of Priority Crime Investigation?'

'It does.'

Graber gave a slight nod. 'Has this "Morris" committed a crime?'

'No.'

'Has he been the victim of a crime?'

'Do you know who he is?'

'We have a very strong suspicion.'

'How?'

'The photograph.'

'He resembles someone your government is looking for?'

'He does indeed. Is he the victim of a crime?'

'He is.'

'A serious crime?'

'Yes.'

'Has he been killed?'

'Who?' Nyathi smiled again, as if he were really enjoying this.

'Paul Anthony Morris.'

'Is that his real name?'

'No.'

'Who do you think he is?'

'Has he been killed?'

'No.'

'Is he in your custody?'

'No.'

That silenced her. Her face was expressionless, but Griessel could see the gears turning.

'Who do you think he is?' asked Nyathi.

'Do you know where he is at this moment?'

Nyathi did not reply.

'Has he been kidnapped?' asked Graber.

'Who is he?' asked Nyathi.

'Colonel, I really need to know whether he has been kidnapped.'

'We really need to know who he is.'

She looked at the photo of Queen Elizabeth on the wall, then back at Nyathi. 'We think he is David Patrick Adair.'

Griessel took out his notebook and began to write.

'Why are you so concerned about Mr Adair?' asked Nyathi.

'Has he been kidnapped?'

'Yes,' said Nyathi. 'All evidence points in that direction.'

'Shit,' said Emma Graber with that mouth which Griessel found so lovely.

She asked them to excuse her for just a minute.

They stood up when she left the room, and sat down again when she closed the door behind her.

Griessel looked at Nyathi. The colonel waved an index finger at the ceiling, then in a circular motion, in the end placing it in front of his mouth.

Griessel nodded. He understood. They were probably being listened to.

Odd world this. He wondered what Nyathi's role in Umkhonto had been. And what Emma Graber's job at the Consulate was. He suspected her interest was not criminal by nature, but political. He wondered who David Patrick Adair was, and why Graber was so careful – yet keen at the same time. And what she had gone to do now. Consult with the Consul General? Or with someone else who might have been eavesdropping on their conversation in an adjoining office? Or was she sitting there herself listening, in the hope that he and Nyathi would start talking?

As if this case needed further complications.

Seven minutes passed before she returned. 'I *do* apologise,' she said, and sat down. 'Now, gentlemen, if you Google the name "David Patrick Adair" you will eventually establish that a man by that name is a King's Fellow in Computer Sciences at Cambridge University, and Professor at DAMTP, the Department of Applied Mathematics and Theoretical Physics, at the same institution. The DAMTP website will furthermore show a photograph of Adair which is almost identical to the one in the counterfeit passport.'

There was a subtle shift in her attitude, businesslike, a greater urgency.

'Last week Tuesday, Professor Adair failed to deliver his usual lecture at the Department. Because of his varied commitments and hectic schedule, this in itself isn't unusual. But he has never failed to let his personal assistant know about such an absence before. She reported this to one of his senior colleagues. Upon investigation by this colleague, it was finally established that there had been a burglary at Adair's house in Glisson Road in central Cambridge. A back door was forced and the interior left in complete disarray. Adair was nowhere to be found. Given the sensitive nature of his work, this colleague had the good sense to notify the right authorities, thereby keeping the matter contained . . .'

'So it was never logged on Merlin,' said Nyathi.

'That is correct,' she answered, without a hint of remorse.

'What is the nature of his work?' asked Nyathi.

'Therein, Colonel, lies the rub.'

13

'For starters, you should know that Adair has been divorced for nine years. He is completely estranged from his ex-wife. The marriage was childless. His next of kin is his younger sister Sarah, lecturer at the School of Mathematics at the University of Birmingham. By all accounts she is an extremely competent academic, but alas, not quite the genius her brother is. We have made highly discreet inquiries as to her knowledge of her brother's whereabouts, and it is clear that she has not heard from him since his disappearance. In other words, there is no need for you to contact her.'

'Ah,' said Nyathi. 'I'm assuming that you have also been . . . monitoring her communication channels since last Tuesday?'

'We are positive that no attempt has been made to communicate with her about her brother since that time.'

'May I ask to which "we" you are referring?'

'I beg your pardon?'

'You said "we are sure" . . .' said Nyathi patiently.

'The British authorities,' she said, with an ironic smile herself now.

'And the nature of Professor Adair's work?'

She nodded. 'Now please bear with me, because this gets a little complicated. But I want to get it right, not least so that you will also understand the great need for circumspection in this matter.'

'Please,' said Nyathi.

Griessel said nothing, just listened.

'An Internet search of his name will eventually lead you to the good professor's responsibility for the so-called Adair Algorithm. To save time, and to enunciate the necessity for discretion, I would like to explain what that is. Have you heard of the Society for Worldwide Interbank Financial Telecommunication, or SWIFT?'

'Vaguely.'

'Very well. Please allow me to elaborate: SWIFT is based in Belgium.

It is a network that enables financial institutions across the globe to send and receive information about monetary transactions. Your bank, for instance, would have a SWIFT code, which is part of this system. Should you receive money from abroad, this code is used, and the information about the transaction is registered on SWIFT's computers. Simple stuff, is it not?'

They nodded in unison.

'Now, shortly after 9/11, the CIA and the US State Department set up the top secret and pretty controversial Terrorist Finance Tracking Programme, also known as TFTP. In a nutshell, this programme provides US authorities with access to the SWIFT database, in order to trace financial transactions that might identify potential terrorist activities. You might have heard of it . . .'

'Yes,' said Nyathi.

'In June of 2006, the *New York Times* ran the first media exposé on TFTP, but the project survived, due to the public sentiment at the time, perhaps, but also because TFTP proved extremely useful right off the bat. However, being a US-only initiative, it was lacking in reach and scope. To be truly effective, it needed to go global. So, the USA invited the European Union to come on board. Of course, Europe was equally concerned about the terrorist threat, and keen to cooperate. But initially the European Parliament rejected an interim EU–US TFTP agreement, because they felt it did not offer EU citizens enough privacy protection. Are we still on the same page?'

'Yes,' said Nyathi.

'Good. This is where David Adair enters our story. He was invited to become a member of the EU evaluation team of the TFTP agreement, because of his expertise in database search algorithms. Adair took a long, hard look at the US system, and came to the conclusion that it could be vastly improved – not only in terms of privacy safeguards, but also in effectiveness. He then proceeded, as geniuses do, to write a vastly superior algorithm on a whim, and offer it to the authorities. Of course, they gratefully accepted, and in 2010 the EU announced their resumption of the TFTP. The so-called Adair Algorithm then became the standard methodology to sniff out terrorists in the international banking system. It has been responsible for the identification and subsequent termination of at least seven terrorist cells, and an impressively large number of senior al-Qaeda leaders and operatives.'

Emma Graber leaned back in her chair, spreading her hands, palms open, as if she had nothing more to hide.

'Gentlemen, the Adair Algorithm is one of the best-kept and most vital international security secrets in history. If it falls into the wrong hands . . .'

She let the thought hang in the air for a minute, then she said, 'Now please tell me about the nature of the kidnapping.'

Griessel listened to Nyathi skipping over certain details of the investigation.

With carefully chosen words and in perfect English, the Giraffe told Emma Graber about Adair's initial contact with Body Armour, his arrival and stay on La Petite Margaux, the death of the farm worker and two bodyguards, and the signs of struggle in the master bedroom. He described the security measures, and how they thought the crime had happened.

Graber asked Nyathi for the email address of the Paul Anthony Morris alias.

He said he would have to consult their notes, but he would send it on. Griessel remembered the address well, but kept quiet.

Nyathi said not a word about the cartridges with the snake and the letters NM engraved on them. Nor of the missing laptop, iPad, and possible cellphone – the Hawks' only clues.

Griessel suspected it was deliberate, but he wasn't sure.

When the colonel had finished, they negotiated a joint press release to quell the hunger of the media, and relieve the pressure on the families of the bodyguard victims and the wine-farm personnel.

It would state that an unidentified man, presumably a European tourist, was missing after a guesthouse employee and two security officials were shot dead during a break-in. Missing and possible incorrect passport details had made the identification of the missing person difficult at this stage, but he was thought to be male and a British citizen. The Directorate of Priority Crimes Investigation was grateful for the willingness and cooperation of the British Consulate regarding this matter. As soon as a positive identification could be made with certainty, and the sensitivity of the investigation allowed it, the media would be fully informed. In the meantime, no stone would be left unturned to bring the perpetrators to book and to track down the missing person. Various leads were being followed.

Nyathi told Graber they would have to inform one more Hawks' colleague of the identity of David Adair: Major Benedict Boshigo, member of the Statutory Crimes Group of the Hawks' Commercial Crimes in the Cape – their expert in financial affairs. But he could give her the assurance that Boshigo, just like them, would handle the information in confidence. 'Until such time as we agree otherwise.'

'Very well,' she said amiably.

They solemnly agreed to inform each other of relevant developments, as often as circumstances allowed.

Graber walked them to the lift, where they said goodbye.

Only once they turned into Buitengracht, in the direction of Bellville, did Nyathi speak.

'I want you to call the Body Armour boss, Benny, and inform her that the British authorities might contact her. I want you to tell her that divulging any information to anyone other than the SAPS would constitute a crime . . .'

'Sir, I think we should . . . She's a tough one, it would be better not to . . .'

'Threaten her?'

'Yes.'

'See what you can do. But above all, ask her not to share Morris's email address.'

He rang. She answered promptly.

He told her that the Hawks would issue a press release later that night that would relieve the pressure on the families of the two murdered bodyguards. He agreed to send it to her as well.

'I appreciate that,' she said.

'There's a possibility that someone from the British Consulate might contact you. We ask whether it would be possible to refer all their queries to us.'

She remained silent for so long that Griessel thought the connection had been lost.

'Hello?' he said.

'I'm here.'

He waited.

'Here's the deal,' she said. 'I won't tell them a thing. But you tell me everything.'

'That is not possible at the moment.'

'You are going to tell me everything when it *is* possible. I don't want to read anything in the press that I don't know, or I'll phone the Consulate.'

'All right,' said Griessel, and rang off.

'Mission accomplished?' Nyathi asked.

'Yes, sir.'

'Well done. You're pretty good with people, Benny . . .'

He didn't know what to say to that.

'The first thing you have to understand about the intelligence community is that they only tell the truth if it serves a purpose. Their purpose, mostly.'

'Yes, sir.'

'Graber is most likely MI6. Also known as the Secret Intelligence Service, or SIS. She is probably working closely with MI5, the British national security service, which hunts terrorists inside the UK, amongst other duties.'

'Sir . . .' He couldn't sit on it any more. 'You seem to know a lot about all this?'

Nyathi laughed, and Griessel wondered whether it was the first time that he had seen the colonel do that.

'Twenty-six years ago I was recruited for MK Intelligence, Benny. Because I was a schoolteacher, they thought I was intelligent. And I worked in London for a while . . . What I'm trying to say is that lying is part of that profession. And I think she is lying to us. Or at least not telling the whole truth.'

'Why, sir?'

'Two things, Benny. The first one is that she tried very hard to have us believe that this is about terrorism, but she never actually said it. Her problem is that she is working in a foreign country, and she has to tread very carefully not to lie directly. Very bad for diplomacy, should things get out of hand later. She has to keep the back door open, the one that allows her to say: "Oh, you must have misunderstood, would you like to listen to the recording again?"'

'I understand.'

'The second is the channel she's chosen. If this were purely about a potential terrorist act, their High Commissioner in Pretoria would have approached our Minister of Security. Musad and I would have been called by him, not by them.'

Burly Brigadier Musad Manie was the commanding officer of the Hawks in the Cape.

'You think this is about something else, sir?'

'All I know is that Adair probably is who she says he is. As for the rest, we'll have to see.'

Griessel began to understand. 'Is that why you did not just send me and Vaughn when they called, sir? You knew, when they called this late on a Monday evening . . .'

'I suspected something might be brewing.'

'And that's why you did not tell her everything, sir?'

'Yes, Benny. When you're working with intelligence people, you should always have an ace up your sleeve. Always. We have a few, and I want to keep it that way. So, the first thing you do, is send her the wrong email address for Paul Anthony Morris. Just a small typo . . .'

He wondered whether he detected a note of nostalgia in Nyathi's voice.

Griessel had always experienced him as a fair, thoughtful man, but quiet and modest, largely unreadable and enigmatic. Tonight he had also discovered a keen intelligence, a feel for this strategic game that Benny would have trouble matching.

The colonel had enjoyed himself in the Consul General's office, that was clear to see. And now, here in the car, there was enthusiasm, a sparkle that he had not previously detected in the Giraffe. How had it felt after the adrenaline and excitement of spying in London, to fill a senior command – really mainly personnel management, administration, and strife from the higher-ups – in the SAPS?

Did he enjoy his job?

When they had gone past Canal Walk, Nyathi asked him to call Cloete, the liaison officer, and ask him to come in. And also Major

Benedict 'Bones' Boshigo. 'Tell Bones to come directly to my office, and not to talk to anyone.'

When that was done – and Bones had responded with a 'that's never a good sign, hey' – he and the colonel decided what they would say to their colleagues.

14

'Wait a minute,' said Cupido in the big IMC room. 'They let you ride all the way, this time of a Monday night, jus' to tune you the passport is a fake? They could have told you that over the phone.'

'It's called diplomacy, Vaughn,' said the much older and more experienced Frankie Fillander. 'You should try it some time.'

'Show me some love, Uncle Frankie. I smell a rat.'

'What kind of rat?' asked Griessel.

'This was a professional hit, pappie, and *jy wiet* who sanctions professional hits. Gangstas and governments.'

'That's true . . .'

'Any news?' asked Griessel, to change the subject.

'Nothing yet,' said van Wyk. 'And we're still waiting for Ulinda and Lithpel. It's going to be a late night.'

'Then you'd better go home so long,' said Griessel to the Violent Crimes detectives. 'I'll call if there's anything.'

They murmured their thanks. Only Cupido stood a while and looked at Griessel. Then he nodded and left.

'*Ja*, I know about the Adair Algorithm. *Maar dit maak nie sense nie, nè*, it just doesn't add up,' said Bones Boshigo in his characteristic mix of languages, after they had told him everything. He owed his nickname to the fact that he was mere skin and bone, thanks to his murderous marathon-training programme. He was also one of the most intelligent detectives that Griessel knew, a man with a degree in economics that he had earned at the University of Boston's Metropolitan College.

Behind his desk, Nyathi just raised his eyebrows.

'Kidnap him, Colonel? Why?' asked Bones. 'Everyone knows what the algorithm does, even the terrorists, and there's nothing anyone can do to stop it. Al-Qaeda must have figured out long ago that moving money through conventional banking channels is pretty stupid. Last I heard about TFTP is that it helps to nail a few small operators. I think this is really about the Adair Protocol, *nè*?'

He noticed his two colleagues hadn't the faintest idea what he was talking about.

'They didn't tell you about the Adair Protocol?'

'No,' said Griessel.

'*Nogal* funny. This *ou*, David Adair, he wrote a paper on the use of his algorithm, about two years ago . . . early 2011, just after the EU joined TFTP. He basically said the scope of the programme was too small, and that his algorithm had the capability to do much more – the authorities had a moral obligation to employ it. He published the paper in a scientific magazine, and it became known as the Adair Protocol.'

'The capacity to do much more what?' Nyathi wanted to know.

'Tracing other dubious financial transactions. His main argument was that the black market is worth about two thousand billion dollars per annum internationally, and tracking that money can have a huge impact on the containment and prosecution of organised crime.'

'OK,' said Griessel, struggling increasingly to keep up. The day was growing very long.

'So they're doing that now?' asked Nyathi.

'No, sir.'

'Why not?'

'The banks didn't like it, *nè*. And you can understand – they're making big bucks from black market money and the whole laundering process. If TFTP starts looking at their organised crime clients, they will lose them all, quickly, to obscure little off-line banks in the Cayman Islands. So they pleaded invasion of privacy concerns, and the EU Parliament and the British government sang the same song.'

'Bones, I don't understand, if TFTP isn't being used against organised crime, why can this kidnapping be about the Adair Protocol?' asked Nyathi.

'Adair is an agitator, *nè*. *Baie* liberal, *baie* vocal. *Hy bly nie stil nie*, he makes a lot of noise. Two months ago, he was saying in *The Economist* that the British Conservative Party is in cahoots with the banks and basically assisting organised crime. He's canvassing, Colonel, all the time. I think the gangstas would maybe really like to get rid of him, before he gets public opinion on his side.'

'So you think they killed him?'

'*Yebo*, yes.'

Jy wiet, *who sanctions professional hits. Gangstas and governments,* Cupido had said. But Griessel also knew that Bones was in essence a numbers guy, not a homicide detective. 'No,' he said.

They waited for Griessel to explain. He took a moment to gather his thoughts. 'Organised crime . . . Bones, when they order a hit, they want to make a statement. They would have left him dead at the guesthouse.'

'No, Benny, not in the current political climate. Then the British press will say Adair was right, there will be big pressure on government to institute the Protocol. The way I understand this whole thing, nobody knows for sure that Adair came to South Africa. If they can make him disappear, *nè*, no names, no pack drill . . . Problem solved. And maybe they want him to suffer first, Benny. You know how the gangstas are.'

'Maybe,' said Griessel, because aspects of the argument did make sense. 'But for that reason they could have murdered him here, and then the media would have said: Look how dangerous South Africa is . . .'

Nyathi's phone rang. The colonel answered, listened, said a few times: 'Yes, sir', and then: 'I'll wait for him.'

After putting the phone down, he looked at Benny. 'That was our Hawks commissioner, in Pretoria,' he said. 'He asked me to receive a representative of our very own State Security Agency. To share the details of the case.'

'But how did they know . . . ?' asked Griessel.

'They monitor the Consulate, of course,' said Nyathi. 'Probably their telephones too.'

'All cloak and dagger, *nè. Dis 'n lekker een dié*, what fun,' said Bones. 'Colonel, thanks for including me. Much more exciting than investigating pyramid schemes. Let me go do a little digging on Adair . . .'

When Cloete came in, Griessel went straight to his office to send Emma Graber the incorrect email address for Paul Anthony Morris/

David Patrick Adair. The one that Cupido had confirmed was Paul_Morris15@gmail.com. He thought for quite a while before deciding on a false address. Nyathi had asked for a typing error, something that could be explained as a simple error, should Graber realise the address was false. One possibility was to swap letters around, but that was too easy. The one he eventually sent to the British embassy was Paul_Morris151@gmail.com – making him feel ever so slightly like a spy.

Then he walked back to IMC.

Captain Philip van Wyk said they had searched the national databases and there were no references to bullet cartridges with snake engravings or the letters NM on them. And all the other processes were still running.

At twenty-two minutes past ten, Griessel sat down in his office, bolt upright, so that the fatigue and despondency would not overcome him too quickly.

In truth, they had nothing.

If you thought about it.

Now that they knew who Morris truly was, the cellphone and computer records wouldn't really help.

And if Bones was right, that meant Adair was already dead, and the murderers would likely feed his remains to the sharks, or bury them.

Once again foreign mischief brought over here. Just what this country needed.

Seven detectives, Forensics, IMC, and Nyathi's whole day dedicated to something that would come to nought, he knew it already.

Maybe the Spooks of the SSA should take over the whole thing.

He should rather just go to sleep.

But he didn't want to. That *fokken* snake on the cartridge, that was the thing that had snagged his attention, that would not let go.

What sort of fool made a stamp of a spitting cobra, and then marked his ammunition, every round? Which would take a hell of a lot of time. For what?

Leaving them on the crime scene like a visiting card . . .

With the letters. NM. Initials? Nols Malan or Natie Meiring or Norman Matthews, like the pretentious number plates of the rich that said 'look how *fokken* common but cute I am'.

Then he made the international connection, and he got up and he walked back to IMC, his brain back in gear again.

'We will have to do an Interpol enquiry,' said Griessel to van Wyk. 'About the cobra and the letters.'

'Good idea.' Van Wyk halted. 'You know they also have a database of stolen and lost travel documents. Shall I look up Paul Anthony Morris on that?'

Griessel knew it wouldn't help, but he kept up appearances. 'Please.'

He turned and walked back to his office. While he waited for Nyathi and the SSA agent to finish talking, he wanted to bring his admin up to date. The file would have to be created. He must write an email to his team, remind them to forward him their interview reports and witness statements for Section A. Then he must write out his own interviews and notes, and in Section C, he must fill in the investigation journal on the SAPS5 form, a detailed, chronological history of the case.

It made him wonder: should he leave out the discussion with the Consulate entirely? Or just not mention the full content?

Nyathi called him within fifteen minutes.

'They want to be kept in the loop,' said the colonel. 'So now I have to liaise with an SSA agent as often as I deem necessary.'

'Sir, if we ask the SSA to look in their database for a hit man who engraves his shell casings . . .'

'I did not tell him about the engravings, Benny. I had to tell them about Adair, because I don't know what they might have eavesdropped on. But I told them no more than we told Graber.'

'OK.'

'Anything new?'

'No, sir.'

'Go and get some sleep, Benny. Tell Philip's people to alert you only if they find something big.'

15

He drove home.

Alexa would still be awake.

She was a true creature of the night, staying up till all hours. In the evenings she answered emails and talked on the phone when he wasn't there. She went over the figures from the record company while she listened to demo CDs of hopeful artists ('One never knows . . .'), and she talked with him about his day when he eventually arrived home.

And she cooked for them. He suspected it was her method of suppressing the urge to drink, an attempt at a degree of normality, to create a homely atmosphere after the chaos of her first marriage, and the bohemian nature of her world. He also suspected that she thought that he expected it of her, even though he had denied it.

But Alexa was no chef. She had no natural aptitude for cooking, and she was easily distracted if a text or a call came in, so that she couldn't remember which of the ingredients she had already added to the pot. And her sense of taste was decidedly suspect. She would carefully taste the pasta sauce, declare it perfect, but when she dished it up and began to eat, she would frown and say: 'Something is not right. Can you taste it too?'

He would lie.

But these were insignificant untruths. White lies.

The big lie, the unmentionable, unshareable and increasingly unbearable lie, the fraud that assailed him now on the dark, silent N1 on the way to Alexa, was the one about sex.

He swore out loud in the car.

Life just never gave him a break.

If you drank as he used to drink, seven days a week, sex was not a big priority. When lust sometimes overcame him, his alcohol-soaked equipment wouldn't cooperate anyway.

But then you dried out, and that had consequences. The biggest problem of being on the wagon was the desire for the healing powers of the bottle. Close on those heels was the return of the libido, at a time when you have way too much mileage on your middle-aged clock, and desirable women were not necessarily queuing up to accommodate you.

Which was what was so damn ironic. Six months ago he was head over heels in love with Alexa, and a big chunk of that was his desire to make love to her, good and proper. Look, he was a sucker for a beautiful mouth, and she certainly had one, broad and generous and soft. And like most guys, surely, he appreciated a royal pair of jugs – as Cupido, faced with an impressive bust measurement, would longingly, admiringly describe them.

And there was Alexa's voice, and her attitude, and that look in her eyes, as if she knew what you were thinking, and she wanted you to keep on thinking just that. He had always had a thing for her, from way back, when she first hit the limelight and he was just one more nameless fan staring at the sexy singer on the TV screen, harbouring his unseemly secret thoughts.

He was crazy for her.

But then, after the chaos of the Sloet case, six months ago, it happened for the first time, and it was everything that Benny Griessel had dreamed of. Lord, that woman could kiss, and her body was just the right combination of soft and firm, even though she was closer to fifty than he was. She was so instantly responsive, her hands all over his body. Her eagerness, her spontaneity, she didn't mind showing her pleasure, shouting, in her jubilant velvet voice: 'Oh yes, Benny, yes. Good, Benny, so good, more, more, more,' along with a few other things that you wouldn't ever mention to anyone, but that were thrilling all the same.

Afterwards, he would lie beside her, spent and wet with perspiration, in love, lost, and so immensely pleased with himself and with her, and with them. He thought, fuck, finally life had given him a break, this sexy creature, this fabulous woman.

And from there on it only got better.

Between her busy schedule and his unpredictable work, at least once a week – now and again two heavenly times – they would repeat the miracle in her big double bed. A couple of times in the sitting room, and once in the shower, soaking wet and slippery with soap. They learned more of each other's tastes and bodies and pleasures, grew relaxed and easy, and Griessel was happy for the first time in he didn't know how long.

And then he went and moved in.

'It would be so nice to have just a little more of you, Benny. Even if it is a half an hour in the morning, or evening.' That's how Alexa brought it up.

He thought that, if it was so amazing when he saw her so seldom, it could only be better when he saw her more. Logical argument. In addition, it made economic and practical sense. She was alone in that rambling house, he was cooped up with his cheap furniture in his cramped bachelor flat.

And they loved each other.

So he gave up his flat, and took the furniture back to Mohammed 'Love Lips' Faizal's pawn shop, and with the proceeds he took Alexa to her favourite restaurant, Bizerca, where he, SAPS Detective Captain, sat eating oysters in the knowledge that his constant struggle was over, life was good. That first moving-in night they fucked like teenagers, and he knew it had been the right decision.

The second night, when he came to bed, Alexa slipped her hand under the elastic of his pyjama bottoms and she stroked and teased and kissed him, and he *njapsed* her again.

The third night, the same thing. His soldier struggled to stand quite to attention, and his performance was not what you'd call first rate, but he pressed through.

And by night four he knew he was in trouble.

In his twenties, when he and his ex, Anna, were young and horny and newly married, he could do the deed two, three times a day.

But that was in the old days. A quarter century and a thousand litres of Jack Daniel's ago.

Now it was altogether a different matter.

So, what did you do?

He couldn't say to Alexa 'no, *fok weet*, this is a bit much'. Not when she looked at you with those eyes full of love and compassion and sexual need, not when you had been *njapsing* her with such abandon for the past six months. Not if she had bought you clothes and an iPhone, and treated you like this big hero.

There was no way he could sit in front of a doctor and say 'I want a prescription for Viagra'. His sexual prowess had nothing to do with anyone, he didn't have that sort of courage, and he couldn't swallow those pills every day. Then he would be addicted all over again to something new, walking around with a permanent Jakob Regop – a constant boner was trouble that he really didn't need.

All he could do, was to sleep over at work. To get the lead back in his pencil.

Which meant he looked rough in the morning, and lied to all and sundry, and his boss and his colleagues thought he was drinking again.

He knew it couldn't go on like this.

But what was he to do?

He was fucked. He knew it.

She met him at the door, kissed him, clucked over him, led him to the kitchen 'for lasagne, it didn't come out exactly as I hoped, Benny, but you must be terribly hungry'. She sat with him in the kitchen. He ate, and told little white lies about the taste of the food. She asked about his day. He told her everything, except the part about Adair. She listened so attentively, was so impressed. Then she said: 'My master detective. You'll catch them.'

He asked about her day. She told him about the negotiations and recordings, about the battle to get publicity and time on air for her artists. 'The market is getting a bit overcrowded.'

They went to the bedroom.

He brushed his teeth, put on his new pyjamas. She sat in front of the mirror chatting, taking off her make-up, told him she had left Woollies food in the fridge for while she was away in Johannesburg from tomorrow. She said she would miss him. And he must keep safe. And phone when he could, she had a horde of meetings and one appearance at Carnival City, but by Thursday she would be back again.

He made the calculations. Two nights to recover, to reload his pistol.

She undressed, rubbed her body with creams and oils. She put on her nightclothes, switched off the light. She lay down close to him, held him tightly, her mouth against his neck.

'I love you, Benny.'

'And I love you too.'

Her hand moved to his belly, slipped under the pyjama bottoms.

'Where's that rascal?' she asked playfully.

The ringing of his cellphone woke him.

He saw it was the DPCI number. It was 2.12 in the morning. He picked it up and walked out so as not to disturb Alexa any more. It was cold in the passage without the pyjamas that still lay bundled up somewhere under the sheets.

'Griessel,' he answered.

'Benny, this is Philip. I'm sorry to wake you . . .'

'No problem,' he said, and tried to keep the sleepiness out of his voice.

'I thought you should know: we have just received a call from Senior Superintendent Jean-Luc Bonfils from Interpol in Lyon. It's about the snake on the cartridges.'

He went into the sitting room. There had been a heater on when he came in earlier.

'Do they know something?'

'Yes, "something" is probably the best description. He received our query, and he's sending us everything they have within the next hour, but in the meantime he wanted to tell me: this is the sixteenth international murder that they know of with that "snake trademark", as he calls it . . .'

'*Jissis*,' said Griessel. The heater in the sitting room was off, but the room was not as chilly as the passage. He turned it on, up to maximum while he listened and stood wide-legged over it.

'I made a few quick notes,' said van Wyk. 'The details are not quite right, but here is what I have: the first crime scene where such a marked cartridge was found, was seven years ago in Portugal. I'll come back to that just now. Most of the consecutive murders were in Europe – Germany, France, Spain, Holland, Poland, Belgium, and Italy. One was in Britain, one in New York, and one in Reykjavik, Iceland. He says there may be one or two in Russia, but these have never been officially handed over to Interpol. This one in Franschhoek is the first in the southern hemisphere.'

'Each time the cartridges had the snake on them?'

'That's right.'

'And the targets?'

'That's the funny thing. He says they have no doubt it is a hired assassin, but there is no specific pattern, except for the engraving, of course. In Poland, Spain, and France, the victims were definitely organised crime. The one in New York was a woman of eighty-two, a multimillionaire and an art collector. In Germany it was a young dotcom entrepreneur, and the other a very pretty teacher in her thirties. They were not connected in any way, and the murders were fourteen months apart. I could go on. Bonfils said their theory was that he works for anyone who is prepared to pay. And apparently he charges a lot. A hundred thousand euro per victim, at least.'

'Do they know who he is?'

'They have a few interesting theories, really just based on a single informant who doesn't know the whole story either. Bonfils says the snake on the cartridges is most probably the Mozambican Spitting Cobra, and the letters NM stand for *Naja mossambica*, the Latin name for the snake. Apparently very poisonous, and deadly accurate . . .'

He struggled to link a European hit man with an African snake. 'Mozambique? That's . . . odd?'

'Indeed. And that's where the story gets interesting. The hit man is known as the Cobra, and Interpol think he is Mozambican. Bonfils says the reasons for that are all in the report, but it starts with the first murder, in Portugal.'

'He's sending it now?'

'That's what he promised.'

'I'm coming in . . . You should get some sleep, Phil.'

'I will, as soon as I have read the report.'

Griessel rang off and stood there, cellphone in hand.

A Mozambican. A British professor. On a Cape wine farm belonging to a German.

Where were the days when this land was the polecat of the world, when no one came here? When at least you knew the suspect would be a local *fokker*?

Then he grew aware of the musky scent of sex rising along with the warm air from the heater. He looked down at his penis, now small and shrivelled.

Rascal.

In the big dark room he laughed quietly, mockingly at himself.

16

Just past three in the morning, in the perfect silence of his cramped office beside the IMC hall, van Wyk gave Griessel the print-out of the email and said: 'Read this first . . .'

He took the page and read.

Jean-Luc Bonfils <j-lbonfils@interpol.int>
To:philip.vanwyk@saps.gov.za
Re:Cobra (Cobra/B79C1/04/03/2007)
Dear Captain van Wyk

It was a pleasure talking to a fellow law enforcement officer on the graveyard shift, albeit a continent and hemisphere away, and under these circumstances.

Allow me to start with the most important:

1. I am not the Interpol officer assigned to the Cobra dossier. This is Supt. Marie-Caroline Aubert, and she will be very anxious to assist you in any way. I will share all our communications with her later today.

2. May I respectfully request a copy of your investigation records for our database as soon as your schedule allows? If you could please also keep me informed, should you make positive progress (or, of course, an arrest). Interpol is keenly interested in this subject, especially given the fact that this is the first reported homicide committed by the Cobra in the southern hemisphere.

3. Please find attached twenty-one (21) documents, which is the full complement of available material at Interpol, and includes notes on all the known Cobra dossiers.

4. Please allow me one clarification: you will notice that the Légion étrangère (L.E. or French Foreign Legion) photograph is of very low resolution, and that the information supplied by the L.E. is limited. This is not an omission on the part of Interpol. Usually the L.E. does not release any information on their enlistments to law enforcement (not even French authorities). However, they do screen all applicants for serious crimes through an agreement with Interpol before acceptance. It was this connection we leveraged for the little information on Curado that was released (unofficially, as a favour).

Please let me know if we can be of assistance in any way, and best of luck with your investigation.
Jean-Luc Bonfils (Superintendent)
INTERPOL
200, quai Charles de Gaulle
69006 Lyon
France

'OK,' said Griessel.

Van Wyk pressed his finger on a bundle of documents. 'This pile contains summaries of all the relevant murder investigations in the northern hemisphere,' he said. 'There isn't anything new, but the cartridges are there every time. The only interesting thing is that the Cobra began using a new Heckler & Koch MK23 in 2009 and 2011. But it seems as though he acquires the latest model every two years . . .'

Van Wyk pushed more print-outs across to Benny. 'Read *these* first. That's how they put two and two together.'

Griessel picked up the top page.

INTERPOL
General Secretariat
200, quai Charles de Gaulle
69006 Lyon
France
Intelligence report: Cobra/B79C1/04/03/2007/19/03/2009
Report date: 2 May 2010
Report submitted by: Stefano Masini, Procura della Repubblica presso il Tribunale di Milano
Interview by: Stefano Masini, Procura della Repubblica presso il Tribunale di Milano
Interview with: (Name withheld, paid informant, Bari.)
Interview venue: Bari, Italy
(Edited Transcription, translated by M.P. Ross, Interpol, 19 May 2010)

SM: The shell casings found on the scene of the Carnevale killing are engraved with a snake, and the letters N and M. Do you . . .

X: (Expletive.) That's bad, man.

SM: Have you ever heard of such markings?

X: Yes, yes, I've heard the rumours, lots of rumours. It's the Cobra. Very dangerous guy.

SM: Does he work for 'ndrangheta?

X: No, (expletive) no, he's a freelancer, he works for anybody, he's a gun for hire. Very expensive, hundred thousand euros for a hit, but they say he never misses, he always delivers. If the Cobra takes a contract on you, you're (expletive) dead, man. For sure.

SM: Do you know who he is?

X: Nobody knows this guy. He's a ghost. Just bullshit stories . . .

SM: What stories?

X: Bullshit, man. Some say he was in the French Foreign Legion, and he lives in Amsterdam, or Madrid, or Marseilles, but they don't know. Nobody knows. Lots of stories, lots of rumours. The wannabes, they talk about him, they want to be him, man. If you want a clean hit, no come-backs, you get the Cobra. (Expletive) psychopath, man, they say he has the eyes of a snake, you know? He never blinks, cold eyes . . . That type of shit, people make it up. They even say he killed his own father, I mean, you know, there's a new . . . how do they say? A new . . . twist every time . . .

SM: How did he kill his father?

X: It's crap, man.

SM: I'm sure. But let's not waste a good story.

X: (Expletive.) Don't write in that report that this came from me. I need the money, man . . .

SM: Of course . . .

X: OK. So . . . They say, he killed his father, because he needed a refer-ence, you know? To get business. Three, four years ago, in Portugal. His father was this retired Russian Army colonel, worked in Africa most of his life teaching those baboons to shoot each other with an AK, you know? What do they call them? Military advisor? So this Russian colonel (expletive) some black woman in one of those hell-hole countries, got her pregnant. And then he just left, never cared for the kid or the woman. Big suffering. But she knew his name and everything. So this kid grew up and he joined the French Foreign Legion, became a real killer, you know?

A badass soldier. No fear. Nobody (expletive) with him. And then he left, and became The (expletive) Cobra, man, they say it was his first hit. He traced his father, the guy had retired to Portugal with all his stolen African money, and that was the Cobra's first hit with the snake on the bullets. That's where it all started.

    SM: So he's a mulatto?

    X: That's what they say.

    SM: Who?

    X: You know. The rumours. Just guys talking shit.

    SM: Guys in the trade?

    X: Yes.

    SM: Has anybody actually seen him?

    X: Maybe the bosses.

    SM: Capos?

    X: Yes. They say, two of them have met the Cobra. But in the beginning, few years ago, when he was selling.

    SM: Selling what?

    X: His service. You know. He had to market himself, in the beginning. As an assassin.

    SM: Anything else?

    X: Not really. OK maybe . . . But you know this is really all (expletive) crap. Because of the snake on the bullets, they make up new things.

    SM: Tell me anyway.

    X: They say there's this tattoo he has. Bird and a snake. On his arm. Right here. Guy must love snakes.

    SM: That's it?

    X: There's nothing else to tell. Oh, they say, if you want to contact him, you place an ad on . . . what's it called . . . . ? Loot. That's it.

    SM: Loot?

    X: Yes. It's a website in England where you can sell anything. So you place an ad and you use the word snake, like 'snake for sale' or something, some special code. And then he will contact you. (Expletive) snakes. I mean, you have to be a psycho man, to be that into snakes.

Griessel looked up at van Wyk. 'There's a lot of speculation.'

Van Wyk nodded. 'It gets better. Read the next one.'

He picked it up and read.

INTERPOL
General Secretariat
200, quai Charles de Gaulle
69006 Lyon
France
Intelligence report: Cobra/B79C1/04/03/2007/27/6/2010
Report date: 27 June 2010
Report submitted by: Superintendent Marie-Caroline Aubert,
InterpolGeneral Secretariat, Lyon
Investigation: Murder of Zakhar Perminov, Vila Praia da Ancora,
Portugal on 13 September 2006
Source: Dossier of the Polícia de Segurança Pública, and personal inter-
view with Superintendent Christóvã Formigo, Polícia de Segurança
Pública, Lisbon, Portugal
(Translated by P.A. Shilling, Interpol, 28 June 2010)

At 07.55 on the morning of 13 September 2006, the body of Zakhar
Ivanovich Perminov was found (by a Portuguese cleaning woman) in the
living room of a villa on the outskirts of Vila Praia de Âncora, a coastal
holiday resort in northern Portugal, about five kilometres south of the
Spanish border.

Perminov had been shot twice – once in the forehead, and once through
the heart. Bullets recovered from the crime scene indicated a Heckler &
Koch MK23 (a weapon popular with American Special Forces) and Cor
Bon ammunition (45 ACP +P 230 grain).

Two shell casings that were found on the scene match this firearm and
ammunition. The casings were engraved with the likeness of a snake with
a flared head, and the initials/letters NM (capitalised, no full stops).

The villa had no security measures, and no sign of forced entry was
found. According to a statement by the cleaning woman the villa's glass
sliding doors leading to the pool were never locked when Perminov was
in residence.

No forensic evidence of the intruder, other than the shell casings and
bullets, was found on the scene. No arrests were made, and the dossier is
still open.

Perminov, the deceased, was a Russian citizen. The Russian Embassy
in Lisbon supplied limited details about the deceased's career, but it was
confirmed that he was a retired former Russian paratroop colonel.

Perminov served as reconnaissance squad leader for the 103rd Guards Airborne Division in Vitebsk in Belarus, and was deployed to Mozambique as military advisor to the Mozambique Liberation Front (FRELIMO) from 1978–1980. He also served in Angola as a member of the staff of the Soviet chief military advisor, Lieutenant-General Leonid Kusmenko, in 1986.

Re. Intelligence Report Cobra/B79C104/03/2007/19/03/2009:

After a written submission to the Mozambican Embassy in Paris, it was confirmed that Zakhar Ivanovich Perminov was registered as the father of Joaquim Curado. Joaquim Curado was born on 27 January 1979 in Cuamba, Mozambique, to Dores Branca Curado (herself born of a Makua mother and Portuguese father).

The Mozambican authorities also confirmed that the same Joaquim Curado is still a citizen of that country. A passport was issued to him (in the name of Joaquim Curado) in 1999, and was replaced by a new passport in 2003. (Note: It is common practice for the Légion étrangère [L.E. or French Foreign Legion] to confiscate enlistees' passports, which might explain the replacement.)

This 2003 passport was used for a return journey from France to Mozambique in 2006, but no further legal entries/exits were logged.

It was further established that a Joaquim Curado, a Mozambican citizen (passport number corresponded with first issued Mozambican travel document), served in the Légion étrangère from 2000 to 2005 as Legionnaire 1e Classe (Lance Corporal/1st Class Legionnaire) in the 1st Foreign Regiment (1° RE).

(Note MCA: The insignia of the L.E.'s 1st Foreign Regiment [1° RE] is a framed bird of prey [black] and a snake [green]. See Intelligence Report: Cobra/B79C1/04/03/2007/19/03/2009, page 2: 'There's this tattoo he has. Bird and a snake. On his arm. Right here. Guy must love snakes.')

According to his partially and unofficially released L.E. records, Curado received special forces training, and showed no exceptional leadership skills. However, he was regarded as a proficient soldier and excellent marksman, and served with distinction in several African operations.

He is 1.89 metres (6 ft 2 inches) tall, and weighed 95 kg (209 lbs) at induction into the L.E.

Curado was honourably discharged from the Légion étrangère at his own request in 2005, having served his compulsory five-year term. In the same year, on the strength of his L.E. service, he was granted French citizenship, and thus now holds dual citizenship of Mozambique and France. A French passport was issued to him on 19 January 2006. The passport has not since been used for travel outside the European Union.

No current address was found for Joaquim Curado.

(Note MCA: A theory might be formulated that Joaquim Curado is the assassin known as 'the Cobra'.)

* A photograph of Curado was supplied by the L.E. and is herewith attached. It was taken during his L.E. induction in 2000.

17

INTERPOL
General Secretariat
200, quai Charles de Gaulle
69006 Lyon
France

Intelligence Report Addendum: Cobra/B79C1/04/03/2007/04/07/2010

Report date: 14 September 2010

Report submitted by: Superintendent Marie-Caroline Aubert, Interpol General Secretariat, Lyon

Investigation: Series of murders in the European Union connected to 'The Cobra' (Original dossier Cobra/B79C1/04/03/2007)

(Translated by P.A. Shilling, Interpol, 15 September 2010)

With reference to the series of nine murders in the European Union (2006–2010) where bullets recovered from the various crime scenes indicated a Heckler & Koch MK23 and Cor-Bon ammunition (45 ACP +P 230 grain), and shell casings were engraved with the likeness of a snake with flared head and the initials/letters NM (capitalised, no full stops):

A theory might be formulated that the snake engraving represents the Mozambique Spitting Cobra:

1. The engraving shows a high likeness for Mozambique Spitting Cobra – also the scale and the size of the hood.

2. The genus name of Naja mossambica corresponds with the initials NM.

3. Interpol Intelligence Reports Cobra/B79C1/04/03/2007/19/03/2009 and Cobra/B79C1/04/03/2007/27/06/2010 indicate a credible link between the suspected hired assassin 'The Cobra', and Joaquim Curado, a Mozambican and French national.

4. It is believed that 'The Cobra' is mulatto in complexion. In every homicide where his involvement is suspected, the victims suffered at least one shot between, near, or through the eyes. Note the behaviour (accuracy, eyes as target) and the colouring (tawny brown) of the Mozambique Spitting Cobra:

(Source, quoted verbatim: http://www.africanreptiles-venom.co.za/mozambique_spitting_cobra.html)

The colour varies between olive-grey, tawny brown or grey, with the scales in-between a black colour. The distribution includes Natal, Lowveld, south-eastern Tanzania and Pemba Island, and west to southern Angola and northern Namibia.

Behaviour:

This snake is a nervous and highly strung snake (sic). When confronted at close quarters it can rear up to as much as two-thirds of its length, spread its long narrow hood and will readily 'spit' in defence, usually from a reared-up position. By doing this the venom can be ejected at a distance of 2–3 metres (5½–8¼ feet), with remarkable accuracy. The spitting cobra does not often actually bite despite its aggressive behaviour, and also displays the habit of feigning death to avoid further molestation.

Venom:

This is probably the most dangerous snake, second only to the Mamba.

Its bite causes severe local tissue destruction (similar to that of the Puff Adder). Like the Rinkhals, it can spit its venom. The venom is ejected from two small holes near the tip of the teeth, usually aimed at the eyes. The effect is instantaneous causing intense smarting and inflammation and if not washed out with milk or water will cause permanent blindness.

The photograph of Joaquim Curado was small, scarcely two by three centimetres. It was printed in colour, but faded.

The face that stared out at Griessel was somewhere between boy and man. His hair was cropped very short, the features almost feminine in their refinement – high forehead, even, strong jawline, big dark eyes, straight nose, full lips, in the photo completely neutral. It reminded Griessel of a police drawing. There was no emotion – it was a face waiting to be filled in by life. But by no means the 'cold eyes' the Italian informant had speculatively described.

And there was something about the width and musculature of the neck that created the impression of an athlete.

Nearly 1.9 metres. Just under 100 kilograms. And that was before he started training with the French Foreign Legion. He would be a handful to arrest now.

'Can we make a bigger photo?' he asked van Wyk.

'Not without losing resolution. Maybe a centimetre or two . . . It's thirteen years old, Benny.' ·

'I know . . .'

He had that light-headed feeling that came with only three hours of sleep, his thoughts erratic, flitting and floundering.

He wanted to read all the Interpol documents carefully. Then he wanted to compile a time line of Adair's last week. He wanted to consider how the photo of the Cobra could help them.

He wanted more sleep.

He looked up at van Wyk, now pale, his bloodshot eyes weary. 'Phil, I want to work through this stuff carefully first. You should go home now.'

'OK, just two more things. Lithpel and the guys came back just after twelve. We managed to isolate Morris's computers from the other farm people by the IP address . . .'

'Computers?'

'Technically speaking. It's an Apple computer, and an iPad. Lithpel said Morris visited a lot of financial news websites. *The Economist, Financial Times, Bloomberg* . . . And then he was on his Google mail at least five times. Lithpel says you must talk to him when he gets back; he might be able to get into the emails.'

He nearly said 'Adair's email?' Stopped himself in time and said 'Morris's email?'

'That's right. Lithpel says there is a way.'

'But not through the channels?'

'No.'

He sat in his office and started with the documents, right from the beginning.

He read the summary of each of the Cobra assassinations – sixteen since 2006 – concise descriptions of the victims and murder scenes. Some reports contained notes by 'MCA', whom he subsequently realised must be Marie-Caroline Aubert.

She sometimes speculated about the possible motive behind the murder, made comments about the quality of the investigations, and carefully suggested theories.

Slowly, he gained respect for the way her head worked. Griessel picked up his pen and circled two of her notes. The first was an insert, in brackets, to the murder of the American billionaire in New York in 2011: *(Note MCA: One possible consideration is that the Cobra does not brand all his hits with the marked shell casings. If one takes into account the fact that he has averaged only two assassinations per annum since 2006, for an assumed (relatively modest for his skills and talents) yearly income of €200,000, there is the distinct possibility that he has completed other contracts on a more anonymous basis. An Interpol database search on H&K MK23 murders in Europe since 2006 shows eleven unconfirmed and forensically unmatched possibilities. For further investigation.)*

The second was in the murder of an Iranian engineer in Warsaw in 2012: *(Note MCA: During a telephone interview with the investigating officer, it became apparent that the victim, Omid Rostami, was involved with the Iranian uranium enrichment project. It is suspected that Rostami was in Warsaw to seek a black market uranium or nuclear equipment contract. It is further suspected that this was a Mossad hit, subcontracted to the Cobra.)*

It reminded him of Cupido's words: *This was a professional hit, pappie, and* jy wiet wie *sanctions professional hits. Gangstas and governments.*

Mossad. Intelligence Services. They knew about this hired assassin. And they were prepared to contract him.

What about other intelligence people? Such as Emma Graber of MI6?

Griessel pulled an A4 pad from his top drawer and paged past the rough notes of his previous dossiers, till he had a clean page.

At the top he wrote *Morris/Adair.*

He consulted his notebook, then the calendar on his iPhone. He wrote:

Monday 24 June: Break in at Adair, Cambridge.
Tuesday 25 June: Adair reported missing.

Wednesday 26 June: Adair phones Body Armour (as Morris).
Thursday 27 June: Adair sends passport scan and flight number to Body Armour.
Friday 28 June: Adair arrives in Cape Town.
Sunday 30 June: Adair abducted/murdered, Franschhoek.

He sat staring at his timeline, trying to make sense of it.

So many things, such a short time. And his head wasn't clear.

The break-in at Adair's flat was just over a week ago. *A back door was forced, and the interior left in complete disarray,* Graber had said.

That meant someone had been looking for something.

The room in La Petite Margaux guesthouse was in the same condition. As if there had been a search.

He made a note: *Who is looking for what?* Bones Boshigo said *everyone knows what the algorithm does, even the terrorists, and there's nothing anybody can do to stop it.* Why then were people searching through Adair's flat and guesthouse room?

Last Monday Adair had got away just in time before the burglary at his home. Or perhaps he hadn't been there at the time, maybe he came home after the incident, saw the chaos and fled? Where to? And why?

He wrote: *False passport?* The question was: Did Adair already have one at his disposal? Or did he acquire one in haste between Monday and Thursday last week? Both possibilities had interesting implications. A Professor of Mathematics who kept a false passport handy? Or knew where to get one at short notice?

Didn't sound right.

And then the big question: How did the Cobra – or the people who hired the Cobra – know that Adair was in a guesthouse on a wine farm in Franschhoek?

If they knew where Adair was before his flight to South Africa, surely they would have kidnapped or murdered him there?

But somewhere between last Monday and yesterday they found out where he was, and sent the Cobra from Europe to do his job.

If Adair was lying low, with his false name, false passport, and false email address, how did they know?

He put the pen down, opened his steel cabinet, and took out the rolled-up camp bed. He put it together, set his iPhone for seven, turned off the light, lay down on his back, and closed his eyes.

He only wanted a few hours of sleep so that he could think this through with a clear head, do what he needed to do. Such as, that he must get a bulletin out to all stations to let them know, should the body of a white man in his fifties be found somewhere. Such as, the fact that someone must sit down and compare all the video material from Oliver Tambo and Cape Town International Airport since Friday with the old photo of Joaquim Curado.

Perhaps luck would be on their side.

18

Tyrone Kleinbooi's Casio G-Shock wristwatch woke him at 6.45.

He had stolen it one Sunday morning last year on the common in Green Point, from a mountain biker whose attention was distracted by his sexy cycling partner.

Tyrone tuned the radio to Kfm, because he wanted to hear the weather forecast. Isolated showers, clearing towards midday.

That was a relief. For his industry.

He made instant coffee. He ate Weet-Bix with milk and sugar. Brushed his teeth, showered, shaved, and dressed. Black, slightly faded Edgars chinos with deep open pockets. Old black T-shirt, reasonably new black polo-necked jersey. *Black is beautiful, Tyrone. Smart. And invisible. You can be anything in black.*

He pushed up the sleeves of his jersey to just below the elbows, he could work better that way. He put the silver Zippo and the hairpin with the small yellow sunflower in his left trouser pocket. He picked up the light blue Nokia Lumia 820, put it in the small neat rucksack that he had bought, because the size and the material and look were important. It mustn't rustle, mustn't look cheap, and it mustn't interfere with his hand movements. But it must be able to hold the loot, cellphone, and his rain jacket.

He had taken the Lumia out of a businessman's pocket up in Kloof Street – the man had been occupied with his coffee and croissant at Knead, reading the sports pages of the *Cape Times,* did not look like the Windows phone type. And no self-respecting fence was going to pay for a Windows phone, zero second-hand value, so Tyrone just kept it for himself. So he could at least phone Nadia, and she him.

He locked his room and walked around the Slamse's triple garage, along the wall to the gate. He typed in the security code. The gate clicked open. He walked out, to the city.

Weather looking OK.

He walked briskly. Tuesdays were not your best days of the pick-pocket week, but the early bird catches the worm if you keep your eyes open between the suits in Strand, Waterkant, Riebeeck, Long and Bree, and you blend in with the office workers hurrying along in groups, late for work, take-away coffee in one hand, as you squeeze in through the doors with them, up the escalators or in the lifts.

He was a man on a mission. Twenty-one thousand bucks by the end of Jan.

Tall order.

But every journey starts with one small step.

That wasn't one of Uncle Solly's. He'd heard that one time in St George's Mall, this pretty whitey girl trying to motivate her hangdog loser boyfriend.

And he liked it. So he didn't steal anything from her, except the quote.

Out of habit he looked north, across Table Bay. He saw the cruise ship, beyond Robben Island. He smiled. Tin can full of marks, that boat would be here in an hour or two.

Rich pickings.

Griessel dreamed a giant snake was chasing him, the mouth agape, spitting, so that it dripped off the back of his head and he felt the sour venom burning down the back of his neck. The alarm was a sudden reprieve, catapulting him to the silent safety of his office.

He folded up the camp bed and stowed it away, took the toilet bag and a worn old towel from the filing cabinet, and went to shower in the bathroom on the third floor.

While he shaved, he realised he felt rested. Fresh. Just over two extra hours of deep sleep, and the cobwebs were gone.

Perhaps because he knew he was alone for at least two nights. He and his rascal, solo.

A little less pressure.

He stood looking at himself in the mirror, and he felt the urge come over him. The urge to catch the Cobra.

Something inside him revolted against the concept of a hit man with a trademark. It was sociopathic, arrogant, it represented every-thing that was wrong with this world. Everyone was obsessed with money and status and fame. More than ever, it seemed, it was the root of evil, the source of more and more crime.

The murdered bodyguards, B.J. Fikter and Barry Minnaar, were former members of the Force, and not one of the highly advanced, First World detective services had been able to apprehend the Cobra so far. After all the mess of the past few months, with the SAPS derided as never before, it would be good to show the world . . .

And catching men was what he did. At least, all that he did well. There was no denying that he often struggled, made mistakes, but that moment when you clicked the handcuffs around the fucker's wrists and said 'You're under arrest', there were few things that measured up to that, it was when the universe balanced out, just for a moment.

He wiped off his face, packed his toiletries in the bag, checked himself in the mirror. One of his new shirts, only slightly creased, with the blue jacket.

This morning no one would think he was drinking again.

Just before seven he knocked on Nyathi's door jamb.

The Giraffe waved him in and said, 'Benny, I think we should tell the team everything.'

'Yes, sir,' he said in relief. He had been feeling guilty since yesterday about lying to IMC.

Nyathi gathered up his papers. 'I have to go and chair the morning parade. You get your guys into your office. Just your team, Bones, and Philip van Wyk. Make it very clear: we trust them completely, but they have to be utterly and completely circumspect. We cannot afford a single leak.'

'Yes, sir. But we are going to need more people.'

'Something happened?'

'Interpol has a lot on the assassin. He's called the Cobra.'

Nyathi checked his watch. 'Walk with me, please.'

On the way to the morning parade, Griessel told him in broad strokes about the new information, the thirteen-year-old photograph, and what he planned to do.

'Good,' said the colonel. 'Go ahead, and keep me posted.'

'Just one more thing, sir. Philip says Sergeant Lithpel Davids can get into Adair's email . . .' And he left that hanging there so that the colonel could draw his own conclusions.

Nyathi stopped and looked at Griessel. 'Do it,' he said, barely audibly.

First he thanked the detectives who had worked very late. Then he told the team everything.

They joked about the Cobra's nickname.

'The bastard probably has a Twitter account too,' said a surly Cupido, his reproachful eyes on Griessel.

They studied the photograph. Griessel explained his strategy. He asked Ndabeni and Radebe to liaise with the SAPS office at O. R. Tambo Airport in Johannesburg, and to fly up as soon as possible to study the video material of the Arrivals Hall. Liebenberg and Fillander must do the same at Cape Town International.

'It's a long shot,' said Radebe.

'It's one of the few shots we have,' said Fillander.

'We are only looking at international flights since Thursday,' said Griessel. 'We know he's coloured, we know he will probably be wearing a hat or glasses, he will be aware of cameras, so he will look away or keep his head down. What we really want, is a name, because then we can link it to a passport, and the way he paid for the flight. Maybe a credit card number . . . That's more than Interpol has now.'

'If he killed Adair, he's long gone,' said Bones.

'Maybe,' said Griessel, 'but someone searched Adair's house in England, and his room in Franschhoek. I don't think they found what they were looking for. I think that is why Adair could still be alive.'

'That's how a Violent Crimes cop thinks, Bones. Live and learn,' said Fillander.

'Touché,' said Bones.

'Don't talk of my girl like *that*,' said Mooiwillem Liebenberg.

They laughed.

'Bones, have you anything new on Adair?'

'Now learn how the genius department thinks, *nè*. I looked at everything, and here's the thing: *daars niks nuut nie*, absolutely nothing new. Now, for you hot-headed blood-lust cops that would mean *nada*. But look at the bigger picture: until about four weeks ago Adair was blogging and writing lots of letters to the press, and gave interviews, all about the Adair Protocol. And then he went quiet.'

'So?' asked Cupido.

'Why, Vaughn? Why did he stop agitating?'

Cupido shrugged.

'Something happened, *nè*,' said Bones.

'You don't know what,' said Cupido.

'Not yet,' said Bones. 'Not yet.'

When they were finished and walked out, Cupido approached Griessel. 'I thought we were partners, Benna.'

'Vaughn, I was under orders.'

'But still,' said Cupido, deeply wounded, 'where's the trust?'

Tyrone was early enough, so he walked into the Parkade Mall in Strand Street, opposite the Cape Sun.

Seven storeys of parking. A lot of cars, a lot of people. And they all had to go down in those lifts, to the street. And there were no cameras in the lifts.

He rode them, up and down.

Lots of coloureds. He didn't steal from coloureds.

Darkies and whiteys were fair game.

He chatted up a sexy, slinky dolly on his second trip down in the lift, but she wouldn't divulge her cell number.

He talked to an aunty on the fifth descent. He made her laugh. He enjoyed that.

He stole two cellphones and two wallets. He rode down to the first storey, and checked his loot in privacy behind a black BMW X5.

A new BlackBerry. Worth three-fifty from the fence. An iPhone 4S. Eight hundred bucks. Three credit cards, fifty each. One driver's licence, fifty bucks. Seven hundred in cash.

Total of about two K. Not bad for an hour's work.

He dumped the empty wallets under the X5.

Time to rob a shipload of tourists.

19

Griessel concentrated hard on understanding Sergeant Lithpel Davids. Cupido sat there too, arms folded, his mouth a straight, sulky line, saying nothing.

'Cappie, you know it's illegal. Fun, but illegal,' said Lithpel. Just one 's' in the entire sentence, easy to follow.

'I know,' said Griessel, 'but Morris is not a suspect. We won't have to explain it in court.'

'Cool. Now to hack a Gmail account, that's easy. You can phish, or you can download an app, or you can use your own Gmail account,' was more or less the translated version, once Griessel had filtered out all the lisps.

'OK,' said Griessel.

'Phishing does not apply, since the dude has been kidnapped, right?'

'OK.'

'And we don't want comebacks, we don't want to leave tracks, so I'm not going to use my own Gmail account.'

'OK.'

'Which leaves us with the app. And it just so happens *lat ek een hier het*, right here on my system. Keeping up with the dark side, Cappie, if you know what I mean.'

'OK.'

'You haven't a clue what I'm on about, Cappie.'

'That's right.'

'No worries. Just sit back, relax, and watch me work.'

Body language, Tyrone. Be a student of body language.

That was how he spotted the woman. She came walking past the Cape Union Mart, in the direction of the V&A shopping centre on the Waterfront. She was somewhat lightly dressed for this weather, jeans, and a thin, blood red sweater. She gripped the handbag tightly under her arm as though it contained a fortune. She looked scared. She walked quickly, looking around as though she didn't know where to go. In the crush of tourists from the ship.

And she was pretty, Mediterranean dark. His age.

What's not to like?

He kept behind her, two, three metres.

She looked around once. He looked away.

He would have to strike before she got too close to the shopping centre. There were cameras.

He pushed his hand into this left pocket, grasped the hairpin. Increased his pace, caught up.

Four women approached from the left, cutting between them, so that he fell behind again.

She was only five metres from the amphitheatre.

He must turn back, it was too near the cameras.

She held the handbag, with its easy clasp, so anxiously. He knew that attitude. It usually meant there was something valuable inside. Cash? Jewellery? Carried by someone who was not accustomed to it.

A real challenge.

He jogged faster.

Just before the steps to the rows of seats in the amphitheatre. There were a lot of people.

He took a chance, tapped her on the shoulder, the hair clip held up in his fingers.

She was startled, looked around at him in confusion. Scared.

He smiled his most charming smile, relaxed and helpful. 'I think you dropped this, ma'am.' His shoulder against hers, his right hand at the handbag.

She looked at the clip, then at him, frowning, not understanding.

She was *very* pretty, he registered. 'The hairpin. You dropped it.'

His hand was at the flap of the handbag, while he twirled the pin in his fingers and kept on smiling.

'Oh,' she said. 'No . . .'

His right hand was under the flap. He felt the leather of a purse.

'You sure it's not yours? Take a good look.'

At that instant, when she gave her full attention to the hairpin, he bumped her with his right shoulder, just lightly, as though someone had pushed him from behind, as though he had lost his balance for a second, and he slipped the wallet out and pushed it, lightning fast, into his trouser pocket.

'No,' she said, looking left and right, worried.

'Sorry, then,' he said, and lowered the pin. He turned around and walked, away from the shopping centre.

Only six paces away, the security man grabbed him from behind, a steely grip on his wrist.

He jerked. His arm came free.

He ran.

Then the second security guard tackled him to the ground.

'And we're in,' said Lithpel Davids.

Griessel leaned forward to see.

'Only one mail in his in-box,' said Lithpel.

On the screen, beside a yellow arrow, he read **Lillian Alvarez** *(No Subject) Arrived in CT. Phone on and working.* And to the far right: *8:12 a.m.*

'That bold means he hasn't opened the mail yet,' said Lithpel. 'But no worries, we can open it and then mark it as unread again.'

'OK.'

Lithpel clicked on the message.

'That's it,' he said. Because there was nothing more than *Arrived in CT. Phone on and working.* 'Sent about an hour ago. Do you want to look at his other mail, Cappie?'

'Please.'

On the navigation bar on the left, Davids clicked on 'More', and then 'All Mail'.

Only the single post from Lillian Alvarez appeared.

'Talk about good housekeeping,' said Davids.

'What does that mean?'

'It means he's cleaned up everything. There is no other mail. Everything he sent or received, is gone.'

'*Fok*,' said Griessel.

'Shall I try to find out who Lillian Alvareth ith?' asked Lithpel Davids.

★   ★   ★

The security guard with the pimples held onto his left arm and the one with muscles pulled his right arm painfully up against his back.

'Let me go!' said Tyrone, his voice shrill and frightened.

'We've got him, control, we're bringing him in,' said Pimples, white and young, into his radio. Then to Tyrone: 'Not as clever as you thought, hey?'

They pushed and dragged him towards the shopping centre.

'What are you talking about?' Tyrone tried to bring his fear under control, tried to sound indignant, but his heart beat in his throat. *Deny, deny, deny, Tyrone. And when that won't help any more, then you lie.*

'*Maaifoedie, fokken* pickpocket,' said Muscles, the coloured one. 'We've been after you for a long time.'

Bystanders made way for them, staring.

'Pickpocket?' said Tyrone. 'Where you come with that?'

'No. It's where *you* are *going*,' said Muscles, and he pressed Tyrone's arm even higher 'Now shut up.'

Through the pain he thought: They don't have anything, the cameras were too far away. They must have been following him, he hadn't spotted them in the crowd of tourists, he was too focused on the woman and the handbag. He must get her wallet out of his trouser pocket. It was the only evidence they had. But he wouldn't be able to get his arm free.

He was stuffed – that knowledge came down suddenly like a black curtain.

Christ, what would Nadia say?

Who would pay for her studies?

A good thing Uncle Solly was dead. All that training, and he let himself get caught like an amateur. A total disgrace.

Fear gnawed at his guts.

They took him into the shopping centre via a service door, and down the stairs. Their radios crackled and rasped, excited voices echoing down the wide corridor. Two sharp turns, then he saw the sign: Security: Control Room. A security man came out, stood waiting. He had stars on his shoulders. A general probably. He was white. He smiled, but not in a good way. 'Little shit,' he said, 'we've got you.'

The general stood aside so they could bundle him through the door.

Two more men sat inside, both coloured. They looked up. '*Ja*, that's him,' one of them said.

Big room, one wall was just TV monitors, a number of radios were recharging on long workbenches down the walls. A double door right at the back, and a single door just here, beside the map of the V&A against the wall. Photos of people, low resolution, as if they were print-outs of TV screen shots, on a noticeboard beside a handwritten notice saying NO TIME SHEETS, NO PAY!!!! Tyrone saw his picture there. Maybe four months old, he was in just black chinos and a black T-shirt. Summer time.

He was fucked. More adrenaline, more fear shot through his body.

Muscles let go of his arm and the relief was instant. His rucksack was pulled off, and Pimples shoved him into a chair. The general took the rucksack, came to stand in front of him, feet planted wide. Pimples and Muscles covered the door like two soldiers on guard.

'Check this,' one of the coloureds in front of the TV monitors said to him. Sneering.

There was Tyrone standing beside the Mediterranean beauty, the hairpin in front of her, frozen and beautifully zoomed in on the screen.

From a camera that he had never seen.

'Call the SAPS,' said the general.

'So I wanted to give her back her hairpin,' Tyrone spoke in desperation.

'And now her wallet is in your trouser pocket,' said the general. 'And we're going to leave it right there, until the police come. So they can get your fingerprints nicely. Call them, Freddie. And tell Vannie to bring the girl in, she probably still doesn't know she's been robbed.'

'She dropped the wallet, look there on your cameras,' said Tyrone. If only he could gain some time . . .

Freddie was one of the guards who were sitting at the monitors. He picked up a phone. They listened in silence as he reported the whole thing.

'Police on their way,' said Freddie, his eyes searching the screens. 'But the girl . . . I don't see her . . .'

Two minutes later it was not the police who came.

20

It was an odd noise that came from the direction of the door, almost like an asthmatic cough, then a low, sick sound. Pimples dropped like a sack of potatoes. Tyrone felt a spattering on his face.

A cartridge clinked on the bare floor.

Blood ran out of Pimples's head.

That sound again, and Muscles went down, right beside him. The same story.

Tyrone saw the man appear in the doorway. The pistol, the long black silencer. The general looked around, indignant that his authority was being undermined. Another quiet shot. The general collapsed. The delicate metallic sound of a bullet cartridge against the wall, then the floor.

It was surreal. Tyrone felt he wasn't really there, he was paralysed, a mingling of fear and shock and relief. '*Jirre*,' he said, and looked at the shooter, who now stood directly in front of him. A coloured man under a faded grey baseball cap, eyes like an eagle, all-seeing, looking through you. A fleeting thought: Who is this guy? Had he come to rescue him? Why was he shooting everyone?

The pistol swung towards Tyrone.

The security men at the TVs screamed.

The firearm was aimed at Tyrone, between his eyes.

Freddie jumped up, rushed towards the shooter.

Pistol swung away, to Freddie.

Tyrone did not think, it was just a sudden knowing: One chance.

He dived blindly, under and past the gunman, grabbing the rucksack beside the general. It snagged, he looked back, a strap was looped around the general's arm. Everything happened in a weird slow motion, like someone was holding back time. Freddie screamed, then the scream was cut off sharply. Freddie fell. Tyrone let go of the rucksack, because the shooter was turning towards him. He leaped at the door, adrenaline giving him strength and speed. The pistol was pointed at him again. He was at the door. The pistol coughed as he kicked off to the left, and out, he felt the burning pain across his shoulder blades. He was shot. He screamed, and ran the way they had brought him in. *Jirre*, Thank God for the sharp turns in the passage. One, two, and then the steps were ahead.

Up the stairs, yelling in terror. The second to last step hooked his foot, he fell forwards, reached out his hands to fend off the closed door. He banged his head hard, a thundering, against the wood, just above his right eye. Scurried to his feet, half dizzy, grabbed the door, jerked it open. He heard the footsteps behind him, ducked instinctively and suddenly as he went out, a bullet smacked against the door jamb. He was outside, he ran to the people, the tourists, he ran as he had never run before. He didn't look back, he sidestepped suddenly left, then right, he ran till he was in the midst of the crowd, he kept running, weaving between them. He felt blood run down his face, and down his back. Through the wide esplanade, into Mitchell's Waterfront Brewery, right through to the kitchen, people standing dumbfounded. He ran out of the back door, turned right, up the steps to Dock Road.

He wiped his hand over the blood, to get it out of his eyes.

He felt his back was soaking wet. The gunshot wound was bleeding.

He ran right in front of a car on Dock Road, tyres screeching. hooter blaring, it only just missed him. He ran over the central island, down to the Granger Bay car park, running right through, between parked cars, then took the stairs to the Coast Road level.

Outside. Turn right, his chest was on fire. He looked back. Saw no one.

Ran across the street, through the gate at Somerset Hospital, then through the big wooden doors.

Someone at the reception desk shouted after him.

He ran past, down the long cold corridors, past frowning nurses, and out of the back.

Hospital grounds.

He kept directly south, ran around buildings, past cars. Looked back again.

Nobody.

He saw the ruins, a building half demolished. Abandoned. He aimed for it, into it.

He found a dark room with no windows. He staggered against the wall, his breathing like a bullet train, sweat pouring off him. Loose bricks, broken planks in the worn floor. The stink of cat piss.

He picked up a length of wood, like a truncheon.

He turned to face the door-less opening, raising the wood high, and stood there waiting, gasping.

On Facebook Lithpel Davids found eighty-seven people with the surname of Alvarez, of whom only one had the first name Lillian.

'At least we know it's most likely a woman,' he said drily.

Cupido was still sitting back, not participating, while Benny Griessel and Lithpel went down the list. To number twenty-two. Beside the small photo and an icon of a house it said *Cambridge*.

'That one,' said Griessel.

David clicked.

A Facebook page opened up. A big photograph on top showed a kitten sleeping on the keyboard of a laptop. A smaller photo beside her name showed a young woman in her twenties, with long black hair and a sultry dark beauty.

'Looks like a Spanish dolly,' said Lithpel.

Griessel did not hear him, his eyes scanned further down: below 'Work and Education' it stated *Research Fellow at Applied and Computational Analysis (ACA) at DAMTP.* He said, 'That's her.'

For the first time Cupido sat up straight. He looked at the screen. 'I don't like this.'

Griessel waited for him to explain. It took a while.

'Is this Adair married?' Cupido asked at last.

'The Consulate said he's divorced.' And then he remembered Emma Graber's little games, and how positively she had passed on that information. As though she didn't want them making further enquiries.

'I'm calling Bones,' said Griessel.

★ ★ ★

Tyrone Kleinbooi stood with the piece of wood in the air for a long time.

But nobody came.

His hands and knees began to shake uncontrollably.

He lowered the plank slowly. He felt his face. The blood had begun to clot. He put the wood down without making a sound, and stretched an arm around his back. His jersey was torn across his back. Wet. Sore, but not unbearably so.

He sat down, his ears still pricked. His heart hammered and his body trembled slightly.

Shock. He was in shock. So this is what it feels like. He let his head drop, tried to slow his breathing down. He would survive, for now. I survived, Uncle Solly. Escaped. And then he thought of his rucksack, and the blows began to hit home. His cellphone. All the cash from this morning's work. The video. The radios that had crackled . . .

They were going to find the cellphone, the police. They would see there was only one name and number in the address book. Nadia's. If the police phoned with it, she would say: 'Hello, Tyrone.'

Then they would have him.

He had to go back. He had to get the rucksack before they came.

It was too late. His face was bloody, and his back, and his clothes.

He was large as life on that TV screen, the image frozen. His photo on that noticeboard.

When the police walked in, they would see it. They would play the whole video back, of how he stole the wallet.

There were other security guards at the V&A who would have heard over the radios that they had caught the pickpocket. That they had taken him to Security.

Everyone would think that he had done the shooting. They would put his face on national TV, and in the papers. *Crazy pickpocket killer on the loose.* Police all over the country would be hunting him.

Nadia would see all of that.

Jirre.

He would have to phone her. He would have to tell her some story. A story she would believe.

He had to steal a phone. Quickly. He would have to lie low. Quickly.

But first he had to get to his room, and wash, and put on clean clothes, and get his cash stash.

He better get going.

Bones let them carry on while he searched for information. He found it. 'No, Adair is not married. That's what Wikipedia says, *nè*. A bachelor.'

Griessel relayed the information.

'OK, so maybe she isn't his *skelmpie*,' said Cupido. 'But still. Check out that chick, pappie. She's *fokken* prime, she works with the *donner*, and she arrives here in the Cape saying: "Come into my arms, you bundle of charms." Doesn't that make you wonder?'

'About what?'

'About the whole thing, Benna.'

'I don't understand.'

'There's a lot that doesn't make sense in this thing. I mean, nothing quite fits. So I think it's time that we consider a few alternative theories. Let's say he's the one who did the shooting. I mean, Benna, we really don't know what went down there on the slave plantation.'

Griessel wondered if Cupido was being deliberately obtuse because he was still unhappy that they hadn't taken him into their confidence. 'Why would he shoot them?' he asked. 'The people looking after him?'

'It's not as wild as you think, Benna. This guy has his hands on the whole financial system. Now that's a very big temptation, doesn't matter who you are. And he's an expert, he knows how the whole system works. How difficult can it be to skim off the top. Just tell the system, just pay me two cents off every transaction, and I'm telling you, within months you're a millionaire. Huh, Lithpel, that's possible?'

'Pothible, but they will catch you, thooner rather than later.'

'And that's my whole point,' said Cupido.

Griessel tried to object, but Cupido held his hand up in the air. 'Just hear me out, Benna. With an open mind. Let's say it's something like this. Let's say the professor had a big scheme, and he planned it a long time ago. And he knew, sooner or later, someone would realise it. You have to leave tracks, I mean, everyone knows you're the guy who wrote this software. They know you've got your fingers in the pie, you'll be suspect, eventually. So you build an exit strategy . . .'

'Hell, Vaughn, I think that's . . .'

'No, Benna. Here we have an academic who suddenly has a false passport? How? I don't buy it. Here's this innocent professor who has a whole other Morris identity, and he makes his Gmail cleaner than a virgin's conscience? I mean, come on. Here's a man who for months protests about terrorists and organised crime, and then he goes suspiciously quiet? Here's a middle-aged *bok* with a pretty young thing, but what can he offer her? A university salary? I don't think so. And I ask you, where's the soft spot in the whole bodyguards and safe house set-up? Inside, pappie. You'd never see it coming . . .'

'But what about the cobra on the . . .'

Griessel's cellphone rang. He took it out of his jacket pocket.

UNKNOWN.

He answered. 'Griessel.'

'I have information for you about David Patrick Adair. I will call you back in two minutes. Make sure you are alone.'

In the lecture hall Nadia felt the vibration of her phone. She peeped, saw it was Tyrone phoning. Three times.

She waited for nine minutes, until the lecture was over. Then she walked out and phoned him.

'Hello?' an unfamiliar voice.

'Who is this?' she asked.

'I'm the guy who picked up this phone on the street. I called you, because your number is the only one on here.' It was an accent she could not place, but the man sounded polite.

'Oh,' she said. 'It's my brother's phone. Where did you pick it up?'

'Here in the city. He must have dropped it – it was just lying there. Where can I contact him?'

'You are a good person,' she said. 'I . . . His phone is the only way . . .'

'Sorry, what is your name?'

'Nadia.'

'OK, Nadia, I can take the phone to him. Where does he work?'

'I . . . He's on a painting contract, somewhere in the Bo-Kaap. I'm not sure . . .'

'I'm flying out today, so I would really like to get it to him.'

'That is very nice of you. Uh, let me . . . Can I give you his home address? He has a . . . There might be people at home, at the place where he has a room. Or you can drop it in the mailbox or something?'

'Of course. What is your brother's name?'

21

Griessel walked out into the corridor. The voice over the phone was a woman's, full of self-confidence and authority. Speaking in Afrikaans. About something to which only the Hawks and the British Consulate were privy. It made no sense.

His cellphone rang again. He answered quickly. 'Griessel.'

'Are you alone?' The same voice.

'*Ja.*'

'Let me just tell you up front, you can try to track these calls, but it won't work.'

'Oh?'

'Your name is Benny Griessel. You're a captain in the Directorate of Priority Crimes Investigation in Bellville. You have an eighty-three per cent crime solving rate, but you have a serious drinking problem. Your ex-wife's name is Anna Maria, your children are Carla and Fritz. In 2006 and in 2009 you were involved in disciplinary hearings with the SAPS. Every time you were acquitted. You have three outstanding traffic fines against your name.'

He said nothing, felt deeply uneasy.

'The point is, I have access to information. That is all you have to know. If you doubt my trustworthiness, ask me a question.'

'Who are you?'

'Call me Joni.'

'Joni who?'

'Joni Mitchell.'

'The singer?'

'Yes.'

He had never been crazy about Joni Mitchell, she hardly ever used decent bass guitar. But he just said 'OK', because he smelled Intelligence Services. Spooks.

'Your only problem is, you can't talk about these calls. Not to anybody. If I hear you blabbing, they will stop. Do you understand?'

'Yes.'

'You should also know, this is not one-way traffic. *I* give a little, *you* give a little. Understand?'

'It will depend on what you give.'

'Naturally. I will give what I can, when I can . . .'

'Why?'

'Good question. Because I want to. That is all I am going to say.'

'OK.'

'Here is an example so long: last night at 20.42, the British High Commissioner in Pretoria asked via the Department of International Relations and Cooperation for a talk with the Minister of State Security. This meeting took place at ten o'clock at the minister's house. The rumour is that you are going to receive an order not to proceed with the investigation.'

'Someone will have to investigate it . . .'

'SSA. The State Security Agency is going to take it over.'

'That is . . . It doesn't work like that.' But his guts started to contract, nobody was going to take *this* case away from him.

'We'll see,' said Joni. 'I don't have much time. Emma Graber told you about the Adair Algorithm.' It was a statement, not a question.

Now he was sure that Joni was a Spook. 'Yes.'

'It's an old trick. Divulge part of the information to create a false trail. There is more, Captain. According to my information, Adair loaded a new version of the algorithm into the international banking system some time in the past six weeks, without permission.'

He waited, but she said nothing more. 'Why?' he asked. 'What is different about the algorithm?'

'I don't know yet.'

He thought of Cupido's theory, and he wondered suddenly whether he had something there. 'Would Adair have . . . Could he channel money out of the system?'

She was silent for a moment. 'It's an interesting theory,' she said with a measure of respect. 'And surely a possibility . . . Now you must give me something. The correct email address that Adair used as Morris.'

The question surprised him, because he had only sent the incorrect

email address to Emma Graber of MI6. By email. That meant that
Joni had intercepted it. And she was a Spook who spoke Afrikaans.
That meant SSA. Who didn't trust Zola Nyathi to reveal all the information. And if he gave her the correct Morris address, the SSA would
know about Lillian Alvarez. And *that* he did not want.

But he also didn't want to spoil this new information channel. You
never knew . . .

He gave her the correct address.

The line went dead.

Griessel ran back to Lithpel Davids.

The stolen wallet in Tyrone's trouser pocket yielded four hundred
British pounds in notes, and just over two thousand five hundred
South African rand. The urgency made him use some of the rand for
a taxi home – from the stop in Portswood Street.

The driver looked at his injuries and asked: 'Now who *bliksemsed*
you, my brother?'

'You charge me two hundred rand for a trip of four kilos and then
you want to get personal with me too?'

'*Ek vra ma net*. Just asking.'

'*Fokken* rip-off.'

'So why don't you take the bus?' And a few seconds later, 'No
wonder you look like you do.'

He almost lost his temper, the anger welling up, a surge of jumbled
emotions. He suppressed it with difficulty, knowing with a deep
certainty that he had to stay calm. He had to plan his way ahead, the
next step, the urgent things.

He made the taxi drop him off at the corner of Longmarket and
Ella Street, in case this *doos* went to the cops when the paw-paw hit the
fan, he didn't want a specific address to be available.

'No tip?'

Tyrone just shook his head. He waited for the taxi to disappear over
the curve of Longmarket. Then he jogged home. He hoped that the
rich Muslim's oldest daughter, who hung around the house during the
day, wouldn't see him come in now, not with all this damage.

In his room he undressed. He saw that the bullet had made a long
tear across his sweater. It was caked with dried blood. He tossed it in

the corner and turned around so he could see the damage to his back in the mirror.

He gave a moan to the heavens: there was a lot of blood. But no fresh bleeding. The wound was a thick stripe across his shoulder blades. Trouble was he wouldn't be able to reach it. He would have to rinse off in the shower and hope for the best.

He quickly checked his face. He had to get out of here. He had to call Nadia, the clock was ticking. Thank God for a dark skin. Because once he had washed thoroughly, he would look OK.

He hurried to the tiny bathroom.

At 9.27 the SAPS sergeant at the V&A shopping centre radioed the charge office at the Sea Point Station, breathlessly and somewhat disjointedly, to report 'a bad shooting'.

The constable on radio duty had the good sense to run down the passage to tell his station commander the news.

The station commander was a captain with twenty-two years' service. He pushed the pen he had been using into his pocket, stood up quickly, asked precisely what had been reported, and ordered the constable to tell his two most experienced detectives to meet him at his official SAPS car. 'As in *now*.'

While he hurried to the car park, he thought of the style of the meetings he had had with the provincial commissioner over the past months. And the bulletins that had been issued in that time with monotonous regularity, all in support of the same basic message: the president, the minister and the national commissioner were deeply concerned about the fact that the SAPS' reputation stank. In the last year there had been the Marikana massacre, the Oscar Pistorius case, and the video of a police van dragging the Mozambican Emidio Macia to death. Trumpeted out from here to *Time* magazine and the *New York Times*. It had to end now. Keep our individual and collective butts out of the media and out of trouble. Maintain discipline in your people. Don't let raw *blougatte*, still wet behind the ears, mess up your crime scenes. Don't let inexperienced people be placed in a position where they need to take important decisions. Take them yourself. With wisdom and balance.

Or bear the consequences.

The Sea Point commander had three children at school, a bond on his house of over a million, and a wife who thought he worked too much and earned too little. He didn't want her to bear the consequences. He frowned, feeling the tension in his body. And the urge to go to the V&A Waterfront himself. Along with his two best detectives. Because the Waterfront was a key area, an international tourism jewel. It was the sort of place where 'a bad shooting' would bring down the media vultures in hordes. Including those of *Time* magazine and the *New York Times*. It was the sort of place where you could very quickly land very deep in the soup if you didn't make the right decisions – with wisdom and balance.

The two detectives approached, their jackets flapping in the cold wind. 'Bad shooting at the Waterfront,' said the station commander. They quickly got into the car. The captain switched on the sirens and the lights, and they drove away.

At the main entrance to the V&A Waterfront in Breakwater Lane, the station commander parked on the pavement. A SAPS sergeant had heard the sirens and came running up. This was the one sent out after the original call from the Waterfront security about the pickpocket. The one who had discovered the scene of the homicides.

'This way, Captain,' he said, eyes wild.

'How many?' asked the station commander as he and the detectives jumped out and ran after the sergeant.

'At least five, Captain.'

Christ. He didn't say it though, just thought it. 'Where did it happen?'

'At the security centre. It's a bloodbath.'

And it was. Standing in the doorway of the *Security: Control Room*, the station commander saw five people crumpled into the characteristic helpless awkwardness of death. As he stared at the blood and brain spatter, the pools of blood, the spray and the footprints, he knew it was going to be impossible to keep anyone's collective butt out of the media, thank you. The best he could hope for was to keep everyone's butts out of trouble.

So he turned around and led the whole team of two detectives and the uniformed sergeant, and the seven black-clad security men who stood in stupefied curiosity in the corridor, to the door that opened into the shopping centre (where he spotted a bullet hole in the door frame). He walked out, closed the door, and said: 'Nobody goes in here.'

And then he phoned the Hawks.

Brigadier Musad Manie was the commander of the Directorate of Priority Crimes Investigation, the 'Head Hawk Honcho', as Cupido sometimes referred to his coloured brother with a measure of pride. Manie's nickname in the DPCI was 'the Camel', because 'Musad', one of the Hawks detectives had learned from a Muslim friend, meant 'camel set free' in Arabic. And the Hawks, like most SAPS units, liked to give each other – and especially senior officers – nicknames. But Manie didn't look like a camel. He had the looks of a leader. He was a powerful man, broad of breast and shoulder, with a granite face of strong lines and a determined jaw.

It was this jaw that entered Nyathi's office first. In his deep but always muted and calm voice he said, 'Zola, there has been a shooting at the Waterfront. Five security guards dead, as far as we know. Sea Point has requested our assistance.' Only the final word was coloured with a light shade of irony.

'What sort of assistance?'

'Full crime scene and investigative assistance.'

They exchanged a look that said: 'Can you believe it . . .'

'I can send Mbali.'

'That would be perfect.'

'And I'd better get Cloete out there too.'

22

Griessel hurried back to Cupido and Davids. He had asked Davids to make a copy of Lillian Alvarez's email to Adair urgently, and then delete it. 'Quickly, Lithpel. Please,' he said, with Cupido's suspicious gaze on him.

When it was done, he asked that the Facebook photo of Lillian Alvarez be sent out as a bulletin to all SAPS stations. And as he walked out of Lithpel Davids's kingdom, he said to Cupido, 'I want to show you something.'

Cupido followed him with a half-spoken 'What?' forming.

Griessel held a finger to his mouth and trotted down the stairs, to the basement, with Cupido in pursuit.

Right at the back, beside the 'clubhouse' door, he stopped.

'I don't see anything,' said Cupido.

'I didn't want to talk in there. I think the SSA is eavesdropping on us.'

'The SSA?'

'Yes.'

'*Jissis*,' said Cupido. 'Benna, are you serious?'

'I had a call from a Spook. And she didn't mind me knowing that she had intercepted my email.'

'*Now*? That call that you took just now?'

'Yes. And she said she would know if I told anyone about the call.'

'How do you know she's a Spook?'

'Put two and two together. She knows about Emma Graber, the MI6 agent at the British Consulate. The thing is, I think they tap our cellphones, and I wouldn't be at all surprised if there were microphones in some of our offices too.'

'She could be CI also,' said Cupido, now muted and wary, as if they were being listened to here as well.

Griessel considered the possibility. It wasn't far-fetched. 'CI', as the

SAPS Criminal Intelligence unit was known, had become a sinister place in recent years. First there was the fiasco with Lieutenant-General Richard Mdluli, the former station commander for Vosloorus, who had been appointed as head of Criminal Intelligence – and who was subsequently sacked due to alleged involvement in fraud, corruption, attempted murder, and conspiracy. Now rumours were flying about his successor, the new acting chief of Criminal Intelligence, especially about his close ties with the highest authority of the state. In the halls it was whispered that this unit concerned itself more with the dirty laundry of the president's enemies, than with collecting evidence to fight crime.

'I don't think so. CI wouldn't bug the Consulate. It's SSA . . .'

'Crazy country, Benna,' said Cupido. 'Crazy world . . . OK. So what did the bitch say?'

Griessel told him everything.

'Why now, Benna?'

'I don't know.'

'No, I mean, why trust me now?'

'Vaughn, it was a mistake. I didn't have a choice.'

'Apology accepted. And you believe me now about Adair and the great digital bank robbery?'

'Hell, Vaughn, anything is possible, but that would mean that Adair or an accomplice knew enough about the Cobra to use the same pistol and engravings. So that it looked like the Cobra had done the shooting . . .'

'No, Benna, I've been thinking . . . Adair might have hired the Cobra. Remember, he's for sale to anybody. And if Adair had been skimming off dough, then money is no problem.'

Sometimes he battled to keep up with Cupido's wild mental leaps. The problem was, his colleague was right at least sixty per cent of the time.

Tyrone put an old T-shirt on first. In case his shoulder started bleeding again. Another T-shirt, then the grey Nike sweatshirt. His raincoat was in the rucksack. He would have to buy a new one. And a new rucksack. Because he would have to run now. To Johannesburg? Durban? He didn't know any of those places. He only knew the Cape.

Where would he go?

He put his black beanie on. *You never wear a beanie, Tyrone. Makes you look like a criminal. Baseball caps too. Hats are better if you want to change your profile, but in the Cape wind* daai's *difficult.*

It's a crisis, Uncle Solly. Camouflage.

In the bathroom he climbed onto the toilet, pushed up the trapdoor in the ceiling, reached for the hot-water cylinder, and loosened the pack of notes that he kept there. Two thousand rand. His emergency stash. He put the trapdoor back neatly.

He jumped in fright when the intercom at the door sudden growled.

The cops were here.

So soon?

He was shaking now, but he grabbed the stolen wallet and the iPod on his bed. The intercom made that irritating sound again. He stuffed the wallet, the stash, and the iPod in his trouser pockets, and pressed the button.

'What?'

'There's a guy at the gate asking for you,' said the rich Muslim's daughter. She always spoke English.

'A guy? What kind of a guy?' The cops were here. His heart jumped.

'I don't know.' Irritation. 'Just a guy.'

'What does he look like?'

'Coloured guy, grey baseball cap.'

And then Tyrone had a horrible suspicion, as dread descended on him. 'Black windcheater?'

'Yes. I'll buzz him in.'

'No! Tell him I'm not here.'

He knew his voice would convey his panic, and he waited in suspense for her to answer. *Jirre*, please, don't let her *gooi* that fat rich girl mentality, he thought.

'What have you done?' she asked. She was *mos* always suspicious.

'Please. Just tell him I'm not here. Please!' Then he grabbed the doorknob, opened it quietly, and slipped out, grateful that the gunman could not see him here in the backyard. He jumped up against the back wall.

That man was going to shoot her.

He jumped down again, ran back to his room, pressed the intercom.

'Be careful, lock your door, the guy is dangerous. He'll kill you. Call the cops. Now!'

He ran out, jumped up against the wall and clambered over.

On the other side a *moerse* big dog came for him.

Nyathi found Griessel and Cupido in the passage. 'I was looking for you. Can I see you in my office?'

As usual, the Giraffe displayed no emotion.

Nyathi closed the door behind them. 'Sit, please.'

They did so.

'The brigadier had a call from our commissioner. We have to hand over all case material to officers of the Department of State Security.' He put 'officers' in quotation marks with his fingers. 'And stop the investigation.'

Griessel saw Cupido trying to make meaningful eye contact. He was too afraid that Nyathi would ask what was going on. He was afraid of microphones.

'Yes, sir,' he said quickly.

Tyrone screamed, the sound slipping involuntarily over his lips. The dog, huge and growling, teeth bared, rushed at him.

One hot summer night, hanging out with some mates on a Mitchell's Plain street corner, one of them said if a dog attacked you, you should do two things. You rush at him with your arm like this, hanging out. Because they train dogs to go for the arm. And then, just before he grabs your arm, you hit him on the nose.

That's the first thing that came into Tyrone's head.

He didn't think, just rushed at the dog holding out his skinny arm. *Jirre*, wasn't his body hurting enough already?

The dog skidded to a halt in cloud of dust and Tyrone could swear he had a look of 'what the fuck?' in his eyes. The beast stood still as Tyrone ran past, alongside the house. He didn't know if there was anyone home.

And then the dog came for him again.

For all his failings Vaughn Cupido was always quick on the uptake.

When Griessel took out his notebook and pen and put them on the desk to make a note, his colleague realised the Giraffe was going to say something about it.

'State Security? That's bullshit,' said Cupido indignantly.

Griessel hoped Cupido would not overdo it, it sounded melodramatic, and he had never talked to Nyathi like *that* before. He scribbled hastily: *Office bugged? Talk outside*, and slid it over to the colonel, while Cupido said, 'With all due respect, of course, sir. But what does State Security know about investigating a criminal case?'

Nyathi read and nodded.

'I'm sorry, gentlemen, but that's the way it is. If you could bring me all relevant documentation, please.'

And he wrote in Benny's little book: *5 mins.*

Griessel replied with: *Clubhouse*.

He was almost at the high railing fence at the front of the neighbour's house. But the dog was too close, Tyrone had to spin around to confront the creature.

This time the animal didn't stop. He came at him, jumping at Tyrone's midriff, his crotch, which in that moment seemed so unfair to Tyrone, so totally unacceptable – what sort of person taught his dog to bite a guy's dick? – that rage drove away fear, and he hit out blindly, connecting with the dog's muzzle. A sudden sharp pain in his fist. The dog yelped.

'Hey!' A voice came from one of the windows. A man.

It made the dog turn away, and Tyrone ran and leaped. Adrenaline made him agile, and suddenly he was over and on the pavement, he wasn't sure how.

He just ran.

23

Captain Mbali Kaleni was the only woman in the DPCI's Violent Crimes team. For six long months now. She was short and very fat. She was never to be seen without her SAPS identity card on a ribbon around her neck, and her service pistol on her plump hip. When she left her office, there was always a huge handbag of shiny black leather over her shoulder. Her expression was usually grim, as though she was constantly angry at someone. It was a defence mechanism, but only two of her colleagues understood that.

She had an honours degree in Police Science, and an IQ of 138. Her name meant 'flower' in Zulu. Behind her back she was called 'the Heavy Hawk', 'the Flower', 'Cactus Flower', and sometimes, when she had once again antagonised certain male colleagues with her unbending rigidity, 'That *fokken* Mbali'.

Nyathi knew Mbali Kaleni and Vaughn Cupido did not necessarily see eye to eye.

The Flower could recite every article in the Criminal Procedure Act, and every ordinance of the Hawks. She always acted strictly according to these regulations. While Cupido saw everything as a vague, voluntary guideline. Nyathi knew that these divergent philosophies were frequently a recipe for conflict. Which he had to manage.

That was why he had not included his female detective in Griessel's Franschhoek team, so she was now free to be sent to the bloodbath at the shopping centre.

The Sea Point Station commander stood at the door of the Waterfront Shopping Centre. He saw Captain Kaleni waddling towards him, filled with fire and purpose. His heart sank; her legendary reputation preceded her. He knew she was clever, but she was difficult.

He greeted her politely. He stretched out his hand for the door.

'No,' said Mbali, 'you are not wearing gloves.' All he wanted was to keep his station's collective butt, and his own individual one, out of trouble. He didn't say that many hands had already touched that handle. He merely nodded and watched as she dug a pair of gloves out of her handbag and put them on.

'Don't you have gloves?' she asked.

'In the car,' he said.

'Go and fetch them.'

He nodded, and asked one of his detectives to fetch them.

'Do you have shoe covers?' she asked.

He called to the detective to bring them too.

Mbali shook her head in disbelief. 'You wait until you are properly attired. And then you come in. Only you.'

'But the sergeant was first on the scene . . .'

'I will question him when I come out.' She pointed at the other detective, and the uniform sergeant. 'You guard this door.'

Then she walked in.

'What makes you think they've bugged our offices?' Nyathi asked.

They were standing in the underground car park, beside the club-house door, where no one could see or hear them: the Giraffe, Griessel and Cupido.

'It was something she said, sir,' said Griessel. 'When she warned me not to tell anybody. "If I hear you speaking out, the phone calls will stop." She didn't say "if I heard", but "if I hear". Maybe I'm wrong, but it made me very uneasy.'

Nyathi stood there for a long time, his head tilted. He sighed. 'They are already monitoring our email and our phone calls. The sad thing is, you might be right. And we have to assume that you are.'

'Yes, sir.'

'You go back, and you make copies, just the two of you. Don't talk to anybody about it. Just do it. Bring me all the original material and I'll hand it over when the agent comes.'

'Does that mean we continue the investigation, sir?' asked Cupido.

'Damn right it does,' said Nyathi.

Mbali Kaleni wanted to cry.

It was her greatest secret, greater than the secret packets of crisps or KFC or chocolate that she ate alone in her office. Greater than the fantasies about the actor Djimon Hounsou that she sometimes allowed herself in bed at night. At a murder scene she wanted to cry. It was all about the loss, the senselessness, tragedy, but above all the human capacity for evil. *That* broke her heart, and she often mused on this with great solemnity and concern. Why did people do it? What was it that, especially in this country, drove people to rape and maim and murder? The heavy burden of the past? Or was it something that came from the bedrock of South Africa, a demonic energy field that unsettled people's minds?

She was purposefully strict with the SC back in the passage, because she really wanted to come in here alone. That way she would not have to work so hard to hide the tears. She knew, just one sign of weakness, and her male colleagues would be crowing. But now, at least, she could let her shoulders sag and allow the silent tears to well up. She dug in her handbag and took out a bunch of tissues, gripping them in her fist as she looked at the five lifeless bodies. This afternoon their loved ones, fathers and mothers, wives, children, would be torn apart by grief. A few days only in the headlines, but this deed would last so much longer, would ripple outwards creating single breadwinners and greater poverty and misery, far into the future, when a son or daughter of one of these men would say to a social worker or a magistrate: 'My father died when I was four . . .'

She wiped away the tears, pushed the tissues back into her handbag. She straightened her shoulders, and began to study the crime scene.

Tyrone Kleinbooi ran across August Street, over the empty plot, and jumped up against the high concrete wall of the school. He wanted to be among people, that was his only defence up here in Schotsche Kloof, where the houses were too few and the streets too wide.

He clambered over the wall. The school grounds were quiet.

Holidays, he had forgotten it was the holidays.

He ran past the school buildings, down to the main gate, next to the netball court. An ageing security guard with a military cap set on askew, struggled across a concrete area, shouting and waving a knob-kierie stick at him.

Tyrone kept on running.

The main gate was high and locked, but the chain was long, so that he could force it open a crack and squeeze his skinny body through.

He looked back.

He didn't see anyone, except for the old uncle with the cap, gesticulating wildly and shouting inexplicable things.

He was through. He ran past the Schotsche Kloof flats, the ugly housing projects where washing flapped from windows. An aunty shouted from up there: 'Hey, look at him run now.'

He was grateful it was downhill. He swerved left, through backyards, into the upper end of Church Street.

He looked back again.

Nobody.

They made hurried copies of everything. Griessel passed the documents on, and the more technologically skilled Cupido copied them.

Griessel's phone rang. He took it out, annoyed by the interruption while they were under so much pressure. MBALI on his screen.

He answered.

'Benny, I'm at the Waterfront. There's been a shooting. Five security people dead . . .'

Griessel suppressed the '*Jissis*', because Mbali didn't like expletives or swearing.

'I think you'd better come,' she said.

'Mbali, we're very busy . . .'

'I know. But the colonel briefed us on the Franschhoek shooting at morning parade, and he said there were shell casings with the etchings of a snake . . .'

'Yes?'

'There are a lot of them here, Benny. And I mean a *lot*.'

Fok, thought Griessel, he should not have been so impatient and hasty – his cellphone was being tapped, now the whole SSA knew it too.

'I'm on my way,' he said.

'Can you bring Sergeant Davids too? There's a lot of technology we'll have to figure out.'

'OK,' said Griessel, and rang off.

★ ★ ★

Nadia Kleinbooi sat at the bottom of the Neelsie, the student centre of the University of Stellenbosch, at a long wooden table with some of her classmates. Her cellphone rang. She barely heard it, because it was a noisy environment, the voices of students, music playing.

TYRONE, she read. The guy must have delivered the phone.

She covered one ear and put the phone to the other. 'Hello?'

'I'm really sorry to bug you, but there's nobody home.' The Good Samaritan's voice again.

'No, please, you're not bugging me. My brother works in the city, he'll only be back tonight. I . . . Can you maybe put the phone in the mailbox? I will try to . . .' Tyrone lived in the back room, and she didn't know if the Muslims would realise that it was his phone. She didn't know what to do.

'I'll bring the phone to you,' said the man.

'No, I'm in Stellenbosch, it's far away . . .'

'Stellenbosch . . .' His voice became clearer. 'I have to go there, before I fly out.'

'Really?'

'Yes. My hotel is there.'

'Oh. That is . . . You are a very kind person.'

'No, no, I know about losing a phone. It is a . . . *grand dérangement.*'

'You are French?'

'*Mais oui.*'

'That's so cool.'

'So where do I find you?'

'Oh, yes. I have class until one o'clock. Where is your hotel?'

'Right there in Stellenbosch. I will call you when I get there?'

'OK, just after one. Call me just after one.'

24

Further down the corridor, in the belly of the Victoria and Alfred Waterfront shopping centre, was the office of the head of security. At two minutes past twelve, Mbali sat on one of the visitors' chairs. A coloured security official sat opposite her. The Sea Point Station commander stood against the wall.

'I was on duty at the Red Shed when I heard them on the radio,' said the security man. He was shocked and nervous.

'What time was this?' asked Mbali.

'I can't say exactly.'

'More or less?'

'I'd say about nine. Maybe . . . maybe quarter to, ten to nine . . . I'm not sure.'

'OK, what did you hear on the radio?'

'That they've caught Knippies.'

'Who is Knippies?'

'He's the pickpocket. We've been trying to catch him for a long time now.'

'Is that his name? Knippies?'

'That was what we called him. He's . . .'

'What is his real name?'

'I don't know.'

'Did your colleagues know?'

'No. Nobody knows.'

'What do you know about him?'

'We . . . He . . . We've had complaints, for a long time, two years, maybe longer. People who report they've been robbed. By a pickpocket. Every time, it's the same thing, this guy, Knippies, he would come up to them and ask if they dropped this hair *knippie*, what do you call it, a hairpin, you know, the thing women put in their hair, with a butterfly or a flower on it. Sometimes he would use a lighter, like a

Zippo, when it's a guy he wants to rob. And they all said it's a black guy, slim, about one point eight metres tall, wears black, sometimes blue denim. So, for a year . . . maybe more, we were looking for him, all the security officials, we would look for a skinny black guy. And the control room would scan for him, and tell us there's a suspect . . .'

Mbali put her hand in the air. The security official stopped talking.

'The control room is where the CCTV is?'

'Yes.'

'This Knippies, how often did he rob people?' she asked.

'Once a month. Maybe . . . It . . . I don't know, sometimes it would be two on one day, and then nothing for weeks.'

'But about once a month?'

'About.'

'OK.'

He said nothing.

'Go on,' she said.

'Oh. OK. I . . . Yes, once a month. But he was clever, he knew where the cameras were, so he always robbed people where there weren't any cameras. And then about a year ago, maybe less, maybe August . . . I'm not sure . . .'

'That's OK.'

'OK. Thank you. So, maybe August, they put in extra cameras, the small ones. And in March – yes, it must have been March – they caught him on camera, just by the pier, at the charter signs. They caught him on video stealing from a guy, a photographer, he stole a lens from his bag with the lighter trick. But they didn't see it live, he is very slick, very quick. When the guy came in to report it, they played the video back, and they saw him. And then we had a shot . . . a photograph of Knippies. Turns out he's coloured, but dark, you know? So they showed all of us the photograph, and the video . . .'

'That's the same photograph that is on the wall? In the control room? The one that looks like the guy on the TV screen?'

'Yes, that's Knippies.'

'OK. And this morning?'

'I heard it on the radio.'

'Exactly what did you hear on the radio?'

'I heard Control call Gertjie and Louw. They patrol the

amphitheatre. Control said they had spotted Knippies, and Gertjie and Louw must look for him. There were a lot of civilians, we had the cruise ship in this morning, so Control was directing them, you know. Go left, go right. And then I heard Louw call it in, they caught him.'

'Is that what he said?'

'Yes, but in Afrikaans. "*Ons het hom, Control, ons bring hom in.*"'

'And then?'

'Then everybody called in to say well done. And Control said: "His ass is grass, he's on video."'

'And then?'

'Then I heard Jerome call on the radio about the shooting.'

'Who is Jerome?'

'He's an official.'

'A security official?'

'Yes.'

'Like you?'

'Yes.'

'What time was this?'

'I don't know. After nine. Some time after nine.'

'How did Jerome know about the shooting?'

'He had his tea break, and he said he wanted to take a look at Knippies, so he went to the control room, and he saw everybody was dead.'

'Where is Jerome now?'

'He's in the bathroom. He's throwing up. A lot.'

Tyrone stole a Samsung S3 in St George's Mall, from a man's windcheater.

He hated Samsung S3s, because they have seven sorts of screen lock. Most people used the pattern, the nine dots that had to be connected in a certain order.

He tried the three most popular patterns.

Nothing. The thing stayed locked.

He didn't have time. He tossed it in a rubbish bin and looked for his next victim.

★ ★ ★

They threaded their way through the traffic on the N1, blue lights on, but sirens off. Griessel drove. Cupido blew off some steam about Mbali.

'Last week she tells me, a man's worth is no greater than his ambition. Just because I was taking a break with Angry Birds. I mean, can't a man take a break now and then . . .'

'Who is Angry Birds?'

Lithpel Davids laughed from the back seat.

'Not "who", Benna, "what",' said Cupido patiently. 'It's a game. On my phone. You should try it, there's an iOS version too. Great stress reliever. Anyway, so then I want to say to her: "Mbali, if I had as much ambition as you have, I would also be a *doos*," but *fok weet*, then you would never get her to shut up about your swearing, and how that's also a sure sign of weakness, she's always got a *fokken* quote. What's wrong with swearing? I mean, it's just another word. What really pisses me off is people that want to say "*fokken*", but then they *gooi* "*flippen*" instead, and that's OK. It's not *fokken* OK, they mean the same thing. And intent is nine-tenths of the law, pappie. But you can *ma'* say "*flippen*" in front of Mbali, *daai's* cool. I mean, Benna, there's no justice when it comes to that woman.'

'Possession.'

'Huh?'

'Possession is nine-tenths of the law.'

'OK. True. But what is possession without intent?'

'Also true.'

'*Fokken* Mbali . . .'

Cupido was quiet for a while, and Griessel thought of a conversation he had had in the Wimpy at the Winelands Engen service station on the N1, one morning on the way back from a case in Paarl. Over coffee, Mbali had hauled a textbook out of her massive handbag. *The Law of Contract in South Africa.*

'I'm sorry, Benny, I have an exam tonight.'

He hadn't known she was studying again. She, who already had an honours degree in Police Science. So he asked.

'I'm doing a B Iuris at UNISA.'

'Do you want to leave the Service?'

'No, Benny.' She had hesitated and looked at him in a measured way, then decided she could trust him. 'I want to be the commissioner. One day.' There was no arrogance in the statement, just a quiet determination.

He had accepted that she meant the national commissioner, and he had sat thinking in amazement. About people. About himself. His trouble was that he had never wanted to be *something*. He had just wanted to *be*.

A man's worth is no greater than his ambition.

Perhaps that was why he had become a boozer and fuck-up. Perhaps you should have three- and five- and ten-year plans for yourself, higher aspirations. But how do you get there if you are still struggling with all the trouble that life throws at you?

What was he to do about this trouble between him and Alexa?

His only 'ambition' was to avoid a *njaps*.

What did that say of his worth?

Maybe it said everything.

Where did you get an agenda for this sort of trouble, a three-day plan. Or was he the only one who battled with this kind of shit?

25

Pickpocketing is a lucky dip, Tyrone. You take what you can get. That's why you need more than one fence. 'Cause everything's got value for someone.

But what do you do, Uncle Solly, if you don't have time for the lucky dip, if you need to steal a phone *specifically*, and opportunity doesn't exactly come knocking? And you've never really thought about this before, and you don't have the time or inclination to ponder on it? 'Cause the clock is ticking like crazy, and you can't phone your sister from a public phone, 'cause that's exactly the problem, right, they are public, especially the row of coin and card phones up in St George's Mall. You can't just go stand there and say: 'Nadia, I'm in deep trouble, if the cops phone you, say you don't know who the call is from.' It's noisy there by the phones, it's not like you can stand there and whisper. Or you waltz into a restaurant and say here's a hundred bucks, please let me use the phone, it's an emergency. And the maître d' hangs around suspiciously to check that you're not phoning Beijing. And Uncle Solly, Nadia is going to *skrik*, she'll be so scared, and she'll ask: 'Now what's going on?' and if I don't say, she'll worry. 'Cause I'm all she has. I've always been all she has.

And in his urgency, his haste, eyes flitting from one pedestrian to the next, it hit him suddenly, out of nowhere: How had the gunman known where he lived?

The thought made Tyrone stop in his tracks, and shiver.

When the fat Muslim chick buzzed him, he thought it was the cops. But it wasn't, and he hadn't had the time to work that one out.

How the fuck?

Did the shooter tail him?

Must have. He didn't want to shoot Tyrone in public. He wanted no eyewitnesses. So he tailed him, all the way behind the taxi. He's good, never saw it coming.

He looked around, slowly, carefully, his eyes scanning for the man in the grey baseball cap. Or a reasonable facsimile thereof.

He saw nothing. He moved on, searching for possibilities.

The time, time was running out.

Why did that bro' want to shoot him?

Because he was a witness.

Why had that bro' come in there with a silenced gun like a secret agent and blown all those mall cops away?

Maybe a big heist in the mall?

Probably drugs, and the mall cops were all dealers who were skimming. That's the only thing that would have brought a coloured bro' out of the woodwork with a silenced gun.

Tyrone searched for a mark, to steal a phone.

And then he thought, what a *blerrie* fool he is, that's what stress will do for you. Don't steal a phone. Buy one.

The Sea Point Station commander was still leaning against the wall of the security chief's office. He listened to Captain Mbali questioning Jerome, the official who was first on the scene. All stuff he would have asked, he thought, it wasn't as though she was *that* clever.

Jerome was clearly still in shock. He was as white as a sheet, his voice muted, and he hesitated before each answer, as though he didn't want to recall the events. He said the roster was such that only one official was off duty at a time. His break was from 'oh nine hundred hours', but he was on duty at the Clock Tower car park, and he first had a chat with a friend on his way back to the tea room. And then he wanted to see what Knippies looked like in real life, and so he went to the control room. He wasn't even sure the super would allow him to look at the pickpocket, but he thought he would take a chance, as they had looked for the *ou* for so long.

'So you came in?'

'Yes.'

'And the door was open?'

'Which door?'

'The one to the corridor.'

'No. It was closed.'

'Did you see anything out of the ordinary?'

'Jeez, lady, I saw all of them dead . . .'

'That's not what I mean. Before you got to the control room. Did you see anybody or anything that did not belong there?'

'No. It was just very quiet.'

'Did you touch anything?'

The Sea Point Station commander's cellphone rang. He saw Captain Kaleni give him a dirty look. He wondered: How does she think I can help it? He recognised his station's number and walked out of the office as he answered it.

It was his charge office, and the constable's voice was weighted with drama. 'Captain, we have another shooting. Up in Schotsche Kloof.'

'Yes?' His heart sank, but he mustn't show it.

'A woman phoned at eleven thirty-three, Ella Street number eighteen, and reported an intruder at her gate, he was busy climbing over the fence. So I asked her, are the doors locked and she said yes. So I sent a van, they were there at eleven forty-four. The gate was still locked. They rang the bell, but no one answered . . .'

The SC's patience ran out. 'Is she the one who was shot?'

'Yes, Captain. They found her there inside. One of the windows is broken . . .'

'I'm coming.'

It was not his day.

Tyrone bought a phone from the Somalians in Adderley. First they tried to palm an LG E900 Optimus 7 off on him for R900.

'Nine hundred for a hot Windows phone. Do you think I'm stupid?'

'It's a good phone. Not hot. Cool.'

'I don't care if it's a good phone. I'm not paying nine hundred for a hot phone. And I don't want a Windows phone. Nobody wants a Windows phone. What else do you have? For under two hundred?'

'No. Two hundred? Nothing for two hundred. We only sell good phones. Not hot phones.'

He didn't have time to tell the Somalian with his soft eyes and big smile that he was talking shit. He shook his head, turned, and walked off.

'Wait,' said the Somalian, as Tyrone knew he would.

'Two hundred.'

'For that? It's a relic. One hundred.'

'One seventy-five. It has a SIM card. It works.' The man switched the phone on.

'Let me test it.'

'No. I will show you. I will call my friend.' He typed in a number and held it out so that Tyrone could listen. It rang. Someone answered.

'You see. It works. Pay as you go, you can top up. Not a hot phone.' He switched it off.

'How much time on the card?'

'Ten hours' talk time.'

'OK.' He didn't believe the man. Probably closer to an hour or two. But that was all he needed. He took out the stolen wallet.

'So, did you touch anything?' Mbali asked again.

'No,' said Jerome, the security official.

'What about the outside door handle?'

'Yes, I touched that.'

'And inside?'

'No, nothing. Wait. I touched the inside door handle too. And the toilet door, and the basin and . . .'

'I'm talking about the crime scene.'

'No, I never touched anything in there.'

'OK. Did you look at the TV screen when you were in there?'

'Yes. But just for a moment. I mean, all my friends . . .'

'I understand. Is that Knippies on the screen?'

'I think so.'

'So there is a video of Knippies that was taken today?'

'Yes, they watched him, and all the cameras are recording.'

'OK. Thank you.'

Tyrone ran up to the Company Gardens so that he could phone Nadia without a hundred ears listening.

She didn't answer. He got her voicemail, drew a breath to leave a message, then reconsidered and rang off. What could he say that wouldn't frighten her?

Her phone was on silent. She was in class. It was twelve minutes to one. She would probably come out just after one.

By that time the cops would have got hold of the rucksack, and probably the phone too.

He would *have* to leave Nadia a message. He would just say that this was his new number . . . No, he would say it was a temporary new number, he had lost his old phone, and please phone him, there was something urgent . . . no, there's something important he wanted to tell her. Phone as soon as she can.

He took a deep breath so that she wouldn't hear the tension in his voice, and pressed the numbers.

For the first time Mbali saw the bullet hole in the door that led into the mall. She studied it carefully, and then she tried to understand the meaning of it, in the context of the whole crime scene.

She opened the door and walked into the corridor of the shopping centre. She still had her gloves and her shoe covers on. Her eyes searched for a camera that could have covered the door to the control room.

She found one, ten metres away, high up on the wall.

She measured the angle from where it was. Perhaps it hadn't covered the door, but it would at least have caught a great deal of the wide corridor in front of it.

'Mbali?' She heard a familiar voice and turned. Benny Griessel. He, Vaughn Cupido, and Lithpel had arrived. She steeled herself. Griessel was her favourite colleague. Sergeant Davids' apparel and grooming were a bit of a scandal, but he did his job well, and he knew his place. Cupido she could not stand. But she was a professional woman. She must be able to handle everything.

She greeted all three, then went and stood in front of the door that led out of the mall's walkway. 'The crime scene starts here. You'll have to put on protection.'

26

Nadia Kleinbooi walked out of class.

In the corridor a guy behind her said, 'Do those jeans come with the cute bum, or is that an optional extra?'

She looked and laughed at him, a passing flirtation. She enjoyed the attention. She wasn't as skinny as her brother. 'You got the calves that they forgot to give me,' Tyrone always said.

Then she would reply, 'And you got the looks.'

'There's nothing wrong with your looks. *Jy's* beautiful.' But she knew he was the good-looking one. All her girlfriends used to hang around Uncle Solly's house in the hope that Tyrone would be there. But Tyrone wasn't there much. Though he was always there when she needed him.

Only once she was outside, in the weak winter sun, did she take out her cellphone.

Two SMSs beeped immediately.

You have two missed calls.

You have two voicemail messages.

At that very moment it rang, and she saw it was Tyrone's phone. She answered.

'Hi,' said the guy with the sexy French voice. 'I'm in Ryneveld Street.'

But he pronounced it 'Rinerval', which made her smile. 'There's a building here, I think it says Geology.'

'I know where that is. I'll be there in two minutes.'

'*Très bien*,' he said. 'I am at the entrance to the parking. With a silver Nissan X-Trail.'

'OK,' she said, and rang off.

She wondered what the Frenchman looked like. It was such a sexy, sexy accent, and his voice was nice – there was a hint of laughter in it, as though he found the whole situation very amusing.

★　★　★

Griessel held the cartridge in his glove-protected fingers.

'It's the same snake. And the same initials.'

'OK,' said Mbali, and gave them a short, bullet-point summary of what had happened, according to the security men.

'The Cobra is a pickpocket now?' Cupido asked, shaking his head scornfully.

Mbali ignored him.

'That's not the Cobra.' Cupido pointed at the screen, and then at the photo on the noticeboard. 'This guy is too dark. And that's not racist, Mbali. That's just a fact.'

She didn't look at him. She told Griessel the hardest decision they had to take now, was at what stage Lithpel could sit down in front of the video console so that they could look at the material. Because the console was in the middle of the crime scene, and there was the risk that they would disturb forensic evidence if they were all standing around, among the dead. But Thick and Thin were on their way, and their procedures, the video and photography department's recording, the pathologist's *in-loco* examination, and the removal of the bodies could take hours. The longer they waited, the more likely it was that any possible video evidence would prove useless. While the culprit fled further afield.

'Easy decision,' said Cupido. 'There's no big mystery here. He came, he shot, he left. And we're already in. Let's do it.'

Mbali looked only at Griessel.

'He's right,' said Griessel, 'but we still have to be very careful not to disturb the scene.'

'OK,' said Mbali. 'There's one other problem. Because the shooting was localised, and the Sea Point SC managed everything appropriately, it has not attracted much attention yet. But when Forensics and the pathologist and the ambulances arrive, that will change. Someone needs to go and tell the shopping centre management. They will want to manage the public and media attention.'

'Don't look at me,' said Cupido.

'Where's the SC?' asked Griessel.

'He had to leave. He has another shooting somewhere to attend to.'

'What shooting?' asked Griessel, heart sinking, because he didn't believe in coincidences.

★ ★ ★

Nadia saw him standing beside the silver X-Trail. A blond man in old denims and a white T-shirt with a cellphone in his hand. Looking around, as though he was searching for someone. Brush cut, narrow hips, broad shoulders, white skin, but tanned, like a surfer. Maybe he was a surfer.

A pity he was on his way back to France . . .

But as she approached, while he looked enquiringly at her and she waved and nodded, she realised he was probably in his mid-thirties. Too old for her. Although . . .

He held the phone up and asked: 'Nadia?'

'Yes.'

He smiled broadly. White, even teeth.

'How can I thank you?' Out of the corner of her eye she saw two other men in the X-Trail.

'It is only a pleasure.' He held out the phone to her.

She reached him and put out her hand to take the phone from him. Then he grabbed her arm.

Two male students in a Volkswagen Citi Golf drove out of the car park beside the R.W. Wilcocks building. The passenger was busy on his cellphone. It was the driver who saw it – the white man grabbing the coloured girl. The rear door of the Nissan X-Trail opened, and he half carried, half dragged her into the vehicle.

'What the fuck?' he said and wound down his window.

'What?' asked the passenger.

'That *ou* . . .' He saw the X-Trail pull away calmly. He pressed the hooter of his car three times, short and urgent.

'What is it, bro?' asked the passenger.

The X-Trail drove on.

The driver bellowed out of the window. 'Hey!'

'Cool it, bro,' said the passenger.

'Those guys in the Nissan kidnapped that girl right now . . .' He accelerated, and set off in pursuit of the X-Trail.

'What girl?'

'The one in the car.'

'You're not serious.'

'I *am*. Call the police.' The X-Trail turned right into Crozier.

'There's no girl in that car . . .'

The driver hooted again, reduced his following distance so that he was on the tail of the X-Trail. 'They're pushing her down. I'm telling you, call the police. I *saw* it.'

The passenger wasn't convinced. 'Bro, we can't just call the police. I mean . . .'

The driver swore, a staccato of reproach. He took his cellphone out of his shirt pocket. 'I will *fokken* phone them myself . . .'

The X-Trail turned right into Andringa. They followed, the driver had to look up from the cellphone, then down again, to type in the number.

'Watch it!' said the passenger.

The driver looked up quickly. The X-Trail had stopped suddenly. The doors opened and two men came running back, each with a pistol in hand.

'*Fok*, bro, reverse!' screamed the passenger. But the driver hadn't even stopped yet, and when he did, with a short shrill screech of tyres, it was too late. The men were right there, moving impossibly swiftly. And surely. One aimed a weapon at the front wheel. A soft explosion, then the hiss of the tyre going flat, and then they were at the doors of the Golf, jerking them open, grabbing the cellphones from their hands. Then they slammed the doors, ran back to the X-Trail, jumped in.

The X-Trail drove off.

The students sat there.

'*Jissis*,' said the passenger.

The driver let out a sound that was just like a tyre deflating.

Benny Griessel didn't use his cellphone. He phoned the Sea Point SC from a telephone beside the video console in the control centre.

The first thing that the station commander said to him was: 'There's a cartridge here with a snake on it.'

'How do you know about that?'

'I was present at Captain Kaleni's interrogation at the V&A. She phoned someone and talked about "shell casings with the etchings of a snake" . . .'

'OK, who is the deceased?'

'She hasn't been identified yet. Young coloured woman, she seems to have been alone at home. Intruder gained access via a broken window in the sitting room. He forced open the woman's bedroom door, the lock is broken. And he shot her once, in the forehead.'

Jissis, thought Griessel. What the fuck was going on? 'OK,' he said, and tried to keep the vexation out of his voice. 'It's definitely linked to two other murder cases. I'm sending Captain Vaughn Cupido, if you can just seal the scene so long.'

'Already done,' said the SC.

'Thank you, Captain,' said Griessel, with relief. And satisfaction, because the SSA didn't know about *this* one yet. 'What's the address?'

'Ella Street number eighteen, up in Schotsche Kloof'

Griessel rang off. And then everything happened at once.

'Vaughn, I'll have to send you to the Bo-Kaap,' said Griessel.

'It's that girl.' Lithpel Davids pointed a finger at the TV console where a video was being played back.

'*My fok*,' said Cupido.

'That is very unprofessional language,' said Mbali.

Griessel's cellphone began to ring.

'What girl?' asked Mbali.

'The Facebook girl. Alvarez,' said Lithpel.

They climbed slowly and carefully over the bodies of the security men to reach the TV screen.

'What Facebook girl?' asked Mbali.

'It's her,' said Cupido.

Griessel's cellphone kept ringing, but his eyes were glued to the screen. Lillian Alvarez stood with her face to the camera. She stared at a hairpin in the hands of the pickpocket. Knippies's face was turned to her, his hand touching her handbag.

'What Facebook girl?' asked Mbali again.

From outside came the voice of Arnold, the short, fat Forensics guy: 'Hallooo? Anybody home?'

Griessel answered his phone: 'Hello?'

'You had better hurry,' said the woman's voice, the one who called herself Joni Mitchell. 'SSA are on the way. They are going to take over the scene.'

'The Waterfront scene?'

'Yes.'

Then she rang off.

'He stole something from Alvarez,' said Cupido.

'*Liewe ffff . . .*' said Jimmy, the skinny Forensics detective, when he saw the five lifeless bodies. But he never completed the word because Captain Kaleni shot him a withering look.

27

'Out,' said Benny Griessel to Thick and Thin.

'Don't you think it's you who should leave?' said Jimmy. 'You are occupying the whole—'

'Out!' said Griessel more sharply.

This was very unlike the Griessel they knew. They just stood there.

'Jimmy, please, go and wait out in the corridor. And hurry up.'

They heard the urgency in Griessel's voice, and responded.

'Is somebody going to tell me about this Alvarez girl?' asked Mbali.

'Later, Mbali,' said Griessel. 'We have very little time. The SSA are on their way . . .'

'Shit,' said Cupido.

'The SSA?' asked Mbali in disbelief. 'The State Security Agency?'

'Please, everybody. We'll talk later. Right now we need to look at that footage. Quickly, Lithpel, play it back.'

Tyrone walked up and down the Company Gardens path. Once again Nadia had forgotten to turn her phone back on. Not for the first time.

He phoned again.

It rang. For a long time.

His heart sank more. He was going to get voicemail again.

Then she answered. 'Hello?' and he could hear in that single word that something was wrong. The cops had already phoned her.

'Nadia, it's me. I can explain, doesn't matter what they told you, it's not true . . .' He heard something on the line, a hiss, as if Nadia were in a car.

'They've got me, *boetie* . . .' There was fear in her voice, fear as he had never heard it, and his gut contracted.

'The cops?'

'Is this Tyrone?' A man's voice. But it wasn't a cop accent.

'Who's this?'

'Tyrone, I have Nadia, and you have something I want. If you give it to me, we will let her go. If you don't, I will shoot her, right between the eyes. Do you understand this?'

Tyrone began to shake uncontrollably. 'I don't have anything . . .'

'You stole a wallet at the Waterfront this morning.'

He said nothing.

'Do you have the wallet on you now?'

'Maybe.'

'Why are you being funny, Tyrone. Do you want me to hurt your sister?'

'No.'

'Do you have the wallet on you now?'

'Yes.'

'I want you to look in the wallet. There should be a memory card in there.'

His heart leaped. A memory card? There was no memory card there. 'There's just cash and credit cards . . .' he said.

'I want you to look very carefully, Tyrone. Take your time.'

'You will stay on the line?'

'I will stay on the line.'

He sat down on a garden bench, put his cellphone down beside him, took out the wallet. Trembling, his fingers riffled through the cash. There was nothing slipped between the notes.

The wallet had three flaps for bank cards. He went through each one.

He found it in the back flap, when he pushed his fingers into a sleeve that seemed empty from the outside at first. He pulled it out.

A blue card, light and thin. *Verbatim SDXC. 64GB.*

He grabbed the phone. 'I have it.'

'I want you to look at the card, Tyrone.'

'I'm looking.'

'That card is your sister's life. If you lose it, she dies. If you break it, she dies. If you damage it in any way, and I can't read the data, I will kill your sister. I will shoot her right between the eyes . . .'

'Please!' screamed Tyrone, and squeezed the memory card tightly in his hand. 'I will give it to you.'

'That's good. Where are you now?'

'I'm in the Gardens.'

'Where is that?'

'In Cape Town.'

'That's good. Did you call your sister from a mobile?'

'A cellphone. Yes.'

'And you will keep this phone with you?'

'Yes.'

'And you will keep it on?'

'Yes.'

'That is good, Tyrone. I will call you.'

'When?' he asked with fear in his voice.

But the line was already dead.

Mbali, Griessel, and Cupido watched Sergeant Lithpel Davids play the video back for them. They saw Knippies, the pickpocket, catch up with Lillian and attract her attention. He held the hair clip up in front of her while his right hand fiddled with her handbag.

Smooth as silk, and fast. They observed the thief's skill, the woman's nervousness.

'Lithpel, stop. What did he steal out of the handbag?'

Davids rewound the video. They watched again, but the pickpocket's hand was too fast. The item could not be identified.

'Try slow motion,' said Cupido.

'Won't help,' said Lithpel, but he did it.

The stolen item was still only a light brown, fast-moving blur behind the thief's hand.

'It's a package of some sort,' said Mbali.

'Play it further,' said Griessel.

The camera turned slowly to follow Knippies when he walked away, showing how the two security guards grabbed him and escorted him to the shopping centre door, until they disappeared out of the image.

'That bro is a pro,' said Cupido. 'But they all get caught in the end.'

'You see that screen there?' asked Mbali, and pointed at one of the smaller CCTV screens.

'Yes,' said Lithpel.

'Can you get the video to play back to the time of the crime?'

'Of course.'

'We'll have to hurry,' said Griessel.

Lithpel operated the mouse, moved the cursor on the computer screen. A new image appeared on the main screen – the scene in the corridor of the shopping centre outside the control room – and then became a comical fast-moving blur of people hurrying backwards when he rewound it at high speed. In the bottom corner a time indicator ran back just as fast.

'Around nine o'clock,' said Mbali.

Lithpel rewound past the two officials bringing Knippies in. He stopped the video, fast forwarded, missed it again. 'Dammit,' he said, then found the right moment and played it back.

The time code said 08:49:09:01. The guards pushed and pulled Knippies, the pickpocket's arm pressed up high against his back.

'Now just let it roll.'

'We don't have time,' said Griessel. 'Can you speed it up a bit?'

'OK.'

The speed doubled. The three people disappeared, camera left.

Shoppers hurried past. Everyone on a linear path to the inside or outside.

Only one man walked diagonally across the walkway, in the direction of the door. Disappeared.

'Stop,' said Mbali. 'That guy.'

Lithpel manipulated the video, wound it back, played it at normal speed.

The man was athletic, tall, light brown complexion. Black windcheater, his right hand in his pocket. The head in the baseball cap was subtly but unmistakably bowed, as though he was aware of the cameras. At 08:49:31:17.

'That's him,' said Cupido.

'I don't know . . .' said Griessel.

'That's him, pappie,' said Cupido.

'Who?' asked Mbali.

'The Cobra.'

She drew a sharp breath to ask something, but Griessel pre-empted her.

'I'll tell you everything later,' he said, and looked at his watch. 'Lithpel, speed it up. I want to see who comes out.'

Fast forward. Just over five minutes later, and a dark figure sped diagonally across the walkway. 'There he is,' said Lithpel. He worked the console, found the right point. 08:55:02:51. Normal speed. Knippies ran, long skinny legs stretched, arms pumping.

'Stop,' said Griessel, and leaned closer. 'Can you make it sharper.'

'No,' said Lithpel. 'Motion blur, nothing you can do.'

'OK,' said Griessel.

'Play it, Sergeant,' said Mbali.

Lithpel let the video run. Knippies disappeared from camera range. And then the man in the baseball cap ran across the image. With a rucksack in his hand.

'Look,' said Mbali.

'Wait,' said Griessel. He raised his hands, as though to make everything stand still for a moment. He closed his eyes for a moment, thinking over what they had here, and what lay ahead.

His colleagues looked at him expectantly.

Griessel opened his eyes. 'Vaughn, the passage door out there. See if it locks from inside. If the SSA come, delay them for as long as possible.'

Cupido smiled happily and left in a hurry.

'Lithpel, can you hide the videos? Or put them on a system where only you can find them?'

'The files are too big, Cappie, we don't have time. All I can do now is delete them.'

'Do it.'

'Benny, that's tampering with evidence,' said Mbali, deeply concerned.

'Mbali, we've already seen the evidence. The SSA are not criminal investigators.'

'You will be in trouble.'

'Yes,' he said. 'Lithpel, erase the videos.'

'Roger, Cappie.'

They heard someone hammering on the door.

Griessel moved fast. He took his iPhone out of his pocket. 'Does your phone have a camera?' he asked Mbali.

'Yes.'

Griessel aimed his cellphone at the notice board and took a picture of Knippies. 'If you could take the same photo? Just in case . . .'

'OK,' she said, and dug in her handbag.

Bellowing, indignant voices out in the corridor.

Suddenly the doorway darkened. 'Everybody out,' said the herd leader of the State Security Agency. 'Right now.'

28

Tyrone sat curled up on the bench in the Company Gardens, cell-phone and wallet in one hand, memory card clutched in the other. He scarcely heard the footsteps that shuffled up to him, and only properly registered when the shadow fell across him.

'Brother,' came the voice abruptly, making Tyrone jump.

'What?'

'*Askies*, brother, I didn't know you were meditating.'

It was a *bergie*, a little, crumpled man, bent right over. The tramp's apologetic grin was nearly toothless.

Tyrone was back in reality. He stood up, pushed the wallet and cell-phone instinctively and hastily into his pocket as he walked away.

'Now where you going, brother? No offence, five rand for a loaf of bread, children didn't eat last night, you've got it good, I saw.' The whining words came ever faster as Tyrone walked away. The beggar pursued him. '*Moenie soe wies nie*, brother, hey man, don't be like that. Show some solidarity, show some charity, just five rand . . .'

Charity. Tyrone stopped.

The *bergie* was startled by this turn of events. He took a step backwards.

Never forget charity, Tyrone. To ease another's heartache is to forget one's own.

Tyrone took out the wallet. He carefully put the memory card away in its original place. He remembered an Uncle Solly quote: *But you don't just give when you have. A bone to the dog, that's not charity. Charity is the bone shared with the dog when you are just as hungry as the dog.*

He took out a fifty-rand note from the stolen wallet and gave it to the man.

'God bless you, brother.' The little grubby hands made the note disappear like a stage magician, and then he, too, melted away, as though he were afraid Tyrone would regret his lavishness.

Tyrone began walking towards Queen Victoria Street.

Keep moving.

He could think while he walked.

A pickpocket can't afford to hang around. Keep moving.

He could handle the dreadful tension inside better if he was moving.

OK, so this is what happened. He stole the wrong wallet, on the wrong day.

It wasn't a drug deal gone south.

The mall cops were dead because he stole the wrong wallet, at the wrong time.

And now they had Nadia. For the same reasons.

Keep moving.

It didn't help to beat himself up over this mess. He had to get Nadia out of there. Then he would worry about himself.

It was easy. He would just swap the card for his sister.

Then why are you so afraid?

He walked along Perth and Vredenburg, towards Long Street.

He was afraid, because that *guy* with those eyes, a guy who strolled in so calm and collected and shot mall cops, like one, two, three, four, five, fish in a barrel, no emotions . . . That guy wasn't going to stand there and say: 'Thanks, my brother, pleasure doing business with you'. He was going to take his memory card, and he was going to shoot him and his sister just like that.

He shivered, because he had got Nadia involved in all this. If they laid a finger on his sister . . . His heart beat in his throat. He turned left into Long Street and walked south, towards the mountain.

Keep moving.

Get those pictures out of your head. Think.

Tyrone Kleinbooi slowly suppressed his fears, and he walked, and he thought. He went through the whole thing from the beginning. He must forget about what happened to him, he must get into the mind of the man with the cool eyes, he must get a bird's-eye view, that's what he needed.

He walked over the Buitesingel crossing and up Kloof Street, through the hubbub of students, business people, tourists, slim models, and *bergies* trying to guide motorists into parking places. He walked to the front of Hudsons The Burger Joint Est. 2009. Then he stopped, his hand resting a moment on the back of his head, deep in thought.

Tyrone turned around and began running in the opposite direction.

Griessel drove with Mbali to Schotsche Kloof so that he could tell her everything. He left nothing out.

It wasn't easy. She was a painfully law-abiding and over-cautious driver. And she was upset. She interrupted him, shaking her head, over the interference of the State Security Agency, over the 'colonial tendencies' of MI6, over the fact that she was an accessory to the destruction of evidence in a robbery and five murders.

Griessel pressed on. He only finished when they had been parked in front of the house at 18 Ella Street for five minutes, beside the ambulance and the six SAPS patrol vehicles.

'This is completely unacceptable,' said Mbali.

'I understand. But it is what we have,' said Griessel.

'This is a democracy,' she said.

'You think so?' said Cupido.

'*Hhayi*!' said Mbali as if he was committing blasphemy.

'That's why I asked you to switch off your cellphones at the Waterfront,' said Griessel. 'Because I am now absolutely sure they are eavesdropping on our calls, and they can track us. We don't want them to know we are here. We must remember they have access to exactly the same technology as us, but they don't need subpoenas. And there's a good chance our offices are bugged . . .'

Mbali shook her head.

'We have to assume,' said Griessel.

She merely nodded.

'I'll ask the Green Point SC to suppress the info of the cobra markings on the shell casings. If this shooting,' Benny pointed at the big house, '. . . leads us anywhere, we'll stay ahead of them.

'Now, let's talk about what happened at the Waterfront. With the pickpocket, I mean. Mbali how did you see it?' He hoped Cupido would understand what he was trying to do, and shut up now.

Mbali was quiet for a long time, her hands on the steering wheel.

From the back seat Cupido sighed impatiently.

'I think that this Cobra person kidnapped David Adair, and he is still alive.'

Griessel heard a detached note in her voice. Her usual self-confident matter-of-fact manner was missing.

'OK,' he said.

'I think Adair contacted Lillian Alvarez, because she had to bring something from Cambridge to Cape Town. Something this Cobra person wants. I think she was going to hand it over to him at the Waterfront, but then the pickpocket stole it.'

'I'm not sure that makes sense,' said Cupido.

'Why?' asked Mbali.

'Because that pickpocket is quick. We couldn't see what he stole, and I saw nobody in that video of the theft itself that looked like the Cobra. So, if he didn't see, he couldn't have known.'

'Maybe he spoke to Alvarez just after the wallet was stolen, and she told him what happened. Maybe he saw it happen, from a distance. Maybe he wasn't sure what was stolen. We could have seen all that on the other cameras, if we hadn't destroyed the evidence. And then this Cobra person followed the security officials, he was only about twenty seconds behind them on the video. And he shot everybody. The pickpocket escaped.'

'Maybe . . .' said Cupido, but he wasn't convinced.

Mbali shifted in her seat, eventually, turned to them. 'The backpack is important,' she said.

'Why?' asked Cupido.

'The pickpocket had it on his back when he was arrested. But when he ran out, it was not there. The man who might be this Cobra person was carrying it in his left hand.'

'So?'

Mbali shrugged.

Griessel nodded. 'Vaughn? You sound as if you have another theory.'

'There's no evidence that the Cobra thought Knippies still had the stolen item. Maybe he found what he was looking for, and just ran away from the crime scene . . .'

'He would not have run if he had what he wanted. He's a professional,' said Mbali.

'Maybe. But my theory still stands: Adair skimmed money on TFTP. And the Cobra is after the money. Alvarez brought something that said where the money is, or how you can get it. Swiss Bank account number . . .'

'She could have emailed that,' said Mbali.

'Maybe,' said Cupido.

Griessel nodded, and opened the door. 'Let's go and see how this fits in with the rest.'

From the sitting room of the big house, where he sat with the grieving owner, the Green Point SC saw the three detectives approach. In front walked the stout, short Mbali with her big handbag swinging from her shoulder, then the taller Vaughn Cupido in a black coat that made him look a bit like Batman, and then Benny Griessel, in height just nicely in the middle between the Zulu and the coloured man. His tousled hair needed a trim, and he had strange Slavic eyes. Everyone who had been in the Service for more than ten years knew about Griessel, the former Murder and Robbery detective who had once arrived at a murder scene so drunk that they had to load him in the ambulance along with the victim's corpse.

These were the Hawks, thought the SC. The crème de la crème. A *vetgat*, *windgat* and a *dronkgat*. The fat, the vain, and the drunk.

What was going to become of this country?

Woodstock lies only two kilometres from the heart of Cape Town's business district.

Two hundred years ago it was a farm, and an outstretched white beach where the wintry northwester spat up the wrecks of sailing ships like driftwood. A hundred and thirty years ago it was the third biggest town in the Cape Colony. And fifty years ago it was one of the very few suburbs in South Africa where brown, black, and white could live undisturbed side by side under apartheid, before it decayed ever faster into poverty, with all the social evils that brought with it.

The minibus taxi dropped Tyrone off in Victoria Road, where the neighbourhood was going through a systematic revival – new boutiques, décor, and old-fashioned furniture shops existed comfortably beside old businesses selling hardware and motor vehicle spares. Office buildings, warehouses, and old bakeries were being restored, and to the south more and more yuppies were buying the pretty old houses.

But when Tyrone jogged north up Sussex Street, this sense of resurgence evaporated rapidly. The little houses here were dilapidated, squat and poor, despite the lovely old Cape architecture. Like the one on the corner of Wright Street, a corrugated-iron building bearing a weathered, insignificant sign, red letters on a blue background, indicating that it was the home of PC Technologies.

The veranda was secured with heavy-duty, white-painted burglar bars, and the door to the street was protected by a security gate. Apparently to keep thieves out. But also to allow for time, should the SAPS appear with a search warrant. Because PC Technologies belonged to Vincent Carolus, a specialist in the handling, cleaning, and fixing of new, second-hand *and* stolen computer and related equipment.

Carolus grew up in Begonia Street, Mitchells Plain, only three houses from where Tyrone and Nadia lodged with Uncle Solly. Nobody knew how he acquired his first personal computer, but everyone knew that at fourteen he was already a technology wizard. He had been called 'PC' ever since.

He was one of only five people at this present moment who knew what Tyrone's true occupation was. The other four were also dealers in stolen goods.

Tyrone stood gasping for breath at the steel door. He pressed the button under the video camera, hurriedly and perhaps a touch too hard.

It took fourteen seconds before the electronic lock opened.

29

The owner of the big house in Ella Street wept unashamedly, uncontrollably. Mbali sat beside him. She held the man's hand tightly, her face twisted with sympathy.

'How am I going to tell my wife?' the man kept asking.

'I'm so sorry,' said Mbali every time.

They waited for him to calm down a little, then asked him the usual questions.

In Cape English he told them that his daughter had been studying fashion design. She had so many plans. She was only twenty-four years old. 'And now she's gone.'

Mbali comforted him again.

They asked him whether anything was missing from the house. He said nothing that he had noticed.

They asked whether his daughter had been to the Waterfront today.

'No, she was home. She would have called if she . . . She did not go out much.'

Griessel took out his cellphone, retrieved the photo of Knippies, and showed it to the man.

'Do you know this person?'

'Was it him?' he asked, shock and horror in his voice.

'No, sir, we don't think it was him. Do you know him?'

'Yes, he is my tenant. Why are you showing me his photograph if it wasn't him?'

'We think the person who came into your house might have been looking for him. He rents a property from you?'

'No. Yes . . . He lives out in the back. In the servants' quarters. What has he done?'

'Right here? At the house?'

'Yes, behind the garage.'

Cupido moved towards the door. 'I'll go and look.'

Griessel nodded. 'Does he work for you?'

'No, we are renting it as a flat . . . What has he done? What is he mixed up in?'

'Sir, please,' said Griessel, 'at this stage we know very little. And we are hoping you can help us.'

'I'm sorry. It's just . . . I always thought . . . I never believed him.'

'We want to know everything, but right now, can you please tell us his name?'

'Tyrone Kleinbooi.'

'Do you know where we can find him?'

'I don't know. He is . . . He says he's a painter. He does contract work, all over. We . . . I hardly see him.'

'OK. How long has he been renting from you?'

'From the beginning of the year.'

'Do you have a prior address for him?'

'He used to live somewhere in Mitchells Plain. I don't have the address.'

'Do you have any information about his family?'

'I don't know if he . . . I . . . I don't know. We advertised the flat, last year in November. And he came to see us. He was very well mannered, looked like a good boy. He told us this story, about him being an orphan. Him and his sister, they were . . . they lived in Mitchells Plain, with old people who brought them up, and then they died. And he said his sister was going to university to become a doctor, and he was a painter, and most of the work was in and around the city, so he wanted to rent. He had the deposit, he paid on time, every month. My wife . . .' He began to sob again, they could see him struggling to bring himself under control. 'My wife really liked him. He would come and talk to her. Just talk. Like he wanted . . . like he would to a mother . . .'

'Sir, do you know at which university the sister is studying?'

'Stellenbosch. That's what he said. But I . . . I thought it was a little too sad to be true, being orphans, you know. And her studying medicine. I thought he just told us all that to get the flat, because there were other people who wanted it too. But my wife said we must help the less fortunate, and that he's a good boy . . .'

He began to cry again, then said, 'How am I going to tell my wife?'

★ ★ ★

'That's heavy encryption, my bru,' said PC Carolus. He was two years older than Tyrone, but short and swish – always decked out in modern labels. Even the big black-rimmed glasses were fashionable.

'How heavy?' asked Tyrone in the dusky room. They were both staring at the computer screen where PC had opened the memory card.

'AES heavy. 128-bit heavy.'

'What's that supposed to mean?'

'AES is Advanced Encryption Standard. That's way heavy.'

'But you can do anything.'

'No, not that. Maybe if I had months.'

'So what is it?'

'It's an encrypted ZIP file, Tyrone.'

'Like I know what that means.'

'It's like . . . a ZIP file is like a box. Something is stuffed into the box, but you don't know what the contents are until you open the box. And this box can't be opened because there's a lock on it. A heavy lock, that's the 128-bit encryption. And you can only open it if you have the key. And I'm assuming you don't have the key?'

'I don't.'

'I rest my case.'

'So what do you think is in there?'

'Tyrone, *wiet jy* what's in a box if you just *look* at the box?'

'Well, if it says fragile on it, then you know . . .'

'But here's *fokkol* written on the box. It can be anything – a few porn movies, a shit-house full of documents, pirated software . . . anything digital. You understand?'

'OK. But you can copy it?'

'Now let me get this straight. You come in here, it looks like you've been beaten up real good, you walking funny, and with all due respect, you look *kwaai* jumpy to me. But you say nothing and you know I won't ask. Now I scheme you want to pull a digital scam. You, who don't even know what a ZIP file is?'

'It's not a scam, PC, it's an ace in the hole.'

PC shook his head. '*Wiet jy wat jy doen?* Do you really know what you're doing?'

'*Ek wiet, ja.*'

'And you're not going to tell me?'

'Not now.'

'OK, cool, my bru', a man's got to do what a man's got to do. *Ja*, you can copy it. Anybody can copy a ZIP file. You just can't open it if you don't have the decryption key.'

'OK, and you can substitute it, so no one can see the difference?'

'If you decrypt it, yes, you will *mos* see it's not the same stuff in the box.'

'I understand that, but *sê nou* you make a box that looks just like this box. And when the guy looks he just sees a box, but he doesn't know there's other stuff in the box. Can you do that?'

'Of course. If you make the file the same size, and you make the file name the same, and you push it through 7-ZIP for AES encryption, nobody will know the difference. But if they try to decrypt it, then you're in your *moer*.'

Tyrone thought for a moment.

'Maybe if you tell me what you want to do, I can help you,' said PC Carolus.

Tyrone hesitated, weighed up the possibilities. He said, 'Here's the deal. There's a guy who wants this card with a sore heart. But he owes me. And if I give him the card, he can take it and run. And I don't get what I want.'

'So you want insurance.'

'Just so.'

'Why didn't you say so?'

In the little room where Tyrone Kleinbooi lived, the cupboard doors and drawers were pulled open. The floor was strewn with clothing, most of it black, dark grey, or dark blue. Cleaning products and cloths, a few bits of cutlery, and some documents were spread in front of the sink.

'Even if the pickpocket was in a big hurry, I don't think it was him who did this. It was the Cobra. And he was looking for something,' said Cupido. 'But look at this first.' He led Griessel to the bathroom.

In the corner of the small room lay a thin black sweater. Cupido picked it up with his rubber gloves and held it up for Griessel to see. It had a long, blood-clotted tear across the back. 'That's a lot of blood,' said Cupido, 'looks like he was badly cut. And look there by the shower and the basin. Blood washed off. The pickpocket was here. In the last hour or two.'

'Shooter followed him?'

'Must be. And no fresh blood. The pickpocket escaped, I think. Maybe he saw the Cobra coming.'

'His sister is a student, Vaughn, we must . . .'

'Look, there on the floor, in there. Those invoices from Stellenbosch. For a Nadia Kleinbooi.'

They walked back out to the room. Cupido had to pick up the documents, because Griessel was not wearing gloves.

'There's an address. West Side 21, Market Street, Stellenbosch 7613.'

Griessel looked up from the document in concern. 'Vaughn, the shooter could have seen this too.'

'*Fok*,' said Cupido.

And right on cue, Mbali appeared in the doorway, like their conscience.

Tyrone sat at one of the little tables in Shireen's Kitchen. The aroma of the peri-peri chips Gatsby made him realise suddenly how terribly hungry he was. He gobbled his food in a hurry, washing it down with Coke. Before he was finished, his mouth still stuffed with bread and chips, the Nokia rang, an ancient tune as ringtone. It was the first call that he had received on it, and he didn't immediately realise it was his phone. He gulped the food down, took the phone out of his pocket.

Nadia's number.

'Hello,' he said as he rose to his feet, not wanting the man behind the counter to overhear. He walked out into the cacophony of Victoria Street where the hooters of the minibus taxis shrilled and bellowed back and forth like migrating herds.

'Nadia tells me you don't have a car.' The same accented voice.

'Yes.'

'But you have the wallet you stole?'

'Yes.'

'So you have money.'

'Yes.'

'I want you to take a taxi. Do you know the Fisantekraal Airfield?'

The pronunciation was so odd that he couldn't decipher the words.

'The what?'

'Fisantekraal Airfield.'

'No, I'm not going.'

'What did you say?'

'I'm not going there. If you want the card, I will tell you where we will meet.'

'You want me to kill your sister?'

'No, I want my sister alive. But you want the card. Let me tell you where I will meet you,' he said, and he wondered whether the man could hear how wildly his heart was beating.

30

It was while he was walking away from the Company Gardens an hour ago that Tyrone had begun to understand the whole thing.

He realised that there was something on the memory card that this guy wanted so badly that he, cool like a swimming pool, strolled in at the V&A and blew away five mall cops, in cold blood, with not even a blink of those chilly eyes. The man had shadowed him all the way to Schotsche Kloof, then had gone and kidnapped Nadia in Stellenbosch. Broad daylight. Capital crimes. Serious, serious stuff.

You didn't do that for a memory card with your holiday snaps on it. You did that for something with more value than Tyrone could imagine. And you wanted it back with a vengeance.

He realised it was a fact he could use. Leverage. And that was what he needed. Because he had to get Nadia out of this mess, clean and quick.

And that was when he grew angry. What sort of cunt involved innocent women? If you want the card, motherfucker, you come after *me*. But nobody messes with my sister. He had never tolerated that, not since he was five years old. And he was going to keep it that way.

Tyrone wanted to hurt the bastard. He wanted to punish him. Get revenge.

Then he thought, steady now, don't get ahead of yourself. Just get Nadia back first, keep her safe.

But how was he going to do that?

You ask yourself, Ty, what is your exit strategy? Doesn't matter where you steal, you've got to have an exit strategy. Just in case.

And slowly he put together a rough plan, and with PC Carolus, he added the finishing touches. And now Tyrone stood on the pavement in Victoria Street, with buses and lorries, cars and taxis rushing and rumbling by, the tension gnawing at him, cellphone to his ear, as he waited for the man to answer. It took some time, and it sounded as though the man was holding his hand over the phone.

Then the voice was back suddenly. 'Where?'

'Be in Bellville at ten to three. And then you call me on this phone.'

'No. You will meet me next to the Fisantekraal Airfield at that time.'

'No.'

With as much firmness as he could muster.

'I am now going to hurt your sister. I am going to shoot her through the left knee, and then the right one. She will be . . . *un infirme* . . . a cripple. Then I will shoot her in the elbows . . .'

Tyrone's body twitched, but he knew there was only one way to get himself and Nadia out of this alive.

'If you touch my sister, if you hurt her in any way, I will burn this card. I am not stupid. I saw you kill five guys. I know you will kill us anyway when you get the card, so don't try to fool me. But I swear I will give it to you if Nadia is there and she is not hurt. I will give it to you when you have let her go. But if you touch her, I will destroy this card.'

Again the phone was muffled. Then, 'You think you are very clever. It is a bad mistake. I warn you: if you are not alone, I will shoot your sister, and I will shoot you. If you don't show up, I will kill her, and I will hunt you down, and I will kill you slowly. If the card is not there, or if it is damaged, I will kill you.'

'OK.'

Fear made his voice hoarse.

'Where in Bellville?'

'At the corner of Durban and Voortrekker Roads. Ten to three. Then call me. And bring a laptop or something. I want you to check the card. I don't want any misunderstandings.'

Griessel and Cupido switched their cellphones on when they were on the N1.

The instruments beeped in a duet of text messages. Benny saw he had five voicemails, four from the same number: the Hawks' Bellville office.

He called, and listened. Nyathi's voice: 'Benny, I need you to contact me very urgently. I need you to terminate the investigation of the Cobra case immediately and return to the office. You, Vaughn, and Mbali. Immediately.'

He deleted the message and listened to the next three. All from the Giraffe, all to the same effect, but his voice growing increasingly urgent and impatient.

The last one was from Alexa: 'Benny, I left you some meals in the fridge – there's something for every evening. Miss you already. I will phone tonight, when the function is over. Love you. Bye.'

He felt guilt at the relief that washed over him. He could sleep at home. And his little rascal was safe, for the next few nights at least.

He put the phone down. Cupido had also finished listening.

'Nyathi?' he asked.

'*Ja*,' said Cupido. 'We have to go to the Kremlin. Mbali as well.'

'Call her.'

'Do you think The Flower is going to answer her cellphone while she's driving?'

Griessel slowed down and moved to the left lane. They would have to wait for her to pass and then try and get the message to her through the window. All a waste of time. They had to get to Stellenbosch. He was deeply concerned about Nadia Kleinbooi.

The Metro train station at Woodstock had recently been refurbished. The concrete and steel building was painted the green and blue of the sea, but it was already looking shabby.

Tyrone barely saw it. He waited on the platform for the train to Bellville, and thought about his scheme. He knew he could not make it work on his own. He needed an assistant.

A pickpocket has no friends, Tyrone. You can't trust anyone, that's why. Nobody. So, if you want to be the life of the party, if you want to make friends and influence people, go and sell insurance.

He would have to buy a friend. And that never comes cheap.

He would have to exchange the four hundred British pounds for rands. And that was always a losing deal, because the Nigerian money-changers ripped you off. The exchange rate was thirteen rand to a pound. If you got eight, you were lucky.

Three point two K was a lot of money if you wanted to buy friends.

But he must spend the minimum, because if it all worked, he *and* Nadia would be on the run. And that was going to be expensive.

In his mind, he worked through the plan, and he thought, *jirre*, there are a lot of holes in this scheme.

But it was the only thing that could work.

They sat around Brigadier Musad Manie's round conference table. Colonel Zola Nyathi twirled a pen thoughtfully in his hand. Griessel and Cupido looked like guilty schoolboys. Mbali looked angry.

'Benny, did you remove or destroy evidence from the Waterfront scene?' The Camel's voice was heavy and solemn.

'No, Brigadier.'

'You did not delete the video material?'

'No, Brigadier.'

Manie looked at Mbali. 'Is this true?'

'Yes, sir. Benny did not touch any evidence whatsoever.' She said it carefully, as if choosing her words like steps in a minefield. Griessel felt a rush of gratitude towards her. He knew how painfully honest she was, how this technical skirting of the truth would conflict with her principles.

'I want you to understand that this is a very serious matter. The national commissioner phoned. From the office of our minister. According to the Department of State Security you deliberately wiped out video material, and hindered a task team from SSA in their investigation of a matter of international importance. International security Mbali. There's a lot at stake here. Not only the reputation of this unit and the SAPS, but of our country. Is that understood?'

'Yes, sir.'

'So I want to ask all three of you again: did you or did you not destroy evidence at the Waterfront?'

'Brigadier, why would we do such a thing?' asked Cupido.

'Answer my question.'

'No, Brigadier, not one of us did,' said Griessel, following Mbali's strategy. Because Lithpel Davids had deleted the evidence. And the brigadier hadn't mentioned the sergeant's name.

Manie looked at them, one after the other. 'If I find out that you have lied to me, I will suspend all three of you. Is that clear?'

They confirmed their understanding with grave nods.

'And do you understand that you are officially off this case?'

'Which case, sir?' asked Mbali.

'Excuse me?'

'There seems to be more than one case, sir. There is the Franschhoek case, and the Waterfront case . . .'

Griessel didn't want her to say anything about the Schotsche Kloof case. Not now, not *here*. For various reasons, of which one was that all hell would break loose. And the other one was that Zola Nyathi had perhaps told Manie about possible bugging devices. And that Manie was playing along.

'Both, Mbali,' said Manie. 'You are to hand over anything and everything that you think might aid our colleagues at the SSA, on both these cases. Am I making myself very clear?'

It was the emphasis on 'both' that gave Griessel hope.

'Yes, sir,' said Mbali.

'Benny? Vaughn?'

'Yes, Brigadier,' they said.

'Very well. You are excused.'

Nyathi gestured to Griessel, an index finger pointing downwards. Griessel understood.

Griessel led the way down the long corridor of the DPCI building. He was in a hurry, his mind on Nadia Kleinbooi. She was the same age as Carla, his daughter. Still a child, though students considered themselves adults. They would have to go and look for Nadia, and they would have to watch over her. They would have to use her as bait, because that was all they had. And time was running out, and there was so much uncertainty, because he didn't even know if they really should drop it. Apparently, Musad Manie's tirade had been for the benefit of the possible bugging devices. He hoped. Because if Manie was serious, they had a major problem.

And there was another thing gnawing at him, a profound sense of unease, a hunch, but he hadn't had time to formulate it yet.

They walked down the stairs, and out into the basement. Griessel stood beside the clubhouse and waited for them all to form a circle.

'Colonel, we need to tell you . . .' began Griessel, but Nyathi stopped him with a 'No' and a shake of the head.

'We'll really have to let it go, Benny. The pressure on the brigadier is immense. Just let the whole thing go.'

Griessel wanted to tell him about Nadia Kleinbooi, but it was Mbali who said, 'No, sir, we can't let it go.' Not in her usual decisive tone, the one that Cupido confused with arrogance. Her voice was strange now, almost despairing.

Nyathi looked at her with a frown. 'I don't think you understand, Captain. It's a direct order.'

'I am sorry, sir, but I am not going to stop investigating this case.'

All three men stared at her in disbelief. Nyathi was the first to come to his senses. 'You're not serious.'

'I am very serious, sir.'

'Mbali, do you want to be suspended? Do you want to get the whole lot of us fired?'

'Let them try.'

There was still no confrontation in Mbali's voice. It confused Nyathi. 'Captain, you are very, very close to insubordination. What the hell has got into you?'

'Sir, I am wondering the same thing about you and the brigadier . . .'

'Captain, I am now officially warning you that you are going too far. One more word, and you are suspended.'

'Sir, you can suspend me or you can fire me, I don't care . . .'

Nyathi's eyes narrowed and he drew a breath to respond, but Captain Mbali spoke with a passion and conviction that none of them had heard before. 'My father used to tell me stories of how he did not dare use his phone, because the security police were always listening. He was part of the Struggle, Colonel. Back when the secret services conducted all the important criminal cases, when they told the police what to do. When everybody was spying on each other. And everything was hushed up by the media. And the public knew nothing. Today it is happening again. Now Parliament is passing this Security Bill. Why? Because they want to hide things. Now this. State Security eavesdropping on us, and taking over a criminal case. Just like in the apartheid times. We are destroying our democracy, and I will not stand

by and let it happen. And it will, if we let it. I owe it to my parents'
struggle, and I owe it to my country. You and the brigadier too. You
owe it to all the comrades who gave their lives for the cause. So, no, I
will not stop. And if you try to stop me, I will go to the press and I will
tell them everything.'

31

Zola Nyathi, the inscrutable, stood there, his intense gaze fixed on the fat captain. For perhaps the first time Griessel saw emotion on the colonel's face, rage that was gradually replaced with something else. Regret? Shame?

The Giraffe suddenly turned his back on them and raised his eyes to the stretch of Market Street that was visible between the rear wall and the vehicle entrance. He clasped his hands strangely in front of his chest, almost as if in prayer.

Silence, just far off the sound of traffic on Voortrekker Road, and an ambulance siren on the way to Tygerberg Hospital. Seconds passed while Nyathi stood stock still.

He turned back to them. 'What do you think, Vaughn?'

'I never thought I'd say this, Colonel, but I'm with Mbali.'

Griessel thought he actually had no right to ally himself politically with his colleagues. He had been a law enforcer under the former regime, and he couldn't pretend he'd been something he wasn't. But Nyathi did not spare him, he looked him in the eyes and asked, 'And you, Benny?'

'Sir, I don't think we have a choice. There is a young woman in Stellenbosch who might be in real danger, and we are the only ones who know . . .'

'What young woman?'

Griessel told him.

'Jesus,' said Nyathi. Another first, as far as Griessel could remember.

The colonel raised his hands in frustration, and dropped them again. He looked at the three of them, then in the general direction of the entrance to the building. 'Oh, what a tangled web we weave . . .'

'Amen,' said Mbali.

'And have you thought how you would approach this?' Nyathi asked Griessel.

He hadn't.

'Sir, I . . .' His thoughts raced as he spoke. 'I want Mbali and Vaughn on the team, sir.' Then his discomfort and suspicions found words and he said, 'And Bones. Because we need to try and find out why State Security wants control. It's about Adair, that's what this case is really about, and Bones is the only one . . . Just the four of us. We'll report to you. Here, where no one can listen. But we need to get to Stellenbosch fast, and we need to get clean cellphones.'

'I can get the cellphones,' said Cupido.

'Where from?'

'You don't want to know, sir.'

Nyathi was quiet. He shook his head as if he was about to do something crazy, like jump off a cliff. Then the expressionless mask was back, control restored. 'This is not just about losing our jobs. If they find out, they will prosecute us. Aggressively. At worst, they'll send us to prison. Or permanently ostracise us, at best. We will never work for the government again. Do you understand?'

'Yes, sir.'

'I have children. So do you, Benny.'

'Yes, sir.'

'I'm going to try and keep the brigadier out of this. For as long as I can. I don't want to destroy his career as well. So you'd better get it right. Do you understand?'

'Yes, sir.'

'Switch off your phones. Check your cars for tracking devices. Get moving.'

Griessel told Cupido to go and buy the five cellphones, and bring one each for Nyathi, Bones and Mbali. 'I'm going to drive to Stellenbosch so long, meet me at the girl's flat. Vaughn, we don't know if they're following us. Just keep an eye on your rear-view mirror . . .'

'Vigilant, pappie, that's my second name.'

He asked Mbali to bring Bones to the underground car park and brief him fully. 'You have to tell him everything, and you'll have to give him a choice. He has a family too. Bones said he'd do more digging on Adair. Ask him if he's found anything, and let me know on the new number. And I want you and Bones to start calling every hotel and guesthouse in the city. Use your land lines in the meantime. It's a risk, but I'm sure they'll be monitoring our cellphones, and there are simply too many Telkom lines going out.' He hoped he was correct. 'Check at the hotels if a Lillian Alvarez has booked in. She must be staying somewhere. Start with the City Lodges, that kind of place – she's a student, she won't be staying at the Cape Grace . . .' He saw the misgiving on Mbali's face, and then: 'I know it's a needle in a haystack, but if we find her it could help a lot. Our biggest problem is that we don't know who we are chasing.'

'OK,' she said solemnly before she began to walk away.

'Mbali,' Griessel called after her.

She turned around.

'Thank you for not saying anything. About the video. I know it must have been difficult.'

'No, Benny. My father said he had to lie many times, under apartheid. He believed, most of the time, that the truth will set you free. But under certain circumstances, a lie can do the same thing. I often pray for the wisdom to know what circumstances those are.'

'You've always been a wise woman.'

'I know,' she said in all seriousness.

He lay under his Hawks' vehicle, the BMW 1 Series. He was looking for tracking devices. His cellphone rang and he nearly bumped his head on the undercarriage. He should have switched the damned thing off. Griessel wriggled out from under the car. On the screen he read *UNKNOWN*.

He had a suspicion who it might be.

'Griessel,' he said, as he straightened up.

'There are bugging devices in Musad Manie and in Werner du Preez's offices,' said the woman's voice. Joni Mitchell.

Colonel Werner du Preez was group head of the Hawks' CATS unit, an abbreviation for Crimes Against the State. It made sense that the SSA would monitor him too, but Griessel was infuriated. Why was she still bothering him? She was part of the organisation that had taken over the case now.

'And you people are listening to our cellphones,' he said angrily.

'We are?' she asked, as if it were a light-hearted game.

'You work for the SSA,' he said.

'Interesting conclusion. How did you arrive at it?' Still playful and teasing.

'My phone is bugged by the SSA, but you phone me on it. That means you know when it's safe to call.'

'I did hear that you're not stupid.'

'What do you want?' He saw no point in this conversation, and time was short.

'Information. I gave you something, now I want something in return. That was the agreement.'

'And now we're off the case. Your information is no use to me.'

'I had hoped you wouldn't be so easily discouraged . . .'

'What do you mean?'

'Exactly what I said. I hoped you would go on with the investigation discreetly.'

It made no sense. 'Why would you . . . ?' He'd had it with these games. 'I can't talk now, I've got work to do.' He got into the BMW.

'What work?'

He switched on the engine. 'I have other cases too. Goodbye.'

He rang off. And he drove.

His cellphone rang again immediately.

UNKNOWN.

She had warned him, at the Waterfront, that the SSA were on their way. And now: *I hoped you would go on with the investigation discreetly.*

He stopped at the exit to Market Street, and answered.

'Please,' she said seriously, 'we *must* help each other.'

'What for?'

'I know you found something at the Waterfront. On the video you deleted. I know all three of you turned your cellphones off after that, and you went somewhere where you were busy for more than forty minutes. I think it also had something to do with the investigation. Something tells me that you don't so easily drop a matter just because another state department wants to take over.'

'I really have nothing more to say to you.'

'You don't have to say anything to me. Just don't drop the investigation.' For the first time she sounded desperate.

He couldn't understand what game she was playing.

'Are you there?' she asked.

'Wait,' he said, and dug the iPhone's earphones out of his pocket, plugged them in, before he drove again.

'I will lose my job if I investigate the case.'

'They won't know.'

'Now who is "they"?'

'I work for them. But I don't share their agenda. Please.'

'I don't trust you.'

'That I can understand. Ask me anything.'

'What are you doing at SSA?'

She hesitated. 'You drive a hard bargain.'

He didn't answer.

'I am head of the monitoring programme.'

'And eavesdropping on us.'

'Yes.'

That was why she could phone. 'What is your name?'

Again a silence. Then: 'Janina.'

'And your surname?'

'Mentz.' With a sigh of resignation.

Janina Mentz. Joni Mitchell. The same initials. Not very original. 'Why does the SSA want us off the case?' he asked.

'I can't put my head on a block, you must understand that. I am senior management, but not part of the top management, I don't have access to all the information. But I have a theory, based on a strong rumour doing the rounds. That Adair wanted to embarrass the British government. Two years ago he published a memorandum on the Internet in which he said a new version of his algorithm could expose a whole string of dodgy bank transactions, and that Britain and the USA had a moral obligation to implement it . . .'

'The Adair Protocol,' said Griessel.

She remained quiet for a moment. 'I underestimated you. I won't make that mistake again.'

'Go on,' he said.

'We suspect that he deployed this new algorithm on the SWIFT system without sanction. We suspect he gained access to information in this way about corrupt activities of British parliamentarians, of much greater scope than that which was already known. Bribe money from media interests, from weapons manufacturers, from interest and pressure groups. Large amounts in Swiss bank accounts. And it goes up to very high levels. Up to the cabinet. Then he tried to blackmail the British government. Something like "use the Protocol to fight organised crime, or I'll make this public".'

'It still doesn't explain why the SSA wants to take over the investigation.'

'If we can get Adair, Captain, we can get all that information. And in the diplomatic sphere, that has incalculable value. You know that the British Department of International Development wants to halt their financial support to South Africa in 2015?'

'No.'

'Our government is very unhappy about that. And that sort of information could definitely make the Brits reconsider.'

He mulled over this for a moment.

'OK. But what is your agenda?'

'Are you familiar with the Spider-Man-principle?'

'The what?'

'The Spider-Man-principle. With great power comes great responsibility. That sort of information would give our government great power, Captain. I don't think our government can be trusted with such great responsibility.'

32

Under normal circumstances Tyrone Kleinbooi liked Bellville Station. It reminded him of Uncle Solly's stories about District Six – the *mengelmoes* of people and colours, the hustle and bustle, the music blaring out, competing from every point of the compass, the aromas of food stalls and takeaway cafés wafting at you as you walked by. His favourite clothing store just around the corner, in Durban Road: H. Schneider Outfitters. A *continental* name. And *Outfitters.* The sound of sophistication, just like their pinstriped suits and shoes and colourful waistcoats. And there, on the square at Kruskal Avenue and among the informal traders' stalls in the alleyways and malls, you found more characters and shysters per square metre than any other place in the Cape. Look any which way and there's counterfeit brand clothing and accessories from China, so much of it, such a racket, that you couldn't even take a picture. If you took out your phone to snap something, the stall owners were on to you at once, 'No, brother, please, no photos.' They asked nicely, but there was a vague, veiled threat behind it.

It was no place for his industry – mostly poor and lower-middle-class moving through here – for him it was a place to relax, to check things out, to shoot the breeze. Because the other great feature of the station was that you almost never saw a policeman here. He had already worked it out for himself: law enforcement turned a blind eye to all the counterfeit, and probably also the stolen goods, because there's no serious crime here. Maybe because everyone was in transit, and there weren't *kwaai* valuables to steal. Perhaps because all the shysters and counterfeit traders looked out for each other, did their own policing.

So the cops don't scratch where it doesn't itch, and they don't bother you here.

Which was a good thing right now.

Logic told him the cops were already looking for him. A nationwide manhunt, for the fugitive from the Waterfront killings. Tomorrow morning his face would be on all the front pages, but now his CCTV star appearance was probably a Kodak moment in every policeman's breast pocket.

Here he didn't need to worry about it. He could just look for helpers. And that was where his trouble lay. It wasn't going to be easy. There were a few coloured businessmen, mainly in the Bellstar Junction in front of the station. Rich cats, they weren't going to do any monkey-business for a brother for just a few hundred rand. The Nigerian money-changers and drug dealers were also a no-go area. They had the good taste to make themselves invisible in small apartments on the second and third floors of the buildings in the area. And they didn't come cheap either.

But mostly, on the ground, it was all Little Somalia here.

And your trouble with Somalians is that they're cat-footed. They tread warily. Because of the xenophobic attacks. And the fact that so many of them are illegal aliens. They don't trust anybody except fellow former countrymen. You see it in their sceptical Somalian eyes. If you didn't buy anything at his stall, if you loitered, or you came to *gooi* a scheme, then they checked you out doubtfully, talk about *under suspicion*. And the shake of the head came early on, no, no thanks, not interested.

But he had better get an assistant quickly. Because his time was running out. It was twenty past two.

Griessel told Janina Mentz to text her number to him. He would think everything over and phone her back. Then he rang off, and he switched off his phone, and drove to Stellenbosch by the Bottelary Road, because it was easier to spot a tail on that route.

And when he crossed the R300, his eyes constantly checking the rear-view mirror, the whole situation crashed down on him. Not gradually, but with a sudden, crushing weight.

And with it, as always, like a whirlwind, the thirst for booze descended on him: he instantly felt the smooth, cool weight of a glass in his hand. Short. Neat. No ice. No mixer, just the raw, rich taste of Jack Daniel's on his tongue, and the heat down his throat. He shivered and gripped the steering wheel; his body craved the tingle of alcohol, *now*. '*Jissis*,' he murmured. His mind told him there were places he could go, here in Kraaifontein, shebeens and a few bars, and nobody would even know.

But what about Nadia Kleinbooi?

Just a quick stop. Five minutes. Brackenfell or Kuils River, it was just a little detour, two lightning doubles, line them up, barman. Christ, the bliss that would flow, slip, slide through his veins and fibres to the deepest reaches of his body. Only two, they would heal him, of every-thing, they would last him till tomorrow, and tomorrow everything would be better again.

Saliva gushed into his mouth, his hands shook. It had been months since he had last had this uncontrollable thirst. Part of him was aware of what was happening. He knew the trigger. The 'secondary one' was what Doc Barkhuizen called it. When he realised how rubbish and useless and irrelevant he was. And he needed the drink to confirm it, and he needed the drink to heal it.

Phone Doc.

Fok Doc. Doc didn't understand. Doc's life worked; his did not. He was hopeless, useless, bad. His work was increasingly becoming a joke. He had drunk away his life, lost his wife, the respect of his children. He could hear it in Fritz's voice when he talked to his son. Fritz just kept him informed, but he *talked* to his mother. His colleagues gave him one look on a bad morning, and immediately jumped to the conclusion that he had hit the bottle. They were merely tolerating him, that uneasy sympathy you have for the handicapped. And Alexa Barnard, she would drop him as soon as she had her alcoholism and her life under control again, as soon as she saw through him once more and realised how shit he really was. He, who lied and ducked and dived from her because his *fokken* rascal couldn't keep up. And why couldn't it keep up? Because he had poured his libido, along with the rest of his life, down his throat.

He put his indicator on to turn left in Brackenfell Boulevard. There were drinking holes down near the hypermarket, his old, old hangouts when he used to pour one last *dop* before going home. Warm places in this wintry weather. Welcoming.

At the back of his mind there was a voice asking: What about Nadia Kleinbooi? She was Carla's age, Christ, would he go drinking if it were *his* daughter?

He turned the indicator off again. It was faster to make a quick stop in Stellenbosch. Buy a little bottle. For the afternoon and the evening.

That's what he would do. He settled on that.

Only once he drove past the entrance to the Devonvale golfing estate, did he focus on the true origin of his self-hatred and the urge to drink.

Mbali Kaleni had spoken with so much feeling about the devastation of democracy. And then Janina Mentz said this government could not be trusted with such a great responsibility. The fuck-up was that they were both right. And therein lay two big problems. First and foremost was déjà vu. Because he still remembered what it was like under apartheid. It didn't matter how hard he used to believe he was only fighting the good fight against crime, that he was on the side of the good guys, there was always the niggling little voice in the back of his head. You couldn't avoid the hatred in the others' eyes, or the rage of the media, and the grubby association with colleagues who were doing evil things – even a few senior men in what was then the Murder and Robbery Squad. It wore you down slowly, because when you worked with death and violence and everything that was sick in a community, impossible hours for a ridiculous salary, then you wanted to, no you *had* to, believe you had good and right on your side. Otherwise you lost your self-respect, your faith in the whole business, and you began to ask yourself: What was it all for?

That had been one of the reasons for his drinking. That pressure. They all needed to soften the sharp edges of reality.

And then came the New South Africa and the great relief: now he could do his job in the bright, clear daylight of justice and respect.

It was what carried the SAPS through the first decade after apartheid, through the massive transformation, and the mess of national commissioners who were fired under one dark cloud after another. But now it felt like it was back to the bad old days again. A government that was slowly rotting. And it was catching. More and more policemen were doing stupid things, and there was more and more mismanagement, corruption and greed, sinking the Service deeper and deeper into the quicksand of inefficiency and public distrust. Despite the new national commissioner, who tried so hard, despite the work of thousands of honest and dedicated policemen, despite senior officers like Musad Manie and Zola Nyathi, whose integrity was entirely above suspicion.

Just as in the old days, he was increasingly reluctant to tell people he was a policeman.

Where did that leave him? A rat on a sinking ship. Once again. He couldn't leap off, he had one child at university and another that wanted to go to a *fokken* hellish expensive film school. At forty-five he was just a stupid career policeman who could do nothing else.

Which brought him to the second problem that Mbali and Mentz's words had revealed: his inability to think about stuff like the powers of the government, information laws, and Struggle history. What was wrong with him that he was stuck at ground level, always wrestling with such basic, mundane things? So that he was embarrassed when Mbali pointed out the bigger picture, the deeper principle, with so much passion and integrity.

What was wrong with him? He had become irrelevant in a vocation that demanded deeper thought and insight and intelligence. In a country and a world that was changing far faster than he could adapt to it.

What was *wrong* with him?

Just about everything.

But nothing that drink would not put right.

The irony did not escape Tyrone Kleinbooi.

Beggars can't be choosers, he thought, but to go and choose a beggar?

He had no choice: time was running out, and fast. He was hurriedly scanning the stall in front of Bellstar Junction for a helper, a sidekick, and then this *ou* appeared beside him, as abrupt and unexpected and embarrassingly silent as a wet dream. Filthy, and with many hard years on the clock. But under the brown layers of sunburn and lack of personal hygiene, he saw to his surprise that the guy was a whitey. In a faded blue overall jacket, ragged orange jersey underneath, eyes bright blue in a red-brown face, he said, 'Brother, I haven't eaten today.'

At first Tyrone wanted to say, 'Brother? *Watse* brother, nowadays you're a brother of everyone that lives and breathes, what's up with that?' But he thought better of it and looked more closely at him. This *ou* would pass for a coloured.

He'd never thought to ask a whitey. Because the ones you could trust wouldn't help with a coloured man's troubles. And the rest . . .

'Show me your hands . . .'

'Excuse me?' said the man.

'Show me your hands.'

The man slowly lifted his hands, palms up. Tyrone looked. He saw no tremor.

'You're not on *tik*?' Tyrone asked.

'That's not my drug.'

'What is your drug?'

'*Boom*,' he said with a measure of pride.

'When last did you smoke weed?'

'Day before yesterday. But I'm hungry now, brother.'

'What's your name?'

'Bobby.'

'Bobby who?'

'Bobby van der Walt.'

It was such an unlikely name for a bum that he felt like laughing. 'OK, Bobby, so you're looking for a bit of money?'

'Please.'

'You can earn it, Bobby.'

He could see the man lose interest instantly. 'Just a small, easy job,' said Tyrone quickly.

The blue eyes were suspicious. 'What kind of job?'

'A legal job. Easy money. A hundred bucks for ten minute's work.'

'What must I do?'

'Do you see that flyover?' Tyrone pointed at the M11 flyover that ran past the station building on concrete pillars, high in the air.

'I'm a smoker, but I'm not stupid,' said Bobby van der Walt. 'I see it. It's the Tienie Meyer Bypass.'

'Fair enough, brother,' said Tyrone. 'Now let me tell you what you must do.'

When Benny Griessel drove into Stellenbosch, and his eyes began searching Bird Street for an off-licence, he thought: four hundred and twenty-three days clean. Four hundred and twenty-three long difficult days. He didn't have a political struggle, he had a drink struggle, a life struggle. His whole being said, Fuck it all, but somewhere in his head there was an objection: You will have to tell Doc why you threw away four hundred and twenty-three days. You will have to tell Alexa as well.

At the Adam Tas traffic light he stopped.

Phone Doc.

He couldn't. His cellphone had to stay off.

Phone Doc. The SSA would not be able to draw any sensible conclusion from the fact that he was in Stellenbosch.

He sighed and turned on his phone.

33

At 14.40 Tyrone stood in front of the Sport Station in the Bellstar Junction shopping centre. The shop's name was on a big sign on the wall behind him. When he had first walked up to it he thought for a fleeting second that they were *lekker* stupid when they made that logo because there was one giant S that had to serve for both words. But it didn't really work – at first glance it looked like *Sport Tation*.

But his mind was focused elsewhere now. He had the cellphone in his hands, he kept an eye on the time. He was shaking, his heart pounding in his chest, too fast, too hard. He wondered about Nadia, how scared she must be. What had they done to her? Tied her up? Hurt her? He didn't want to think of it . . . He *must* believe she was OK, and afterwards she was going to be heavy the *moer in* with him, that fury that transformed her into a spitting, hissing feline creature. If she was heavy angry, her eyes went a funny colour, and words streamed out of her mouth fast and furious, like a waterfall. *What were you thinking, Ty? Are you mad? I thought I knew you.*

But that was all OK, as long as she was *orraait*.

He had begun to work out a story that he would spin to her, but he didn't know if she would fall for it. And if the cops put the CCTV footage on the TV, he was going to have his work cut out for him.

Jirre, he hoped she was OK.

If they so much as touch her . . .

14.43.

He had a view from here, all down the broad corridor from the shopping centre, between steelwork curved into triumphal arches, to the entrance of Bellstar Junction. Happily he could see across Charl Malan Street, under the M11 freeway. Not a perfect view, because there were always people in the way, people coming and going, everybody always moving, moving.

He could see Bobby van der Walt, a forlorn figure up there beside the concrete barrier of the flyover. Bobby's eyes were on him. He could hear the hiss and hum of the traffic racing past behind Bobby.

He kept still, made no gestures, in case Bobby thought it was The Sign. With dagga smokers you had to be careful, the brain cells weren't always firing in sequence.

That *blerrie* whitey better do his part today, bum or not.

14.46.

When he'd recruited Bobby and explained carefully what he would have to do, he'd asked Tyrone, 'Is that all?'

'That's all. But you have to wait for my sign.'

The narrowed eyes were still suspicious. 'For a hundred bucks?'

'I told you it was easy money.'

Bobby's expression showed it might be *too* easy. There had to be a catch, somewhere.

'It's an important job, Bobby. That's why I'm paying you properly.'

'OK.'

Tyrone could see how his head was working. Bobby liked it that he had been sought out for an 'important job'.

Then he took Bobby along and went to talk to the Somalian at the clothes and backpack stall. Bobby stood and listened attentively, keen to know how payday was going to work.

That Somalian was called Hassan Ikar.

'Hassan, I want to buy this backpack.' Tyrone pointed at a compact black rucksack.

'I'll give you good price.'

'No, Hassan, I don't want to pay a good price. I want to pay full price, and a little more, but I need a favour.'

And he quickly explained to Hassan Ikar: he was going to pay him a hundred and twenty rand too much for the rucksack. Out of the change he must give Bobby van der Walt a hundred. The rest he could keep. But only when Tyrone phoned Hassan and said Bobby had done his work correctly and well.

'Do we have a deal?'

Ikar thought it over. He couldn't see any risk. Then he nodded. 'OK.'

'So give me your phone number.'

Tyrone phoned Hassan Ikar's number to make sure it was working. Bobby stood listening to everything, and eventually agreed with a nod.

The plan was made.

But was it going to work?

14.47.

Tyrone checked the cellphone's battery. More than enough juice, one of the few advantages of the Nokia 2700. Yesterday's tech, but there weren't a thousand apps sucking up the power.

A group of coloured labourers walked from the direction of the platform.

'Are the trains running on time?' asked Tyrone.

'Just about,' one called back. 'Few minutes late.'

That was OK. A few minutes late. 'Cause he was cutting it fine. If everything went according to plan, if he and Nadia got away, he wanted to catch Metrorail 3526, at 15.08 on platform 9, to Cape Town. And he could use 'a few minutes', just in case.

Tyrone breathed deeply. Get a grip, you had to be cool and calm and collected. He looked up again at Bobby van der Walt – the figure was still standing there, solitary. Keep looking at me, Bobby, don't let your concentration lapse . . .

14.49.

The security guard came walking towards him, a young black guy in a red beret with a fancy metal badge on it. 'Can I help you?'

'No, thanks, I'm waiting for my sister.'

'OK.'

Then the cellphone in his hand rang and his whole body jumped and the security guard gave him a keen look.

'That must be her now,' he said, his voice hoarse.

The security man didn't move.

Tyrone looked at the screen. Nadia's number. It was them. He answered. 'Hello.'

'I am at the corner of Durban and Voortrekker Roads.'

Same voice, same accent.

'Is my sister with you?'

'Yes.'

He wanted to ask to hear her voice, but the security man was still standing right beside him, keeping an eye on him. He said, 'I need you to come down to Bellville Station. There's lots of parking . . .'

'I don't know where the station is.'

'OK. You carry on straight down Durban Road. When you cross Church Street, you start looking for parking. There are always a few spots available. And then you call me again.'

The man didn't answer him. He waited, heart hammering in his chest. The man broke the silence, 'OK.'

Tyrone cut the connection. The security man gave him one last look, turned, and walked away. Tyrone looked up at the M11 bridge.

Bobby had disappeared.

Griessel battled to find the entrance to West Side in Stellenbosch's Market Street where Nadia Kleinbooi lived. The apartment blocks were hidden behind an old Victorian house, the sliding gates had to be opened electronically with an access system. And when he parked outside and walked to the entrance, he saw there was no reference to a caretaker on the small keyboard beside the gate.

It was good news, he thought. If they wanted to harm her, they would have had trouble getting in.

He pressed twenty-one on the keyboard. Nadia's flat number. There was no answer.

He pressed twenty in the hope of finding a neighbour home.

Silence.

He worked from twenty-two up.

Eventually, at twenty-six, a man's rough voice rasped over the intercom: 'Yes?'

'Captain Benny Griessel of the SAPS. I am looking for Nadia Kleinbooi from number twenty-one.'

'I don't know her.'

'Can you open up, please.'

'How do I know you are from the police?'

'You can come to the gate and see.'

Ten seconds later the gate began to roll open.

Panic scorched like a veld fire through Tyrone. His eyes were glued to the concrete rail of the M11, visible just above the Shoprite banner that screamed *U Save* in red and yellow letters. Bobby's silhouette was gone.

Never trust a whitey. Now Uncle Solly's warning thundered through him. *Never trust a whitey, you steal from them, but never do business there, because when the chips are down, we coloureds are the first ones they sell out.*

But he didn't have a choice, he hadn't had time. He looked at the clock on the cellphone. 14.51.

It would only take that guy four or five minutes to find parking in Durban Road. Another three minutes to walk to the end of Kruskal.

He had seven minutes to track down Bobby van der Walt. And the memory card. Because it was in the pocket of Bobby's faded, dirty blue overall jacket.

34

Don't panic, don't panic, don't panic.

But he panicked anyway, because he didn't know what else to do. If he ran, it was nearly three hundred metres from here to where the Tienie Meyer Bypass dropped down to Modderdam and you got access to the M11. It was the shortcut route that he had made Bobby take – but you had to also climb over two high wire fences. Not difficult, but it took time. Which he did not have. It would take him at least four minutes to the Modderdam crossing, where he would have a view over the highway. If he didn't see Bobby then, he was fucked, six ways till Sunday. Because then he would not have enough time to get back and stand here again.

And the memory card was in Bobby's pocket.

Jirre.

He dithered, this way and that, he tried to control his breathing and the lameness in his knees, he knew he must keep the panic off his face, because that damned security guard with the red beret was lurking around, getting kickbacks from every counterfeit-selling stall owner to keep the suspicious and the overly curious away.

He had got Nadia into this mess. Now he had better get her out.

14.54.

He would just have to stand here and wait, there was no other choice.

If the guy phoned, he would have to play for time.

But that's going to wreck the schedule, because the next train to Cape Town from Bellville D was only at 15.35, platform 11, and the trains were running late, and that meant twenty to, or quarter to four, and that gave that guy twenty minutes to find him and Nadia at the station and take them out with that silenced gun. If he could walk in at the Waterfront and shoot people left, right and centre, he wouldn't be scared of Bellville Station.

The blur of a lorry raced over the flyover, but Bobby was missing in action. Had the idiot stood too close to the road, and got run over, the memory card now in its glory?

14.55.

The cellphone in his hand rang.

Deep breath.

'Yes?'

'I have parked.'

'OK. Find Wilshammer Street, you should be close to it. Then walk down Wilshammer Street . . .' He had to think hard about compass directions, the sun came up on that side: '. . . towards the east, to the corner with Kruskal.'

'The corner of what?'

'Kruskal.' He spelled it in English, slowly and clearly.

'OK.'

Again he wanted to ask if Nadia was there, if she was safe, but he didn't. He wanted the guy to think he could see them.

'Call me when you get there. But not from Nadia's phone. You give her phone back to her, and you use your own phone from now on.'

And he rang off.

After two flights of stairs Griessel knocked on the door of 21 West Side. There was glass set into the apartment door. He kept an eye on it, but saw no movement, heard no sound from inside.

Perhaps she was on campus. Safe.

He knocked again, but he knew there was no one home.

He turned away, looked out over Stellenbosch. The place that Vaughn Cupido called 'Volvoville'. With the usual tirade: 'Volvos, Benna? Why Volvos? *Daai is* the most boring cars in automotive history. And ugly. But the rich whiteys of Stellenbosch all drive Volvos. Explain that to me. Just goes to show, money can't buy you style.'

That Cupido, really. He didn't drink – instead he spewed out insults. That was his safety valve. Maybe Griessel should try it too.

He heard footsteps on the stairs to his right. A young man appeared, walking up. Big and athletic, broad shoulders in a fashionably weathered leather jacket. Griessel's hand dropped to his service pistol. The young man looked at him, curious.

'*Middag*,' said Griessel.

'*Goeie middag.*' The Afrikaans greeting made Griessel relax. Black hair, dark brown, smiling eyes. Carla's age. Must be a student.

'Do you live on this floor?'

'Twenty-three,' he said and walked past Griessel.

'I'm looking for Nadia Kleinbooi.' Griessel nodded towards the door of number twenty-one.

The student stopped. 'Oh.' He looked at the flat, then back at Griessel. A frown appeared.

'I'm from the police,' said Griessel. 'Do you know her?'

'The police?' It was as though something fell into place. 'Why are you looking for Nadia?'

'Do you know her?'

The student came closer. The frown had disappeared, but now there was a different anxiety on his face. 'Is it about the kidnapping?'

'What kidnapping?'

'On campus. The whole varsity knows about it.' His voice became anxious. '*Was* it Nadia?'

'I'm not aware of any kidnapping,' said Griessel.

The man's eyes narrowed. 'Are you genuinely from the police?'

Just wing it, thought Tyrone, there was no other choice now. His eyes were glued to the M11 bridge, in the dwindling hope that Bobby van der Walt would appear. Just wing it. It makes no sense. Didn't the bum know he was throwing away a hundred bucks? That's what you get when you do business with *dagga* smokers.

Tyrone stood on tiptoe to see if he could spot the Waterfront shooter and Nadia on over by the stalls.

Nothing.

Out of the corner of his eye a movement, someone rushing up to him from his right. He leaped in alarm.

It was Bobby, he realised – eyes wide, gasping for breath, mouth agape. 'Sorry, brother, sorry. *Fokken* traffic cop stopping there . . .' a grubby finger pointed in the direction of the flyover '. . . and asked me if I was planning to jump. And I said: "Do I look like a jumper?" and the *doos* said: "Yes" . . .' Bobby stood bent over with his hands on his knees, wheezing long breaths back into his lungs. 'Can you believe it?'

Tyrone wanted to laugh and cry at the same time. 'Where's the memory card?' he asked.

Bobby slapped the pocket of his overall jacket. 'Right here.'

'OK,' said Tyrone, and he stood thinking.

'Can you believe it?' asked Bobby, starting to catch his breath. 'That cop stood there and he says to me: "You look a lot like a jumper to me." And I say: "*Nooit*, I'm just admiring the view." And he says he doesn't want to argue with me, and he doesn't want a traffic jam. If I want to jump, I'd better jump, just don't fall anyone *moer toe* down below. So I just ran. Sorry brother, what do we do now?'

Tyrone didn't hear him. His brain was working overtime. His plan had been that Bobby would wait on the flyover for his signal, and when the guy let Nadia go, then he would throw down the memory card. And the guy would have caught it. He might have believed that it was Tyrone up on the highway, he would have known he couldn't get at him up there. His attention split between the flyover and Nadia. Bobby would have been out of harm's way. Nadia would be free, he would have grabbed her arm just before the Sport Station, they would have run for the train . . .

What the hell was he to do now?

His cellphone rang.

Bobby stood waiting, his eyes wide and impossibly blue.

Tyrone looked at the phone. It wasn't Nadia's number, but it was a familiar one. His own. His phone that had been in the rucksack, at the Waterfront.

He answered.

'What makes you think it was Nadia?' Griessel asked the young man in the leather jacket.

'They said on Twitter it was a coloured girl,' he said, but his attitude had changed. He was suspicious now.

'The girl who was abducted?'

'*Ja*. If you're from the police, how come you don't know about this?'

Griessel barely heard him. 'Do you have a cellphone?'

'Of course I have a cellphone.'

'Could you please make a call for me?'

'Don't you have your own phones?' He took a step back.

Griessel took his wallet out of his jacket pocket, and showed him his SAPS identity card. '*Meneer*, please, will you make a phone call. My phone is out of order.'

The student's body language was antagonistic now. He studied the identity card, then said, 'Sorry, but it looks fake to me.' He started to move away, towards the stairs.

Griessel sighed, opened his wallet and put it away. 'I am going to ask you one more time to make a call.'

'Now you're getting weird.'

Griessel unclipped his service pistol from the holster, and pointed it at the young man.

'What is your name?'

The student froze, raised his hands. Waxen. 'Johan.'

'Take out your phone, Johan.'

The student stood there with his hands in the air.

'Drop your hands, take out your phone and call the police station.'

The mouth opened and shut twice, then he realised what Griessel had said. 'You want me to phone the police?'

'That's right. Stellenbosch Station.'

With visible relief he said, 'I don't know the number. Can I google it?'

'I'm at the corner of Wilshammer and Kruskal,' said the man over the phone.

Tyrone stared down the long passage, over Charl Malan Street and the alley between the stalls, but there were too many people, he couldn't see Nadia or the man. And first he had to give Bobby new instructions, a new plan, cobbled together with a slim chance of success, but he was out of time, he had no more choices.

'Wait there,' he said. 'Stand in the middle, between the stalls, so that I can see you. So that I can see that Nadia is OK.'

Silence.

'We are standing in the middle.'

'OK,' said Tyrone. 'I will call you back.'

'*Merde*,' said the man.

Tyrone didn't know what that meant. He rang off and told Bobby, 'Listen carefully.'

35

The student phoned the number of the Stellenbosch SAPS.

'Tell them you want to talk to Brigadier Piet Mentoor,' Griessel said.

The student followed instructions with a voice of new-found authority.

'Now tell him to hold for Captain Benny Griessel of the Hawks.'

The student looked at Griessel with apologetic respect and whispered a low '*Fokkit*'. Then the brigadier must have come on the line, because he said his piece and passed the phone to Griessel.

'Brigadier?' said Griessel.

'Benny, to what do I owe this privilege?'

'I hear there was an alleged abduction this morning, Brigadier, on campus.'

'You *okes* are wide-awake, *nè*. It's a strange one, Benny.'

'How so, Brigadier?'

'Only one eyewitness who swears high and low that a coloured girl was forced into a car in Ryneveld Street, a Nissan X-Trail. Then he followed the vehicle. In Andringa Street the Nissan stopped, two white men jumped out, shot up the tyres of the car pursuing them, grabbed their cellphones, and raced away. There were five witnesses who saw that happen. But not one of them saw the girl in the Nissan. So we are at least sure of cellphone robbery.'

Griessel tried to make sense out of it. 'What time did this happen, Brigadier?'

'Must have been just after one, when the classes stopped for lunch. What's your guys' interest in the case, Benny?'

He hesitated. 'Brigadier, it might be connected to the thing in Franschhoek. Sunday.'

'*Bliksem*. Any idea who the girl might be?'

He would have to lie. 'No, Brigadier. I gather there was more than one person in the car that was following the X-Trail?'

'Yes, the one who saw the kidnapping, and his friend. Students, both of them. Trouble is, the friend didn't see anything. They only got a part of the registration. We are following up on that. And there's one other thing. The bloody students picked up both of the bullet casings in the road. That's after the tyres were shot out . . .'

Griessel knew what was to come. 'Forty-five calibre?'

'That's right . . .'

'With a snake engraved on them.'

'Hell, Benny . . .' The brigadier didn't complete his sentence. Griessel guessed he was putting two and two together.

'Brigadier, are the eyewitnesses absolutely certain there were two gunmen?'

'Yes, Benny. And probably another chap who stayed behind the steering wheel.'

'Three in total?' He couldn't believe it.

'That's what most of them say.'

'And both the gunmen fired off shots?'

'Each one blew one of the front tyres.'

'The snake engraving – was it on both the casings?'

'Both of them. They are here with the detectives, totally contaminated, of course. You can come and have a look.'

'*Fok*,' said Griessel.

'OK,' said Tyrone over the cellphone. 'Look towards the south. There is a big banner that says *Shoprite, U Save*. Do you see it?'

'Yes,' said the Waterfront murderer.

'I want you to walk towards it. Slowly.'

'*D'accord.*'

'Please speak English.'

'OK.'

'And stay on the line.'

Tyrone moved to his right, just in front of A. Gul Cash & Carry, so that he could use the corner of the opposite side of the shopping centre as cover. The guy knew exactly what he looked like, and he didn't want to be spotted now. But his greater concern was that Nadia would see him, and run to him. Or do something else that could spook the gunman.

There were people blocking his view. He had to twist from side to side to see. He focused on Charl Malan Street, just in front of the flamboyant entrance to Bellstar Junction.

Still nothing.

At least Bobby van der Walt was still standing, ten metres away, right in front of the Hello Mobile cellphone shop, his eyes on Tyrone, his forehead furrowed in concentration.

Then he saw Nadia, and it was like a sudden pain in his chest. Her head hung low and she looked scared and forlorn – she was looking at the ground like someone who had lost all hope. The big bag she always carried over her shoulder to class seemed too heavy for her now. Then the stream of people opened up for a second, and Tyrone saw the man beside her. He had a hoodie over his head now, and he held her right arm tightly, his other hand hidden under his grey hoodie jacket. But from the angle of the elbow and forearm, it looked as if he was holding a firearm.

Must be a hands-free kit, thought Tyrone. That's why he's not holding a phone.

'Stop!' said Tyrone over the phone.

Hoodie and Nadia halted.

Hoodie turned his head slowly. He was checking out everything.

He looked like a whitey. He didn't look exactly like the guy from this morning. Maybe it was just the hoodie. But Tyrone's unease deepened.

'Now cross the road. Slowly.'

He lost them again in the press of the crowd. He zigzagged, he stooped, he stretched up to see over shoulders, careful not to show too much of himself, and also not to make Bobby think it was some kind of sign.

He caught sight of them again. 'Keep walking until you are exactly below the Shoprite sign.'

And he gave Bobby the signal: his index finger, held up in the air, to show Bobby he must get ready, the hand-over was near. 'But after that don't look at me again, Bobby,' he had explained urgently earlier. 'That's crucial, understand?'

To his annoyance, Bobby now gave a thumbs-up, acknowledging the signal.

Tyrone nodded vehemently.

Bobby turned away.

The bum had remembered.

Maybe this would work after all.

Hoodie and Nadia had crossed the road. He steered her past the steel railing, to right under the Shoprite sign.

'OK. Stop, I can see you clearly. Did you bring a laptop?'

'Yes.'

'Where is it?'

'On my back.'

For a moment they were out of sight again, behind a knot of people. When there was a gap again, he saw Hoodie had turned sideways. He could see the rucksack now.

Tyrone breathed deeply. Everything depended on the next few minutes. 'Now listen very carefully. You know there is a ZIP file on the memory card? Fifty-six gigabytes in size.'

'Yes.'

'And you know that the ZIP file has a password?'

'Yes.'

'OK. I had the ZIP file encrypted again. With a new password. Do you understand that?'

'*Va te faire foutre, connard!*'

'Excuse me?'

'You are playing games, *connard*. I will shoot your sister. I have a gun, right here.'

'I know you have a gun. I'm telling you, if you don't follow my instructions, you will never get the password. If you hurt Nadia, if you don't do what I say, I will not give you the password.' Tyrone shot a lightning prayer heavenwards that he would get the words right that PC Carolus had so patiently taught him. 'The encryption is AES 128 bit. It will take you thousands of years to decrypt it without the password. Do you understand?'

There was tangible fury in the silence, before Hoodie answered, 'Yes.'

'Right. You must also know I haven't written the password down. It is in my head. So if you kill me, you won't have the password.'

Hoodie did not reply.

'The password is sixteen letters. Remember that. First, I will give you the disk. Then you can test it on your laptop. OK?'

'Yes.'

'When you see that the file is there, we will start to open it with the decryption key. But then you have to tell Nadia to start walking, slowly, straight ahead, and around the corner, past the hairdresser. As long as she walks, I will give you a letter of the key. Do you understand?'

'Yes.' Impatient now.

'Now, I want you to look up the passage, between the shops. Straight ahead,' said Tyrone.

Hoodie stood still, his features shadowed by the hood, but he was facing in the right direction.

'Do you see the shop with the big green sign that says Hello Mobile?'

'Yes.'

'Do you see the guy with the blue jacket standing next to the door?'

'Yes.'

'He has the card, and he will give it to you when you reach him. If you hurt him, I will not give you the password.'

'OK,' said Hoodie.

'Walk towards the guy now. Slowly.'

36

Griessel gazed out at the Stellenbosch mountains, the student beside him momentarily forgotten.

At La Petite Margaux he had had a vague suspicion that it could have been more than one assailant, but the cobra on the bullet casings had muddled his thinking. The same engraving, the same shooter. That was the logical assumption, though instinct had argued against it. He had made the same mistake as Interpol. And their report had reinforced his error.

He should have known. Two highly trained bodyguards, a reasonably good security system, the abduction of a man who did not want to be caught at all costs – naturally there would have been more than one operator. Now it made absolute sense.

Cobra was not one killer for hire. It was a group.

That explained superintendent Marie-Caroline Aubert's speculation over the different pistols used. And that there were hits that did not carry the Cobra trademark.

It changed a whole lot of things.

Also the fact that a single operator would always be harder to catch. But three men working together, who had to stay together, travel together, move around together, were perhaps slightly more obvious.

Griessel looked back at Nadia Kleinbooi's door, saw the student waiting there eagerly. He would have to temper that enthusiasm.

'Johan, I want you to understand one thing very clearly,' he said strictly. 'You can't repeat anything of my conversation with the brigadier. It's very sensitive information. If it leaks out, I'll have to arrest you for obstructing the law.'

'Never, Captain.' But Griessel could see his disappointment.

He took his wallet out of his jacket pocket and took out a twenty-rand note.

'We need to make one more call,' said Griessel, and held out the money.

'That's OK, Captain, keep it,' said the student.

'You're going to hear more things that you would love to tell your friends, but if I hear you've repeated a single word, I will lock you up. You stay off Twitter, and off Facebook and What's Up . . .'

'WhatsApp.'

'That's right. Understand me?'

'Yes, Captain.' Solemnly.

'Thank you.' Griessel looked at the phone in his hand. It was a BlackBerry Z10. The screen had locked.

'Can you show me how to phone from this thing?'

The student tapped in his code, brought up the dialling panel and passed it to Griessel. He phoned the DPCI's land-line number, and asked to speak to Mbali Kaleni.

The first thing she said was: 'Benny, Ulinda Radebe called from O. R. Tambo. He thinks he has identified the Cobra.'

Tyrone watched Hoodie and Nadia slowly climb the steps under the Shoprite banner and walk towards Bobby.

Don't look at me, Bobby – whatever you do, don't look at me.

Bobby stood still. He looked worried. He looked around, but he didn't look at Tyrone.

'When the guy has given you the card, tell him he can go.'

Hoodie did not answer.

Nadia still looked as though she was in a daze. She kept looking down, as if she didn't know what was going on.

Had they drugged her?

Four metres from Bobby. Three. Two.

Bobby noticed them.

Don't look at me, Bobby. Please.

Hoodie and Nadia reached Bobby.

'You have the card?' Tyrone heard Hoodie say.

A fat couple obscured his view for a second. When he could see again, Bobby was taking his hand out of his pocket. Too far away to see if the memory card was in it, but Hoodie put out his hand, it looked as if he took something.

'You can go,' Tyrone heard Hoodie say.

Bobby's head turned in Tyrone's direction.

Don't look at me, you idiot.

But Bobby looked at Tyrone, as if he wanted to know if he had earned his money, if he could really go now.

Tyrone ducked behind the corner of the shop. He didn't know if Hoodie had seen him. He counted one, two, three, four, five. He peered around the corner of the shop. He saw Bobby was walking away towards Kruskal. He would be heading for Hassan Ikar, the Somalian, for his pay. That's for sure.

Well done, whitey, even though you did look when you shouldn't have.

'Your sister not here yet?' The voice took Tyrone by surprise, because all his attention was on Hoodie.

It was the security man with the red beret. He came and stood right in front of him, too close, no respect for personal space, this guy, so that he couldn't see Nadia.

Tyrone shook his head. He couldn't talk now, it would confuse Hoodie, it would make him look around. And identify Tyrone, if he hadn't already.

'I can't let you stand here for so long,' said Red Beret. 'You must go wait on the platform.'

Probably a complaint from a shop owner: What's that guy doing there so long?

Tyrone nodded. *Go away, please,* he thought.

Red Beret stared at Tyrone in disapproval.

'OK,' said Tyrone. He covered the phone as much as he could. 'Just a few more minutes, please. She says she's almost here,' and he pointed at the phone.

For what felt like an eternity, Red Beret did not move. Then he walked away, to the left, with a smug swagger.

Tyrone looked anxiously at where Hoodie was standing.

Hoodie made Nadia hold the small laptop, right up against the row of bright yellow MTN logos of Hello Mobile's display window. The man's fingers were busy on the keyboard.

'Can you see that the memory card is in working order?'

'Wait,' said Hoodie.

Tyrone saw Red Beret standing on the other side of the passage, arms crossed, watching him with a dissatisfied scowl.

I'm running out of time, the trains are coming. How long would it take to check the memory card?

He quickly looked at the cellphone's clock: 15:04. Could it be? It felt like the whole thing had taken an eternity. He had nine minutes, maybe ten, before the Metrorail 3526 left for Cape Town. If the train was five minutes late. Please.

'The card is good,' said Hoodie at last over the phone.

'OK,' said Tyrone. 'The first letter of the password is "Y". Now tell Nadia to start walking towards the sports shop straight ahead. Sport Station. You can see it from where you are. And when she gets there, she must turn left, towards the station entrance. I can see her, and I will give you a letter for every step she takes, until she turns the corner. But you don't move. You stay exactly where you are. Or I will stop giving you the code.'

'OK.'

'Tell her.'

Five schoolchildren in rust brown jerseys and blazers walked between them. Then he saw Hoodie had the laptop in his left hand, and he was talking into Nadia's ear.

Nadia began to walk.

'The next letter is the number zero.'

Griessel had forgotten about Radebe and Ndabeni, who'd been sent to O. R. Tambo Airport. In the mix-up of the Waterfront shooting no one had thought to recall them.

'Ulinda sent a photo,' said Mbali to him over the student's phone, her voice excited. 'Taken at the airport's scanner. And it might be him, Benny. He arrived on Saturday morning, on a flight from Paris. He is wearing a grey baseball cap and dark glasses. A coloured man, very athletic. They matched the guy to the passport control records, and he is travelling under the name of Hector Malot, a French citizen. Vusi checked all the flights to Cape Town, and the same guy was on an SAA flight that arrived just after two on Saturday.'

'That's very good, Mbali,' said Griessel. 'Are Ulinda and Vusi still at O. R. Tambo?'

'Yes, Benny. We had to recall them, of course. They're waiting for their flight back.'

'Tell them to cancel the flight. Tell them Cobra isn't just one guy. There are at least three of them. We are going to need all their names.'

Tyrone gave Hoodie a letter for every step that Nadia took towards him.

'U.'

'M.'

'Zero.'

Hoodie wasn't writing anything down – the laptop was folded shut under his arm. It didn't make sense, but it wasn't Tyrone's problem.

'T.'

'H.'

'The number three.'

'R.'

Nadia was now in front of the door of Hair International, just five metres from the corner, only eight metres from him. She didn't look up, not to the left or the right. Just walked, slowly.

'F.'

'U.'

'C.'

That was when he saw Red Beret look at Nadia. Intently. And then he began to walk towards her.

37

Mbali asked him how he knew that the Cobra was not a single indi-vidual, and he said he was talking on a borrowed cellphone, he couldn't say right now.

'Oh. OK, Bennie, I will tell them.'

'Get them to call you from a pay phone first.'

'Of course.'

'What did Bones say? Is he in?'

'Yes, he's in.'

'Has Vaughn brought the phones yet?'

'No, we're still waiting.'

'Please tell him I'll be at Nadia Kleinbooi's flat. I'm going to try and find a caretaker to unlock the door, and then search it.' Griessel saw the student beside him shake his head. He gave the young man a querying look.

'You don't know Oom Stoffel,' said the student.

Red Beret walked right up to Nadia.

Tyrone knew why. She was moving like a sleepwalker, it looked as if there was something wrong with her.

'What is the next letter?' Hoodie asked over the phone.

Red Beret was next to Nadia. He said something to her, aggressively.

She looked at him in a daze.

'What is the next letter?' Hoodie sounded threatening.

Tyrone could not remember where he had been. 'Wait,' he said.

C. He had given the C last.

'K,' he said.

Red Beret gripped Nadia's arm.

She was startled, pulled away and looked around her, confusion on her face.

Tyrone knew he could no longer just stand there.

'The number three.' And he began to walk towards Nadia. Hoodie was going to see him, but he had no choice. 'There's one more letter. I will give it to you when Nadia is safe.'

He was close enough to hear Red Beret say to Nadia, 'Are you drunk?'

He reached them. 'Leave her alone,' said Tyrone. 'She's my sister. She's sick.'

Nadia looked at him. That's when he knew for sure they had drugged his sister. That was when his fear and anxiety gave way to fury.

'*Boetie*,' she said with a crooked smile.

'*Sussie*.' He felt like crying.

'She looks drunk to me,' said Red Beret.

Tyrone put his arm around Nadia. 'Come,' he said. 'We must hurry.' He pulled her along, they needed to get away. He knew Hoodie's eyes were on them now, the train was already at the platform, they would have to run for it. But Nadia didn't look like she could.

'Hey, I'm talking to you,' said Red Beret, and pulled his baton out of a ring on his wide black belt.

He wanted to tell the man to 'Fuck off', but he didn't.

'What is the last letter?' asked Hoodie over the phone.

They were around the corner, out of sight.

'R.' said Tyrone and cut the connection. Then he reached his arm around Nadia's back, took a firm grip of her shoulder, and pushed her carefully forwards so they could begin running.

Red Beret was next to them, the baton threatening. 'Stop,' he said.

And right in front of Tyrone stood the gunman from this morning, the guy from the Waterfront, the coloured one with the baseball cap and the eyes that made you shiver. He blocked the way to the station entrance. He had the same silenced pistol in his hand, and it was pointed straight at Tyrone's forehead.

Weird, was the word that stuck in his mind at that moment. How did he get here?

He ducked, instinctively jerking Nadia to get her out of danger. But she stumbled and a knee gave, weakened by drugs and the heavy bag of textbooks and stationery and who knew what. She fell, pulling him down with her.

The pistol's aim followed them. There was a shot, a muffled, almost apologetic noise, and his sister's body twitched as she fell back onto him.

Griessel and the young man walked down the stairs.

'Oom Stoffel is a *drol*,' said the student. 'Difficult arsehole. He'll never unlock for you. Unless you have ten documents saying you have permission from Nadia, her grandma, and the state president.'

'We shall see,' said Griessel.

'You can always threaten to shoot him too,' the student urged him on with relish.

Tyrone grabbed Nadia in his arms and screamed, all the fear, all the tension, all the despair released in a single, raging bellow.

People turned to look.

The gunman stood patiently, the pistol stretched out in front of him, waiting for Tyrone to keep still so that he had a clean shot.

Red Beret, hidden behind Tyrone and Nadia, stepped around them, his baton raised. He moved surprisingly fast for the somewhat plump body. He shouted a reprimanding '*Hhayi!*' The shooter's response was smooth and skilful. He aimed the pistol at the guard. He fired, just a fraction of a second before the baton hit his right wrist. Tyrone felt the blood spray over his face, saw Red Beret sink down, and the pistol clatter on the brick paving. The gunman swore, bent down to the ground, trying to pick up the pistol with his left hand; his right hand hung limply.

Tyrone kicked him with so much desperate violence that he lost his balance, because of the growing weight of Nadia in his arms. He knew that it was their only chance of survival. He hit the man against the side of his face, across his jawbone and cheekbone and temple, with the full length of the bridge of his foot. He felt the pain in his foot, and it gave him a moment of satisfaction. The gunman dropped like an ox.

Tyrone wanted to pick Nadia up and run.

The pistol lay right there in front of him.

He steadied his sister with his left arm, bent and picked up the firearm, quickly shoved it into the deep pocket of his trousers, then swept Nadia up, cradling her in his arms. He saw the blood on her left breast. '*Sussie.*'

It was a whisper, a sob. He had to get her to a hospital. The train was no longer an option. He ran to the right, to the eastern exit of Bellstar Junction, staggering under Nadia's now-unconscious weight.

He saw the delivery van in Charl Malan Street, a white Kia. Two brothers unpacking cartons at the back. Ossie's Halaal Meats on the side. He staggered up to them and cried out, 'My sister, please, she's been shot, I have to get her to a hospital.'

He knew his voice was high and shrill, he felt the wet blood spatter on the left side of his contorted face, Nadia's blood glistening on his hand.

The two men stopped what they were doing and stared at Tyrone, mouths open.

He ran up to them.

'Please, my brother,' he begged. 'She's all I have.'

The older one reacted first. 'Get in,' he said. He looked at his colleague, and pointed at the boxes on the pavement. 'Look after the goods, *nè*.'

Oom Stoffel, the caretaker, was a sour old man, somewhere in his sixties. His flat was opposite, in Block One. He opened the door, without a word, didn't even look at them. Just pointed at the sign on the wall. *Caretaker. Hours: 09:00 to 12:00. 13:00 to 15:00.* He made a big show of looking at his watch. Then he began closing the door again.

Griessel put a foot between the door and the frame. 'SAPS,' he said. 'And if you do that again, you're in trouble.'

Now Oom Stoffel looked at him under heavy raised brows. 'SAPS?'

'That's right. I am Benny Griessel . . .' He took out his wallet and identity card.

'He's from the Hawks, Oom,' said the student helpfully.

'The what?'

'The Directorate of Priority Crimes Investigation,' said Griessel, and displayed his card. 'Will you please come and unlock number twenty-one. It's a crime scene now.'

Oom Stoffel took his reading glasses from his breast pocket, put them on and studied the identity card.

'He's *mos* genuine from the Hawks, Oom,' said the student.

'Where are your papers?' the caretaker asked Griessel.

'Here.' He waved the identity card.

'No, where is your warrant?'

'Are you certain you want to be difficult, *meneer*?'

'I know the law,' he said stubbornly.

'Then you should be acquainted with Articles Twenty-Five to Twenty-Seven of the Criminal Procedure Act.'

'All I know is, you can't just go in there.'

'Now listen to me, *meneer* . . .'

'He's got a gun,' said Johan, the student.

'Shut up,' said Griessel. He looked at Oom Stoffel again. 'If you want to sleep in your own bed tonight, you had better listen. Article Twenty-Five, Three B says I may enter the premises if I believe the obtaining of a warrant will subvert the purpose of it. Article Twenty-Seven says I can lawfully search any person or any premises, I can use such force as may be reasonably necessary to overcome any resistance against such search or against entry of the premises, including the breaking of any door or window of such premises, provided that I first audibly demand admission to the premises and notify the purpose for which I seek to enter such premises. I'm telling you now, in the presence of a civilian witness, the legal resident of number twenty-one is the victim of an alleged crime. Unlock it, or I will lock you up, and break down that door.'

'He's not joking, Oom Stoffel,' said the student, enjoying every moment.

Tyrone held Nadia tightly.

'Gangstas?' asked the guy at the steering wheel.

'Something like that,' said Tyrone, his eyes on Nadia's face.

'To Tygerberg?'

'No, uncle. There's a private hospital just on the other side here, near the police.'

'Louis Leipoldt. It's a Mediclinic. Those people are expensive.'

'I know, uncle. But she's my sister.'

'OK.'

And just before they turned off in Broadway, Tyrone remembered Bobby. He dug his cellphone out of his pocket, and phoned Hassan Ikar.

38

Tyrone knew the Mediclinic people would phone the cops. It was the law, if a gunshot wound came in. That's why he was anxious about how long it was taking.

They had put Nadia on a stretcher in Emergency. He also told them someone had drugged her, they ought to know.

An administrative aunty approached and asked, 'What drugs?'

He said he didn't know.

'What drugs does she use, sir?' In white Afrikaans, adamant and strict.

It made him angry. 'She doesn't *use* drugs. They forced her to take them. She's studying to be a doctor, she's not some *hierjy*. Get her to the doctors now, please.'

'Calm down, sir. First we need the details of her medical aid,' said the admin aunty.

He pulled out his wallet, took out three thousand rand in cash, and gave it to her. 'There is no medical aid, aunty. This should cover it for today. If you need more, let me know, but please, get her in there to the doctors.'

Her heart softened a bit and she said to the nurses, 'Take her in.' She turned back to Tyrone. 'It's a gunshot wound, we have to notify the *polieste*.' This time speaking naturally, *Kaaps*.

'Tell them, aunty, she has nothing to hide. She's pure class.'

'Your girlfriend?'

'No, aunty. She's my sister. I'm rubbish, but she isn't.'

'*Nee, wat*, a man who looks after his sister like that, he's also pure class.'

'Thanks, aunty.'

'Where did they shoot her?'

He hesitated.

'I have to ask, because the police will want to know.'

'Down by the station, aunty.'

'Bellville?'

'Yes, aunty.'

She shook her head in horror. 'Gangstas . . .' She looked at him. '*Ai*, do you know how you look, with all that blood all over you?'

'No, aunty.'

'Here's her bag, you'll have to keep it with you, or let us book it in for safekeeping. Come, let's get you cleaned up, then you will give me all her details for admission.'

He told her he had to go to the toilet first. He wanted to move the pistol from his trouser pocket to the backpack he had bought from Hassan Ikar. Then he came back and sat with the admin aunty to give her the admission details. And also so he could know when she phoned the cops.

Oom Stoffel muttered, all the way down the stairs of Block One, across the car park, and up the stairs of Block Two. Under his breath, but Griessel picked up a phrase here and there. 'Can't recite the numbers of the laws, but I know my rights . . .' was more or less the drift.

He knew people like the caretaker, wielding a little bit of power that they obstinately abused, after a lifetime of being victimised in the same way. There was only one way to deal with them: give them a dose of their own medicine. Then they crumbled.

Griessel let the man go ahead while he fetched his homicide case from the boot of the BMW. The student trotted enthusiastically after him.

They rejoined Oom Stoffel at Nadia's door, where he was searching through a big bunch of keys for the right one. He found it, unlocked, stood back, and waved his arm theatrically.

'There you go,' he said.

Griessel took a pair of gloves out of his case. 'Please wait for me here.'

'I have things to do,' said the caretaker.

'Like what?' asked the student.

'You've got no business here,' said Oom Stoffel.

'I'm supporting the Hawks,' said the student.

The old man snorted.

Griessel picked up the case, opened the door, and went in. He closed the door behind him again, with a measure of relief.

The flat was tidy. A small kitchenette to the right, a sitting room ahead, and the bedroom behind that, to the left.

He was in a hurry, gave it only a cursory going over. He saw no sign that anyone had searched the place yet. It looked as if she had been the last one here.

A porridge bowl, spoon, and coffee mug were on the drying rack, washed. A few photos were stuck on the fridge. Group photos of four or five students. In one he recognised Tyrone Kleinbooi, from this morning's video clips. He was with a girl he assumed to be Nadia; Tyrone's arm was draped protectively around his sister's shoulder.

Griessel opened his case, took out a plastic evidence bag. He took the photo off the fridge and put it in the bag.

In the sitting room there was a beige couch, covered in corduroy, old and a bit frayed, but clean. And a pine wood coffee table. Two books on it. The uppermost one showed an attractive woman eating pasta from a bowl. *Nigellissima: Instant Italian Inspiration.*

He went into the bedroom.

A single bed, made up. A teddy bear propped against the cushion stared at him with all-knowing glass eyes. An old easy chair covered in faded red material. One of the wooden legs was mended, soundly, but not very skilfully. Against the wall was a long table of Oregon pine. There was a mouse and a power cable, but no laptop. Textbooks in a row against the wall. More books on a small bookshelf below the window.

Griessel opened the built-in wardrobe.

The subtle scent of a pleasant perfume. A young girl's clothing filled half the space. Jeans, blouses, a few dresses, a denim jacket. Below, six pairs of shoes. To the left, on different shelves, neatly piled and arranged, were her underwear, jerseys, T-shirts, and a shelf with perfume, a jewellery case. And a cellphone box for an iPhone 4. He picked up the box and slid it open.

Inside was a Vodacom information card for a pre-paid account. With the IMEI and phone number on it.

He held it between his fingers and walked to the front door. He went outside. Oom Stoffel stood there, arms folded, face thunderous. Beside him, the student looked very pleased with himself.

'Can you please phone this number?' asked Griessel and showed him the Vodacom card.

'And now? Don't the police have their own phones?' asked Oom Stoffel.

'His one is broken. So I'm helping him,' said the student.

'Typical.' A disparaging snort. 'God save our country.'

'Please pass it to me as soon as it rings,' said Griessel.

The student phoned, listened for a moment, and gave Griessel the phone.

He stood listening to it ring, without much hope.

They sat in front of a computer at Admissions, Tyrone opposite the admin aunty.

'Is that your phone?' she asked when the ringtone sounded.

He was very tired. The terrible day weighed down on him, a veil over his thoughts. And he was worried about his sister – his thoughts were inside with her. 'No,' he said.

Then he realised the sound came from Nadia's bag. Hoodie must have pushed it in there. He leaned over, took it out, looked at the screen. A number on the display. If it was one of Nadia's contacts there would have been a name.

'You'd better answer,' said the aunty.

'Hello,' he said.

'Who's this?' The voice of a white man.

'Who do you *want* to talk to?'

'To Nadia Kleinbooi.' There was authority in the voice.

'She isn't available.' Adrenaline flowed again and the fatigue was gone.

'Who am I talking to now?'

Tyrone smelled police. He knew the aunty was listening, but he had to get off this line. They could do a lot to trace the call; they would know where he was.

'Hello?' said the voice. 'Who am I talking to?'

'OK,' said Tyrone for the benefit of the aunty. 'OK, I'll give her the message. OK, bye.'

He ended the call and put the phone back in Nadia's book bag.

'One of her classmates,' he said. 'Where were we?'

★ ★ ★

Griessel stood with the phone in his hand and he thought: that was Tyrone. It had to be. He didn't know how it worked, he didn't know how it all fitted together, but his instinct told him that was the pickpocket. The man had a shade of Cape Flats in that accent, and something else: a caution, a suspicion, a wariness.

And he was somewhere with people that he could not speak in front of.

The Cobras had Tyrone too.

That was the only explanation.

He took out his wallet again, fished out thirty rand in notes and pushed them into the pocket of the student's leather jacket.

'No, Captain, really it's not . . .'

Griessel was tired of struggling with other people's phones, with the whole bloody situation. 'Take it,' he said. Then he realised how it sounded. 'Please. I have to make one more call.'

'Any time. It's our duty to help the police,' said Johan, looking pointedly at Oom Stoffel.

The old man snorted again.

Griessel phoned Mbali.

When she answered, he said: 'We need to track a number, Mbali. Very urgently.'

'*Ingels*,' said Oom Stoffel. 'There's your problem, right there, when our police have to start talking English . . .'

39

He had to get away from here, Tyrone thought.

He must phone PC Carolus and ask how long it would take someone to check where a phone was, but he thought it would be quick, the cops just checked on their computers. He might have ten minutes or so, then they would be here.

'Aunty, please, I have to get back to work, they gonna fire me, but first I must know if my sister is OK.'

'I've *mos* got your number here on the system. I'll let you know.'

He thought. The cops would swarm all over this place. And they would find out everything. That Nadia was here in the hospital, and that she had been shot. They would interview her when she recovered. And they would tell her her brother was a pickpocket, and that he had shot people at the Waterfront, and she was going to get a shock, in her state. And there was sweet blow-all he could do about it, 'cause she needed serious medical attention, he couldn't get her out of here now.

But at least she'd be safe. And he would phone her, and he would tell her nothing was like it seemed, first she must recuperate, then he would tell her everything.

Now he had to get out of here. Get rid of this new phone, 'cause the number was on Nadia's phone, from when he talked to Hoodie. He was traceable.

He must become invisible again. So he could do what had to be done.

It was payback time.

'Are you OK?' asked the aunty.

'Can I have your number, aunty, please; I'm not allowed to take calls at work.'

'Now what kind of work is that? Surely they will understand if your sister is in the hospital.'

'Paint contractors, those people are *kwaai*, aunty.'

She shook her head over the unfairness of it. Then she grew serious. 'The police will want to talk to you. About what happened.'

He thought about that. 'OK, give them my number. But I have to go. If aunty could just quickly go and see if she is *orraait*. Please.'

'Sign here so long,' she said, and pointed at a document she had printed out. 'Then I'll see what I can do.'

Griessel had told Mbali to keep Vaughn Cupido at the DPCI head office when he returned with the cellphones. He stretched yellow crime-scene tape across the door of number twenty-one and threatened dire consequences if the caretaker allowed anyone access.

'Except if they also throw article sixty B around here,' the old man muttered

Griessel ignored the sarcasm.

He thanked the student again.

'Any time, Captain, any time.'

'And not a word from you.'

'My lips are zipped.'

For how long, Griessel wondered, and ran down the stairs to the BMW. He put the siren on, stuck the blue light on the dashboard, and drove off as fast as he could.

On the N1, just beyond the Winelands Engen, he switched his cellphone back on. It beeped, and he saw that he had four voice messages.

They would have to wait, he didn't want to waste time putting on his earphones now.

Tyrone grew anxious, as the minutes ticked away, the cops must be on their way already. His ears were pricked for sirens, but he heard nothing.

Maybe it takes a while to trace a phone. And if he just ran out of here, the aunty would know he was not innocent.

To his immense relief she returned with a smile. 'Your sister is going to be OK, they say she was very lucky, that bullet must have hit something in front of her, because she only has broken ribs over here.' She indicated the side of her upper torso. 'There's no internal damage or bleeding there, just external. And it's very sore, the ribs. She's stable so you can stop worrying.'

Stop worrying. Not for a while.

'Thank you very much, aunty,' he said while he tried to think what the bullet could have hit. He recalled that moment, Nadia stumbling and falling in front of him, the pistol making its dull bark. And then he had a hunch and picked up her bag, and began unpacking it on the admin desk. He held up the thick textbook: *Chemistry & Chemical Reactivity*. Kotz, Treichel & Weaver. At the top end was a mark, a piece of the thick hard cover and a chunk of pages were shot away.

'Saved by chemistry,' said the aunty. 'Can you believe it.'

'I'm going to leave the bag here, aunty. So she can get it when she wants her stuff.'

'That's fine.'

'How long is she going to be here?'

'I can't say myself, but I guess four or five days.'

'How much money must I still bring, aunty?'

'For safety sake, another three thousand, then we can just settle at the release.'

He didn't think he would be here at the release, he was a wanted man. And a hunted man. But he said 'OK', thanked her, said goodbye, and left.

On the N1, at a hundred and forty-five kilometres per hour, disgust overcame Benny Griessel. At himself, and at the SSA. It was their fault that he couldn't use his phone. That he had to make calls in front of two idiots. With a *fokken* borrowed phone.

He should have phoned Nadia's number again. He should have talked to Tyrone. If it was Tyrone. But who else could it be? A straight line of reasoning ran to Tyrone. The bullet casings at the abduction scene showed it was the Cobras. The eyewitness said it was a coloured girl who was kidnapped. The Cobras had been in Tyrone's rented room in the Bo-Kaap, and they knew Nadia was studying at Stellenbosch. They were looking for her. And they found her. To get at Tyrone, because he had something they wanted. The Cobras were foreigners. They didn't speak Afrikaans. It had to be Tyrone.

Somehow or other he had got hold of his sister's phone.

Borrowed maybe?

Didn't make sense. He should have phoned again. He should have said: 'Come in. We won't arrest you for anything, just come in, and tell us everything. We aren't after you, we want the Cobras. And your sister.'

But it was the one number rule that he could not call from his own phone. Because it would give the SSA a short cut.

He swore and turned off the N1, onto Durban Road, the sirens still wailing. The traffic opened up for him. He just hoped Cupido was already there with the new cellphones.

'*Jissis*,' said PC Carolus. 'What have you got yourself into?'

Tyrone walked up Duminy Street, on the way to catch a taxi on Frans Conradie Drive, cellphone to his ear.

'Nothing I can't handle. Tell me now, what info can they get from a cellular number?'

'Everything, Tyrone. Where you are, where you've been. Who you phoned, who phoned you. SMSs, the works. They can even read your SMSs, brother, so I hope you kept it clean.'

'OK, how long will it take?'

'Depends. Who are the people who want to trace your phone?'

'I don't know them.'

'Now you're lying to me. Is it private individuals or the cops?'

'What's the difference?'

'The cops have to get a warrant first. That takes time. Private individuals can do what they like, if they have the right equipment. Within half an hour, then they find you.'

He wanted to ditch the phone. Now. Because these guys, Hoodie and the Waterfront shooter, you didn't know what they could do. They got Nadia so fast, they knew where his room was, they stalked him there at the station. They were sly bastards. And they wanted him dead.

'OK, thanks, PC . . .'

'Don't thank me. Just stop all the monkey business. You're not a player, you're a pickpocket, for fuck's sake.'

Griessel found Cupido in Mbali's office busy putting SIM cards into cellphones.

Mbali was talking on the land line. 'Alvarez,' she said into the receiver. 'With a "z" at the end. No, I'm not going to hold. This is a serious police matter. You stay on the line, and give me the information . . . You know I'm a police officer because I am telling you I am. And I don't need a room number, I just want to know if you have a booking . . .' She looked up at Griessel and shook her head in frustration.

'Vaughn, I need to use a phone.' Griessel pointed at the cellphones on the desk.

'This one is ready. Take it for yourself.' He passed one to Benny. 'Battery's not completely charged yet. ZTE F Nine Hundred, sorry, Benna, it's all I could get. Earphones are still in the plastic.'

Griessel had never heard of a ZTE. It was a simple phone with a keyboard. At least he would know how to use it.

'Thanks,' he said as he took Nadia's Vodacom information card out of his pocket.

He phoned the number.

It rang for a long time.

'Thank you,' said Mbali over the land line. 'That wasn't so hard,' and she put the receiver down.

'Hello?' said a woman's voice over Griessel's ZTE.

'Nadia?' he said in surprise.

'No, this is Sister Abigail Malgas of the Louis Leipoldt Mediclinic. Who's speaking?'

Mbali's office door flew open and Bones's face appeared. 'I've found Lillian Alvarez,' he said in triumph. 'Protea Hotel Fire & Ice!, New Church Street.'

'Hello?' said Sister Malgas. 'Are you there?'

40

You're not a player, you're a pickpocket for fuck's sake.

Not a player?

Tyrone stood in front of Brights Electrical in Frans Conradie Drive and he thought, sure, he was a pickpocket. And usually he lived according to Uncle Solly's code. *Steal from the rich. Never use violence. Be kind to the less fortunate.*

Yes, he had never been a player. Until today. Until these guys changed the game. Till they introduced a whole new set of rules. Until they shot him and chased him. Until they messed with his sister, kidnapping and drugging her, and he didn't want to think what else. And then they shot her too.

Enough is enough. Code or no code, you don't do that. Not to the Kleinboois of Mitchells Plain.

Now he was a player. Now they would pay. Because now Nadia was safely in hospital, the police would be on the scene there soon, and he was beyond fear. Now he was the hell-in.

He called his old phone number, and he hoped they still had it, and that it was on. The phone rang and rang, until at last Hoodie answered it.

'Yes.' All formal and semi pissed off, like a man taking a call from his mother-in-law. And Tyrone liked that, because he knew Hoodie would not be pleased to hear from him. Because he had kicked Baseball Cap a *snotskoot* that he hoped gave the cunt a migraine for a week.

'Listen, motherfucker, did you think I'm stupid?'

'What do you want?'

'It's what you want. I have a small surprise for you.'

'Yes?'

'I'm not stupid. I knew that a guy who just walks in and shoots people is a crazy motherfucker. So I got myself a little insurance.'

'What insurance?'

'That ZIP file on the card is bullshit. You used the password I gave you?'

'Yes.'

'And you saw another ZIP file?'

'Yes.'

'If you use the same password I gave you, it will open, sesame. And you will see a hundred and two high-res, full-colour photographs of the beauty of Cape Town, for your viewing pleasure. You want to do that now, to see if I'm pulling your chain?'

Silence over the line.

And Tyrone thought, Take that, MoFo, put that in your pipe and smoke it.

It was a while before the man asked: 'Where is the original file?' But cool and calm.

'I have it right here, in the famous stolen wallet, motherfucker. Do you want it?'

'You are a dead man.'

It was just a statement, no emotion, and Tyrone shivered, but he said, 'Fuck you. Do you want the original file?"

A heartbeat of silence, then, 'Yes.'

'Then you are going to pay.'

'How much?'

It was a question he had thought deeply about, all the way from the Mediclinic. His gut feel was one million, but then he thought, these guys are not local, that accent is continental, they work in euros and dollars, one million is chump change.

'Two hundred thousand euros. That's about two point four million rand. And that's how I want it. Local currency.'

No hesitation. 'That is not possible.'

'Tough shit, motherfucker. Then you can kiss the ZIP file goodbye. Hang on to my phone. I will call you again later tonight, in case you change your mind.'

And he took the phone he had bought from the Somali, still switched on, and he dropped it in the dustbin in front of Brights Electrical. Let the cops or the Hoodie gang trace it now.

Fuck them all.

He ran for a taxi.

★ ★ ★

In Mbali's office he held his hand up in the air for silence. He said to Sister Abigail that he was Captain Benny Griessel of the SAPS Directorate of Priority Crimes Investigations, and they were urgently looking for Nadia Kleinbooi.

'Yes, the phone belongs to Nadia. You are very lucky, Captain, I was on the way to take her personal effects to storage when you phoned. She was admitted about an hour ago for a gunshot wound. We have already reported it to the Bellville Station. They said they would come as soon as—'

'Is it serious?' asked Griessel, while his colleagues stared at him in silence.

'No, thank goodness, it's not critical. They are busy treating her wound now, but she is conscious.'

'Sister, thank you very much. We're on our way.' He ended the call and told his colleagues the news. Mbali said something in Zulu that sounded like a prayer of thanks.

'Bones, is Lillian Alvarez at the hotel?'

'I didn't ask, Benny. But she has definitely checked in.'

'Vaughn, can you and Bones go and find out?'

'Of course we can,' said Bones enthusiastically. He was a member of the Statutory Crimes group of the Hawks' Commercial Crimes branch. For the most part his daily routine involved wrestling with financial statements, but like most Hawks detectives he would never pass up a chance to be part of a violent crimes investigation.

Cupido laughed. 'There's a phone and a charger for everybody. Watch the batteries, plug them in whenever you can. I'll drop off the Giraffe's on the way out. And I'll SMS the numbers to everybody.'

Griessel thanked him and said to Mbali, 'Let's go talk to Nadia.'

The taxi stopped in front of Parow's small, grey Metrorail station, Tyrone got out and walked straight to Station Street, nowadays a lively pedestrian market with a host of colourful stalls. It was different from Bellville, here it was mostly South Africans doing business – in cheap Chinese bric-a-brac, vegetables, fruit, sweets, cigarettes. But between the butchers, fast food, clothing and furniture shops that flanked the street, there were at least seven cellphone shops. And one of them was Moosa Mobile.

That was where he went, as fast as he could, even though he felt the fatigue in every fibre of his body, and the pain across his back, even though he wished he could just lie down on a soft bed somewhere and go to sleep.

Eat your veggies first, Ty. Work, then play.

That's what I'm doing, Uncle Solly.

He had come to Moosa Mobile because, in his industry he had heard that if you want to peddle a hot phone in the northern suburbs, Moosa was the fence to see. Tyrone didn't do business in this area, so Moosa didn't know him. But he was looking for three second-hand phones that were not traceable.

He walked in and said straight out what he wanted. And the little man gave him that look, and he knew he looked awful, but at least no one was going to take him for an undercover cop. The man took out three phones from the back, no boxes, no trimmings, just the instruments and their chargers. Cheap stuff, that the little man put in a Pick 'n' Pay plastic bag. Then Tyrone bought three prepaid SIM cards: Vodacom. MTN. Cell C. He put sixty rands of airtime on each one.

Then he walked to the stalls and bought a small, cheap travel case, two shirts, white and blue. A smart pair of black trousers, a grey pullover, a purple windcheater – because that was the only colour they had in his size – six pairs of underpants, four pairs of black socks, and a dark grey tweed jacket. Because a jacket, Uncle Solly used to say, is the ticket.

And then he walked back to the station. He would have liked to be near Nadia. But it wouldn't help him; he couldn't afford to go near there, that's what the cops would expect. But still, the urge to be close to her was strong. To protect her. But he must do the smart thing. The northern suburbs were a foreign country. He must get back to the city. That was his hunting ground. That was where he was at home.

Sister Malgas told Griessel and Mbali what she knew. Someone had drugged Nadia Kleinbooi, and then she had been shot, at Bellville Station. Her brother Tyrone had brought her in.

Griessel took out the photo of Tyrone and Nadia from his jacket pocket, and showed it to her.

'Yes, that's the brother.'

He asked if Tyrone was still around, but he already knew what the answer would be.

Had he left a contact number?

Sister Malgas said the number was on the system – she looked it up and gave it to him. 'But he can't take calls.' She explained about a strict boss at a paint contractor.

Griessel nodded as if he believed it, and asked if they could see Nadia.

No, they would have to wait. Perhaps in the next hour.

She had spoken of Nadia's personal possessions. Could they look through them?

She would ask the superintendent. She made the call, got the OK, and went to fetch them.

While he waited, Griessel phoned the SC of Bellville police station to get the details of the shooting. He heard that a security guard had been fatally wounded, and a girl had been admitted to Louis Leipoldt. That was all the station commander could say for sure now, because his detectives were still at the scene, busy questioning witnesses. But he thought it was gang-related, most likely drugs.

'Colonel, at what time did this take place?'

'Just after three.'

While he had been in Stellenbosch, the Cobras had shot people, less than a kilometre from the Hawks' headquarters.

'We are at Louis Leipoldt now to interview the wounded girl. If you retrieve any bullet casings, let me know. And when the detectives are finished, ask them to phone me. We suspect the case is related to an urgent matter that we are investigating.'

'I'll do that.'

Sister Malgas approached with a bulging shoulder bag, which she put down on the desk in front of them. Mbali took out rubber gloves from her equally large handbag, pulled them on, and began to unpack Nadia's belongings: textbooks on biology, chemistry, physics, and maths.

'Look here, the bullet hit the book,' the sister pointed out.

Two notebooks. A bright yellow zipper bag for pens and pencils. A transparent lunchbox with a sandwich and two sticks of dried fruit. A charger for an iPhone, and the phone itself. A small toilet bag with a comb, make-up, and women's things. A purse, of denim fabric, with Nadia's student card, a cash card from FNB, a few cash slips for groceries from Checkers, prepaid airtime from Vodacom, and just over a hundred and fifty rand in cash. Two packs of chewing gum, one half empty. A single condom. And last, a key ring with the black and white yin and yang symbol on it, with a round chip for an electronic gate, and a key that would probably fit her apartment's front door.

Griessel took the phone and began to look at the call register. TYRONE was listed for all the calls from ten o'clock this morning and just after one. Her brother had been phoning her continuously. Or she him. After that, numbers that were not identified in her contacts. The last call, before his own, new phone number appeared, was just before five.

He saw that there was not much charge left in the battery, but he used Nadia's phone in any case to call Tyrone's number

Perhaps he would answer.

It rang for a long time, and then went over to voicemail.

'Hi, this is Ty. You're looking for me. Why?'

The same voice that had answered Nadia's phone a while back.

With the leaden feeling of frustration and disappointment he rang off, without leaving a message.

This whole thing had played out at Bellville Station. And David Patrick Adair's death warrant had been signed there.

41

'Cool,' said Vaughn Cupido as they walked into the Protea Hotel Fire & Ice! and he spotted all the neon lights, the slick fittings in glass and wood.

'Funky,' said Bones.

They walked to reception, Cupido's long coat tails flapping.

Bones showed his SAPS identity card to the woman behind the desk. 'Major Benedict Boshigo, Priority Crimes Directorate of the SAPS.'

Cupido could hear how his colleague relished saying it. He knew Commercial Crimes were mostly desk jockeys; they didn't get the chance to flash plastic every day.

'How may I help you, sir?'

'We called earlier about a Miss Lillian Alvarez. You told us she has checked in.'

'That must be our reservation desk, sir.'

'Could you please give us her room number?'

The woman was uncertain. 'I . . . Our policy . . . I'll have to check with my manager, sir.'

'Could you call him for us?'

'Her. Just a minute . . .'

Cupido looked at an iPad that stood on the counter. Photos of the hotel's rooms flashed up and dissolved on a constant loop, and below that, Today's tariff: R899.00 per night (Room Only).

'Can't be doing too badly as a research fellow to be able to afford that,' said Cupido. 'Unless the rich, digital bank robber of a sugar daddy is paying.'

'That's nothing if you're from England, nè,' said Bones. 'Less than sixty pounds.'

Cupido only nodded, unwilling to discard his financial fraud and mistress theory.

A woman came walking up on black high heels, accompanied by the receptionist. Late thirties, black skirt and jacket, white blouse, thin smile. She knew the SAPS were not good news.

'Gentleman, how may I help?'

Cupido knew Bones was eager to speak. He stood back.

Bones explained the situation to the manageress. She asked for their identification cards, and studied them carefully.

She looked up. 'Is there some sort of trouble?'

'No, she was the victim of a pickpocket this morning. We would just like to talk to her.'

'A pickpocket? That does not seem like a priority crime.'

'Uh . . .' Bones was taken by surprise.

Cupido stepped forward. 'Ma'am, please, we don't want to do this the hard way.' His expression was stern, but he kept his voice low and courteous.

The manageress's smile disappeared entirely She looked at Cupido, thought for a moment, then nodded to the receptionist. 'You can give them the room number.' While the younger woman consulted the computer, the manager said, 'If there is something I should know . . .'

'We'll tell you, of course,' said Cupido. 'Thank you.'

Griessel and Mbali had to wait in the hospital restaurant until they could question Nadia Kleinbooi.

They walked from Emergency in Voortrekker Road to the new wing of the hospital on Fairway Road. He walked half a step behind his colleague, still trying to process and express his disappointment. At least the girl was safe, he thought.

And he hadn't had a drink today, though it had been close, so fucking close. He shivered as if someone had walked over his grave. It was always a danger, when there was so much chaos in an investigation, so much crazy rush and pressure. And trouble. He just mustn't let the lost battle with the Cobras mess with his head as well. Let him first test his theory on Mbali.

He looked at her, saw how she turned up the collar of the blue SAPS windcheater to keep out the cold late afternoon wind. There was a quiet strength in her walk. On the way to the hospital she had been very quiet, and in the interview with the nurse she was as solemn as ever. But he knew she had been like that from this morning, since the conversation in the car outside the house of the Schotsche Kloof murder. The disapproving frown, the determined, almost arrogant attitude had given way to something else – dismay.

He thought he knew what it was. And he understood.

He had walked that path himself, when he had been appointed by Murder and Robbery – and before he started drinking. Christ, it was a lifetime ago. He had been so full of fire and full of himself and his status, and his responsibility as a Servant of Justice. As Detective. Because when you worked at Murder and Robbery, your role was spelled with a capital letter. What you did *mattered*.

Part of his smugness was because he had started to run with the big dogs then. The living legends, the guys whose investigations, break-throughs, interrogation techniques, and witticisms were passed on in seminars, tearooms and bars, with an awed shake of the head. They were his role models and his heroes long before he joined them – in the beginning he was wide-eyed with respect and awe.

But the longer he worked with them – through intense days and nights, weeks and months where he learned to know them as they really were – the more he realised they had feet of clay. Each and every one of them. Everyone had weaknesses, deficiencies, demons, complexes, and syndromes that were laid bare by the inhuman pressure, the violence, the homicides, the powder keg of politics.

It was a depressing process. He had tried to fight against it, rationalise and suppress it. Later he realised that it was partly out of fear of the greater, inevitable disillusionment: if they were fallible, so was he.

And so was the system.

He remembered having a moment of insight, after a few years with Murder and Robbery, when his drinking was still under control and he still spent time pondering such things: life is one long process of disillusionment, to cure you of the myths and fictions of your youth.

Mbali was going through that now, and there was not much he could do.

But she would handle it better than he did. Women were stronger. That was another lesson he had learned over the years. And Mbali was one of the strongest of them all.

★ ★ ★

Cupido knocked on the door of Room 303 of the Protea Hotel Fire & Ice! Not loudly, not urgently; he wanted it to sound like room service.

In case Lillian Alvarez was there. Which he very much doubted.

They stood and waited in silence. He kept an eye on the peephole for a movement, a shadow.

Nothing.

Cupido raised his hand to knock again, perhaps a little harder. Then something moved in front of the peephole, and it went dark. A voice, female and frightened, said, 'Who is it?'

'Miss Alvarez?' asked Cupido.

'Yes?'

'I'm Captain Vaughn Cupido of the Hawks. We would like to talk to you, please.'

'Of the who?'

'The Hawks. The elite investigative unit of the South African Police Service.'

The peephole went light again. Bones and Cupido looked at each other. Cupido thought, it's the third floor, and the way he pictured it, there were no balconies or places to climb down, surely she wouldn't . . .

The door opened.

There she was, the woman from the Facebook photo and the Waterfront video. She was in her late twenties, sultry and beautiful, far more striking face to face.

She looked at them with big, dark eyes, from the lean marathon athlete to the tall, broad-shouldered Cupido. Emotion marred the beauty – her generous mouth twisted, her eyes red and tearful.

'Please tell me you really are from the police.'

'We are,' said Bones.

'Why are you here?'

'Because of David Adair, and what happened at the Waterfront this morning.'

'Is he OK? Please tell me he is OK.'

'We are trying to find him, ma'am. That's why we're here. We hope you can help us.'

'Oh God,' she said. And then her face crumpled and she began to cry. When Bones put his hand out to touch her shoulder in sympathy, she moved instinctively forward so he could hold her.

'I'm sorry,' she said.

'Don't be sorry. It must have been a rough day,' Bones comforted her and gave Cupido a meaningful look.

'I'm so glad you came,' she said, and began to sob.

Cupido thought, fuck, why wasn't he the one who'd put his hand on her shoulder?

The Sunwind restaurant was small. Griessel didn't know what the name had to do with a hospital, or with food. It was probably meant to refer to the Cape. But not this sunless winter.

They studied the menu at the self-service counter. Decided on the Grilled Beef or Chicken Burger, for only thirty rand. He chose the beef, Mbali asked for the chicken, 'But no rocket, please, and the chips must be hot.' But with less authority than usual.

While they waited for the food, he said, 'I want to test my theory on you.'

'Please, Benny.'

He said he thought she was correct: Lillian Alvarez had brought something from England that the Cobras wanted from David Adair. She would have handed it over to them at the Waterfront, but Tyrone Kleinbooi stole it. They knew the Cobras had been at the Schotsche Kloof house. Perhaps they had followed the pickpocket there, but then he managed to get away, with the stolen article still in his possession.

Mbali nodded. She was still in agreement.

He said there was a university account in Tyrone's room with Nadia's address on it. But the Cobras did not kidnap her at her flat, it had happened on campus. That didn't make sense. The only thing he could think of was that the Waterfront gunman left with Tyrone's rucksack. Something in that rucksack allowed them to identify Nadia, and to track her down on campus.

'It's possible,' said Mbali.

'And once they had Nadia, they knew how to contact Tyrone. To set up a meeting and an exchange: the article for his sister. That happened at the Bellville train station. And in the process, she was shot.'

'Yes.'

'It means they now have what they want, Mbali. They have no further need of Adair.'

Again she nodded, despondent. Then she said, 'We have the name on the passport for one of them. If he keeps travelling with that passport, we might be able to apprehend him at an airport.'

'Perhaps we should let the SSA know. They probably have better systems for tracking travellers.'

'No, Benny, don't do that,' said Mbali quietly, as their burgers arrived.

42

Cupido asked Lillian Alvarez to accompany them to the hotel lounge, knowing that an average hotel room was not designed to seat three people comfortably.

She asked them to excuse her for a moment, disappeared into the bathroom and closed the door.

They waited patiently.

'She's very beautiful,' whispered Bones.

'Yes,' said Cupido. 'But you're a married man.'

'And she smells nice.' Teasing, because he was the one she had embraced, and he had seen what an impression that had made on his colleague.

'You paid a big *lobola* to your wife's parents, pappie. Don't make me phone her,' said Cupido.

'But I'm allowed to look, *nè*. And allow myself to be hugged.'

'Strange accent,' said Bones. 'She's not English.'

'She looks like a South American.'

'Latin American,' Bones corrected him in his schoolteacher voice. 'When I was studying in the States . . .'

'Here we go again,' said Cupido, teasing, because Bones was known for being eager to talk about his time there – he was very proud of the B degree in Economics from Boston University's Metropolitan College.

Bones grinned. '*Ja, ja*. But seriously, in Boston there were lots of Latin American chicks. They were all stunning. And I wasn't married then . . .'

The bathroom door opened. Alvarez appeared. Her hair was brushed, her make-up and her self-confidence were restored. She was even more breathtaking now.

'Let me just get my bag. And my phone,' she said with a small, self-conscious smile when she became aware of their undisguised admiration.

'In case Professor Adair calls,' she said when she returned, putting her phone away in the brown leather handbag.

In the lift she asked, 'How did you find me? I mean . . .'

'We'll explain everything in a minute.'

'God, it's nice to get out of that room.' Her earlier emotions had subsided, and her relief was palpable.

'You've been in your room all day?' asked Cupido sympathetically.

'Yes. I didn't know if David – Professor Adair – would call . . .'

'Shame,' said Cupido, resting his hand gently on her shoulder.

She just smiled gratefully at him.

While Mbali ate, Griessel's burger and chips grew cold. Because his sense of duty made him call Nyathi – he knew he could not postpone it any longer.

He brought the colonel up to speed with the afternoon's events. The Giraffe clicked his tongue when he heard about Nadia Kleinbooi, and he said he would personally phone the commanding officers of the Stellenbosch and Bellville stations to ask them to keep the engravings on the cartridges quiet.

'I think they now have what they want, sir,' said Griessel. 'All we can do is to try and apprehend them if they attempt to leave the country through a major border post. If we can get a bulletin to Customs Admin. We have at least one possible passport we can track.'

'I'll do it myself, Benny.' A brief silence, and then a deep sigh. 'The question is, will they now kill Adair?'

'Yes, sir.' He knew they were thinking the same thing: if Adair's body was found somewhere in the Cape, there'd be hell to pay with the media. And if they started digging, and found out about the SSA's bullying tactics, and the Hawks' attempts to suppress evidence, everyone's name would be stinking mud, at home and abroad, all over again. And it always came out, because when there were slip-ups, there were always scapegoats and blame, to save other arses and reputations and careers.

'Thanks, Benny. I'll be here when you get back.'

They looked for a quiet corner in the lounge, on the modern sofas and chairs, and asked Lillian if she would like something to drink.

'Oh God, yes, a whisky, please.'

Cupido beckoned a waiter nearer, and ordered the drink for her, and coffee for them.

'We know you've been through a lot, Miss Alvarez,' Cupido said sympathetically, as he took his notebook and pen out of his inside pocket. 'We know what happened this morning at the Waterfront. We know you work for David Adair, at the university. And we know he has gone missing. But we would like you to tell us . . .'

'He's gone missing? I mean, I know something's not right, but I thought . . .'

She appeared agitated and looked to Cupido for an explanation.

'If we can hear your side of the story, we might be able to explain,' he said. 'Could you tell us, please?'

'You don't know where he is?'

'Not at this time. But perhaps you can help us find him. Please. Tell us what happened.'

'Well,' she said. 'I . . . Professor Adair called me on Monday morning, very early . . .'

'Ma'am, sorry, could you start with your . . . you work for him, is that right?'

'Yes. I'm his assistant.'

'Like a secretary?'

'No, no, I'm his research assistant. I'm doing my Masters Degree in Applied and Computational Analysis. I'm a research fellow at the Department of Applied Mathematics and Theoretical Physics, where Professor Adair teaches. He's my supervisor. But I also do research for him on some of his projects.'

Cupido noticed her leaning forward, focused and serious. And a little bit tense. And he thought, she keeps referring to the man as 'Professor Adair' in such a pointed way, every time the inflection just a little bit over-emphasised and forced. Or was that his imagination?

'You don't sound British at all,' said Bones.

'Oh, no, I'm from the United States.'

'Where in the US?'

'Kingsville in Texas. Small town, nobody's ever heard of it. It's near San Antonio.'

'I ran the Rock 'n' Roll Marathon in San Antonio,' said Bones. 'Pretty place. But the heat . . .'

'You know it?'

Cupido knew Bones was going to use the opportunity to bring up his studies again. He pre-empted him, 'If we can get back to Professor Adair?'

'Sure. Where were we?'

'How long have you worked for him?'

'Since the beginning of the Lent term.'

'When was that?'

'This past January.'

'And you see him every day?'

'Well, not every day. He is a very busy man. Maybe two or three times a week, at the department.'

'When did you last see him?'

'On the Thursday of the week before last.'

'Where?'

'At DAMTP.'

'On campus?'

'Well . . . yes, at his office.'

In his eleven years as a detective, Vaughn Cupido had questioned hundreds of people – first at the Mitchells Plain police station, later with the Organised Crime Task Force in Bellville South, and over the last few years with the Hawks. Thanks to this experience, and the many lectures and courses with the SAPS Forensic Psychology section, he had learned a great deal about the art of lying. He knew the ability to tell an untruth varied radically from person to person. Some did it so naturally, skilfully, and smoothly that you couldn't help but admire them, even after you had arrested them. Others telegraphed all the predictable signs of lying with an astounding clarity and awkwardness, but so totally oblivious to what they were doing, that they were still highly indignant if you confronted them about it. And then there were those who fell somewhere on the sliding scale between the two extremes. Lillian Alvarez was not an accomplished liar, but for an amateur she wasn't doing badly. It was not her eyes, her body language, or gestures that betrayed her, but the timing and tone of her words. That over-eagerness to be helpful, to please, that touch too much obvious sincerity: 'Look, see how honest I am.'

The way to handle people like this was to pretend you believed them, give them more rein, let them paint themselves into a corner.

'And he was . . . Did you notice anything different?'

'Not at all. He was his usual witty self. He can be very funny – he's always making mathematical puns . . .'

'I see,' said Cupido, as if he understood. 'And he didn't mention that he was going to travel?'

'No.'

'So, the next thing you hear from him, is the call yesterday morning?'

'No, Monday . . . Yes, yesterday! It seems longer . . . Well, I had an appointment with him last week, Tuesday, for a progress report, but he wasn't at the office, and nobody seemed to know where he was. But it's not all that unusual. Because of all the work he does for the financial industry, and the fight against terrorism, you know . . .'

'You mean his algorithm.'

'Exactly. Usually he'll send me a text or an email to cancel. But still, I didn't worry too much.'

The waiter brought the whisky and coffee. Bones reached for his wallet, but Cupido was faster. 'Keep the change,' he said.

When the man had gone, Cupido said, 'OK. And before his call yesterday morning, nobody contacted you about him?'

'No.'

'OK. Now, yesterday morning . . . You said it was very early. Can you remember the time?'

'It was around three o'clock in the morning. Maybe that's why it feels so long ago . . .'

'UK time?' Bones asked.

'Yes.'

'About five o'clock South African time?' said Bones.

'I suppose . . .'

'The call, was it from his own phone?' asked Cupido.

'How do you . . . ? Oh, you mean, did it show on my phone that it was him?'

'Yes.'

'That's a good . . . I can't remember. I don't think I looked. It was . . . He woke me up, so I was a bit sleepy.'

'Could you take a look now? On your phone?'

'Sure, I should have thought of that.' She opened her handbag and took out the phone. Her deft fingertips managed the screen with practised finesse, till she found what she was looking for.

'No,' she said in surprise. 'It's from a different number . . . And it was at seven minutes past three in the morning.'

'Could you read the number to me?'

She read out the number, which began with a +44. Cupido scribbled in his notebook.

'Do you recognise the number?'

'Not at all.'

'OK. So what did he say?'

'He apologised for the time of the call, and I said it's not a problem. Then he asked me if I could do him a big favour . . .'

'How did he sound?'

'Apologetic.'

'Not stressed?'

'No, I wouldn't say he was stressed out . . . He's very calm, always, so I . . . No, not stressed out.'

'OK. And then?'

'Well, I said of course I would do him a favour. And he said he's in a bit of a bind, it's very embarrassing, so it's a really big favour, and it's going to mean I have to travel halfway around the world, but he's asking me because I've said more than once that I would love to visit Africa, and if I don't feel comfortable, I should just say so, he would fully understand. So I said, wow, that sounds exciting, when did I have to go? And he said he's booked a flight for me . . . Well, you know, in that very polite British way, he actually said he really hopes I don't mind, but he's taken the liberty of booking a flight for me, and it leaves at seven thirty on Monday night, from Heathrow, for Cape Town in South Africa.'

43

Griessel was still eating, without enjoyment. Mbali pushed her empty plate away, wiped her fingers with the paper serviette, and said, 'Bones has found something interesting about David Adair.'

'Yes?'

'It might not . . . I'm trying to figure out what it means. Adair apparently belongs to a group of British scientists who are starting a protest group against government secrecy, and invasion of public privacy.'

Griessel raised his eyebrows, and Mbali continued, 'Bones and I thought it was strange too. Because Adair's algorithm does exactly that. It infringes on the privacy of anyone who uses banks.'

'They are *planning* to start a protest group?'

'Well, Bones says he only found one reference, and that is perhaps significant too. He says there was so much on the Internet about Adair and his protocol, and his algorithm, and his other academic work, that he almost missed it. He came across a small item in a weekly scientific newspaper, in the USA. It reported that a group of British scientists attended a conference on the Association . . . no, the . . . Project for Government Secrecy. It was held by an association or a federation of American scientists at the end of last year in St Louis. The leader of the British delegation was a political scientist, who told the newspaper that they were planning to start a similar project in the UK. And that they were very worried about their government's suppression of information, but also the hijacking of new technologies to infringe the privacy of citizens. The newspaper listed one of the British team members as a Professor D. P. Adair.'

Griessel tried to fit this information in with what they knew, but it would not make sense.

'I've been thinking, Benny, we know the UK ambassador has been talking to our minister of state security. And then MI6 and the SSA got involved very quickly, and we were taken off the case. So, now I wonder if this whole thing about Adair is maybe not about his banking software. I think it might be about government secrets. And with our government now passing legislation to be even more secretive . . . That's maybe why they are cooperating so enthusiastically with the British.'

Lillian Alvarez took a gulp of her whisky, and she said, 'That really woke me up, so I said, wow, that's a real surprise, it would be incredible, but don't I need a visa or something? And he said no, US citizens don't need a visa, and he will email me the ticket a little later. So, I asked him how long would I be staying, you know, I had to know what and how much to pack. But right then, he didn't answer me, he just said there's something else he needs me to do. So I said, sure, and he said, I should go to his office, and find a book. He told me where the book was on his shelf, and he told me where to look in the book, because there is a memory card, and I should take the card . . .'

'What kind of book?' asked Bones Boshigo.

'*On Numbers and Games.* It's the classic by John Horton Conway . . .' She saw that they didn't have the faintest idea what she was talking about. 'The famous British mathematician? He's one of David's – Professor Adair's – heroes, it's about game theory. The book, I mean. The memory card was stuck to the first page of the First Part, which is really the second part . . . Look, it's one of those mathematical inside jokes that he loves.'

'OK. So he said you must go fetch the card . . .'

'Yes. He asked me to go early, before anyone else arrived at the office. And that I shouldn't tell anybody about his call, or the memory card, he'll explain later, but it was about his security work, and discretion is the better part of valour. He apologised again, and thanked me, and said he would call again later that morning. And then he rang off.'

'Did he call you again?'

'Yes, at . . .' She suddenly remembered she could give the exact time, took out her phone again, and consulted the call register. 'At seven minutes past ten.'

'Yesterday morning?'

'Yes.'

'UK time?'

'Yes.'

'From the same number?'

'Yes.'

'OK, so after that first call, what happened?'

'I set the alarm for six o'clock, and tried to go to sleep again, which wasn't easy. I was pretty excited . . .'

'And not worried?'

'No, not at all. I mean, you know . . . I was getting this trip for free to a cool place, and it was helping this man I respect so very much with something very important and . . . well, interesting, you know? It was only later that I thought it was a little bit strange that he didn't say anything about where I was going to stay, or how long the trip would be . . . He's such an organised man, so very methodical . . .'

'And then you went to his office?'

'At seven sharp.'

'How did you get in?'

'I have a key.'

'And you found the book?'

'Yes.'

'And the memory card?'

'Yes. It was right where he said it would be.'

'Could you describe the card?'

'Well, you know, it was one of those SD cards, sixty-four gigabytes. Verbatim, blue and purple. Not the micro-SD. The regular size.'

'What was on the card?'

'I have no idea.'

'You didn't look?'

'No!'

'And what did you do with it?'

'I put it in my purse.'

'And you kept it there all the time?'

'Yes. Until this morning. The purse was in this bag . . .' She pointed at the handbag that lay between her thigh and the armrest of the chair. 'I thought it would be safe. I always keep the bag with me. Always. And then the asshole stole it this morning.'

He smiled at the word. 'Did anybody see you at Adair's office?'

'Not that I know of. Seven is early for the department.'

'And you went home?'

'Yes.'

'And he called again, just after ten?'

'Yes. But before that, I received an email with the electronic ticket for the flight.'

'From his usual email?'

'No, it was from a Morris guy, which was kind of strange, but then I asked him and he said, don't worry, it was just his security name.'

'Paul Morris Fifteen at Gmail?'

'Something like that. I can check . . .'

'No, that's fine. So you asked him this on the second call?'

'Yes.'

'How did he sound?'

'More together, I think.'

'What else did you talk about?'

'He said he would make a deposit for me, to pay for my accommodation in Cape Town, and asked me if I could do the hotel booking myself. And he said, if I wanted to, I could stay for the week, he'll deposit one thousand five hundred pounds into my account, which should cover a good hotel, and some spending money. Then he said my flight would arrive in Cape Town just before eight o'clock in the morning, and that when I got off the plane, I had to switch on my phone and check that it was working on the local networks, and send an email to the address from which the ticket was sent, the Gmail address. Just to say that I had arrived. He said this was very important, and that I should then take a cab to the V&A Waterfront directly, not go to the hotel first. And when I got to the Waterfront, I should put on something bright red, like a jacket or something, and find the amphitheatre, and he described it to me, he said there was a stage, and I should go and wait at the foot of the stairs leading up to the stage. And I shouldn't talk to anybody, just wait, a guy will come and meet me, and ask me for the memory card, and I should give it to him. But only if he specifically asks for the card. And then I could go to the hotel and have a nice little holiday.'

'And that's all?'

'No. I . . . I asked him . . . how I would know if it is the right guy, and he said I shouldn't worry, only a few people know I'm coming, so as long as the guy specifically asks for the card, I should give it to him. And then he again said, remember to test your phone, send the email, and go straight to the Waterfront, and wear something bright red. He thanked me again, and then he rang off.'

'Did he transfer the money for the hotel?'

'Yes.'

'From his usual account?' asked Cupido.

'Actually, no. It was from his security name. Morris. And a bank in Zurich.'

'I see,' said Cupido, and he knew he had her.

'Do you know which bank?' asked Bones.

'Well . . . I can check . . .'

'Perhaps later,' said Cupido. 'OK. So what did you do? After the last call?'

'I went shopping. For the trip. And then I took the Tube to Heathrow. And the flight was delayed. So I started worrying, will the guy still be there if I was late? But the delay was only twenty minutes, so I thought it would be OK. And when I arrived, I sent the email, and I changed two hundred pounds into rands in order to pay the cab, and then I took the cab, and I got to the Waterfront. And then I realised, I had to do something with my suitcase, I had no idea how far it was to this amphitheatre, and I didn't want to lug the suitcase with me. So I spoke to the cab driver, and he said he'll take it to the hotel for a hundred rand, which is like ten dollars, so I said OK. And after that, everything just went haywire.'

44

'Could you tell us exactly what happened at the Waterfront?' asked Cupido.

'It happened so fast,' she said, and shifted to the edge of her chair. 'I asked the cab driver where the amphitheatre was, and he didn't know, so there was this security guy, and I asked him, and he directed me. So I was walking, there were lots of people, which was a real surprise, so many white people, I mean, you know, you expect . . . No offence, but you know, when you come to Africa . . . Anyway, so I saw the amphitheatre, and I was almost there, when this asshole started bugging me about a hairpin, and I was in a hurry, I was a little worried, because there had been no contact from Professor Adair, and I was about half an hour late because of the flight delay, and getting off the plane, I wasn't thinking—'

'Did you expect the professor to contact you?' Cupido interrupted her deliberately. He could hear her anxiety from the quickening pace of her narrative, her rising tone. He thought this part was probably the truth, but she was providing unnecessary detail – he suspected that since yesterday she had been replaying the incident over and over in her mind, to try to make sense of it, to rationalise.

'No, no, I mean, yeah, I suppose, sort of. Here I was, having flown halfway around the world, I thought, maybe, if he got the email, he would call . . .'

'And he didn't contact you again?'

'No.'

'No email, nothing?'

'No.'

'Even after the Waterfront? This afternoon?'

'No.'

'But you are hoping he'll call?' Cupido pointed at her cellphone.

'Well, you know, I got worried, after what happened . . .' She flipped her hand palm upwards to emphasise that it was a natural response.

'OK. Please continue.'

'Right. So this guy is bugging me, and for a minute there, I thought he might be the guy, you know, for the card, and then he wasn't. And I was thinking: David said, don't talk to other people, it sort of . . . I think anybody, under the circumstances, would have felt . . . Look, I'm not stupid, but maybe I did get a little carried away with the whole clandestine thing, sort of cloak and dagger, you know, and I thought this guy might be, like, the enemy, a terrorist, you know? So I got a little panicky, and I tried to get rid of him, and the bastard stole my purse, and I didn't even know it. So, the thief walks off, and I start jogging, I'm late, I can see the amphitheatre, I'm looking for the steps to the stage, but I'm still ten yards away, and the next thing I know, there's this guy with a baseball cap and shades, and he's really in my face, he says, "Do you have the card?" I mean, I'm not even near the steps yet, it's right after the hairpin guy, I'm still a bit disoriented, I suppose, but he says, "Do you have the card?" and I'm sort of anxious, and I say, "But this is not where I'm supposed to give it to you." I was . . . You have to understand, I was on the plane all night, thinking about what Da— Professor Adair had said I should do, I was all geared up, and I was expecting a . . . I'm really not racist, my granddaddy on my father's side came from Mexico, so please, don't take this the wrong way, but it's just that I expected, you know, an English guy, a white guy—'

'Miss Alvarez,' Cupido interrupted her.

'Yes?'

'I want you to take a deep breath.'

She stared at him, not understanding. Then she took a deep breath, and said: 'I was going a little fast, wasn't I?'

'That's OK.'

'And you don't have to worry about expecting a white guy,' said Bones. 'We understand.'

'Thank you.' She sipped some more whisky, gave a small, self-conscious smile, and took another deep breath. 'It's just that, right then, it got really weird. I mean, this guy is all over me, he's in my face, and he has this strange accent, and when I say, "But this is not where I'm supposed to give you the card," the guy in the cap takes a gun from his pocket, with this black silencer, and he sticks it in my ribs, and there's this commotion behind us, people giving little yelps, and I want to look, and . . .'

She realised she was talking too fast and too anxiously again, and she reined herself in. 'Sorry,' she said, taking another gulp of whisky. When she did continue, she was more measured. '. . . And I was completely freaked out and scared. And he says, "That man stole something from you, do you have the card? Look. Now." And he looks over my shoulder at the commotion, and when I want to look, he jams the gun into my side again, and he says, "Look at me." So I froze, I just completely froze. He grabbed my arm and he shook me, and he asked for the card again, and I stuck my hand in my handbag, and the purse was gone, and I thought I was going to faint I was so scared, and he said, "Do you have it?" and I said, "My purse is gone," and then he said, "It was in the purse?" and I say, "Yes," and he says, "Are you sure?" and I was busy looking in my bag, and I nodded, and I started to cry like a damned baby, and then he ran, and the next thing I know I'm just standing there, amongst all these people, and nobody knew what had just happened . . .'

Tyrone lied.

He had got his story right on the train, thought through everything he must say, just to be on the safe side.

He walked into the Cape Calm B & B in De Waterkant, wearing his new jacket, with his new little suitcase. He looked legit, he had checked that in the mirror of the men's room at Cape Town Station. He had washed his face, combed his hair. OK, maybe he didn't smell like a rose garden, but he was a traveller, after all.

He said to the Cape Calm B & B aunty, a kindly lady, of the type with the exaggerated friendliness that comes from white guilt: 'Hi. My name is Jeremy Apollis,' in his best white English. 'I'd love to have a room for the night, OK, if I pay cash in advance?'

And Uncle Solly was right, the jacket was the ticket, and the cash in advance did not hurt, she came back *daatlik* with: 'Of course, of course, where you from?' He had that worked out too. 'Johannesburg, but I'm from here originally. I lived up in Schotsche Kloof.' He pronounced it 'Scots kloef', the way he heard English people say it.

She asked, 'Here on business?'

He'd anticipated this and wanted to contain the lie – too much detail is a dangerous thing – so he said, 'No, just came to spend some time with my sister. I'm flying back tomorrow night.'

He signed the register and he paid the six hundred and fifty rand and thought that the bed *and* the breakfast better be *blerrie lekker*, it's a lot of money. She took him to his room, and after she had left, he locked the door and put the case on the bed. Then he took out the gun and silencer, and the three cellphones. Put them on the bed, neatly in a row. He took off the jacket, hung it up in the wardrobe. Stood in front of the bed, looking at the cellphones. And he thought, he must concentrate. Use one at a time. And remember which one he was using. Where and when.

He got undressed, went into the bathroom and turned the shower on full, a blast of hot, soothing, beautiful water, and he stood like that for a very long time, so that it would wash away all the day's troubles, would soothe the pain across his back.

It didn't really work.

Griessel felt he should encourage Mbali. He wanted to tell her that at least one good thing had happened – she and Vaughn Cupido had found each other in some way, the antagonism between them was gone. He wanted to tell her that life and the world worked in cycles. Things would come right again, the wheel would turn. It always did.

He wanted to tell her the downturn of the wheel was more frequent than the up, but you had to ride it all the same.

But he didn't, because he thought, why on earth should she believe a middle-aged white drunkard from the apartheid era?

He had no credibility.

And he thought he should phone Radebe at O. R. Tambo Airport to hear if they had found anything more, because the more names they had, the easier it would be to arrest the Cobras at a border post. But he couldn't phone Ulinda, because the SSA were monitoring Radebe's cellphone too, and he thought: Fuck cellphones. *Jissis*, they managed without them for so many years, and they arrested just as many criminals. If not more. Using the old methodology. They investigated. Built dossiers bit by bit, with thorough footwork. They used their heads, thought and pondered and argued amongst each other, and debated, tested theories, outmanoeuvred suspects with clever tricks and snares in the interrogation rooms. They learned to spot a lie a mile off, just by watching and observing.

And now? Now technology had to do everything. And when it failed, then so many of the young detectives sat there saying, no, this case can't be solved.

He didn't like to be reachable everywhere, all the time. He didn't like trying to type a text on a tiny keyboard with his out-sized fingers. People sent messages for any shit that came into their heads, in a language that took you half an hour to decipher, and if you didn't answer, then they wanted to know why.

And the SSA could eavesdrop on you, track you, follow you, because the technology worked both ways – if you could catch a criminal, then someone else could find *you*.

He sighed, and tried to think of something else, but all that popped into his head, was his Alexa dilemma.

And it was not something that he could discuss with Mbali or anyone else, no matter how oppressive the silence was, here at the table.

When he saw Sister Abigail Malgas approaching, he felt relieved.

The nurse had Nadia's big book bag over her shoulder. 'The girl is in a ward now,' she said. 'The doctor said she will be able to talk to you. But only for a half an hour, and the child must give permission first.'

He didn't tell her that Nadia had no choice. They followed her, into the hospital. In the lift, Sister Malgas said, 'They still don't know what those people drugged her with, but it doesn't seem to be something serious.'

She made them wait outside the door to the ward, and disappeared behind the cream-coloured curtains that were drawn around the bed.

45

'So what did you do then?' asked Cupido.

'I tried to call Professor Adair, but he didn't answer. So I left a message, and I sent a text—'

'What was the message?'

'I just said . . . things didn't work out like I expected, I'm sorry . . .'

'Can I take a look at the text message?'

'I . . . uh, sorry, I've deleted it.'

'What did you do then?'

'I started walking. I mean, what could I do? I couldn't go to the police. This was about the professor's security work, he said I shouldn't talk to anybody, I mean, I couldn't just go to the police and say, look, this is . . . You know, I couldn't tell them everything, so what's the use of telling them anything?'

'You're telling us now.'

'Sure, but you guys know, right. About Professor Adair, and the pickpocket. I mean, this morning, I was . . . confused. And scared. And it all happened so fast, and the guy who wanted the card just ran off, and I did not have the card any more, and I thought, the professor will call, eventually, and I could tell him.'

'OK. Where did you go?'

'I walked to the hotel. This guy had stolen my purse, and all my cash. Thank God my bank cards were in my suitcase, with my passport. But I had no money for a cab, so I asked directions, and I walked to the hotel, and it rained a little, and I was damn cold, and my jacket was in my suitcase because I had to wear something red. And it was much further than I thought, I got very tired. And all the time I was so very worried that I had fucked the whole thing up, if you'll pardon my French.'

'Wasn't your fault,' said Bones.

'I know, right?'

'I just want to make sure, when you talk about "his security work", you mean the algorithm – for finding terrorists?' asked Cupido.

'That's right.'

'You said you work with him on some of his projects. The algorithm project too?'

'Oh, no, nobody worked with him on *that*.'

'How many research assistants work with him?'

'Four.'

'So why did he choose you?' asked Cupido.

'Excuse me?'

'Why did David Adair choose you to bring the card to Cape Town?'

'Because . . . I suppose he thought he could trust me? Or he knew I love travelling, and I wanted to come to Africa . . .'

'When he transferred money to your account, why did he not ask for your account details?'

'I . . . He . . . I didn't say that.'

'Did he ask for your details? During that second call, yesterday at ten. Did he ask for your account details to transfer the money?'

'Well, I . . . Yes, I think so.'

'But you specifically said it wasn't from his usual account. It was from a bank in Zurich.'

'Yes, but I . . .' she realised she had talked herself into a corner.

'Do you get paid for your work at the university?'

'Yes.'

'By David Adair?'

'No.'

'So how did you know it wasn't from his usual account?'

She didn't reply.

'You're not telling us the whole truth, are you?'

With fearful eyes, Nadia Kleinbooi looked from Griessel to Mbali, and back at him again.

They stood beside her bed, both on one side.

'You don't have to be scared,' said Mbali.

'We're here to help,' said Griessel.

'Do you know where my brother is?' She was pale and tired, her voice was hoarse.

'No. But we know that he brought you here.'

'Is he OK?'

'How do you feel?' asked Mbali.

'It hurts,' said Nadia, and touched her side.

'Is it OK if we ask you a few questions?'

'Yes. I don't . . . They injected me, in my arm. With something. I was very sleepy, so I can't remember everything that happened . . .'

'You can just tell us what you remember,' said Griessel.

'And if you get tired, just tell us.'

'OK.'

'We would love to hear everything. About the . . .' And then Griessel stopped, because a cellphone was ringing. He thought it was his, because it had the same ringtone, but he touched his pocket, and realised his iPhone was off.

'It's my phone,' said Nadia, and looked at her bag on the chair beside Griessel.

He bent, opened the bag, saw the light from the screen of the ringing phone. He took it out. 'Do you know this number?' he asked as he passed the phone to her.

'No.' She took the phone, answered it. 'Hello?'

She listened for a moment, then they saw her face brighten as she said, '*Boetie*! Are you OK?'

Tyrone had showered and changed into clean clothes. He pushed the pistol into the back of his belt, under the jacket. He put the stolen wallet, where the original memory card was still stored, in the inside pocket of his jacket. After that he took cellphones One and Two, put them in the side pockets, and walked to the Cape Quarter Lifestyle Village on Somerset Road.

He shouldn't have pondered everything that happened that morning, because that's what caused him to make the mistake. But he couldn't help it, it was so close to the Waterfront, and the Schotsche Kloof, and he recalled everything so vividly – how he had been shot, how he had run for his life, the dog that nearly bit him. He relived the fear, and that moment at Bellville Station, when he realised they had drugged his sister. And the heart-wrenching moment when they shot her. It all made him so angry, a fierce anger coiled in his brain, the thirst for revenge overpowering everything.

His mind was still full of it when he switched on the cellphone at the entrance to the Food Spar and phoned Nadia's number.

Nadia's number? What was he thinking, he thought later, get a grip you fool, because he'd actually meant to phone the hospital's number and ask for Sister Abigail, but his head was filled with vengeance, and he was tired, finished, done in, *klaar*. A *kwaai* crazy day, big lapse of concentration. The phone rang and rang, and suddenly his sister answered, startling him. His heart thumped and he wondered, was she alone?

'I'm fine, *sussie*. Are you OK?'

'Where are you? Why aren't you here?'

'*Sussie,* are you OK? What do the doctors say?'

'They say I was lucky. Two broken ribs, and I bled a bit . . .'

'What did those bastards give you?'

'I don't know. Something that made me very *dof*. I got so sleepy. They injected me in my arm . . . Where are you, *boetie*?' He heard fear in her voice.

'I am busy sorting things out. I'll come and get you, as soon as I'm done.'

'What things? Done with what? Didn't you give them what they wanted? I can't remember that well, *boetie* . . . The *polieste* are here now. You must come and talk.'

He had thought as much, that's why he had phoned from here. Thought he was smart and clever and alert. He must finish this call, but he didn't want to leave her like this. 'Don't you worry, *versta' jy*? Everything is going to be all right. You must just get better now. Just tell me, how many of those *ouens* were there that kidnapped you?'

'What things must you sort out, Tyrone?'

She only said Tyrone when she was angry. It was a good sign, that she could be angry at him. 'Don't worry. How many were there?'

'I think four. But you can't say I mustn't worry. What card were they looking for? How did you get mixed up with such people, Tyrone?'

'I will explain everything, *sussie*. I just tried to help someone, then there was this massive misunderstanding . . .' He stopped talking, it wasn't the time for explanation, he didn't even know what she knew.

The cops were sitting there, maybe listening. He must finish up. 'Just get better. Do you need anything?'

'What I need is to know what you mean by "As soon as I'm done".' And he could hear, there wasn't too much wrong with her, she would be OK after all.

Then he made his second mistake, out of sheer relief, and because the anger and revenge still clung to every fibre of his being: 'Nobody touches my sister. I've got something they want. Now I'm a player. And they're going to pay.' It just came out, and he was immediately sorry that he'd said it.

'No! *Boetie*, no! Those are *annerlike* people. Let the *polieste* deal with it.'

'Keep that phone with you. I have to go. And remember one thing: I love you very much.'

He pressed the button to kill the call before he could hear her reaction, then he switched the phone off completely. 'Shit,' he said out loud. He began walking immediately, purposefully, out of the shopping centre.

Fifty metres on, he said quietly to himself: '*Jirre*, Tyrone, you didn't handle that well. Get a grip.'

46

Lillian Alvarez wept.

Bones sat and glared at Cupido.

Cupido knew that his colleague clearly did not understand the very first defence mechanism of a woman caught out in a lie. 'I know you're trying to protect him,' he said with great compassion. 'But if you want us to find him, you will have to tell us the truth.'

Bones stood up, took a snow-white handkerchief out of his pocket, and held it out to her.

'There really isn't anything to tell.' She took the handkerchief, dabbed beneath her eyes, then at her nose, and looked at Cupido, pleading.

Bones sat down again.

'It's not like we're going to call the university and tell them the good professor was having an affair with his beautiful young student.'

She stared at the carpet.

'Maybe that's not the case, Vaughn,' said Bones.

'Maybe,' said Cupido, but the word was loaded with irony.

'I know what you're doing,' said Lillian Alvarez.

'We're trying to save your lover.'

'I watch TV. You're playing good cop, bad . . . Save him? What do you mean, save him?'

'David Adair was kidnapped, Miss Alvarez. By the people who wanted to get their hands on that memory card. So the sooner you start telling us everything, the sooner we can try and save him.'

Her mouth was half open, her tearful eyes expressed shock and reproach. She fought against emotions, and eventually she said, 'I knew it.'

Then she began weeping again.

'My brother,' said Nadia Kleinbooi to Griessel, distress in her voice.

'He's mixed up in something ugly.' She pressed call-back on the number that Tyrone had phoned her from, but a recorded message said: 'The subscriber you have dialled is not available. Please try again later.'

'What do you mean?' asked Griessel.

'Tyrone said they are going to pay, because he has something they want. And he wanted to know how many they were. Those people are going to kill him.'

'Your brother has something they want? A card?'

'Yes. He says he's a player now.'

'A player?' asked Mbali.

'Whatever that means,' said Nadia. 'I don't like it.'

'The people who are looking for the card are the same ones who kidnapped you?'

'Yes.'

'He still has something that they want?'

She nodded anxiously.

'Do you know what it is?' asked Griessel.

'I thought . . . I don't know. It must be the card. But I thought . . . I was very confused . . .'

'What kind of card? A credit card, a bank card?'

'The one Frenchman, he phoned Tyrone after they grabbed me. And he said Tyrone had stolen a wallet, and there was a memory card in the wallet, and he would exchange the card for me . . .'

'A memory card? What memory card?'

'I don't know.'

'But . . . Hang on . . .' Griessel struggled to understand the new angle. 'We thought that was what happened at Bellville Station. Tyrone gave them something, and he got you back.'

'I was very confused. I also thought . . .'

'Nadia, this is very important: What can you remember from the station?'

She closed her eyes, shook her head. 'I don't know . . . The guy held me so tight, we first went to a man in a blue jacket. He handed over something. I couldn't see exactly, something small . . .'

'Wait, slowly. What guy held you?'

Nadia opened her eyes. 'I'm not even sure that things really happened this way.'

'Just tell us exactly what *you think* happened,' said Mbali.

'OK,' she said, with conviction.

'When did you start having an affair with Adair?' asked Cupido.

Lillian Alvarez looked towards the entrance of the hotel, wiped away tears, and blew her nose. She kept looking out ahead of her as though they weren't there.

'Bones, if she doesn't want to save him, perhaps we should just abandon the search. He's not a South African citizen. Let the British Consulate look for him.'

Bones realised what he was doing. 'But they don't have the resources, Vaughn. And his life is in real danger,' he said.

Cupido stood up. 'If she doesn't care, why should we?'

Bones hesitated before he got up. 'Good day, Miss Alvarez,' he said.

'Happy holiday,' said Cupido, and began walking towards the door, and Bones followed suit.

'Wait,' said Lillian Alvarez, before they had taken four paces.

Nadia Kleinbooi told them everything, as she remembered it. They had shoved her down in the Nissan X-Trail, two of them. Frenchmen, she thought. That was the language they spoke to each other. One was white and blond. He looked like a surfer. The other one was bald. Also white. Of the driver, she could only see the back of a head in a cap. The blond one phoned Tyrone and right after that one of them injected her in the arm with something. Then she became very drowsy, and everything was as vague as a dream.

She could remember driving down Durban Road later, the effect of the drug was not so strong then. But then there was another man in the car. Left front. Coloured she thought.

Four, then?

Yes, four.

One was on the phone all the time. He talked about the card. They stopped. Blondie made her get out. Her knees buckled. He swore at her and dragged her with him. To the station, she could remember the stalls, the colours of the stalls. Then they stopped for a while. It was like she was slowly waking up. Then they walked up to a scruffy man in a blue jacket, a workman's jacket, 'with a zip'.

She wasn't sure if the man in the blue jacket had handed over the card. He did give Blondie something. She had to hold a laptop. But then Blondie said she must walk until she saw Tyrone. She walked a long way, it felt very long, then Tyrone was there with her. Then she got very confused. There was a black man who said she was drunk. She wanted to protest, but the words wouldn't come out, it frustrated her so much. She remembered the other coloured one who shot her. It was the other man, who hadn't been in Stellenbosch in the Nissan.

Perhaps, she said, he shot her because Tyrone hadn't given him the card. But that was all she could remember. Except for Tyrone's arms around her in a lorry, on the way to hospital.

'Your brother definitely said he has something they want?' asked Griessel.

'Yes.'

'And that they are going to pay?'

'Yes.'

'Nadia, if you show me the number, we can see if we can trace him.'

She held the phone against her breast. She asked, 'Do you know who these people are?'

'We think so.'

'Do you know how Tyrone got mixed up in this?'

'What does your brother do for a living?' Mbali asked before Griessel could say anything.

'He's a painter. A house painter. He works so hard . . .'

'We think he got into this by accident,' said Mbali. 'That is why we want to help him.'

Griessel knew why Mbali told this white lie. To upset Nadia now with the truth about her brother the pickpocket might cost them her cooperation.

'Yes, that's what I thought. He's a very gentle person. They will kill him.'

'We can help him. If you just show me the number.'

'But he turned the phone off.'

'If we have the number, we can find out where he phoned from.'

'He lives in Schotsche Kloof. I can give you his address.'

'He's not there any more. We went to look.'

She thought for a moment, then nodded and held out the phone to him.

Cupido and Bones sat down again.

The lovely Lillian Alvarez put her feet on the stool and pulled her knees up under her chin. She wrapped her arms around her legs, as if she was embracing herself, and didn't look at them. She said something, but so quietly that they could not hear.

'I'm sorry, but we can't hear you.'

'We didn't have an affair.'

They said nothing.

'An affair is when one person is married. An affair is something . . . fleeting. It's not like that.'

'What is it like?' asked Cupido.

'You will do a lot of damage,' she said.

'We don't need to tell anybody,' said Bones, and he shot a pleading look at Cupido.

'That's right,' said Cupido. 'All we want to do is to find him.' He got up, shifted his chair closer to her, and sat down again. Bones followed his example.

She waited until they were settled, looked from one to the other. 'Do you promise?'

'Yes,' they said almost in unison.

47

Lillian Alvarez did not start talking again immediately. She sat there as though gathering her strength. And when she told the story, the subtle signs of lying were gone for the first time.

She said the last thing she expected was a love affair with her supervisor. She was so grateful and happy when she was accepted by DAMTP for her Masters degree, she looked forward to Britain, to the whole English experience. She wasn't well travelled. Not then. No one in her family was well travelled. Her father had been to Washington, DC. She did graduate studies at the University of California, Los Angeles campus. She had been to Vegas and San Francisco with her student friends, but no one in her middle-class family had even been in New York or Chicago. Never. Not to mention crossing the Atlantic Ocean.

And then she was accepted at Cambridge. Cambridge! One of the best universities on the planet. Another country, another culture, with a history that stretched back thousands of years. The world of the Beatles and Princess Di and the Queen and Prince William and Kate. On the edge of the European continent, with the opportunity of weekends in Paris or Milan or Madrid.

Cupido began to listen. He knew the art of being father confessor. As people started spilling all, you had to shut up, and let them talk, let them free themselves. Sometimes they needed to take long detours.

The university was everything she had dreamed of. The first time she saw King's College Chapel – nearly six hundred years old – it had taken her breath away. To study mathematics at the same institution that produced Newton and Lord Kelvin and Lord Rayleigh. And Charles Babbage, the father of computers . . .

And then, as she knew she could not put it off any longer: 'A week after I arrived, I walked into David Adair's office and I fell in love. Just like that,' with a soft snap of her thumb and middle finger. There was still a sense of amazement to how she said it. It was such a shocking joy, that moment. It was a first. She had waited so long to fall head over heels in love that she had begun to suspect it would never happen to her. She had had relationships before – a school romance, and two friendships of more than a year each at UCLA. She loved them, for sure, but was never intensely in love. And then she said pensively, and without any arrogance, that perhaps it was because neither of them was her intellectual equal.

And then David Adair happened.

She only realised much later that he was actually twenty-five years older than she was. He could have been her father (said with the easy irony and self-mockery of someone who had verbalised it before). But it was never relevant, because their souls were equally old. She said that twice.

They couldn't stop talking. About mathematics, about the world, about life. About people and their ways. About food. Did they know he was a foodie? He was a good cook too, at weekends he prepared them the most delicious meals, just the two of them, Chopin on the hi-fi, the Sunday papers, a good bottle of French wine, and David busy over the cooking pots.

But that was later. She guarded her love for him closely. Thought it was one-sided. It took him nearly two months to confess that he had 'feelings' for her.

She relived it all with a strong voice, with the self-confidence that it was good and right, clearly also trying to portray him as a true gentleman: he had asked her to drive with him, please. He took her to a restaurant in Huntingdon, he didn't want to do this in his office where the power balance of lecturer and student reigned. He bought her lunch. They finished eating. His face grew suddenly serious. He said he had thought over the matter for a long time, but he could no longer remain silent. He had feelings for her. She wanted to respond in jubilation, she said his name, and he stopped her with a hand on hers. He said, please, let him finish. He was sincerely sorry. He would absolutely understand if she wanted to change supervisor. He would help her to make the change, he would take responsibility, he would explain that his schedule had become too full. There would be no embarrassment for her. But his feelings were so strong that sooner or later he was going to do something stupid. That was why he was telling her now, before he humiliated himself and put her in an impossible situation.

'And when he was done, I said, "David, I love you very much".'

While Mbali tried to get the best possible descriptions of the four 'Frenchmen' out of Nadia Kleinbooi, Griessel walked out into the hospital corridor and phoned the colonel. He explained what had happened. That there was a chance that the Cobras were still in the Cape, and that they still hadn't got what they were looking for. And that David Adair might still be alive.

Nyathi was businesslike, and Griessel wondered if someone was there with him. 'Let's meet as soon as you're back, Benny.'

'Yes, sir.'

He stood in the corridor and tried to process that odd feeling – half an hour ago he was resigned to the fact that the Cobras were going to get away. Now there was a chance.

Tyrone Kleinbooi had bought them time. How much, he didn't know.

And the chances were slim. To track someone down quickly in this city, someone with false passports, who took professional precautions, who did not want to be found, was well-nigh impossible.

But there was another possibility. The chances were marginally better.

It depended on what Nadia could remember.

He took a deep breath and walked back into the ward to go and ask his questions.

Cupido thought she was a *kwaai* smart girl, so pretty, but emotionally so immature. Still he said nothing, let her tell the whole story. Alvarez said she and David Adair agreed to keep their affair secret until she attained her degree. Because, although they were both adults, morally unencumbered and not involved with third parties, a relationship between a middle-aged lecturer and a much younger student remained a serious and thorny problem in the corridors of academia. In addition, he was the DAMTP study leader who could best support her with her specific thesis. The most logical alternative was a transfer to another university, but neither of them wanted that. He insisted on the appointment of a fourth external examiner for her degree, and got one from the Massachusetts Institute of Technology. So that no fingers could be pointed when she graduated in a year and a half, and their relationship became public.

And then there were serious problems from what she described as 'his position': on the one hand, his work with highly secret anti-terrorism algorithms, and on the other hand, his protests against the British and European authorities and the banking industry. The 'position' meant that for security reasons he was watched like a hawk, but also that different factions would very much like to shut him up, muzzle and control him, should they get the right sort of ammunition.

'What factions?' Bones interrupted her for the first time.

She answered quickly. Her haste, the tone of her voice betrayed something again. 'Well, politicians, to start with. He had been fairly vocal in his opposition of privacy intrusion, and had been publicly criticising the government for not going far enough in fighting organised crime, for instance. Then there's organised crime itself. You should see the threats he received . . .'

'What threats?' asked Cupido.

'Death threats.'

'From whom?'

'They didn't exactly sign their names, but he knew it was from people in organised crime. He just laughed it off as scare tactics, and posturing. He said they would not dare, because if they killed him, the government would be forced to act. So it wasn't in the Mafia's interest to carry it out.'

'Anybody else? The factions, I mean.'

'Just every terrorist organisation in the world, of course . . . You know . . . You can imagine, I'm sure. Anyway, a lot of factions, so we had to be very careful with our relationship.'

'I don't think you're telling us everything,' said Cupido.

'I swear I'm telling you everything.'

He let it go for now.

'So you had to be very secretive in your relationship.'

'Very.'

'How did you know which bank he usually used?'

'David would transfer money for a plane or train ticket to Brussels or Paris or Zurich, for me to spend a weekend with him.'

'OK, getting back to the past week, could you now tell us the whole truth?'

'There really isn't all that much to say that will make a difference. I lied about last seeing him at the department Thursday a week ago. We actually spent that following Sunday in Ipswich, and much of the Monday night in my apartment. David left just after twelve o'clock that night . . .'

'Where did he go?'

'To his place. That's why I was so surprised when I went to see him at the office the next morning – we had an official appointment – and he wasn't there. I mean, he always told me if he had to travel. But he did mention that it might happen, you know, with all his responsibilities, that he might be called away at short notice. So I wasn't really worried then. But when there was no contact for four days . . . We've never been apart for that long . . .'

'But you had no idea where he was?'

'No.'

'And the call on Monday morning?'

'OK, that wasn't the first call. David called me last Friday night, at about eleven. It was a very short, hurried call. He just said he was fine, he had to rush off on security business, and he might be away for a while. And he said I mustn't tell anybody that he had called.'

'That's it?'

'He did say he loved me. That's it.'

'And the Monday morning call, the early one?'

'It happened almost like I told you. I did ask him where he was, and said that I had been worried, and he replied that he understood, but it's his anti-terror work, he can't talk about it, and everything is fine. But he said that he needed my help. And then he told me about coming to Cape Town.'

'Nothing else?'

'Before he rang off, I told him that I loved him. And he said he loved me too. But . . .' She shook her head slightly, as if she was unsure.

'But?'

'I don't know. He said he loved me, but there was something . . . As if he was the tiniest bit embarrassed. As if . . . I don't know, as if someone was listening?'

'Maybe you're right. And the second call?'

'I asked him where he was staying, because usually he booked us into a hotel, you know, in Paris . . . And he said he has official accommodation. So I asked when I would see him, here in Cape Town. And he said perhaps on Tuesday, if he could conclude his work. Oh, and when I was on the plane, I . . . I know I shouldn't have, but I thought nobody would know, and I was just so damn curious. I mean, I . . . Look, if you're really into what I'm studying, the Adair Algorithm is like the Holy Grail. It's bleeding edge, and it must be brilliant, because David is just so . . . Anyway, I thought, maybe if I can just look at the code, what harm could there be? So I popped the memory card into my Air. And there was a ZIP file. Password protected. So I took it out again. I really don't know what's on the card.'

'Anything else?'

'That's about it, really.'

'You didn't think it was a little strange that he wasn't going to be able to see you in Cape Town?'

'Of course I did. But this was the first time that David had involved me in his other work. I thought, maybe that's just how it was . . . How he was, when he was busy with the security stuff.'

'Who kidnapped him?' asked Cupido.

'I don't know,' she said, too vehemently.

'I think you suspect a specific . . . faction.' Cupido put the last word in quotation marks with his fingers.

'No, I don't—'

'Yes, you do.'

'No.'

'This is life and death, Miss Alvarez,' said Bones. They could see her internal struggle. Her fists were balled, her lovely mouth pinched, her eyes darted.

'The life and death of the man you love,' said Cupido.

'I . . . can't tell you.'

'Even if it means David Adair gets killed?'

'Oh God . . .'

'We're on your side, Miss Alvarez. We are the good guys.'

'I'm really not sure I can share this with you. It's . . . very, very delicate.'

'Do you think this *delicate* group is behind his kidnapping?'

'I . . . maybe.'

'Do you want to save him?'

'Of course,' she said emphatically. 'But he trusted me with some very secret information, and I . . . I just don't know . . . I mean, this is the sort of thing that could . . . It has very big implications. Internationally.'

'Do you want to save him?' asked Cupido, slow and measured.

She began to cry. 'I don't know what to do.'

'Just do what you think is right,' said Bones.

'Oh God . . .' Her head drooped so that the thick black hair hid her face.

Cupido knew there was nothing he could do. They would just have to wait.

She lifted her head. Her eyes were still filled with tears.

48

Tyrone bought a packet of Panados, two chicken-mayo sandwiches, and a half-litre of Coke at the BP service station's Pick n Pay Express on the other side of Somerset Road. Then he walked in the strong, chilly northwester, to the front of the Rockwell All Suite Hotel. He sat down on the low wall between the hotel and the service station, beside the big green recycling bin, where the wall of a storeroom provided shelter from the wind.

The pistol pressed against the small of his back and he had to shift it so it didn't chafe him. He liked the feel of the gun there. Very *empowering*, he thought, and he grinned in the half-dark.

Pickpocket with a pistol. Uncle Solly would turn in his grave.

He swallowed two Panados with a mouthful of Coke. The wound across his shoulders throbbed with a dull, growing pain.

From here he could see the entrance to the Cape Quarter Lifestyle Village. So he could see how long it was going to take before the cops arrived.

He ate and drank. And he thought.

How was he going to get the money? Conclude the transaction without getting shot in the head.

The easy way would have been an electronic transaction, but Uncle Solly taught him long ago: *Stay away from banks, Ty. They have tentacles that pull you in, you don't want to leave tracks, you don't want to be connected with a paper trail if a fence is prosecuted, you don't want the tax man to come asking questions. Cash is King.*

There would be a lot of questions if a coloured *outjie*, formerly of Mitchells Plain, suddenly got two point four million in his bank account.

The exchange would have to be manual. Hard cash, the hard way. But how? He couldn't involve anyone else, because these guys were bent on murder. Look what they did at Bellville Station, even after he gave them the card. And how stupid was that? If he had been lying dead now, all they would have would be a card full of Cape tourist pics.

'Cause they underestimated him, thought he was just a local yokel, too stupid to be a player. Surprise, surprise, motherfucker, *ma' nou weet hulle.* They wouldn't make the same mistake twice.

But the fact remained: he would have to be extremely clever if he was going to get out the other end alive. He had made one big mistake himself. He thought the guy with the eyes was a lone operator. Now he knew there might be four of them.

Four. Against one.

Bad odds.

He would have to be smart.

He thought for an hour, while the wind blew stronger, and fatigue crept up on him again. Slowly he began to formulate a plan. Until the wind became too cold and miserable, and he knew the cops were not too fast when it came to cellular tracking. He stood up, walked west on Somerset, to the corner of Ebenezer. He walked into the Victoria Junction Hotel, past reception as if he belonged there, into the bar and lounge.

He enjoyed the warm interior for a moment. There were only a few guests – three businessmen at the bar, a group of four men and women in a square of couches and chairs in the middle of the big room.

He sat down at one of the small tables against the wall, where he knew no one could hear him. He took out Cellphone Number Two.

A waiter approached, brisk and friendly. Tyrone shook his head to show he didn't want anything.

He watched until the waiter was far enough away, then he turned the phone on and waited for a signal.

He called his old cellphone number.

The guy answered a little faster this time.

'Yes.'

'Hello, motherfucker, how are you?' asked Tyrone.

'I am good, because I have a future. But not you.'

'Do you want the original card?'

'Yes.'

'Do you have the money?'

'Not yet.'

'When will you have it?'

'Tomorrow morning. Maybe nine o'clock.'

'OK, motherfucker, here is what you are going to do: tomorrow morning you are going to stack that money on a table, and you are going to take a photograph. And then you are going to take a bag, and put the money in the bag. Then you take another photograph, of the bag with the money in it. And then you are going to get your buddy to take a photograph of you and the bag. Full length, so I can see exactly what you look like and what you are wearing. Do you understand?'

'Yes.'

'Then you are going to MMS me those photographs to this number. And when I receive them, I will call you with instructions.'

'You will not call on this number again. We will break this phone now.'

'No.'

'Yes. I will not negotiate on that.'

'So how do I contact you tomorrow?'

'On the number we send the photos from.'

Tyrone thought. That should be all right.

'OK.'

'We know your sister is in hospital,' said the guy.

'If you go near my sister again, I will destroy the card,' he said, but he had to concentrate to keep the panic out of his voice.

'We know which hospital. If you don't deliver the card, or if there is something wrong with the card, we will go in there and kill her.'

'The police are protecting her.'

The guy laughed quietly. 'You think so? You think they will stop us?'

Tyrone's hand began to shake.

Then the guy said, 'I will send you the photos tomorrow morning,' and he rang off.

They sat in the Hawks' clubroom, the legendary, hidden bar room where only members of the unit were allowed in: Nyathi, Griessel, Mbali, Cupido, and Bones Boshigo. The only door was locked.

Griessel did not come in here often, but sometimes on a Friday afternoon he stood with the guys outside at the braai. Now he thought, it could be the first line of a joke: 'An alky is locked inside a police bar . . .'

He realised everyone was waiting for him to say something. 'Vaughn, do you want to report first?' He saw his colleague was burning to share something with them.

'The CIA, pappie,' said Cupido. 'Lillian Alvarez says it is the CIA who abducted Adair.'

After the stunned silence, Zola Nyathi asked, 'And she knows that *how?*' Very sceptical.

'It's a long story, Colonel.' Cupido gave them the main points of Alvarez's experiences over the past week. 'But I'll let Bones tell you about the bank stuff.'

'It seems,' said Bones, 'that the good professor unleashed a new version of his algorithm about six weeks ago, *nè*. New, improved, expanded. All in the name of hunting terrorists. Now, the way this algorithm works, is to use SWIFT data to track the source of the money – the country, the bank, and the account – and unique transaction patterns, because terrorists receive and withdraw and use money in a very specific way, aimed at avoiding attention. So the algorithm generates patterns, and Adair's data-mining software then identifies possible suspects, and looks at the names and nationalities of all the account holders and money movers, and spits out the most likely suspects to the intelligence people, who follow it up. But the terrorists are not complete idiots. They know about the algorithm, and they have started to change their financial behaviour and the paths through which the money flows. That's why Adair wrote the new software: to adapt to the new behaviour. And apparently he is the first one who gets the results every day, 'cause he has to study them to see if the whole system is working properly, *nè?*'

The last '*nè*' was a question, and everyone nodded. They were still following.

'So what happened was, Adair started to identify a new category of suspects that had the right financial profile – or the wrong one, depending on your side of the fence – but did not fit in with any of the software's parameters for nationality, origins of names, and other stuff that would indicate terrorists. So he started digging, without telling anybody, because he was very worried that the software was screwed up. And then he realised that this new group of suspects were probably spies. Clandestine operatives, working for intelligence agencies. Alvarez says what gave him the big clue was the fact that if you tracked the money all the way to the original source, a hell of a lot of it came from very obscure Chinese and Russian accounts. The kind of stuff governments bury deep in red tape and dummy corporations and funny names. And there were as many payments going the other way – coming from the Americans and the British, going to people and little companies in the Middle East, Russia and China—'

Cupido could not keep it in any longer. 'So basically he was building a list of all the undercover spies and sleepers and even double agents of the world's major intelligence agencies. And he was the only one who knew, the only one with all this data.'

'Why did he tell Alvarez?' asked Nyathi. 'She's a student, isn't she?'

'Long story, Colonel. Let's just say they are having a red-hot affair, and he was very troubled by this spy thing, and she kept asking him what was wrong, why was he so glum, had she done something to upset him, nagging all the time, until he told her. Poor guy must have wanted to share it with someone, all that pressure . . .'

'How did the CIA find out?'

'That's the thing. About three weeks ago, Adair got very crafty. He went to MI6, and told them what he had. They wanted it all, of course, but he said he'll horse trade. If the British and American governments agreed to take on the banks about their money laundering, to make a real effort to use all the financial data to cripple organised crime, he'd release the spy data to them. But it had to be done with legislation, and real results. And he had some demands about public privacy too, and the limits of government snooping. MI6 was furious, and threatened him with all sorts of legal action, but he didn't budge, *nè*. Then they blocked his access to the SWIFT system and his software, brought in their own people, and tried to find the data themselves. But it turns out Adair suspected they might do just that. So before he went to MI6, he deleted his new software, and loaded the old version again. The spy data was just gone.'

'That's what's on the memory card,' said Griessel.

'Exactly,' said Cupido. 'The girl says she doesn't think MI6 would kidnap their own citizen. If it all goes wrong, they want deniability.

Clean hands. But she says of course MI6 is very good friends with the CIA. And the CIA has no scruples, everyone knows about Guantánamo Bay and drone attacks and all that monkey business. So, if the CIA kidnapped Adair, everything is sweet.'

Mbali shook her head in revulsion.

'It will explain why our very own SSA is so keen to get hold of Adair,' said Bones.

'That's right, pappie,' said Cupido. 'Just think how they could play puppet master with all those spies' names. Talk about horse trading . . .'

Zola Nyathi clasped his hands together, slowly and formally. Griessel knew it was not a good sign.

'I think the girl is wrong,' said the Giraffe. 'Or she's lying.'

They waited for him to explain. Nyathi looked down at his hands. 'When Benny and I spoke to Emma Graber, the woman from MI6 at the British Consulate, the overwhelming impression was that they did not know that Adair was kidnapped, let alone by whom. If it was the CIA and they knew about it, they would not even have bothered to involve us, or the State Security Agency. They would have responded very differently to our passport enquiries.'

They digested the logic in quiet disappointment. Cupido said hopefully, 'So maybe it's the Russians. Or the Chinese . . .'

Nyathi shook his head. 'Sadly, I don't think so. Unfortunately you're not the only members of this unit that have had a busy afternoon. But my news is bad, and perhaps less . . . shall we say, about international intrigue. I have to tell you, if we decide to continue to pursue our investigation . . .' and the colonel looked straight at Mbali '. . . it will lead to further disappointment in our government, and it will be a considerably higher risk to our careers. And it will probably lead nowhere else but into deep trouble, because we have nothing to go on. So I'd like to give you all the opportunity to walk away, right now. I will understand, absolutely and completely.'

49

The northwester was up to gale force when Tyrone walked up
Somerset Street, and then south, up the hill along Dixon and Loader.
He wanted to shelter in the warmth of the guesthouse, take his tired
body to bed and sleep, because tomorrow he must have his mind clear
and sharp.

But there were still two things he had to do. Of the one, the last call
that he had to make, he didn't want to think now. He was focusing on
the other task, getting that last bit of insurance in place.

He walked to the top of the rise, where Strand Street ran around the
belly of Signal Hill. There was no shelter from the wind here, it
screamed in his ears, it shoved and plucked at his body. He waited for
a gap in the traffic, and jogged across the street. Then, on the other
side, he ducked into the bushes.

When he was sure that no one could see him, he took the pistol out.
In the faint glow of the city lights he worked the safety catch clumsily,
aimed at a tree's broad trunk about eight metres away, and pulled the
trigger.

The pistol made a muffled retort, and bucked in his hand.

He walked to the tree.

Missed completely.

Jirre.

He hoped it was just the strong wind.

In the Hawks' bar, no one moved.

'Are you sure?' asked Zola Nyathi.

They nodded, one by one.

'OK,' said the colonel. 'Let me tell you about my afternoon. The
brigadier and I had a telephone conference with both the National
and the DPCI commissioners. We were asked if we had terminated
our investigation. Several times. The brigadier told what he thought

was the truth. I lied. Several times. I am ashamed of that, because
Musad Manie is a good man, and he trusts me. I'm not sure the
commissioners believed us. Then they asked us if we had destroyed
any evidence, because there is a strong indication that we did. Both the
brigadier and I told them what we thought was the truth. I am not
going to ask you about that again, but if they can disprove it, our
careers are over, and we will drag down the brigadier as well. But be
that as it may, the point is that both commissioners were clearly under
extreme pressure from above. And we all know what that means.
About forty minutes later, the brigadier had a call from the acting
head of Crime Intelligence. The general told him that CI is sending in
a team to, and I quote, "oversee the conclusion of our investigation,
and to inspect our systems for compliance". They are flying in from
Pretoria tonight. I'm expecting them any time now.'

'*Hhayi*,' said Mbali under her breath.

'Yes, Mbali,' said Nyathi in sympathy.

Vaughn Cupido hissed through his teeth, a fricative that sounded
very much like the suppression of a swearword.

'Then it's probably not about spies and the CIA,' said Bones.

'No, it's probably not,' said Nyathi.

Mbali was correct, thought Griessel, when she said in the hospital
that this was about South African government secrets. But as
Criminal Intelligence was involved that high up, most probably it
meant very specific secrets. Because it was common knowledge that
the head of that unit frequently received calls from the highest office
in the land.

'I must tell you,' said Nyathi, still sombre and deliberate, 'that I had
no choice. After the calls, I told the brigadier everything. I offered him
my resignation. He did not accept. He did, however, demand an
apology for the fact that I did not trust him to support us. He then
asked me what I was going to do. I told him that I was going to have a
meeting with you all and tell you the truth. And the truth is that, as
noble as the cause may be, we have nothing. We are being investigated,
watched, listened to. We have no room to manoeuvre. We are not going
to discover what is on that memory card, and we are not going to save
David Adair. So you have to ask yourself: why do you want to endan-
ger your lives and your careers by chasing quixotic windmills?'

Nobody moved. The atmosphere was heavy, heads were hung low. Everyone's except Griessel's.

Tyrone fetched the third cellphone from the guesthouse.

This time he walked towards the city. Despite the wind that propelled him with an invisible hand, and the cold that penetrated his jacket, he concentrated on the call he had to make. He had considered phoning the hospital, but he didn't know if that would help. He would have to talk directly to the cops. And he would have to be convincing.

How had Hoodie and his henchmen known she was in the hospital?

Who were these men?

What was on the *fokken* memory card?

They shot her, and they must have known what he would do – take his sister to the nearest hospital. They knew her name, and his. Doesn't take a genius.

The cops would have to look after Nadia. Lots of them. Because these guys were afraid of nothing.

If something happened to her . . . For a moment he considered dropping the whole thing. Just telling the guy tomorrow, I'll leave your card somewhere, take the thing and go away, leave us alone.

It's not worth the trouble.

But of course, it wasn't that simple.

Even if you took the anger away, at what they had done, to him and Nadia. He couldn't carry on like this. Every day it got harder to work in his industry. The cameras everywhere. The cops, the patrols in the city, the security, wherever you found affluent marks, there was law enforcement. And he had targets to meet so that Nadia could study and he could survive. And he was getting further and further behind, and the pressure was growing. And the more pressure, the more he had to take risks. And taking risks was trouble, no matter how you looked at it.

Two point four million.

A lot of money.

It could take away all his troubles. All the pressure. All the risk.

Long-term security.

It was Nadia's bursary. And maybe even he could better himself – finish school, and go and study to run a business. Something small, a hat shop for men, an exclusive clothing shop. Tyrone's Outfitters. He would like that.

And maybe that train trip across Europe.

But only if he could get the cops to protect Nadia.

He sheltered on the threshold of a big closed door, just a few metres from the Zanzibar restaurant in Castle Street. It was deserted in this weather.

He called Vodacom directory enquiries and got the number of the Bellville cop shop.

In the oppressive silence of the Hawks' bar Griessel said, 'It doesn't matter what is on the card.'

They looked at him, caught unaware by the positive note in his voice. While disappointment and disillusionment had wafted through the room, he had had a sudden moment of clarity and insight: he was the only one here who knew how it felt to work in a broken system. He had been through it all before. Even if he was a drunk and a fuck-up. Maybe *because* he was drunk and a fuck-up. In those days, in the darkest years of the old system, he had to find a reason to get up in the morning and do his work, despite everything. It was the only thing that stood between him and total devastation and despair.

It made Benny Griessel here, now, suddenly feel useful again. Relevant. For the first time in months. Or years, he didn't think he could remember. It was almost a euphoric experience: he could think of more important things than life's meaningless little frustrations. He could make a contribution. A difference. That was why there was excitement in his voice.

And now he had to find the right words to explain it. Without making a total fool of himself.

'It doesn't matter why the SSA is involved, or CI, or MI6,' said Griessel. 'It doesn't matter where the pressure is coming from, or if we are disappointed in our government, or our commanders . . .'

He saw Mbali looking at him, hurt and disappointed. 'We don't work for the president, or the minister or the commissioner,' he said. 'We work for the people who were killed in Franschhoek and in the

Waterfront, and for their families. We are all they have. We are the police. We enforce the law, the law that says if you kill someone, you have to pay. That is what I want to do: catch them, and make them pay. It is the only thing I can do. It is the only difference I can make. And I just think . . .' and he wondered, where all this shit was coming from that he was going to say now, but he said it anyway, in the full expectation that Cupido would laugh out loud '. . . if we all . . . if everybody in this country can just try to make a difference, then everything will be OK.' In the silence, only the humming of the big beer fridge in the corner could be heard.

Then Mbali said, 'Benny, that was beautiful.'

And Bones nodded in agreement, and Zola Nyathi had a little smile on his usually unreadable face.

Vaughn Cupido, however, was never one for hallowed moments. 'But how do we catch them, Benna, if we don't know what is on that card?' he asked.

'Like you taught me,' said Griessel. 'With technology. Cellphones.'

'Benny, with CI coming, there is no chance we can use IMC. They will be sifting through everything. I've already terminated all the existing cellphone tracking.'

'Sir, we can use an outside operator,' said Griessel. 'An independent.'

He knew they weren't going to like this. The biggest problem was that the SAPS, according to the Criminal Procedure Act, was not allowed to use independent cellphone tracking operators. Any evidence or testimony that was acquired in that manner would be angrily rejected by the court, and they would be crucified in the media. In addition, the private digital detectives were not popular with the police, because they frequently worked in the shadows and on the margins of the law, and sometimes paid key people at cellular companies a little something under the table.

But they were fast and frequently effective.

When no one responded, Griessel said, 'We're not looking for evidence. All we want to do is find the pickpocket.'

'And those guys don't need subpoenas,' said Cupido with rising enthusiasm. 'They're off the grid, sir.'

'But we're going to have to pay them,' said Griessel.

Nyathi didn't look as though he liked the idea.

Griessel wondered if he was worried it would get out. 'Sir, the private operators have to be discreet. It's the only way they can stay in business.'

The colonel stared at his hands.

'Do we have phones to track?' asked Bones Boshigo.

'Yes,' said Griessel. 'One to start with. But we are going to need a bit of luck.'

'How much money are we talking about?' asked Nyathi.

50

Griessel turned his iPhone on when they were standing in the parking area. Seven voice messages.

He sighed, not in the mood for this now, they had a plan, they had little time, and he wanted to get going. He wanted to catch the fuckers.

He phoned his voicemail number. The first message was from Janina Mentz of the SSA.

'I have information that can help you. Call me.'

Fuck you, he thought and deleted it.

The second was from Alexa. 'Hello, Benny, I just wanted to tell you I'm safely here. Remember the food in the fridge. I'm going to miss you so much tonight, not having you beside me in bed. I love you very much, don't work too hard. Bye.'

He deleted it.

The third was from Emma Graber of the British Consulate.

'Captain, I would really appreciate it if you could give me a call.' She provided her personal cell number, and concluded: 'It's really urgent.'

Fuck you, he thought, and deleted it.

The fourth was from Janina Mentz again. 'We're reasonably sure now why the Brits got our government's cooperation so easily. This could help you. Call me.'

He deleted it, not without a measure of satisfaction. Because all of them – along with the arrival of Criminal Intelligence, and the calls from the national and the DPCI commissioners, meant only one thing: the bastards of the SSA had made no progress with the investigation. They were all desperate now.

The fifth voicemail was from Bellville SAPS commander. 'Benny, *hier's nou 'n ding*. Something's come up. Call me, please.'

He called.

'We had a strange phone call at the charge office, Benny,' the colonel said. 'A guy who said the shooting at the train station was Flats gang-sters. And the girl in the hospital is a target, she knows the big guns, she has information that could be very damaging to them. And there's a contract out on her: now I want to know, does that match with the thing you are investigating?'

It took Griessel a while to realise what was going on. 'Yes, Colonel.'

'So there is a real risk?'

'Yes, Colonel. Will you be able to allocate people for protection?'

'I have already sent two uniforms.'

Griessel shook his head. Two uniforms, against the Cobras. 'They might not be enough, Colonel. These guys are dangerous.'

The colonel sighed. 'I don't really have more people, Benny. And my overtime budget . . . You know how it is.'

Griessel pondered the dilemma. There was no one at the Hawks who could help. Not with CI on the way, not with SSA eavesdrop-ping, not with the danger that each of them that they coopted could lose their job and career. But he knew what would convince the colonel.

'I understand, Colonel. It's just . . . if the media finds out you knew about the risk . . .'

The station commander sighed deeply. 'Yes, I know. Let me see if I can spare two more.'

Griessel suspected that even four constables would not be enough.

They had to hope that things would work out so that more compre-hensive protection of Nadia Kleinbooi would not be necessary.

The sixth message was from Jeanette Louw of Body Armour. 'Captain, I would love to know how the investigation is going. Remember your promise.'

What could he tell her now?

And technically speaking, it was SSA's problem now.

He deleted her message.

The seventh message was from Ulinda Radebe. 'Benny, we're back. Where are you? We have five photographs and names. Five potentials. Call me.'

He ran back to Nyathi's office to discuss this development.

'We can't involve them too, Benny,' said the Giraffe. 'Ulinda has four kids. Vusi takes care of his mother. Given the choice, I'm sure they'll both insist on taking the risk, but I'm not going to do that. Let me handle it. I'll get the names and the photographs, I'll tell them we've been taken off the case.'

'Yes, sir.'

'I'll call you.'

'Thank you, sir.'

Then he ran to the car park, where the others were waiting for him.

They drove to Sea Point – Mbali, Cupido, Bones, and Griessel – to Dave Fiedler, the most respected freelance operator in the business.

On the way, Benny tested his theory on his colleagues. He said the key to the hunt lay in the rucksack that Tyrone Kleinbooi had with him this morning at the Waterfront. The deleted video showed Tyrone had it on his back when he was apprehended by the security men. But when he ran away after the shooting, he was without it. The Cobra team member had a similar rucksack in his hand when he followed Tyrone.

And he was sure Tyrone's phone was in that rucksack, and that cellphone was their only way to catch the murderers.

Cupido asked him why he was so certain the cellphone was in the rucksack.

Because the Cobras, said Griessel, did not track down Nadia in Stellenbosch through her address details on the university account in Tyrone's room in Schotsche Kloof. That account showed her flat address. But Nadia had told him and Mbali how she had been in class the whole morning. And then someone had called from Tyrone's phone, and said he had picked it up on the pavement in the city, and made an appointment to meet her on campus. That was where they had kidnapped her.

'I still don't get it,' said Bones. 'How are we going to catch them based on that information?'

'Because Nadia says as far as she can remember, the Cobras used Tyrone's phone to talk to him. All afternoon.'

'So Tyrone has another phone as well.'

'I think Tyrone has two other phones. Three in total. Or at least one other phone and two SIM cards.'

'How do you figure that out, Benna?' asked Cupido, his technology mentor, who was frequently sceptical of his apprentice's ability to grasp all the nuances.

'There is the phone that was in the rucksack. Let us call it Phone One. That is the one the Cobras have now.'

'Check.'

'There is the phone that he used around one o'clock to call Nadia on her iPhone. The number was on Nadia's register. Phone Two.'

'Check.'

'But tonight, while we were with Nadia at the hospital, he called her again, from another number, but definitely a cell number. Phone Three.'

'Check. That pickpocket is a canny coloured.'

'But now we know Tyrone wants to continue to negotiate with the Cobras. And how is he going to contact them?'

'By calling the phone that was in his backpack,' said Mbali. 'Phone One. Because the Cobras still have it.'

'We hope,' said Griessel.

'So we try and plot Tyrone's phone?' asked Bones.

'We try and plot all three phones,' said Griessel. 'So we can find him and the Cobras.'

Cupido was driving, but he took a moment to look at Griessel with amused pride. 'Who said you can't teach an old dog new tricks?'

'I'm trying,' said Griessel, pleased with himself.

'Then we and Dave Fiedler will have to get a move on. Before the pickpocket completes his payback.'

Tyrone put the three phones in a row on the guest room dressing table. He made doubly sure they were all off. He propped Number Three in his recharger, because tomorrow it was the one that had to be fully loaded.

. He hung up his jacket, trousers, and shirt in the cupboard. He laid out clean underwear for the next morning. He placed the pistol beside the bed.

He gulped down another two Panados, pulled the duvet back, and slid into the bed.

Jirre, that was good.

One day, when all these troubles were over, he would like to ask the aunty here what kind of mattress this was.

He would surely be able to afford one, with two point four million stashed away.

Then he thought about Nadia, and he prayed that the cops would take his call seriously. He had used his best Flats Afrikaans, had used all the slang of the gangs, he had dropped a few names of known mob bosses, he had said there was a contract out for any gang member who walked into the hospital and shot her.

It wasn't easy, because when you said it, then you saw it, here in your head.

And that's the last thing he wanted to see. Because it was his fault.

But he mustn't think about that now. Let him go over his plan. Bit by bit, step by step. He had picked the turf that he knew.

Work the places you know, Ty.

And everything was geared so that, when all was said and done, he could get to his sister quickly.

Just in case. Because he wasn't going to crook anyone, he would keep his part of the bargain.

But you never knew. And he was a pickpocket with a pistol now.

Outside the rain suddenly slashed against the window, rattling and raging.

And he thought, at least his plan was reasonably weatherproof. Unless it rained so much that the trains stopped running.

When they turned out of Buitengracht into Helen Suzman Boulevard, Griessel's ZTE phone rang.

He answered.

'Benny,' said Zola Nyathi. 'I think we can be fairly sure there are five Cobras. The photographs don't show much of their faces, probably because they were aware of the cameras, had their heads down and were all wearing some sort of disguise – hats, caps, glasses, bandanas, or scarves. But they are all mid-thirties, probably. Military types. Which isn't conclusive, of course. But then there are the names. I'm not sure about the pronunciation: Hector Malot, Raoul de Soissons, Jean-Baptiste Chassignet, Xavier Forneret, and Sacha Guitry. I'll SMS them all to you. But Vusi had an idea, while they were waiting for their flight back. He googled the names. And that's why I'm sure they are all part of a team. All the names belong to famous French authors. Famous deceased French authors.'

51

Dave Fiedler handed Griessel's SAPS identity card back to him. 'You've gotta be kidding me, china,' he said in a rich baritone.

He was chunky and hairy – short beard and moustache, hair growing out of his ears, hair out of his nose, hair that pushed out from under the collar of his grey pullover, like plants reaching for light.

They were standing at the door of 2A Worcester Street in Sea Point, the double-storey where Fiedler lived and worked. The four of them only just fitted in under the small porch, with the rain falling in a thick, hissing curtain behind them.

'We're not kidding. Just get us out of the weather,' said Cupido.

Fiedler stood aside and waved them inside, his luxuriant eyebrows raised in disbelief.

'I hope you have a warrant,' he said when Griessel walked past him.

'We don't need a warrant, we need your help.'

'No wonder it's fucking raining,' said Fiedler, and shut the door behind Bones.

'I will not tolerate such language,' said Mbali. 'Have some respect. I'm a lady.'

'Oh, Jesus Christ,' said Fiedler, but so quietly that only Bones, right at the back, could hear him. He walked ahead, to a large room – probably once a sitting room before he had converted it into work space. To the left against the wall was a table with a coffee machine, mugs, sugar, and milk, beside a conference table with eight chairs. To the right was a long, low table with a couple of computers. There were film posters on the walls.

The story was that Fiedler had emigrated here seven years ago from Israel, a former senior member of the Israeli army's legendary Unit 8200. This unit not only produced, according to the rumours, the most sought-after technology alumni in the world, but had also developed much of the programming and apparatus that Fiedler now used to do digital detective work for private investigators, the security industry, and the public.

Nobody knew why he addressed everyone that lived and breathed as 'china'.

'Please, sit down,' he said, and he pointed at the table. 'There's a fresh pot of coffee, so help yourselves. I hope you brought the doughnuts . . .'

They didn't get the joke. He shook his head.

'What's with the posters?' asked Cupido.

'Have you seen the movies?'

Cupido read the titles: *American Pie, Blue Thunder, EDtv, Enemy of the State, The Bourne Supremacy, Minority Report, Cape Fear, 1984, The Osterman Weekend, La Zona.*

'Some of them.'

'What do they have in common?'

Cupido shook his head.

'Surveillance flicks,' said Fiedler. 'And they all get it wrong . . . So the first thing I tell a new customer, if he wants movie tech, he should go watch a movie.' He stood beside the table, clearly still not at ease. 'This is very weird, but I'll play along. What can I do for you?'

Griessel took out his notebook, and tore the page out. 'We want you to plot these three numbers.' He slid the page across the conference table. 'We want to know where the phones are, and we want to know which numbers called them today.'

'For starters,' said Cupido.

Fiedler stared at Griessel with an expression that said he was waiting for the punch line of the joke.

When it was not forthcoming, he said, 'You're from the Hawks, it said on your ID.'

'You'd better believe it,' said Cupido.

'And you want me to plot three numbers for you?'

'Yes,' said Griessel.

'And you can't ever tell anybody that this happened,' said Cupido. 'If we hear even a whisper that you mentioned this, ever, we will make your life a misery.'

Fiedler laughed, a short, deep guffaw. They didn't react. 'It's the end of the world,' he said. 'God's truth.'

Mbali made a disapproving sound.

'You're gonna pay me?' asked Fiedler.

'You talk money, you talk to me,' said Bones. 'What is your rate?'

'This is real. This is actually real,' said Fiedler, pulling up a chair and sitting down. He looked at the numbers. 'Where are the IMEIs?' He pronounced it in the trade lingo, *eye-me-eyes*.

'We don't have them.'

'I should have known. Then it's going to take a while, china.'

At ten thirty-five, Dave Fiedler spoke out, from behind one of his computers: 'That second number has been static in Bellville since four o'clock.'

They sat around the conference table. They were familiar with the art of waiting. Each was busy with his own thoughts.

'Where in Bellville?' asked Griessel.

'Boston. Frans Conradie Drive, about halfway between Duminy and Washington. Google Earth shows a place called Brights Electrical.'

'He's still there now?' asked Cupido.

'Yep.'

Griessel stood up. 'Static. Completely static at the same place?'

'Yep. Phone's on, but no calls or texts. Last call was made at fifteen fifty-two.'

Griessel walked to the computer screen. 'How accurate is the plotting, the position of the phone?'

'About fifteen metres. But because it's been static, I'd say closer to ten.'

Cupido also came close. They looked at the screen, where Fiedler had Google Streetview open.

'Those are flats there beside Brights,' said Cupido. 'On both sides.'

'Could it be in those flats?' Griessel asked Fiedler, and pointed at the screen.

'Yes. Probably the one on the right.'

'And it's near the hospital,' said Griessel. 'Let's go.'

They walked quickly to the door. Griessel stopped. 'And the other phones?'

'I'll tell you in ten . . .'

'Call me on this number,' said Griessel and scribbled it down

hurriedly on a page in his notebook, tore it out and passed it across to
Fiedler.

They drove up the N1 with the siren on and the blue light balanced
on the dashboard, from where it frequently slid off into Griessel's lap.

Just beyond the N7, Fiedler phoned. 'What you call Phone One has
been off for the past two and a half hours, china. Plotting says it was
all over the place today. Smack in the city, then the Waterfront, then all
the way to Stellenbosch, then Bellville . . .'

'What was the last location?'

'The R304.'

'Where's that?'

'It's the road that runs from Stellenbosch all the way to Malmesbury.
Before it was switched off, the phone was about three kilometres from
the R312 crossing. That's the one running from Wellington to
Durbanville.'

Griessel knew the area. 'But there's nothing there.'

'That's right, china.'

'Do you have the call registry yet?'

'Nope. But it's coming.'

'And Phone Three?'

'Phone Three was on for just eleven minutes, about three hours ago.
It made one call. From Somerset Road in the vicinity of the Cape
Quarter mall.'

That was when Tyrone phoned Nadia in the hospital.

'That's it? Just the one call?'

'Just the one. And then it was switched off.'

Cupido switched the siren and light off when they turned out of Mike
Pienaar Drive into Frans Conradie.

Griessel said they would have to use the old trick to get into the flats
without a warrant: tell the residents there was a very dangerous, heavily
armed murderer in the area. He might be hiding in one of the flats at
that very moment, they just wanted to secure everything.

'Then we focus on the flats that don't want to let us in.'

Bones grinned. 'You old salts,' he said, but with respect.

They paired off and went to knock softly on all the doors of the

Darina apartment block in 12th Avenue, Boston. White and brown faces opened doors warily. The team displayed their identity cards, apologised for the inconvenience, and spun their tale.

Everyone allowed them in, wide-eyed, standing frightened at the door while their humble one- and two-bedroom spaces were searched, for Tyrone Kleinbooi.

Less than a quarter of an hour later they were back on the pavement in front of the building.

'Maybe it's that block over there.' Mbali pointed at the flats on the other side of the big, red Brights facade.

There too, and in the rooms above the Boston Superette, they found nothing except shocked and anxious residents.

They called Dave Fiedler, who went through his computers again and said the phone was still there, right where they were.

It was Cupido, ever bold and impulsive, who looked at the long row of rubbish bins in front of the Brights steel gate and said: 'He dumped the phone.'

None of them was keen to brave the minimal shelter of the facade's narrow overhang, where the cold rain splashed down, to rummage in the contents of the filthy rubbish bins.

At 23.52 Mbali pulled the phone from the rubbish.

It was a Nokia 2700.

52

Griessel took his colleagues back to the DPCI headquarters, because Dave Fiedler said there was one call to Tyrone Kleinbooi's Phone One – the device that the Cobras most likely had in their possession now. The number had been active for sixteen minutes in Castle Street, and after that had disappeared off the air.

'Go get some sleep, china. I'll call you if there's any action.'

They met Nyathi down in the basement and informed him of the latest developments.

The Giraffe gave them the photos of the five possible Cobras that were taken at O. R. Tambo Airport – not very useful, but better than nothing. 'These are our five famous French authors. Take them with you. Maybe it will help.'

Griessel agreed with Bones, Cupido and Mbali that they would phone as soon as there was news. It was better to get some sleep. He was going home, his house was only five or ten minutes away from Fiedler, and he would let them know if there was any activity on the numbers.

Then he drove alone to Alexa's house, mulling over the events of the past hour or two.

The pickpocket had deliberately left Phone Two, according to Cupido a 'prepaid special' that you could buy at any backstreet cell-phone shop for a couple of hundred rand, in a rubbish bin at Brights. Still switched on. As if he knew someone was going to trace the number and try to determine the location of the phone.

It made sense. Tyrone knew they would find Nadia's iPhone in the hospital and start analysing it.

So Tyrone was nobody's fool. He knew what could be done with technology. And he wanted to make some kind of statement. 'I'm in Bellville,' perhaps?

Only to make the next call from De Waterkant?

Which was not too far from where Tyrone rented the room in Schotsche Kloof.

Did he go back to the city, to Bo-Kaap, because he felt at home there? Safe?

That's what fugitives from the law often did when the heat was on, when the chase became too intense, and their flight chaotic.

And shortly after Tyrone had called Nadia, a new, unknown number had called Phone One, now with the Cobras.

Jissis, thought Benny Griessel. How many phones did the fucker have?

But then he realised the man was a pickpocket. He had as many phones as he needed.

And if you were negotiating with a team that walked into the Waterfront in broad daylight and shot dead five security guards in cold blood, you'd want to make doubly sure that they can't track you down via cellular technology.

He felt a great sense of determination rising in him. He would have to keep his head, with all the phones, all the technological possibilities. He would have to show he had learned to be a modern-day detective. Even if Cupido called him an 'old dog', and Bones joked about the 'old salts'.

When he got home, he phoned Dave Fiedler and said he also wanted a complete analysis and monitoring of the number that had called Phone One from Castle Street.

'Sure, china, but the meter is running.'

'Just let me know as soon as there is any activity on any of those phones.'

He walked through the cold, empty house to the kitchen. The rain drummed fiercely on the roof.

And suddenly he missed Alexa, her presence, her happiness when she saw him, her embrace, her chatter, every evening so intense and enthusiastic, as if he really mattered. As if she really loved him.

All this he saw and felt, now that she wasn't here.

He took the Woolworths food out of the fridge – chicken and broc-coli, his favourite, which she'd bought specially for him – with a pang of guilt about his relief earlier in the day, at the thought of having the house to himself.

He put the container in the microwave, pinged it on. Two minutes, thirty seconds.

What was he going to do, between the devil of his self-doubt and his inadequate rascal, and the deep blue sea of his attraction to her? And the pleasure of being with her. She was so . . . full. Full of everything. He sometimes wished her *joie de vivre*, her intensity, her naivety would infect him.

She was his perfect polar opposite. He didn't want to, he dared not, he could not lose her. Despite, everything, he had begun to love her very much. And tonight, after he had regained a measure of relevance as a policeman, as a team member of the Hawks – for the first time in his career – he felt optimism. He *wanted* this thing with Alexa to work.

If he could just find a solution to his dilemma.

Griessel ate his supper.

When he had finished, rinsed his dishes and put them on the drying rack, he phoned the Louis Leipoldt Hospital. He asked to be put through to the ward where Nadia Kleinbooi lay, identified himself to the night sister, and asked how the patient was.

'We gave her a sleeping pill, Captain. She's sleeping peacefully.'

He thanked her and said she must see that the four constables got coffee regularly so that they were awake and alert.

The night sister said yes, she'd see to that.

He rang off.

At least he knew now that there were four uniforms on guard.

He went to shower, put on his pyjamas, which still smelled faintly of sex. He made sure both his cellphones were on. He set the alarm on the iPhone for seven o'clock, but he suspected Dave Fiedler would call him long before then.

Then he slept.

53

Twenty to six.

Tyrone woke suddenly from sleep, released from a dream where a man in a grey cap was shooting Nadia, one shot after the other. He felt his sister's body jerk in his arms, and he tried to shield her with his hands, but it didn't help, the bullets went right through, leaving big holes in his palms, but there was no blood, only Nadia bled, and then he was awake and a huge wave of relief washed over him.

Just a dream.

Had he screamed out loud in his sleep, the way he had heard his own voice in the dream?

Moments of disorientation, the strange room, sounds of water dripping off a roof outside the window.

And then, the full onslaught of reality returning. He was here. This was the day he had been preparing for. His body was stiff, his back was sore.

Was Nadia OK?

He wanted to phone the hospital straight away.

But he couldn't phone from here.

He got up and walked through to the bathroom.

Tyrone sat on the end of the bed. He was washed, dressed, packed. He'd taken two Panados already, but the pain still throbbed across his back. The cellphones on the dressing table lay neatly in a row, the pistol next to them.

Phone the hospital. Hear if Nadia is OK.

Switch on the phone the guys are going to send the money photo to.

Twenty past six in the morning? You're too anxious, Tyrone. Get a grip. Take a deep breath. Don't fuck this up.

Turn on the TV. If there was an attack at the hospital, it would be on the news.

He switched it on. The high, exuberant voices of a children's programme were suddenly too loud and shrill for the morning silence. He stabbed at the remote's volume button over and over again until it could barely be heard. Navigated to SABC2 and *Morning Live*. An interview with a darkie dude that he didn't know. The news would probably come on at half past.

Breathe. Go through the schedule.

He wanted to know if Nadia was OK. Watch the news. If there was nothing, phone later, once he was out of here.

He must have breakfast, 'cause it was going to be a hectic day.

He must buy chewing gum, to stick the memory card to.

He must double-check the train times.

He must wait for the photos of the money, the suitcase, and the guy.

And then it was lights, camera, action.

He looked at the TV screen.

Twenty-four past six.

Time stands still when you're not having fun.

The iPhone alarm woke Griessel at seven.

When he switched it off and lay back for a second, holding the phone, he was grateful for the six hours of unbroken sleep. And then he realised that it meant there had been no action on any of the numbers, and he wondered if his plan was going to work.

Perhaps none of the cellphones was still in use.

Wouldn't that be typical: just when he started getting his head around all the technology, it turns out to be useless.

He got up, in one restless, uneasy movement, walked to the toilet, lifted the seat, pulled his pyjamas down, aimed, and urinated.

He suppressed the urge to call Dave Fiedler now.

If there was news, he would have known.

He flushed, put the seat down again, and walked to the hand basin. He must finish up and drive over to Fiedler's.

News item, four minutes past seven, *Morning Live*: 'Western Cape police spokesperson Wilson Bala denied that the SAPS was investigating a shooting that allegedly occurred at Cape Town's Victoria and Alfred Waterfront yesterday. This, despite claims by family members of Waterfront security personnel, and eyewitness reports of extensive medical and law enforcement presence at the shopping centre yesterday morning. Both the centre management and the Blue Shield security company declined to comment on the matter. The alleged shooting even drew attention in parliament today . . .'

What the fuck? wondered Tyrone.

And then a moment of huge relief. His face was not on TV.

But why not?

He watched the news until it was over, his thoughts occupied with possible reasons, his heart fearful of news of a hospital shooting.

It didn't come.

But now he wasn't sure if that meant anything. If the cops were denying that they were investigating a Waterfront shooting? A shooting he had seen with his own eyes.

What was going on?

The urge to move, to get going, to gain momentum, overwhelmed him. He must get out of here. He must phone Nadia.

And then get breakfast, even though he felt queasy now.

07.27

Griessel had a coffee mug in his hand and a mouth full of toast with Marmite, when his ZTE phone rang.

'Hello,' he answered, swallowing quickly.

'China, we've just had action. Phone Number Three came alive four minutes ago and called the same number as yesterday afternoon. Call lasted just thirty-seven seconds.'

'Hang on . . .' Benny plonked down the half full coffee mug and ran to the bedroom to get his jacket.

He grabbed his notebook out of his jacket pocket, riffled through the pages until he found what he was looking for. 'This number?' He read it out to Fiedler.

'That's the one.'

Nadia's iPhone. It was Tyrone phoning her again.

'Where's the phone now? Phone Three.'

'It's gone off air, the call was too short for a good fix, but it was made in the vicinity of the Waterkant and Loop Street crossing, give or take five hundred metres.'

'I'm on my way.'

He rang off, and began calling his colleagues as he jogged to the front door.

Tyrone sat on the planter box of black marble in front of Atterbury House in Lower Burg.

Nadia was OK.

In a manner of speaking.

She was cross with him. 'Tyrone, come in, and leave those things, the *polieste* say you're not in trouble, please, *boetie.*'

'Everything is fine, *moenie worry nie*. Are there cops guarding you?'

'*Ja*, Tyrone, and it's because you won't let this thing go.'

'Everything is going to be just fine, *sussie.*' Then he'd ended the call and walked over here.

Time to check in for the money shot.

He switched the second cellphone on.

On the way, Griessel phoned Nadia.

She said, yes, her brother had phoned, he wanted to know how she was.

Then he heard another call coming in, said goodbye, and took it.

Dave Fiedler: 'Funny thing, china. That fourth number you asked me to keep an eye on, the one that called Phone One from Castle Street last night . . .'

'Yes.'

'It just came alive. I'm trying to get a fix on it now . . . hang on . . . Damn!'

'What?'

'Went off again. All I can tell you is it's in the city.'

Old dogs don't believe in coincidences, thought Benny Griessel. Two phones calling shortly after each other from the city?

Phone Four was also Tyrone's.

07.51.

Tyrone ordered a Big Breakfast at McDonald's in the Golden Acre. And Premium Roast coffee.

He carried everything carefully on a tray in one hand, dragging the suitcase with the other. He sat down so that he could watch the door, although he couldn't quite say why.

Three sugars in the coffee.

He ate and drank. The coffee was OK, the food was basically tasteless.

He would have to dump the suitcase, he couldn't drag it around with him all day, he had to travel light. Be highly mobile. Time to rock 'n' roll, and yes, some running would be involved.

He had only needed it to look legit for the guesthouse. He would leave it here, just put the underpants, socks, and shirts in the rucksack.

When he had finished eating, he switched the cellphone on again. Only long enough to see there were no pictures of the money, the bag, or the guy yet.

54

08.12.

Rush hour, the city traffic was crazy, even though it wasn't raining – the sun broke through dramatic clouds, the sunbeams blindingly bright on the wet road.

That's how the Cape is, thought Griessel when he eventually parked in front of Fiedler's house and office. When rain looked likely, every *fokker* in the Peninsula drove his own car to work, although it then took everybody twice as long.

He got out. His ZTE rang. It was Fiedler. He answered and said, 'I'm at your door.'

'Phone Four was alive for three minutes. I'll open up for you.'

And when Fiedler opened the door, 'Three minutes, and then it went dead again. Still in the city centre. I can't get a close fix.'

'So that's twice?'

'Yes, china. Twice, three minutes every time, then off again, for about five.'

'He's checking in for something. A call . . . ? And he's worried that he will be tracked.'

'If you check in like that, you're waiting for an email, or a text,' said Fiedler. 'Not a call.'

'Yes,' said Griessel. 'Will we be able to see a text?'

'I was afraid that you'd ask that.'

'Why?'

'Because accessing the server is against the law.'

'Can you do it?'

'For a Hawk? Are you crazy?'

'Can you do it?'

'Of course I can do it, china. But it's going to cost a little extra. And you'll have to sign something. I'm not going to incriminate myself.'

'How much extra?'

08.17.

Griessel phoned Nadia Kleinbooi again. He apologised for bothering her.

Anxiously, she asked if there was any news.

No, he said. But he would love to know: did Tyrone have an email address?

She said no without hesitation.

'Are you absolutely sure?'

'Why?'

'We just want to make sure.'

This time she thought a bit before she answered. 'No, he's not into those things.'

'Does he have a car?' Something he should have asked a long time ago.

'No.'

'Does he have access to someone else's car?'

'No. I . . . No, I don't think so.'

Griessel thanked her and rang off. And he thought, Tyrone knew enough about technology to be careful with cellphones, and to hoodwink the Cobras with a memory card. He wasn't so sure she was right.

If the pickpocket had an email address, and that was how he was communicating with the Cobras, they were fucked. Completely.

Metrorail train 2561 on platform 10 of Cape Town Station was full.

At 08.26 Tyrone slipped through the door of the middle third-class carriage and stood in the aisle.

He waited till just after 08.30, when the train jerked and pulled away, before he switched the cellphone in his hand on again.

He held it so that the people pressing against him couldn't see the screen.

He watched it search for a signal, and find it.

It always took a while for an MMS to come through.

At least he was on the move. And he was going to stay on the move, until this thing was finished.

He watched the time passing on the screen.

One minute.

The train picked up speed.

Two minutes.

The train began to lose momentum.

Three minutes.

He felt the action of the brakes as the train slowed to a stop at Woodstock Station.

He waited until it came to a complete standstill.

The doors opened. More people got on.

He switched the phone off.

Still no photos.

Jirre.

08.49.

Mbali arrived first.

'Turn around and drive to Bellville Station,' said Griessel to Cupido over the phone. 'We think he's on a train – we picked him up in Woodstock, and again in Maitland, he was on for about three minutes . . . Hold on, Mbali is here . . .'

Griessel pointed to where Dave Fiedler was busy at the computers. 'We think Tyrone is taking a train. See if you can look at the Metrorail schedule. We need to know which train.'

He turned his attention back to Cupido and the phone again. 'Vaughn, are you there?'

'I'm here. I turned around at the N7, but the traffic is hectic, pappie, it's going to take a while to get back to Bellville.'

'OK. We're trying to find out which train it could be.'

'How sure are you it's a train?'

'He doesn't have a car, and he can't move this fast in a bus or taxi during rush hour. Dave said three minutes is not long enough to get a precise fix, but every time it was within a kilometre of the stations, and the phone is moving, it looks like it's moving.'

'OK, Benna, keep me posted.'

'I'm looking at the Metrorail schedule,' Mbali called.

The front doorbell rang.

'Jesus,' said Dave Fiedler. 'It's like a bloody beehive here.'

Mbali clicked her tongue at him.

Griessel said, 'It must be Bones, I'll open up for him.'

09.01.

At Parow Station Tyrone got off and walked quickly over to the train schedules on the wall in the station building, just to be sure.

Train 3412 ran back to Cape Town, from platform 11. In five minutes, at 09.06.

He jogged around to the platform. Stopped. Switched the phone on. Stood and stared at the screen.

It found a signal.

He waited.

He couldn't go on like this for the whole day, *fok weet*, when were those guys going to send the photo?

Or were they trying to track him?

Good luck with that, motherfuckers.

Train 3412 pulled into the station.

Still no photos, no message.

Shit.

He got on the train, heading back to Cape Town.

'I think it is train 2561. It was at Woodstock at 08.33, and in Maitland at 08.42 . . .'

'He's back on-line,' called Dave Fiedler. 'Hang on, the fix is coming . . .'

Griessel looked at his notes. 'Mbali, I think you're right.'

'He should be in Parow now,' said Mbali.

'Yes, Parow it is,' said Fiedler.

'What time does that train reach Bellville?' asked Griessel.

'Six minutes past nine,' said Mbali.

'*Fok*,' said Griessel, because it was too soon. Cupido would never make it.

'This once, I forgive you,' said Mbali, also dismayed.

55

At 09.14, Tyrone got off at Goodwood Station.

He switched the cellphone on again.

The first MMS came through.

On the small screen he saw the photo. The money, stacked on a table: hundred- and two hundred-rand notes, tied in bundles with rubber bands.

His heart leaped. Could that be two point four million? It seemed so little?

The next photo came through.

A black rucksack, with the money visible through the open zipper. The bag was pleasingly full. That looked better.

The third photo. A man in a blue windcheater and black beanie. High cheekbones, stubble. The rucksack on his back.

Tyrone felt his heart beating. This was a face he had never seen before. It wasn't Hoodie, it wasn't the Waterfront shooter. But this one looked so . . . terrifyingly ruthless.

He felt the phone in his hand tremble.

Stick with the plan, Tyrone.

He steadied himself, tapped the phone to call the number,

It rang.

The guy answered immediately. 'No, don't call me. Send me text messages.'

'Why?' asked Tyrone.

But the line was already dead.

Griessel, Mbali, and Bones Boshigo stood and stared at the photo on Dave Fiedler's computer screen.

'That's a lot of money,' said Fiedler.

'I'm guessing at least a million, million point five,' said Bones.

'Track the number it was sent from,' said Griessel.

'I'm busy . . . He's just called it.'

'Who called what?'

'The train guy . . .'

'Tyrone. Call him Tyrone.'

'OK, Tyrone's just called the number from which the photographs were sent. He's still in Goodwood. I'm getting a better fix, hang on. Yes, definitely at or very near the station.'

'He's clever,' said Mbali. 'He got them to send him a picture of the money. He's selling them the memory card . . .'

'There's another photo,' said Fiedler. 'And another . . .' His hand moved quickly, adeptly with the mouse.

The new photos appeared on the screen, one beside the other.

'*Hhayi*,' said Mbali, because the last one was the one of the man with the rucksack. 'That's a Cobra.'

'A Cobra?' asked Fiedler, but Mbali waddled hastily away to the conference table, where the O. R. Tambo photos of the five suspected Cobras lay. She flipped through them, and found the one that looked like the man in the photo that was sent to Tyrone's phone. She trotted back.

'It's this one.' She held the photo up beside the screen. The resemblance was clear.

'Print that photo, Dave,' said Griessel. 'And send one to Captain Cupido's number.'

'Give me his number,' said Fiedler.

Griessel looked it up on his phone, and held it out so that Fiedler could see.

'Tyrone is very clever,' said Mbali.

Griessel wasn't listening, his brain was too busy now. Tyrone on the train. Tyrone deliberately took the train from Cape Town Station. He could have taken a taxi. He could have taken the bus, but he didn't.

Why?

Tyrone, who travelled to Parow, and was now on the way back towards Cape Town.

'We have a new text,' said Fiedler. He read: '"Why must I only SMS?" That's from Tyrone's phone, to the other guys.'

'The Cobras,' said Griessel, because he wanted their communication to be very clear. What lay ahead was going to be messy enough.

'Who the f—Who are the Cobras?'

'The bad guys.' Griessel read the SMS over Fiedler's shoulder.
Why must I only SMS?
'They must have told him not to call,' said Griessel.
'But why?' asked Bones. 'They can still be traced and tracked, can't they?'
'I think I know, but you'll have to tell me what the hell is going down here,' said Fiedler.
Griessel knew it was the right thing to do now. 'Tyrone is selling a very valuable item to some very dangerous people. We call them Cobras, it's a long story . . . Tyrone is trying to set up the exchange of the item, for the money in the photo.'
'Is it a gang? How many Cobras are there?'
'Five, at least.'
'OK. I think they want him to text so that they can share the message quickly. Doing that on a voice call is tricky in peak time – our cellular network is just too up to shit if you're on the move and you're not using the same service provider.'
They all read the new message from the Cobras to Tyrone on the screen: *Because I say so.*
There was silence in Dave Fiedler's big room. Everyone trying to make sense of the text messages.
'They are setting a trap for him,' said Mbali.
'Yes,' said Griessel. 'They are.'
Fiedler was busy at another computer, while the detectives stood and looked at the screen where the money photos and text messages appeared. Time dragged.
Go to Bellville Station.
'That's Tyrone to the Cobras,' said Bones.
'I have a fix on the Cobra phone,' said Fiedler.
New text: *No.*
'The Cobras are saying "no"?' asked Bones.
'Where is the Cobra phone?' asked Griessel.
'It's moving along the R304, going south, towards the N1.'
Do you want the card?
Nobody said a word, waiting for the Cobras to answer.
Bellville Station too dangerous after yesterday. Choose another place.
'Fair enough,' said Bones.

Nothing on the screen.

Fiedler, at the other monitor, said, 'The Cobras are now on the N1, heading towards the city.'

Griessel wished he could call in the SAPS helicopter, or that he had the time and manpower for a roadblock.

His phone rang. It was Cupido.

'Vaughn, we still don't have anything, I'll phone you back.'

'Roger, Benna.'

'Why isn't Tyrone answering?' Bones asked.

'Because they have messed up his plan,' said Mbali.

Go to Parow Station.

'Trains,' said Griessel suddenly.

They looked at him questioningly, but he picked up his ZTE and phoned Nadia again.

It rang for longer this time. She answered with a scared 'Hello?'

'Nadia, does Tyrone ride the trains often?'

'*Ja*, he comes to me a lot, in Stellenbosch. He's always saying he likes the trains. Loves riding them.'

'First class or third?'

'I think third class.'

'Thank you, Nadia. We still don't have news, but I'll let you know as soon as there is.'

'Thank you.'

He killed the call. He heard Fiedler talking, and Mbali answering, but he wasn't listening. He wanted to make sure his reasoning was correct, that he understood Tyrone. He tried to put himself inside the pickpocket's head. He didn't have a car. Taxis and buses were subject to the flow of traffic. Unpredictable, at best. And also not private if you want to make calls or receive photos of money. The Metro trains were reasonably predictable. In the morning they ran at regular intervals. They were public, but if you wanted to make a call, you could get off and put distance between yourself and your fellow passengers.

It was familiar territory, as well.

And now The Great Transaction. The trains gave Tyrone a moving exchange location – there were not the same dangers of a specific street corner or abandoned building, where the Cobras could hide or stalk him.

Tyrone was clever, as Mbali had pointed out. He knew the trains, apparently he knew the stations. They must be good places to steal from people's pockets. And there would be some small comfort in the crowds of other people, possible eyewitnesses. The Cobras were rightly wary about going back to Bellville. On the rail system, Tyrone could keep moving, in two directions, keep them guessing. Every station offered its own escape routes, within minutes from each other . . .

He phoned Cupido.

'Where are you?'

'Just past Karl Bremer, on the N1. Traffic is a bit better this side.'

'Tyrone is on his way back to Cape Town.'

'*Jissis*, Benna, he's fucking us around.'

'*Ja*. I think you must still go to the station. Take the first train to Cape Town.'

'Then I'll be without a car.'

'I know, but I think he's going to do the whole thing on the trains. He knows the system, and it gives him a lot of options.'

'It's taking a big chance, Benna.'

'It's all we've got.'

56

'Bones, you're going to stay here and you're going to be our controller,' said Griessel.

'Me?' In disbelief.

'Yes. Mbali and I need to get to the city station. I think Tyrone is going to make the handover somewhere along this railway line. At a station or on a train. And the quickest way to get from station to station is by using the train.'

Griessel searched through his pockets, until he found the earphones for the ZTE. He plugged it into his phone, pushed them in his ears.

'Dave, you're going to have to help. You'll have to call Captain Cupido and give him instructions, but wait until I tell Bones what to do.'

'Sweet, china.'

'Bones, call me on this phone. Tell me everything that is happening.'

'I'll do my best,' said Bones nervously.

'You'll be OK,' said Mbali, and adjusted the pistol on her hip.

'You'll have to hide the weapon,' said Griessel. 'And the ID card. We're going undercover.'

Tyrone was on train 3414, from Goodwood to Cape Town.

He stood with bated breath and waited for Black Beanie's answer.

He hadn't expected them to refuse to go to Bellville. He should have thought of that, it was common sense, he didn't want to show his face there either for a while.

But it had made his timetable a bit weird. Because Metrorail's trains ran less frequently until late afternoon.

But it was still OK, if he kept his head.

The phone vibrated in his hand.

OK.

That was their answer.

He let out a sharp, explosive breath.

It was on.

Griessel and Mbali, in the BMW, with the siren and blue light on.

The ZTE rang. Griessel answered, 'Bones?'

'Tyrone is moving again, train 3414 to Cape Town.'

'OK.' He thought for a moment and then spoke loudly, so that Bones on the phone as well as Mbali beside him could both hear him clearly, 'He's moving between the city and Parow. Bones, look at the schedule, is that where the most trains are running?'

'Hang on . . . Tyrone has just replied to the Cobras' text, he said "Tell me when you are at Parow Station".'

'Has Dave called Vaughn yet?'

'Yes. Vaughn is on train 3214, it left Bellville at ten, direction Cape Town. It's the one right behind Tyrone's.'

'OK, tell him we're undercover. No ID, no firearm visible.'

'Roger . . . Benny, you're right. The bulk of the trains will be running between Eerste River and Cape Town from now until about four. Just about twenty per cent go to the Strand.'

'OK, Bones. I think it is going to happen between the city and Parow, maybe Bellville. When is Vaughn going to reach Parow?'

'He's already past Parow, according to the schedule. He should be at Thornton now.'

'Tell him to get off at Maitland. Unless you can see Tyrone leaving his train somewhere.'

'Tyrone still seems to be moving.'

'Hang on.' Griessel wove though the traffic in Strand Street. He had to concentrate on the road for now. Mbali sat staring with wide eyes, clutching the big black handbag on her lap.

Then they were across Adderley, alongside the station. He saw a loading zone, switched off the siren, and parked. Mbali's door was already open, as though she was relieved to be getting out of the car.

'Mbali!' he shouted as they ran to the station. 'We are going to take two separate trains, just to cover more bases.'

'Yes,' she said, already puffing.

★ ★ ★

Tyrone got off at Woodstock.

Where was Black Beanie? Why was it taking so long to get to Parow Station?

They were going to fuck everything up.

He went over to the schedules again. He would have to wait.

Time to begin chewing the gum. He dug in his pocket, took out the pack, put six strips in his mouth, began to chew.

His cellphone vibrated.

We are at Parow.

He shivered. Was his plan going to work?

His fingers trembled as he typed *OK. I know u are 4. Money guy ...* and he looked closely at the time tables ... *goes on train 3520, leaving Parow at 10.36, Plfrm 9. Must be alone, or u won't get card. I will hide card on train 3515, reaching Parow at 10.50. when I have money, will tell u where on train card is hidden.*

And then he waited for them to answer.

Bones's voice was high and almost panicky when he passed on the news to Griessel.

'OK, Bones, Mbali has just left the station on that exact train, so we are covered. I am going to call her now, and I'm going to warn her. Now you and Dave must try to get Vaughn on the same train, Mbali will need backup.'

'Roger, out.'

'No, wait. Where is Tyrone?'

'Woodstock.'

'OK, that's where I'm going.'

If card is not on train, we WILL kill your sister. Just 4 guards at hospital.

How did they know that? wondered Tyrone. Had they been there?

Of course they had been there, you ape.

He would have to get the money, and then take the pistol and go to his sister, these guys just wanted to kill.

Take a deep breath, Tyrone.

He typed on the phone: *If money is right, card is there.*

Train 3515 pulled into Woodstock Station.

Tyrone ran for the train.

Time to put the card under a seat.

Mbali Kaleni saw the pickpocket running towards the train. Her cell-phone against her ear, she told Griessel, cool as a cucumber, 'I see him.'

'Good,' said Griessel.

'He's getting on the train . . .'

'OK.'

'He's in the next carriage, I can see him . . . He's taking off his back-pack. He's sitting down . . . He's opening his backpack, he has taken something out. I can't see what it is. He has it on his lap. Wait . . . Now he's taken something from his mouth. He's looking around . . . Sorry, Benny, I had to look away . . .'

'OK.'

'He . . . Benny, I think he has stuck the card under the seat. Now he's getting up, the train is going to stop at . . . Salt River Station. I think he's going to get off.'

'Mbali, go and see if the card is there.'

She waited until Tyrone had left the train. She watched Tyrone go and stand on the platform. She felt sorry for him, in that instant, he looked so scared and bewildered.

Still she remained seated. Till the doors closed, and the train jerked, and began to move.

Then she got up and walked to the seat he had vacated. She saw Tyrone standing on the platform staring at the departing train.

A young black man sat down on Tyrone's seat. He had earphones on and his head moved in time to the music he was listening to.

Mbali stopped in front of him and said: 'I want you to move.'

He didn't hear her.

She tapped him on the knee and he looked up, irritated by the intru-sion. She gestured that he should move up.

He stared at her, challenging. '*Ungachopha apho,*' he said. You can sit there.

She smacked him against the ear, like a naughty child.

That shocked him, he ducked to avoid another possible smack, and said in agitation, '*Yintoni eyebayo?*' What is *wrong* with you?

But he took in her severe expression, the fearless attitude, and he shifted up, three seats further away. He shook his head in disbelief, trying to regain a little dignity.

Mbali ignored him, sat down, put her handbag beside her, and leaned over. She felt underneath the seat, until she found the wodge of chewing gum. She pulled it loose, and held it up.

She said to Benny Griessel, 'I have the card.'

57

Griessel was still waiting at Cape Town Station for train 2319.

On his cellphone, Bones said, 'Tyrone has just sent the Cobras a message. It says: "Card hidden on train now. Let me know when money is at Maitland Station." And the Cobra said: "OK." But there's a problem. I could not reach Vaughn in time, he says there was no signal. So he missed Mbali's train.'

'Shit.'

'What do you want me to do?'

'Can you tell me where Tyrone is now?'

'He is still at Salt River Station.'

'Tell Vaughn to get off there.'

'OK, Benny.' He rang off.

On platform 7, Griessel saw his train's doors open at last. He jogged up and got in.

He stood, holding on to the metal rail near the roof.

Mbali was going to have to confront one of the Cobras all on her own – the one who would go to find the memory card under the seat as soon as he got on, probably at Parow. There was no time, no one else to help. He would have to warn her now.

Vaughn Cupido got off the train at Salt River Station, and within seconds he spotted Tyrone Kleinbooi sitting on a bench beside the platform.

The pickpocket had a phone in his hand, and all his attention was focused on it.

Cupido walked calmly down the platform, called Dave Fiedler, and told him.

'Hang on, china,' said Fiedler.

Cupido heard Fiedler and Bones talking.

'Captain Griessel will be there in five minutes,' said Fiedler eventually. 'He wants you just to keep an eye on Tyrone.'

* * *

Griessel called Nyathi and explained to him that Mbali, due to an unexpected confluence of events, was alone on a train where, just after Parow Station, she would be confronted by a Cobra who would want that card.

'Sir, if you could just wait for the train at Bellville – we have no other backup.'

'I will take Ulinda with me,' said Nyathi. 'How much time do we have?'

'Not more than ten minutes.'

No anxiety, no reproach, just: 'We'll be there.'

Beyond Maitland, Mbali sat with the memory card held between her fingers, wondering what disastrous data was stored on it. Information that was responsible for the death of at least nine people, and very nearly a tenth as well, an innocent young student.

She stowed the card carefully in a side pocket of her big handbag. She rolled the chewing gum between her fingers until it was one big ball again. She stuck it back precisely where it had been when she found it.

From her handbag she took a little bottle of waterless hand cleaner from Woolworths, and a tissue. She cleaned her fingers thoroughly.

Then, with both hands hidden in the darkness of the handbag, she took her Beretta pistol and made sure it was cocked.

She took her left hand out, but her right hand remained hidden in the depths of the bag, gripped around the pistol.

Benny Griessel had said that a Cobra would get on at Parow Station, and would come looking for the memory card.

And she would be ready for him.

Benny Griessel got off the train at Salt River and phoned Cupido.

'Where are you?'

'On the platform.'

'I can't see you.'

'Platform 11.'

'OK, I'm on the other side, I'm coming. Can you see Tyrone?'

'He is ten steps away from me. He's texting on his phone.'

'I'll be there directly.'

Griessel walked hurriedly down the stairs, heading for the other side of the railway line.

Bones would phone at any moment with news about the text that Tyrone was sending.

If the pickpocket was still here, that meant that he was going to receive the money here.

Good news, because he and Cupido were both here. One to catch the Cobra, and one to follow Tyrone and the money.

The ZTE rang, as he had expected.

'Cobra texted to say he has passed Maitland, then Tyrone answered with this: "When train stops at Salt River, wait until just before doors close again. Throw out money. Don't get out. Stay on train. Just throw out money bag. If money is good, I'll send card details."'

'Have they answered?'

'No . . . yes, just came in. Just "OK".'

'How long before that train comes in at Salt River?'

'Three minutes.'

Griessel began running. 'OK, I'll call you when I have news.'

Cupido saw Griessel running towards him, coat flapping, hair ruffled by the wind. He walked to meet him.

Griessel waited until he was beside his colleague and then explained quietly and breathlessly what was going to happen. 'I'm going to get on that train, Vaughn. You follow Tyrone and the money. If the Cobras are tracking his cellphone too, he's dead. Protect him.'

'Got it,' said Cupido.

Then Griessel walked away, towards the platform.

The money train was visible, a kilometre away.

Tyrone hid behind a pillar, his heart beating wildly. He had put the rucksack down on the concrete and now he looked up quickly to see if someone could see him, put his hand in the rucksack and pulled out the pistol. He pushed the pistol under the purple windcheater, closed the bag, swung it up onto his back.

It was the moment of truth, now.

Maybe they would try to shoot him.

Maybe they would just throw the money out.

Either way, he was as ready as he was ever going to be.

It's worth it, it's worth it, his sister's future . . .

He took the cellphone, typed the message in: *Card is in carriage 3, 3rd class, stuck in the middle of middle bench, table mountain side.*

He would send it when he was sure the money was correct.

The train came in.

He stood ready, behind the pillar, peering at the train.

It stopped.

A few people approached.

A few people got off.

A few people got on.

The train stood there.

The whistle blew.

His eyes scanned up and down, up and down.

A rush of air as the doors closed.

Where was the money?

Right at the back, the furthest from him, the rucksack bounced once, twice across the platform.

The train was leaving.

Tyrone waited.

No one else got off.

His eyes followed the train.

There through the glass, he saw Black Beanie, the man's eyes searching.

Instinctively, Tyrone ducked behind the pillar.

He waited.

The train was gone.

The rucksack lay there.

He looked around.

There was a tall coloured man in a coat, some distance away, with his back to Tyrone. Looked like he had a phone in his hand.

Tyrone waited.

The rucksack lay there.

The coloured man in the coat began to walk away.

Tyrone flew out from behind the pillar and ran to the rucksack.

He grabbed it, raced back to the pillar, opened it.
The money was there.
He sent the text.

58

Benny Griessel made a fatal error.

The chaos of the morning was to blame, the many threads that he had to hold on to and manipulate like a puppeteer, the adrenaline and crazy pace of the chase, the determination to bring the Cobras to book.

He should have stood still for a moment and thought, but he didn't.

Instinctively he shifted his service weapon into easy reach. And he stormed through the train carriage.

He had been standing at the window of the middle carriage, and saw where the rucksack was thrown out. Now he threaded his way between the people in the compartment, to get there, two carriages down. He didn't see the notice stuck in big cartoon strips above the door.

Travelling between coaches is illegal.
Do not board train when full.
Do not hold doors open when train is in motion.

Nobody stopped him when he went from the middle carriage to the next. He saw the Cobra, the one from the photo, with the black cap and the blue windcheater, on the other side of the last door. He put his hand on the Beretta on his hip, pressed the safety off, focused on the man who was staring intently out of the window.

Griessel was unaware of the middle-aged ticket inspector approaching, only noticed him when the man reached him and said, 'You can't travel between coaches.'

'I'm from the police,' said Griessel so as not to attract attention, especially not from the Cobra.

Griessel walked past the ticket inspector. The train was noisy and he didn't hear whether the man said anything in response. Griessel raised his left hand to open the door between the carriages.

The ticker inspector grabbed his right shoulder, to stop him. The man said, 'You can't go through there, it's against the rules.'

'I'm a policeman,' said Griessel, loudly and impatiently this time.

The Cobra saw the movement, turned his head, looked at him.

Griessel jerked the door open with his left hand, pulled out his service pistol.

The ticket inspector shoved Griessel's shoulder, pushing him off balance.

The Cobra was swift and practised. His right hand emerged from his windcheater, holding a pistol. He swung it towards Griessel as he moved forward. To the middle of the carriage.

The door began to close automatically again.

Time stood still. Griessel didn't know how thick the glass was, he would have to shoot before the door closed, before the Cobra could fire at him, there was no time to aim. He jerked his shoulder forwards, and pulled the trigger.

The deafening shot boomed through the train carriage. People screamed. Blood exploded in a fine spray around the Cobra's head and against the window behind him. The Cobra collapsed. The ticket inspector dived at Griessel and tried to wrench the pistol away from him.

Griessel aimed a punch at the man, the pistol was loaded and dangerous, what was the idiot doing? He hit the ticket inspector with an elbow somewhere in his face and the man fell. Griessel staggered forward, up to the Cobra.

The Cobra's lower cheekbone and nose was a bloody, gaping hole.

'*Fok!*' He wanted to know where David Adair was, he'd wanted to question the man.

The ticket inspector tackled Griessel, and both of them stumbled over the Cobra.

Griessel lost his temper, but he pressed the catch of the Beretta so the weapon was safe. Then he hit the ticket inspector angrily across the jaw with the pistol. The man fell down again. Griessel straightened up. He jammed the pistol against the ticket inspector's cheek. 'Are you *fokken* deaf? I'm a policeman.'

'Yes,' said the man, clearly confused.

'Yes, what?'

'Yes,' said the ticket inspector, 'I am a bit deaf.'

Only then Griessel did notice the discreet hearing aid in the man's ear.

Someone pulled the emergency cord so that Griessel completely lost his balance and fell over, on top of the Cobra's corpse.

Mbali sat and waited. She felt no fear. There was just a tingling of adrenaline in her veins.

Her hand was firmly on her service pistol, the barrel pointing straight ahead, even if it was deep in her cavernous handbag. Even though Bones had phoned her and said Benny Griessel asked that she should just watch the Cobra who came to fetch the memory card. At Bellville Station, Captain Zola Nyathi and Ulinda Radebe were waiting. Don't confront the Cobra. Identify him, watch him.

At Parow Station she looked out of the window, to see if she could spot a Cobra.

There were too many people getting in and out of her carriage.

Only once things had settled down, just before the door closed, did she become aware of him.

It was the one from the Waterfront. She knew it, because she recognised the baseball cap, the slender grace of his movement, the shape of his face, the *café au lait* complexion. It was the one they believed came from Mozambique, Joaquim Curado, currently travelling under the name of Hector Malot.

She admonished herself, inaudibly and in Zulu, to keep calm. Her heart began hammering in her chest, her hand perspired on the pistol butt.

He was the one who had shot five people.

The train pulled out of the station.

She watched him count the benches. He came over to her.

'Could you move?' he asked, and pointed at the empty seats on either side of her.

'No,' she said.

She looked into his eyes. She saw death.

She didn't look away.

He hesitated. He stooped, his hands fumbling under the bench to the left of her. He straightened up. He moved to her right side, bent and searched again. He rose, and stood in front of her. 'You will have to move. I lost something. I must find it.'

She sat, a female Buddha, deliberately motionless and stubborn. She sighed deeply, as if it were a great sacrifice. She shifted to her right, slowly.

He waited until she had the full weight of her body in the next seat. He bent down. He searched, until his fingers came to a stop.

She pulled the pistol out of her handbag in one smooth move-ment. She made sure it didn't hook on anything. His face was down near her thigh, while he was feeling about. He saw the movement too late. She pressed the muzzle of the pistol against the edge of the baseball cap, just above the man's temple. She said, 'If you make any movement, I will shoot you, because you are a killer. I am Captain Mbali Kaleni of the South African Police Services, and you are under arrest for the murder of five security officials at the Waterfront.'

He sat stock still, both hands still under the seat. She knew he had his hands on the chewing gum. Let him think the card was still there.

He said something, short and explosive, in a language she didn't understand. She knew it was a swearword.

Mbali banged the pistol muzzle hard against Joaquim Curado's temple. 'Profanity is the effort of a feeble brain to express itself forci-bly,' she said. 'Don't do that again.'

She pulled the handcuffs out of the handbag with her left hand. She stood up carefully, without taking her eyes off the man or taking the pistol away from his head. The handbag slid down to the floor, but she left it. She pressed her knee and her considerable weight against Curado's back.

'Put your hands behind your back. Very slowly.'

He didn't listen.

She pressed harder with her weight, and her knee clamped him against the bench. She banged the pistol barrel hard against the back of his head.

He moved his hands behind him. She saw there was nothing in them. He would think the card was still there under the seat. She clicked the handcuffs first on his left wrist, changed grip and then on his right wrist.

'You are not all that dangerous,' she said, and bent to pick up her handbag. Time to report to her team leader, Benny Griessel.

Tyrone ran across the bridge at Salt River Station, past the coloured man with the coat that flapped like Batman's cloak in the wind. He must catch the train, to Bellville.

His shoes clattered down the stairs, to the platform.

The train wasn't there yet.

Relief.

He realised his grip on the money-rucksack was so tight that his fingers were cramping.

Relax, Ty, just relax. All that he could do now, was to get to the hospital. Extra insurance against an attack, but it shouldn't be necessary. No reason for them to harm Nadia, they had the card, the correct file on it. He had the money. Two point four fucking mill. His struggles were over, Nadia had a future.

The train came in. He walked, he had to sit down, he'd been on his feet since the crack of dawn, he was exhausted by all the worry, he just wanted to sit, just relax, enjoy the ride.

There were a lot of empty seats.

He chose the one at the back, at the end of the carriage.

He couldn't help himself. He pulled the rucksack open again. *Jirre*, that was a lot of money. He pushed his hand in, pulled out a bundle of notes.

Everything is legit.

The dude with the Batman coat came in through the intersecting door of the carriage and looked round. Tyrone zipped the rucksack closed, fastened the buckles. Batman headed towards him. Sat just one seat away. Cellphone in his hand.

Suspicious-looking motherfucker.

Tyrone put the rucksack on his lap.

The pistol was behind him now, in his belt, the butt pressed coldly against his ribs.

Was he one of *them*?

Or just a dude? Wouldn't it be really funny if he got robbed now?

He moved his hand very slowly, until he had hold of the pistol.

Nobody was going to rob him now.

Batman looked at him and smiled. '*Wa's jy op pad heen, my bru?*' Where are you going?

Tyrone was so relieved about the Flats Afrikaans, the smile, the fact that Batman might be a nice *ou*, over the dreadful tension that was broken, that he laughed.

'*Na my suster*,' he said. 'In Bellville.'

'Nice,' said Batman. The phone in his hand rang. 'Sorry,' he said, and answered: '*Jis*, Bones?'

59

Batman said 'OK.' and '*Jissis*' and 'Yes, everything is fine' into his cell-phone, and Tyrone tuned out and thought, can you believe it? He took a few deep breaths and exhaled. He felt light-headed, he wanted to laugh out loud. No, he wanted to dance, but that would all have to wait until he was dead sure the cops were looking after Nadia nicely. What he would do, he would phone them again, *sommer netnou* from Bellville, scare the bejaysus out of them: fifteen gangstas are on the way from the Plain to go and hurt that girlie in the hospital, get your SWAT team in, *manne,* call in the big guns, this is not child's play. All his plans had worked out so well, the whole lot, after all his worries. And now there was the small matter of what he was going to do with his share of the two point four. Nadia had six years of study, about fifty grand a year, let's make it sixty or seventy, let him *maar* let her have some luxuries too, some nice *goeters.* That's more than four hundred thousand bucks, leaves them with another two million. Buy her a little car, nothing fancy, just a little Peugeot or something.

How are you going to explain that to your sister, Ty, don't be stupid.

Not impossible. He could just say he got this *moerse* paint contract . . .

Batman said something.

'Sorry?' said Ty.

'It's not necessary, *jy wiet.*'

'*Ek versta' jou nie, my bru.*' I don't understand.

'You don't need to go to the hospital.'

Did he just say 'to the hospital' by mistake? Hadn't he told him Bellville?

'We've just caught the guy from the Waterfront. A bunch of Hawks are now on the way to the hospital, just to make sure. Your sister is safe. If I were you, I would just stay on the train.'

Tyrone grew ice cold.

'Who are you?' He moved his hand back to his pistol.

'My name is Vaughn Cupido. I'm a captain in the Directorate of Priority Crime Investigations of the Es A Pee Es. They call us the Hawks, pappie. We're the hot shit, the top cops, the main men. And if you have a weapon there under your jacket, my best advice is, forget it. They don't call me Crackshot McKenneth, the Pride of the Prairies, for nothing. I am Quick Draw McGraw, faster than a speeding bullet . . .'

'OK,' said Tyrone. 'I get the point.'

'So just relax.'

'I am relaxed.'

'Have you got a gun?' Cupido's voice was very calm, as if he were asking what he had had for breakfast.

It took a long time before Tyrone could get it out: '*Ja*.'

'Hand it over. Slowly. We really don't want anyone to get hurt.'

Tyrone sat frozen. The thought that he was going to lose everything, that it had all been for nothing, all the blood, the running, the terror, the worry, it made him feel paralysed.

Cupido looked at his watch. 'Time is running out. Just hand it over, everything will be OK.'

Tyrone lifted his hand slowly to his hip, pulled out the pistol reluctantly.

'Hold it like that so the *Hase* can't see it.'

'The *Hase*?'

'It's police-speak for the public. Slow and easy now.'

Tyrone passed the pistol over, low and unobtrusively. The cop dude took it.

'That's better, Tyrone. Tell me, where did you grow up?'

'Mitchells Plain.'

'Me too. What street?'

'Begonia.'

'I know Begonia. Hard times, *da*'.'

''S true.' What did the motherfucker want?

'I grew up in Blackbury Street. It's just other side Eisleben.'

'I know Blackbury.'

'How long have you been a pickpocket?'

Jirre. He knew everything. 'Since I was twelve.'

'Who taught you?'

'Uncle Solly. From Begonia Street.'

'Was he your real uncle?'

What kind of conversation was this? 'No. My foster father.'

'You and Nadia were orphans?'

'*Ja*. Daddy and Mommy died when I was three and she was one.'

'*Daai's* sad, my *bru*.'

'Uncle Solly was a good man.'

'But a pickpocket.'

'Damn fine pickpocket. And he had morals.'

'How much money is in the rucksack?'

That was a surprise. Such an ugly surprise that his body jerked with the shock of it.

He wanted to ask, 'How do you know about the money?'

But something else suddenly dawned on him: the Batman cop wanted a cut. Of course he wanted a cut. Or all of it. Everyone knew the cops were corrupt.

'What money?'

'The money in the photo that they sent to you. Did they hand it over?'

He kept quiet.

'Did they?' Cupido asked again.

'*Ja*.'

'How much?'

What did it help to lie. 'Two point four.'

'Million?'

'*Ja*.'

Cupido whistled softly. 'And it's all there?'

'I think so.'

'That's a lot of money.'

'How much do you want?'

Cupido laughed. 'If it wasn't such a *lekker* day, my bru, I would have bitchslapped you.'

Tyrone dared to look at the cop for the first time.

'*Ek sê*, it's a lot of money. A lot of responsibility.'

'It is.'

'Not many get such a chance. An *ou* who can put his sister through university. And make something of himself. Get out of Begonia Street.'

''S true.'

The cop put his hand in his coat pocket. Tyrone watched the movement. The hand emerged, holding a card.

'This is my business card. Take it.'

Tyrone took it.

'I'm getting off in Bellville just now. You are going to stay on the train. You are going to go all the way to Stellenbosch. Go and stay in your sister's flat, until you get your own place. Don't go back to that room in Schotsche Kloof. There's still people who might try to find you, for a week or two. So, lie low. If you have any trouble, call me. If you want to make absolutely sure the whole thing is over, call me.'

Tyrone nodded, dumbfounded.

'But no more pickpocketing. I am going to check the system. If you ever get arrested, if I see you on a CCTV camera, if you jaywalk, my *bru*, then I will come and bliksem you, and I will put you away, *versta' jy?*'

Tyrone nodded again.

'Make a life, Tyrone. Few people get the chance.'

'I will.'

Cupido put out a hand and squeezed Tyrone's shoulder. 'You're a brave *ou*. Very brave. Your sister is lucky to have you.'

And then the motherfucker stood up, smiled at him, and walked to the door of the railway carriage.

The train slowed. It stopped at Bellville. Tyrone watched Cupido walk away in his long swanky coat. The dude didn't look back, just stepped out when the doors opened. He followed Batman with his eyes, he watched the cocky walk, until he disappeared completely from view.

Tyrone sat there, staring, until the doors closed again, and the train left the station.

Then he shuddered, and began to cry.

He cried all the way to Muldersvlei, his tall, skinny, sore, tired body shaking uncontrollably.

60

They were questioning Joaquim Curado in a small office of the DPCI building in Bellville, away from the suspicious eyes of Criminal Intelligence, when Benny Griessel walked in.

There was blood on Griessel's jacket. His hair was even more dishevelled than usual, he was harried and stressed, but his eyes burned clear and full of fire.

'He won't say a word.' Cupido pointed at Curado, who sat like a sphinx at the table, still handcuffed.

'He doesn't have to talk,' said Griessel, 'but tell me first, who is with Nadia?'

'I've convinced the Bellville SC to send eight more people. They have every entrance covered,' said Zola Nyathi.

'OK. Thank you, sir.'

'How come he doesn't have to talk?' asked Cupido.

'Dave Fiedler has tracked the Cobra phone,' said Griessel. 'We have four other phone numbers. Two are registered with Orange France, and Dave can't do anything with them. The other two are Cell C, they must have bought them here. Dave has been plotting their location over the last twenty-four hours. I think David Adair is on a farm by the name of Hercules Pillar, near the R304.'

Griessel was watching Joaquim Curado closely. When he said the words 'Hercules Pillar', there was an infinitesimal movement of his head and eyes, and he knew that he was right.

'Dave said the place is advertised on the Internet: Rent a farmhouse, privacy and solitude, just twenty minutes from Cape Town. Here is the Internet address . . .'

They walked to Cupido's office, where they could look up the Hercules Pillar website.

'It's perfect,' said Mbali, because the old farmhouse, beautifully

renovated and whitewashed, was situated on a hill. You would be able
to see any intruders coming a kilometre away.

'We'll have to go in with speed and superior firepower,' said Nyathi.
'That is the only option.'

There were eight of them: Griessel and Cupido, Nyathi and Mbali,
Radebe and Vusi Ndabeni, Frankie Fillander and Mooiwillem
Liebenberg. Quietly, in pairs, each collected an assault rifle in the
Hawks' weapon safe, then crept though the corridors to the car
park.

They drove off in four cars.

On the N1, in the leading car, the Giraffe asked Mbali, 'What
happened to the memory card?'

She tapped a chubby hand on her big black handbag.

'What are you going to do with it?'

She looked out of the window. She said, 'I'll keep it as a safeguard.'

'Against what?'

'Against people who want to harm our democracy, and the spirit of
my father's struggle.'

Nyathi just nodded. He couldn't think of a better guardian for it.

In their car, second in the convoy, Griessel asked, 'What happened to
Tyrone?'

'Canny coloured *daai*. He gave me the slip,' said Cupido.

'Yes,' said Griessel. 'We old dogs don't have the speed to keep up
any more.'

Cupido's laugh was a little forced.

And Benny realised what must have really happened.

Their plan was simply to race up to the farmhouse on the hill: there
was nowhere to hide, no room for surprise.

They would drive up to the farmhouse, park the four vehicles
around it. Then they would give the Cobras a chance to come out
before they stormed the house and began shooting.

The plan worked, up to a point.

When all the cars had come to a halt, when they had jumped out
and found shelter, assault rifles cocked and aimed at the windows and

doors behind the wide veranda of the big house, there was only silence. Just the cooing of a few doves, and a cow mooing somewhere.

Nyathi called out over the megaphone, 'You are surrounded. Please put down your weapons, and come out with your hands on your heads.'

They waited, the adrenaline pumping, fingers on triggers, heads shielded behind the safety of the vehicles' metal bodies.

No reaction. Only the afternoon hush, and the shadow of a fat white cloud that came and went.

Griessel looked at the bare ground outside the front door. There were the tracks of other vehicle tyres in the mud of last night's rain. The Cobras had parked in front of the door, with at least two vehicles. Maybe three.

Nyathi repeated the message, even louder.

Nothing happened.

'Sir, let me run to the door,' Cupido said.

'Wait,' said Nyathi.

They waited. The minutes crept by.

'OK, let's cover Vaughn,' said Nyathi. 'Wait for my signal.'

They stood up, lifted the barrels of the rifles over the roofs and bonnets of the cars, pointed them at the door and windows, where there was still no sign of life.

'Go!' yelled Nyathi.

Cupido, in his long, elegant coat, ran across the open yard to the front door, slightly crouched, as if that would somehow help. The automatic rifle in his hand made him look like a character from a 1930's film.

Only his footsteps were audible on the saturated ground.

He was safely at the door.

Silence.

'I hear something,' said Cupido. He knelt down in front of the door.

They waited, dead quiet.

'Yes, there's somebody in there.'

He shifted closer to the door.

'Someone is shouting for help,' he said. 'I think we should go in.'

They found David Patrick Adair in the master bedroom of the house. He was stretched out and tied to the bed, with cable ties and rope. He was unshaven, dirty, and smelly, but unharmed. His first words when Cupido walked in were, 'Are you the cavalry, or a different kind of trouble?'

'We are the Hawks,' said Cupido.

'I'm not sure that answers my question . . .'

Shouts from the other team members, as they declared the house safe, room by room.

'We are the South African Police Service,' said Cupido.

Nyathi and Mbali walked in, then Griessel and Fillander.

'And what a splendid representation of the Rainbow Nation you are,' said Adair, his nonchalant tone trying unsuccessfully to disguise his immense relief. 'You wouldn't happen to know if my student, the lovely Lillian Alvarez, is safe, would you?'

Adair politely requested a chance to shower. 'And, please God, let me brush my teeth.'

He was a tall, elegant man. Griessel saw that he wanted to preserve his dignity at all cost, but the trauma of the past days lay close to the surface.

They waited on the veranda to make sure the Cobras didn't make a surprise appearance. When Adair came out of the bathroom, Nyathi, Griessel, Mbali, and Cupido questioned him in the sitting room.

He said there were three of them during the abduction in Franschhoek. 'They were so terribly efficient. So utterly businesslike.'

They knew about Lillian Alvarez. That was how they found out precisely where he was, because they had tapped Alvarez's cellphone. And like a fool, he had phoned Alvarez last Friday night from the Franschhoek guesthouse.

'They also used her to convince me to hand over the data. They said they would kill her. And that I had to call her, to bring the memory card.'

'What was on the card?' asked Nyathi.

'A lot of data,' said Adair.

'What kind of data?'

'The monetary evil that men do.'

'Can you be more specific?'

'How much time do we have?'

'All the time we need.'

'Well, there is the data on possible terrorists. And possible spies. And possible organised crime money laundering. By organised crime, and by the banks. Damning evidence of dirty banking hands. Not murky little banks in banana republics. Continental, international banking colossi. And then there's the quite impressive and intimidatingly long list of corrupt government officials . . .'

'South African government officials?' asked Mbali.

'I'm afraid so. But let me hasten to add that the data also includes government officials from thirty-nine other countries. My own included. And the evidence is quite conclusive.'

'Can you tell us which South African government officials?'

'Quite a few. MPs. Ministers. Your president, I'm sorry to add.'

Mbali made a small despairing sound.

'That's how they got the SSA and CI involved,' said Nyathi.

'Who?' asked Adair.

'Your MI6 got our State Security Agency and Crime Intelligence Unit involved in the investigation, in the quest to find you.'

'I see. No stone unturned. How comforting. But yes, you might be right. I did mention the corrupt politicians list to my friends at MI6.'

'Who do the Cobras work for?' asked Griessel.

'The who?'

'The people who kidnapped you. Do they work for the CIA?' asked Cupido.

'Good heavens, no. They are working for the banks.'

61

They didn't believe him.

David Adair explained. He said he knew he would only get one chance to go fishing for all manner of evil in the SWIFT system with his extensive new protocol, because he had always been very open about his political and ethical standards. There were so many factions watching him, all waiting to see what he wanted to do with the system – and suspecting that he might be looking for ammunition for his crusades.

So he wrote the programming in such a way that he could slip in a digital Trojan horse afterwards, when everyone was satisfied that the protocol would not be damaging to them.

And the end result, when the data began coming in, was mind-boggling. There were the spying details, the corruption of politicians, the massive extent of large, well-respected international banks looking the other way and cooperating in the laundering of billions for organised crime. But what took him completely by surprise, was a conglomerate of international banks manipulating the financial system: to evade taxation, to fix rates, to tamper illegally with share prices and exchange rates, and to continue to trade in derivative instruments – indecipherable and complex derivatives, despite the huge risk it posed to the world economy.

Executives of banks and financial institutions enriched themselves on a massive scale, at the expense of common people. He was totally unprepared for the greed, the sheer extent of the machinations.

'The problem is, what does one do with such information? To make it public is an act of potential financial sabotage. The system, still very fragile after the meltdown, might well collapse. Or at least trigger a new international recession. The big losers won't be the banking fat cats, but the very people I had hoped to protect. The public. So, just after my dialogue with MI6, I made the mistake of calling the CEO of a very big international bank. Just to tell him that it might be a good idea to start winding down all the illegal and dangerous activities. Or run the risk of being exposed. Yes, it was blackmail, but the cause was good and just, I thought. Soon after, I became aware of a series of strange occurrences. I thought I was being followed, I was pretty sure someone had been in my office and my house. Perhaps to plant bugs? So I took a few precautions. I flew to Marseilles to get myself a false passport, and I put a considerable sum of money away in a new account under the false name—'

'Where would a university professor get a considerable sum of money from?' asked Cupido.

'The European Union has been rather generous in remunerating me for my work.'

'OK.'

'I packed a suitcase, just in case. And when I got home from Lillian's place last Monday night, and I saw that my home had been ransacked, I knew. And I ran.'

'But how do you know it was the banks?'

'I speak French,' said Adair. 'I understood what one of my abductors was saying over the phone to the people who hired them. There is only one conclusion.'

They concealed one vehicle behind a shed a hundred metres away from the farmyard. Cupido, Fillander, Mbali, and Ndabeni stayed behind, since the Cobras' luggage, a few firearms, and travel documents were still in the house.

Griessel and Nyathi took Adair to the city: he'd asked to be taken to Lillian Alvarez as quickly as possible.

Griessel sat in the back of the big Ford Territory, with his and Nyathi's assault rifles beside him on the seat. Adair sat in front beside Nyathi, who was behind the wheel.

On the R304 Nyathi said, 'You realise you are still in danger?'

'I do. But as soon as I've seen Lillian, I will rectify the matter. I will Skype the editor of the *Guardian*. He is a man of the utmost integrity, and I will make a full confession, and give him access to the data.'

'But the memory card is gone.'

'Good.'

'Wasn't the data on the memory card?'

'Of course it was. I was hoping against hope that, if I gave them the data in a tangible format, they would not kill me. But they would have, I'm sure. The data also lives in the cloud. Two or three places. They'll find it, eventually, I suppose. One always leaves tracks . . .'

On the N1, just before the Lucullus Street off-ramp, Adair said philosophically, 'Of course, one contemplates one's own demise, under these circumstances. And then you keep hoping that all the lies, all the deceit, will somehow be uncovered. That the truth will set us all free. But you know, it is such an imperfect world, and it is getting more imperfect every day. So, thank you . . .'

Griessel looked out of the window and thought about Mbali, who had also spoken about how liberating the truth could be. His mind was so filled with the question of secrets and lies that he was barely aware of the white Volkswagen Amarok double cab drawing up beside them.

Later he would not remember whether it was an odd movement, the sun reflecting on a gun barrel, or the vaguely familiar face of the man. Something suddenly made him focus, triggered the alarm in his head. In one move he grabbed the rifle on the seat next to him and shouted, 'Sir!'

It was too late.

The shots boomed beside them, the bullets punched through him, and through Nyathi. Shreds of fabric puffed from the headrests, the wind was suddenly loud in his ears, and a bloody mist, entire droplets, seemed to hang suspended in the interior of the car.

Griessel felt the exploding pain of bullet wounds, the terrible violence of lead slamming, tearing into his body.

Nyathi lost control of the Ford, the vehicle zigzagged across the road, skidded, overturned, and rolled. Griessel tried to hold on. Airbags exploded. He had his seat belt fastened, that was his only thought, he had his seat belt fastened, now he could tell Fritz it was proof that that was the right thing to do.

Just before everything went black, he saw the body of Zola Nyathi, still buckled into his seat, but strangely uncontrolled. Only the laws of physics in charge of his body now, tugging it back and forth. And he thought: how fragile a person's body is. Nyathi had always seemed so indestructible.

★ ★ ★

There was a moment when he recovered consciousness, as he was suspended upside down in the wreckage, watching his blood flow from his body and pooling on the roof of the Ford. A moment when he was aware of the man who rifled through his pockets, hastily and roughly, but thoroughly. The face was devoid of emotion. It was one of them, one of the men on the O. R. Tambo photos. The man's hands searched through all his pockets, coated in his blood.

A shot cracked, one last time, in the shattered space.

Then everything went quiet.

62

He saw Alexa beside the hospital bed, in the middle of the night. She was sleeping awkwardly in the chair. He tried to say something to her, but he was so very tired, he could scarcely open his mouth. His parched mouth.

He was awake. He was at Alexa's house, in the sitting room. His arm was gone. Completely. Alexa said don't worry, there are bass guitar players with only one arm. She puffed on a cigarette.

He dimly realised someone else was here too. Strange, it was daytime now. He opened his eyes. It was his daughter, Carla. She sat hunched over, her elbows on the bed, her face close to his, her expression intense, as if willing him not to go. He saw her mouth move, forming the word 'Papa', but he didn't hear it. He was drifting away from everything. But both his arms were here.

Fritz sat in the chair beside the hospital bed. His son, with a guitar. His son sang to him. It was so incredibly beautiful.

He had a conversation with Nyathi and Mbali. They spoke Zulu and Xhosa, and to his surprise so did he. Kaleni said, Isn't it wonderful?

Yes, said Nyathi.

What? Asked Griessel.

There's no corruption here, said Mbali. Look, Benny, none. It wasn't for nothing after all.

Cupido and Bones and Mbali stood beside his bed, their faces grim.

'Vaughn,' said Griessel.

'*Jissis*,' said Cupido and stood up, looked at him.

'This is a hospital. Watch your language,' said Mbali.

'Get a nurse, he's awake,' said Cupido.

And then Griessel was gone again.

They only told him Nyathi was dead after he had been awake for two days. Nyathi and David Adair.

'They thought you weren't going to make it, Benny,' said Alexa, her tears dripping on the sheet. She held his left hand tightly, the one on the arm that was still reasonably whole. 'They brought you back from the brink of death twice. They said you had no blood left. None.'

Two wounds in his right leg, one in his upper right arm, his right shoulder, his left wrist, two bullets through his ribs and his right lung. But everything would heal in time. There would be stiffness in the limbs, the surgeon said. For many years. He had been in a coma for sixteen days, they said. And he thought to himself, that was the easiest sixteen days off the bottle he had ever added to his tally.

Cloete came and sat with him. 'CNN, the BBC, Sky News and the *New York Times* are all asking for interviews, Benny. Are you up to it?'

'No.'

Superintendent Marie-Caroline Aubert phoned him from Lyon. She sympathised with the loss of his colleague. She congratulated him on the arrest of Curado. She said the one he shot dead was the only French citizen, one Romain Poite. The others that they identified were all Eastern Europeans, but also former members of the French Foreign Legion. 'We are trying to track them down, thanks to your good work.'

Jeanette Louw, the owner of Body Armour, came to sit with him too. He told her everything.

Alexa was there every day, in the morning, afternoon, and evening. Carla came to visit. Fritz. His colleagues. Doc Barkhuizen. His fellow Rust band members. And Lize Beekman, once. 'I'm sorry about your concert,' he said.

'It won't be the last one,' she said. 'Just get better.'

He had done a lot of thinking, in the hospital. When Alexa came to fetch him and take him to her house, his words were ready.

Tired and weak, he climbed into the double bed in Alexa's bedroom. Then he said, 'Come sit here, please. There is something I have to talk about.'

She sat down, concerned.

'I love you very much,' he said.

'And I love you, Benny.'

'Alexa, I didn't know what to say, because it's a difficult thing. But someone said: the truth makes us free . . .'

'What truth, Benny?'

'I can't . . . you know . . .' and all his planned words and phrases, practised in his mind, over and over, deserted him.

'What are you talking about?'

'Before this thing . . .' And he indicated the last of the bandages. 'I couldn't keep up. With the . . . sex. I'm too old and too fucked-up, Alexa. I can't do the thing every day any more. You are very sexy to me, my head wants to, but my . . .' He pointed at his groin.

'Your rascal,' she said.

'Yes. My rascal can't keep up. Not every day. Maybe every second day. We can try.'

He saw how her face crumpled. He saw her begin to cry, and he thought, *fok*, that was the wrong thing to say.

'I'll see a doctor,' he said.

She hugged him tightly. He felt the warmth of her breath, and her tears. 'I was so scared, Benny. I was never enough for Adam. I thought that was why he strayed. I just wanted to be enough for you.'

Adam, her late husband.

'You are more than enough for me,' he said. 'Just not every day.'

'Thank God,' she said.

And then he heard her vibrant, joyful laugh.

GLOSSARY

Ai – ah, oh; ow, ouch, mostly used a little despairingly.

Ag – Very similar to 'ai': ah!, oh!; alas, pooh!, mostly used with resignation.

Annerlike – Cape Flats Afrikaans for 'a different kind of' – often used in a negative way. (Cape Flats slang refers to the Afrikaans spoken on the Cape Flats, a vast area east of Cape Town, where the majority of 'Cape Coloured' people reside. 'Coloured people' refer to the descendants of Malaysian slaves in South Africa (forced migration by the Dutch East India Company), who inter-married with white farmers and local Khoi people – as opposed to Blacks (descendants of the Bantu people) and Whites (descendants of European settlers).

Appie – Diminutive of 'apprentice', someone who is learning a trade.

Baie – Afrikaans for 'A lot', or 'very'.

Bergie - Cape Flats Afrikaans for a homeless person, often a vagrant, living on the side of Table Mountain (berg = mountain).

Blerrie – Cape Flats slan for 'bloody'.

Bliksem – Mild profanity, used as an exclamation or adjective ('Damn!' or 'damned'), a verb (I will 'bliksem' you = I will hit you hard).

Blougatte – When trainee constables attend police college, they wear blue uniforms, and are called 'blue arses', or 'blougatte'. The nick-name is also used to refer to lower, uniformed police ranks in uniform as a slightly derogatory term, as opposed to plain clothes police women and men.

Boetie – Diminutive of 'broer', which means 'brother'.

Bok – Afrikaans for 'goat' or 'deer', but used much more widely. 'Here's a middle-aged bok with a pretty young thing' refers to an Afrikaans idiom 'an old goat likes green leaves', meaning 'an older man likes younger women'. 'Bok' or the diminutive 'bokkie' is also used an as endearment for men or women.

Broe', daai's kwaai – Cape Flats Afrikaans for 'Brother, that's heavy'.

Coloured – See 'Annerlike' above.

Daai, daai's – Cape Flats Afrikaans for 'that' (daai) or 'that is' (daai's).

Daatlik – Cape Flats Afrikaans for 'immediately'.

Dagga – Afrikaans for cannabis.

Die Boer – Literally, 'The Farmer'. It is the name of a famous, intimate music theatre in Durbanville, a suburb of Cape Town.

Die rekening is agterstallig – Afrikaans for 'Your account is in arrears.'

Dis 'n lekker een die – Afrikaans for 'this is a good one'. 'Lekker' is word widely used for anything that is 'good', 'delicious', 'tasty'.

Dof – Afrikaans for 'faint', but also used to indicate a stupid person.

Donner – Mild Afrikaans expletive, literally meaning 'thunder'. Often used in the sense of "I am going to donner you' – I am going to hurt / hit you.

Doos – Afrikaans expletive, comparing someone to female genitalia. Closest English translation would be 'cunt'.

Dop – Afrikaans for 'a drink', referring to alcohol.

Drol – Afrikaans for 'turd'.

Dronkgat – Afrikaans for 'drunkard'. (Literally, 'a drunk arse'.)

Ek kom van die Pniel af – Cape Flats Afrikaans for 'I come from Pniel'. Pniel is a village near Stellenbosch.

Ek sê jou – Afrikaans for 'I am telling you.'

Ek versta' jou nie – Afrikaans for 'I don't understand you'. (Cape Flats vernacular.)

Ek vra ma net – Afrikaans for 'I am just asking.'

Ek wiet, ja – Cape Flats vernacular for 'I know, yes.'

Flippen – Mild expletive, used as an acceptable alternative for 'fucking'. (Afrikaans.)

Fokken – Afrikaans for 'fucking', as in 'that fucking guy . . .'

Gefok – Afrikaans for 'fucked', as in 'I am fucked.'

Fok weet – Afrikaans for 'fuck knows'.

Fokkit – Afrikaans for 'fuck it'.

Fokker – Afrikaans for 'fucker'.

Fokkol – Afrikaans for 'fuck all', meaning 'nothing'.

Goeters – Afrikaans for 'stuff'.

Gooi – Literally, Afrikaans for 'throw', but used as a slang verb substitute for, inter alia, 'sing for us', or 'tell me' . . .

Hase – Literally, Afrikaans for 'rabbits', but used here as the collective name by which members of the South African police refer to the public.

Helm – Literally, Afrikaans for 'helmet'. According to local superstition, when a baby is born with the placenta covering her / his head, it is believed the baby is born with the 'helm', and could have a special talent of foretelling the future, or 'see' or 'feel' evil.

"Here is an example so long" – 'So long' is a typical example of how Afrikaans had influenced South African English. 'Solank' (literally means 'in the mean time') became 'so long', and is widely used.

Hier's nou 'n ding – 'Now here's a thing.' (Afrikaans.)

Hierjy – A nobody, as in "I am not just some nobody'. (Afrikaans.)

Hyahi – IsiZulu for 'No!'. (South Africa has 11 official languages: Afrikaans, English, IsiNdebele, IsiXhosa, IsiZulu, Sepedi, Sesotho, Setswana, SiSwati, Tshivenda, Xitsonga. Township slang transcends all 11.)

Jakob Regop – Afrikaans for the flower zinnia. Literally means 'Jacob standing at attention' sometimes Anglicized as 'Jacob Straight-up', it can also refer to an erect male sexual organ.

Jirre – Cape Flats slang for God, approximates 'Gawd'. (Afrikaans.)

Jissis – Jeez (as in harsher version of the exclamation Jesus!) (Afrikaans.)

Jy's – Abbreivates form of the Afrikaans 'jy is', meaning 'you are'.

Jy kannie net loep nie – 'You can't just walk away?' (Afrikaans.)

Jy wiet. Jy wietie – Cape Flats Afrikaans for 'You know'. Or: 'You don't know' = jy wietie.

Kaaps – Literally, 'from the Cape' or 'of the Cape', referring to anything from the Cape Town region, or the wider Western Cape Province. (South Africa has nine provinces (similar to the states of the USA): Gauteng, Limpopo, Mpumalanga, Northwest, Free State, KwaZulu-Natal, Northern Cape, Eastern Cape, and Western Cape.)

Kak – 'Shit'.

Knippies – Literally, 'knip' is Afrikaans for 'clasp', 'clip' or 'fastener'. Knippies would literally be the plural form, but used here as a nickname for the pickpocket Tyrone Kleinbooi, who uses a hair clip as distraction.

Kwaai – Mostly used in slang form to indicate coolness, it is an Afrikaans word with a very wide application. Literally meaning someone who is hot-tempered, bad-tempered, ill-natured, harsh or severe, it is also often used as an exclamation: 'Kwaai!' = "Cool!' (or 'Heavy!').

Kwaat – Cape Flats Afrikaans for 'angry'.

Lat ek een hier het – Afrikaans (Cape Flats vernacular) of: '... that I have one here.' "And it just so happens lat ek een hier het" means: "And it just so happens that I have one with me / right here with me".

Lekka, lekker – Afrikaans word widely used for anything that is 'good', 'delicious', 'tasty'. ('Lekka' is Cape Flats vernacular, 'lekker' is formal Afrikaans.)

Liewe ffff – Literally, 'dear ffff . . .' US English equivalent would be "Sweet fff...' as in someone just stopping short of saying 'sweet fuck'.

Lobola – (Or Labola, an isiZulu or isiXhosa word, sometimes trans-lated as 'bride price'.) A traditional Southern African custom whereby the man pays the family of his fiancée for her hand in marriage. The custom is aimed at bringing the two families together, fostering mutual respect, and indicating that the man is capable of supporting his wife financially and emotionally. Traditionally paid in heads of cattle, but cash is now widely accepted. (Source: http://en.wikipedia.org/wiki/Lobolo)

Los – Afrikaans for 'loose'.

Ma' – Abbreviated form of 'maar', meaning 'but'. (Afrikaans.)

Ma' nou weet hulle – 'But now they know.' (Afrikaans.)

Maaifoedie – Cape Flats Afrikaans for a scoundrel or rascal.

Maar – see 'Ma" above.

Middag, goeie middag – 'Afternoon, good afternoon.' (Afrikaans.)

Mkhonto we Sizwe – or Umkhonto weSizwe ("Spear of the Nation") or 'MK' as it was more commonly known, was the military wing of the African National Congress (ANC), launched on the 16th December 1961.

The African National Congress (ANC) is South Africa's governing party and has been in power since the transition to democracy in April 1994. The organisation was initially founded as the South African Native National Congress (SANNC) on 8 January 1912 in Bloemfontein, with the aim of fighting for the rights of black South

Africans. The organization was renamed the ANC in 1923. While the organization's early period was characterized by political inertia due to power struggles and lack of resources, increasing repression and the entrenchment of white minority rule galvanized the party. As a result of the establishment of apartheid, its aversion to dissent by black people and brutal crackdown of political activists, the ANC together with the SACP formed a military wing, uMkhonto we Sizwe (Spear of the Nation/ MK) in 1961. (Quoted from South African History Online: http://www.sahistory.org.za/topic/ umkhonto-wesizwe-mk and http://www.sahistory.org.za/organisa-tions/african-national-congress-anc)

Moenie soe wies nie – Cape Flats vernacular for 'Don't be like that'.

Moenie worrie nie – Afrikaans slang for 'Don't worry'.

Moer in – 'Moer' is a wonderful, mildly vulgar Afrikaans expletive, and can be used in any conceivable way. Its origins lie in the Dutch word 'Moeder', meaning 'Mother'. 'Moer in" means 'to be very angry', but you can also 'moer someone" (to hit somebody), use it as an angry exclamation (Moer!, which approximates 'Damn!'), call something or someone 'moerse' (approximates 'great' or 'cool'), or use it as an adjective: I have a 'moerse' head ache – I have a huge head ache. 'Moer toe' means 'fucked up', or even 'dead'.

Mos – Widely used and applied Afrikaans adverb, mostly meaning 'indeed', or 'as you know'.

Nee, wat – Afrikaans expression approximating 'no, not really'.

Njaps, njapsed – Mild synonym for sexual intercourse.

Nogal – Afrikaans word with wide application, mostly meaning rather, quite, fairly . . .

Nooit – Never (Afrikaans).

Nou's dit – Now it is (Afrikaans).

Orraait – Afrikaans version of 'all right'.

Ou, Outjie – Guy. 'Outjie' is the diminutive form. (Afrikaans.)

Panados – A paracetemol pain killer in tablet form.

Poegaai – Cape Flats Afrikaans, meaning 'very tired'.

Rand value – Over the past two years, the value of the South African currency (Rand, or R) has fluctuated between 7 and 110 to the US$, 9 and 15 to the Euro, and 14 to 18 to the British pound.

Sê nou – 'Now tell', or 'do say'. (Afrikaans.)

Shebeens – A shebeen (Irish: síbín) was originally an illicit bar or club where excisable alcoholic beverages were sold without a licence. The term has spread far from its origins in Ireland, to Scotland, Canada, the United States, England, Zimbabwe, English-speaking Caribbean, Namibia and South Africa. In modern South Africa, many "shebeens" are now fully legal. The word derives from the Irish síbín, meaning 'illicit whiskey'. (Quoted from http://en.wikipedia.org/wiki/Shebeen)

Sien jy – 'Do you see?' (Afrikaans.)

Sisterjie – Diminutive of 'sister'. (Afrikaans.)

Sjoe – 'Wow'. (Afrikaans.) With wide, broad application.

Skelmpie – From the (Afrikaans) 'skelm' (noun) meaning rascal, or sly person, or 'skelm' (adverb), meaning dishonest, a 'skelmpie' is the common term for a lover out of wedlock.

Skep, pappie, skep – 'Skep' can mean 'scoop' (as in scoop up water from a well) or 'spoon' (as in spoon up, when eating soup, for instance). Vaughn Cupido uses it in the sense of the Afrikaans idiom 'you have to scoop when it rains', meaning you have to gather your hay while the sun shines. ('Pappie' is the Afrikaans for 'father', and is used in the sense of the African American slang 'dawg').

Slim kind – 'Clever child'.

Snotskoot – Literally, 'snot shot', as in 'I hit him a snot shot' – i.e. right on the nose, or 'hit him in such a way that the snot flew'.

Sommer netnou – 'Soon'.

Sussie – Another diminutive for 'sister'.

Tik – South African nickname for the drug methamphetamine.

Versta'jy – 'Do you understand?' (Cape Flats vernacular.)

Volkies – Derogatory reference to coloured farm workers.

Waterblommetjie stew – 'Waterblommetjie' literally means 'little water flower'. A plant growing in fresh water ponds in the Western Cape (translation 'water blister / hydatid / Cape pondweed / Cape hawthorn / Cape asparagus'), it is famous for its use in a stew with lamb.

Wiet jy – 'Do you know?' (Cape Flats vernacular.)